CAMPTOWN LADIES

MARI SANGIOVANNI

Ann Arbor
2011

Bywater Books

Bywater Books First Edition: December 2011

Printed in the United States of America
on acid-free paper.

Cover designer: Mari SanGiovanni

Bywater Books
PO Box 3671
Ann Arbor MI 48106-3671
www.bywaterbooks.com

ISBN: 978-1-932859-86-7

To Kim, always, for my life.

Also for my sister,
who tirelessly pounds the streets in Provincetown,
harassing all the ladies to buy her sister's books.

One

The Long Haul Wasn't Designed for a U-Haul

My sister's voice always went through my head anytime I saw a fortune cookie, and I heard it now as I ate a stale one from the takeout scraps in my cupboard. "See, a vagina!" My sister Lisa saw vaginas everywhere she went. If she had been in my kitchen, she would have broken the fortune cookie in half, turned the triangle-shaped cookie wide end up, shoved it in my face and said, "See, a *vagina*!" I knew this too: no matter the mood I was in, she could crack me up.

Other vagina sightings ranged from the obvious flowers to a more obscure list that included: puffed rice cereal, pre-sliced hot dog buns, the Toyota logo, a Dorito, tacos, and several varieties of shellfish. When we were kids, she would trap a long, wide blade of grass vertically between her thumbs so she could blow into it to make a whistle, then at some point she should shove her spitty fingers into my face and say, "See, a vagina!"

Lisa always spotted the vaginas before I did—and she said this was my biggest problem. Sure, I could see the resemblance in a fortune cookie, but I maintained that the blade-of-grass-between-two-thumbs-whistle was stretching it just a bit. With my sister around, there was simply no way to hide a vagina, except maybe with her favorite pair of extra-large camouflage boxer shorts.

While Lisa chose camouflage as a fashion statement, there was never anything camouflaged about her preference for the fairer sex. My sister barreled out of the closet (knocking me down with the closet door she'd ripped off its hinges), proclaiming herself a lesbian just as I was starting to wonder about my own preferences. I was the gay tortoise; she was the queer rabbit. While I was secretly reading books in the library on a fact-finding quest after hopelessly falling in love with my straight best friend, Lisa left me in the dust, blazing by me in a friggin' rainbow-colored Macy's Thanksgiving Day float with a turbocharged engine.

The fortune cookie wasn't the only reason I was thinking of my sister. Lisa had threatened to call any minute now, so what I really needed was Cheetos. And not the fake Cheddar Puffs Mom bought when we were kids, but the real deal. I tried to ignore the craving as I settled back on the couch, remembering how Mom would hide the generic Stop and Shop bag deep in the trash and pour the inferior puffs into a white ceramic bowl, thinking us kids wouldn't know the difference.

"See," Mom would say, "same orange stuff on your fingers," then she would offer up the neon evidence as if they were the real thing. But Lisa and I noticed how the fake ones sat uncomfortably in the bowl, with much less of a dramatic curl, looking packed flat, like cheap Chinese food. And we noted the Orange No. 5 was off just a shade (was it Orange No. 6?) and that the color didn't cling to your fingers in the same fluffy-fiber way, but more like thick war paint.

I wished I could spot a faux lesbo just as easily, and I thought of Lorn Elaine for the millionth time. The Actress, the ex. I knew she was never the real deal—or, that she wouldn't let herself be because of her career, or, at least, that was the perfect excuse. The more distressing question was, What made me believe I could ever make her stay? From the very start, being with a woman did not sit easily with her. She, too, always sat uncomfortably in the bowl, and, in the end, she didn't cling to my fingers nearly as long as I would have liked, and I ended up smeared in war paint.

I anticipated the phone ringing as I dozed on the couch, giving into the sudden nap attack, which was brought on by the exhausting prospect of heading out to the store to score that bag of electric orange carbs. After six long weeks without Lorn and my sister Lisa's impending phone call, I hoped that when the phone rang I would be able to stifle the agonizing hope it was Lorn calling to tell me she was coming back. Maybe this would be the time I could hide my disappointment when I heard my sister's voice (or any voice besides Lorn's) and then my sister wouldn't tease me, "Still waiting for The Actress, I see."

I considered letting my answering machine take my sister's call, but I couldn't risk the chance it might be my brother, Vince. His check-in calls were fairly regular, and getting more frequent since he was having girl troubles of his own. Vince had been with Erica for almost as long has I had been with "The Actress"—as my sister and Vince's girlfriend, Erica, called her.

I was in LA when I first met Erica, the woman who would become my brother's girlfriend, and she had introduced herself as "Erica . . . as in *All My Children*," and that nickname stuck for a while. I liked Erica's cocky attitude and had introduced her to my brother, then congratulated myself at quite regular intervals on putting together the world's most perfect straight couple. When I told Vince the unsurprising news that "The Actress" decided she could not be with a woman (again) and it was all over (again) and she was so sorry (again), Vince trumped me with his own news: Vince and Erica, the world's most perfect couple, were also breaking up.

So, I did what any sister would do when presented with these facts: I blamed my brother for blowing the perfect couple I had created. He was mad at me for a week (evidence: he called me only twice). By the following week he'd resumed his normal pattern of calling every other day, eventually realizing it wasn't my fault, since we all knew his track record with women had been spotty at best.

Before Erica, my sister and I could blame our brother's failed relationships on his selection of The Barbie Doll of the Week. This time, it was my reputation on the line. I had made this perfect couple, and he had blown it, big time. Erica and Vince were no more. My sister had been equally compassionate when I had called her to share my news about being dumped.

Lisa had said, "There's something about straight girls you just can't put your finger on . . ." and then she laughed and snorted for several minutes at her own joke.

I snapped back to reality when the phone rang and I opted to pick it up rather than hear my nauseatingly cheerful voice on the answering machine, since I was no longer that person. That person was sporting my pre-dumped voice.

"Hello?"

Lisa said, "Don't get your panties in a twist, it's just me,"

"Don't be an ass, I've stopped thinking she'll call," I said.

"Liar."

"Shut it," I said.

Lisa said, "Don't lose your sense of humor. You fucked a straight actress, she pulled an Ann Heche on your sorry ass, and you got dumped. Now scrape your friggin' shoe and move on."

I said, "Don't pretend you didn't like her."

"Of course I liked Lorn, I like all women," Lisa said. "That doesn't mean I don't know how to kick a dog to the curb if they piss on my leg and try to tell me it's raining."

"So what's going on?" I said.

Unlike Vince, who always called about nothing, Lisa always called with some sort of news.

"Are you sitting down?" she asked.

"I'm lying down," I said, already exhausted. I braced myself, because you never know with Lisa.

This could be the call our family all expected, the call from a prison in Maine for running an Italian restaurant out of her home with no permits to sell food or the gallons of homemade wine she calls "V." She told Mom and Dad "V" stood for Vino, and then she forgot, and told them she named it after Vince, but the triangle-shape label was an obvious and familiar reference. Dad figured it out and would ask for a glass with pure delight, "Give me another shot of that V-jay-jay-juice!" When he got away with that in front of Mom, Dad switched it up to: "Sure am craving some more Vay-jay-jay!"

Lisa said, "You may want to sit up for this. I've decided what I'm going to do with my share of grandma's inheritance!"

"You mean the money you said you didn't want because it would only bring pretentious and empty lives to all who touched it?"

"You and Vince haven't spent my share, right?" she asked.

"No. Dad helped me set it up in a money market for you. He said you'd want it eventually. He's known you a bit longer." Lisa is two years older than me. "His actual words were: 'Even an earthy-crunchy bulldyke from Maine can find a use for a few million dollars.'"

"Not from Maine anymore! Ready? Wanna guess?"

I didn't.

"I've decided to buy a campground in Rhode Island, and you're gonna help me run it!" She sang out this news with that typical "Ta-daaaaa" sound in her voice, waiting for applause.

"No," I said.

"Marie, it's gonna be great! Remember all the fun we used to have camping? The smell of the campfire and the pine trees—"

"I remember a giant hawk dismembering a baby bunny on a picnic table. We were too afraid it would go after us if we made a run for it, so we had to stand still and watch it eat the thing."

Lisa laughed, "I tried to use the remains to get out of dissecting a frog in science, but, no go. Hey, remember all the cool nights by the campfires, the dappled sunshine through the trees, the chocolate and marshmallow s'mores, the hot dogs, the barbeque chicken—"

I said, "My stomach is still on the bunny, but I do remember that really creepy guy who hung around the campground and exposed himself every time we spun around the playground Round-A-Bout."

"That was hysterical," Lisa said.

"Not really."

"You have to admit his timing was amazing. Hey, remember the nights hanging at the teen rec hall?"

"Yeah, except there were no teenagers, just a bunch of us nine- to twelve-year-olds hanging around trading crumpled Star Wars cards."

"Mmmm, Princess Leia," Lisa said. "Don't forget, I got to touch my first boob while camping. Ahhhh, Jennifer Litwieller. I called her Jennifer Tit-Sweller after that, remember?"

"Yeah, she loved that," I said.

"She only let me touch her once, but it never would have happened if our parents hadn't taken us camping."

Lisa had that Woodsy The Owl tone in her voice now, like she was teaching something important: *Remember kids, your best chance to touch a boob before you turn twelve is behind a skanky teen rec hall while camping!*

Lisa was on a roll. "And remember the time we made Vince pee right inside the rec hall because we didn't want to leave all the fun to walk him to the bathrooms, then he ratted us out to Mom and Dad? And you tried your first cigarette, there too."

I said, "Those are reasons enough to buy a campground." I had thrown up from the cigarette and wiped the evidence off my mouth with a climbing ivy plant that turned out to be poison sumac. My lips burned for weeks. Good times.

Lisa continued with a irritating wistful high-pitched tone to her usually husky, matter-of-fact voice, "It's a sweet little spot in the woods in southern Rhode Island, with 250 sites, a man-made pond, a few old cabins, but I plan to build some more, and a huge log recreation hall attached to a camp store. The website pictures look pristine. I told the woman I would have a deposit to her by the end of this week."

"The website?" I said, sitting up, feeling the sharp grit of potato chip crumbs grind into my elbows. "You mean you haven't even *seen* it?"

"Of course I saw it! I just told you, the pictures are sweet! There's even a golf cart to make campfire wood deliveries! Oh, and in the back of the camp store, I might even put a gift shop." By "gift shop," I knew she meant "bar." Anytime we ever went to a hotel she would scan the lobby and say, "Ooooh, look! A gift shop!" and make a bee-line for the bar.

Lisa continued in her disturbing cheerfulness. "The owner was honest with me that the whole campground needs some updating, but I was glad to hear the buildings needed some work, since I want this to be a bit of a project, you know? Leave my mark on the place. It'll be fun! The biggest thing is all the roofs need fixing or replacing, the electrical, too, maybe the plumbing, but, I have the perfect name to go after the dyke clientele."

I said, "Well, it all makes sense now, I mean, since you already have the perfect name."

Lisa shouted into my ear, "Camptown Ladies!"

Then she proceeded to screech her song into the phone:
"Camptown Ladies sing this song,
Dildo, Dildo!!!
Camptown Lezzies, eight inches long,
All the Dildo, Gaaaaaaay!"

Two

Camptown Ladies & Camp, Camp

Lisa had rented a three-bedroom condo for us to share, one town away from the campground, and I was once again reminded how simple it was to make life-changing decisions when you are wealthy. She had done a good job with the condo, aside from the freakishly décor-free environment in the living area downstairs, bare except for a wide screen TV and huge couch to watch Patriots football. The only other sign of life was in the kitchen, which was fully stocked with Italian cooking supplies, and the largest set of chef grade cooking pans available in the free world.

Vince and I were both in such dire need of a distraction, we would have agreed to any of one of Lisa's wild ideas, and within two weeks, Vince had hired a realtor to sublet his California apartment, placed all his things in storage, and I had closed up my own house in the Hollywood Hills. We were running late and Lisa had planned to meet us at the camp but still my brother and I wasted ten minutes to rock, paper, and scissor our way into getting our rooms decided (we played six rounds until he finally got his way).

Now I was in a condo in Rhode Island, showered and changed, my clothes all put away, and I was waiting outside for Vince. My brother could take longer than a teenage girl to go anywhere. As I waited, I thought about how perfect Erica had been for him. She was smart and strong, and she met his strict "knock-out" requirement. She was so strong, that when we first met, I didn't doubt for a moment she was a lesbian. OK, it was mainly since Erica had advertised her contractor and decorating company in the Pink Pages to get gay clientele. Erica turned out to be an ace contractor and carpenter, who, despite her petite size six frame, could work side by side with a crew of three to sledgehammer down a non-load bearing wall in a matter of minutes. When I found out about her strategy to get gay clients, I accused her of being a "Thespian" (a straight chick acting gay)—and I realized in many ways she was the complete opposite of my now ex-girlfriend, the re-closeted actress Lorn Elaine, who had made a career of pretending to be straight.

Erica and I had formed an unlikely business partnership when I first moved out to California, one that was built from hiring her due to my extreme boredom and my inheritance of a ridiculous amount of money from my dead grandmother, which made boredom affordable. Erica certainly didn't agree to work with me from any skill I had that she lacked. I was basically her chief bottle-washer; assistant of all things needing to be nailed (Lisa would say, except women). Most often I was what Erica called her Homo-Depot runner.

I laughed at this memory as I kicked the tires of my old car to see if they were still up for the ride after all this time stored in Dad's garage. Lisa had coordinated getting the car over to the condo for me.

I yelled for my brother. "Vince! What the hell are you doing in there? Let's go!"

He poked his head though a window in the upstairs bedroom and yelled back, "Settle down! The neighbors will know the lesbos have moved in!"

"I wouldn't worry," I yelled back, "no lesbian would wear a shirt that girly!"

He laughed, walked away from the window, and I heard something smash.

"Oops," he said.

If it was Lisa's statue of Martina Navratilova . . . Vince was toast.

I got in the car to distance myself from the scene of the crime. My plan to move out to California had been a simple one after inheriting the family money. I would use my nonexistent career as a screenplay writer to somehow meet (and permanently bed) the elusive actress Lorn Elaine. When I managed to actually pull this off through a freakish series of events starting in Jamaica (a totally implausible story; maybe I should write it up some time) I soon realized that, while other people do it all the time, being a wealthy girlfriend of a Hollywood actress is not really an occupation.

Plus, being with a closeted girlfriend doesn't typically offer up boatloads of opportunity to be out together in public, since this makes more likely the chances of a paparazzi attack. Lorn's career was going well, and I had just come to terms with the fact that my ridiculous dream of being a screenplay writer would likely not pan out in my lifetime. (It turned out that writing my screenplay in order to meet Lorn had been the sole reason for me wanting to be a writer . . . whoops.) So, I decided to do what many wealthy people do—buy myself a career instead.

Rich people do this all the time. They start fundraising organizations, rescue children in far-flung places in the world, build houses for the needy, open soup kitchens, and for a while I thought about doing something similar since my sister could make some damned fine Italian Wedding Soup and various other savory items in the kitchen, including homemade wine, which could turn quite a profit for a good cause. But instead, I made the slightly less noble offer to buy into Erica's successful contracting and home decorating business, which catered to Hollywood's elite. Along with the bargain, I had led my brother Vince to the girl of his dreams, and I was convinced there was no better girl for him than Erica, as in *All My Children* . . . that is, if Erica would have him.

Working as a contractor's nail assistant was a job I grew to love, which surprised me as much as my little brother's ability to nail a girl as damned near perfect as Erica. It was the variety of the job I loved. One day I would be fetching nails, the next day we were courting prospective movie star clients at ridiculously expensive LA restaurants.

"Price of doing business in Hollywood," Erica would say as we ate $50 salads, which barely covered the center of our plates.

The next day, I would be holding my breath, as Erica would be walking like a ballerina on the clay tiles of a Mediterranean style roof overlooking the property that overlooked Spielbergs' pool. The day after that, she would teach me how to rip out a septic system she felt wasn't being done right by the sub-contractors we hired. The following day we would be firing somebody. On those days, I kept a safe distance, like when watching a train wreck. She never fired someone who didn't deserve it, and she never fired anyone who didn't try their best.

Until she fired me.

"Vince!" I yelled. We were really late now, if you could possibly be late to a campground.

Finally, he came running out the front door, hopping down the steps.

"Keys?" I asked him, and he made a face and had to go back in the condo again while I rested my head on the steering wheel and waited again. We were supposed to be at the campground an hour ago. Still, it was hard to get angry at him; he'd been fired by her too.

I remembered Erica and I had been working together for several months, when she vaguely confessed things weren't going well with Vince, though he had not mentioned a word about this to my sister, or to me. I had known only that Vince was head over heels in love, so I feared for my brother's heart. Her confession came while we were splitting a mediocre LA version of a mozzarella and tomato sandwich on the marble dust-covered floor of a rock star's mansion. It had been a big job for us, and the place had reached the stage where we didn't want to break and leave for a real lunch, unless we needed to court the next wealthy Hollywood resident for our next project.

Since we'd lined up several projects, we could relax that we were booked for at least the next six months while we dined alone in our paint-splattered clothes on the mansion's floor, a comfort level we both preferred to the swanky cafés beneath the Hollywood Hills. Maybe it was this comfort level that made Erica confess, "I'm not sure your brother and I are going to make it."

I had been in mid-bite.

"Of course you will," I said, with my mouth stuffed, "you're perfect for each other."

Actually, not true. He may have been my brother, but Vince was still a guy. Generally speaking, it was Erica that was perfect. Smart, successful, and annoyingly attractive in a tool belt, even with her hair pulled back in a sloppy ponytail. God knows, I didn't look good on the job.

She'd stared at me, waiting, I assumed, for a more convincing answer. We ate in silence for a while, and I finally laughed uncomfortably and said, "I bet the two of you will be together long after Lorn and I split."

As I heard myself say it back then, my confession sounded as if I was speaking the inevitable out loud. Since Erica had grown silent and uncomfortable, I told Erica my actress was trying to jump back into the closet I had worked so hard to pry her out of. The sad truth was, Lorn had done exactly what my sister predicted she would do. She came out just enough to keep me and allowed one very public kiss at my uncle's wedding in Jamaica, and the paparazzi ate it up. Soon afterward, Lorn credited Hollywood's attitude regarding her "new" lifestyle for every lost role or missed opportunity, and although I had more than enough money for both of us, she felt the relationship had cost her. Now it appeared I had introduced my brother to the woman who would cost him his heart as well.

Erica looked more sorry for me than for herself, so I tried to sound casual as I said, "I love her, but I just can't see her staying."

Erica nodded and I wished I hadn't said it out loud. Would it have killed her to disagree? The answer was yes, it would have, because Erica wasn't a woman who pretends, ever—well—except for the whole gay thing to get contracting clients. But that was business.

Erica ended our business partnership abruptly a few days later while we were scraping a wall with putty knives, along with two hired hands. We were covered in shards of curled wallpaper and gritty drywall bits, and she tried to talk casually as she brushed away a drywall curl, which had landed weightlessly on her forehead, like the Gerber baby hair curl. (The Gerber baby could only hope to have skin like that.)

"I need to buy back your part of the business," she had said. Then, not waiting for my reply, she continued to scrape an area that was already stripped clean. I watched as each pass of her blade removed another 3 to 5 millimeters of perfectly good drywall. I grabbed her arm to stop her, which must have startled her, because she pulled her arm away with a fierce jerk. The other men stopped scraping.

"Why do you want to buy me out?" I asked, feeling oddly heartbroken. "It's always been your business, I understand that, but did I do something wrong?"

She looked away from me, then dusted off her clothes. "No. Things have gotten worse between your brother and I, and I need to separate myself from your family. That means you, too."

It hadn't once occurred to me back then that my newfound career as Homo-Depot runner had been riding on Vince's ability to keep Erica as a girlfriend, especially a girlfriend Lisa and I had both teased was way out of his league.

"I'm really sorry," she said, looking back to the wall. "I've enjoyed—having you as a business partner, so don't ever think it was about that." She took her gloves off and touched the wall to feel the damage she had done with her bare fingertips, but she never looked at me again. "So, will you let me buy you out?" she asked.

I was crushed at the finality in her voice. Thinking back, she had sounded uncharacteristically sensitive, not Erica's style at all. I couldn't think of anything to say, except the right thing.

"Of course, you can buy me out. I was always just your gopher."

"No, you weren't," she said, but I was, and we both knew it. And just like that, I hung up my putty knife, and walked numbly to the door. "The Homo-Depot receipts are in our—your tackle box." I had called the toolbox a tackle box once, and it had stuck. Many things had stuck, but our friendship wouldn't be one of them.

"I'm sorry, Mare," she said, and I heard the scraping of her putty knife start up again, and knew the time it would take for her to repair it all later, alone. As I walked down the driveway I remembered tears stinging at the corners of my eyes as I thought about how she'd just started to call me Mare, like my brother did.

A week later, possibly escalated by all the time on my hands, which made me more visible to the paparazzi, Lorn called me and made our separation final, asking if I would mail her the last of her things. "I'm sorry, Marie," she had said.

Why was everyone so goddamn sorry?

Erica and Vince didn't have the pressures of the outside world that Lorn and I did, and since I'd built this perfect couple, I was resentful of how casually their relationship was tossed away. Lorn and I had been an expected implosion, one Lisa insisted was long delayed, but my brother's breakup bothered me as much as my own, and I couldn't help thinking, if the two of them couldn't make it, who on earth could?

Vince climbed in the car, startling me.

"What the hell were you thinking about?" he asked.

"Nothing. The Campground."

Vince reached for my hand in an overly dramatic gesture, "I'm scared, too."

"You are fucking on your own if that was Martina Navratilova you smashed up there."

"Yeah, I screwed up. I wanted to post a shot of it online, but at least I didn't break the arm holding the tennis racket. It was the one Lisa uses to hold her boxers." His voice was casual enough, but there was real fear in his eyes, and I must confess I'd really missed seeing it.

I started to giggle. "She is going to Grand Slam your sorry ass."

When my sister and I had last talked, it didn't seem to worry her that the camping season was over, and she didn't seem concerned that anyone she knew with any real experience running a business was gainfully employed and could not be bothered to help fix all that needed fixing or to run a campground. Lisa held fast to her plans to build a team comprised of people who all had too much time, money, and lack of skills on their hands: the Santora family. I knew we would be a pathetic little Italian army before Vince and I even set foot on the place.

Since the road was completely overgrown, the only clue of the camp's entrance was that Lisa was jumping around waving her arms like a lunatic when we pulled up. When I pulled in past her, I saw there was a crudely constructed camp sign that looked equally ancient and under construction. This was just the beginning. Vince and I could tell from Lisa's hard-sell grin and a quick look around as we rolled the car to a stop, that the hard-sell-grinning-her-ass-off was well deserved. I formulated what must have been the top three qualities that made an irresistible campground to an impulsive and wealthy Italian woman: 1. ancient log buildings, all with rotted (or missing) roofs; 2. overgrown woods with completely obstructed campsites; 3. thick beds of pine needles for optimum fire hazards.

I rolled down the window and Lisa shouted in my ear, "Welcome to Camptown Ladies! Oh, I see you brought a girlfriend, excellent."

"Here we go," Vince said with a grin.

I was troubled at the sight of the place. Remarkably, there were trailers with year-round campers there, but many looked abandoned for more than a season or two. My sister had bought this place?

"Lisa, this place—"

"—Now don't be so quick to judge, I know it's a little different than the pictures on the website."

"Website?" Vince said. "Were there any color pictures from this century? Because sometimes that can be a hint that there's a problem."

As if on cue, the weight of an adolescent squirrel sent a chunk of roof on the guard shack behind Lisa splattering to the ground. It was so rotted it landed in complete silence, like a thick serving of overcooked minestrone soup.

Lisa hugged us both roughly as we got out of the car and I surveyed the place over her broad shoulders. I was confident I was looking at the biggest mistake my sister had ever made, and there have been a quite a few. But this one, I reminded myself, would be special, since my brother and I had just signed on to be a part of her crew. I knew Vince was thinking the same, because he was making the girlie noise in his throat he always made when he was trying hard not to laugh.

"Shut the fuck up," Lisa said, as she nailed him in the gut, "I have huge plans for this place."

I had no doubt.

There was so much wrong with our personal lives, all Vince and I could do was follow blindly into step with Lisa's plans. Dad, forever the optimist, had been the first to join Lisa at her breakneck pace of plowing full steam ahead. Dad had already earned the nickname Woody, due to his obsession with making perfect pyramid bundles of split campfire wood, which were stacked into one giant pyramid which he fussed with constantly. He didn't dare mention it to Dad, but Vince called the woodpile The Jenga-Suit, since it would be a lawyer's wet dream the day a camper pulled a piece of wood from the pile and it all came tumbling down.

Dad outfitted himself in an impressive array of lumberjack flannels (an outfit Lisa called Oscar-de-la-lezzie) and a giant ax he got from Wal-Mart, with the handle decorated in a burned wood signature of Paul Bunyan himself. Vince walked by him, swatting him on the back in praise, "Nice attempt with the Bounty guy outfit and the ax, Dad, but Lisa is still the most butch member of Camptown Ladies."

I didn't have the heart to mention that since Dad purchased the wood pre-split, the blade of the ax was destined to never lose its shine, and the butt of the blade would forever stay its pristine Coleman red. (And if he attempted to split the wood into smaller pieces, any missing fingers or toes would not ruin the red paintjob on his ax.)

He was so pleased with himself that the rest of the family agreed not to discuss openly that his new career was less lumberjack and more shrink-wrapper. He rolled and wrapped the wood bundles in clear plastic wrap and shrank them with biggest Conair blowdryer he could find at Wal-Mart. (Unfortunately, it was available only in a tween-pleasing lime green.) He kept the blowdryer at the ready, installed at his hip in a homemade holster he'd fashioned out a large piece of white PVC pipe and an old leather belt. Dad didn't know it, but Vince was campaigning hard to change his nickname from Woody to Mc*Gay*-ver for his ingenuity and dazzling pop of color holstered at his hip.

If it weren't for the 43 rolls of non-biodegradable plastic wrap, the sparkling wood pyramid might have passed for an odd tribute to the wilderness by the rarely seen, non eco-friendly Saran Tribe. This might all have been ignored by a busy camper, if Dad had not found a price-tagging gun in the camp store and hit each one with a florescent hunter-orange sticker that read: $3.99 or 2 for $5.00.

Lisa wasn't troubled by this, as the stack of pine kept Dad busy, and at least once a week my sister walked by and pointed out to Dad a football-shaped knot in a piece of wood and yelled, "See, a vagina!"

No matter where he was in the camp, Dad, aka Woody, never missed it when someone dared to touch his pile.

"Hands off my wood!" he'd shout.

"Most men don't say that," Vince told him as we laughed. But we all worried how he would handle it when the camp reopened and campers attempted to carry the wood away to have it perish in their campfires.

Vince said to me one day, "If we ever get this campground going and they burn any of his wood, do you think Dad will hear the Screaming Of The Limbs?"

"Seriously, we should prepare him that people will be burning the wood," I said.

"Mom is bound to mention it," Vince said, and we agreed to let her break the news.

My Mother didn't have to be convinced to be a part of the Camptown Ladies project, but then, Lisa hadn't told anyone but us that she intended to transform a rundown family campground into a place that catered to gays. Mom was happy to sign onto a project with such a huge chance of failing, securing her a front seat for when it all unraveled and she could say: "I told you so." She shadowed Dad's every project, offering worst-case scenarios from the safety of the cheap seats, waiting until it would be time to take the front row.

Typically, she shouted observations from inside the camp store—by the looks of things, it was the only sound structure on the grounds, and smartly, this was the turf she had claimed as her own. Her first order of business for the camp store was a good cleaning, but she kept the screen door open to allow for a full view of everyone else's doomed activities. Within the first week I had stopped to listen at the store door, since Lisa was giving Mom vague instructions for her plans.

"Mom, I want half the store to be very girlie, you know, Yankee Candles, proper tablecloths, nothing ugly. I want to get some pretty lanterns and lots of tiny twinkle lights, you know, *fairy* lights—in all the colors of the rainbow. Oh, and let's sell porcelain plates in sets of two, not ceramic. Porcelain is actually more durable, less likely to chip, and has a higher perceived value. And no friggin' paper."

Mom's rare silence meant she was baffled. Or pissed that she was being told what to do in so much detail—but time would tell on that one.

Lisa continued, "The other side of the store needs to be for the rough and tumble campers. You know, citronella bug candles, tent stakes, fire starters, basic tools, hammers, saws, and sets of these blue-speckled metal enamel cookware and plates. That's where the paper plates will go, with all the manly stuff on this side of the store. Nothing girlie on this side. You got the picture?"

Mom thought she got the picture and suggested a name for the sign: Guys & Gals Camp Store. Lisa agreed. Later, Lisa confided to me she planned to change "Guys" to "Gays" with the flick of a paintbrush. What Mom didn't know was that Lisa planned a Fairy & Dyke divided camp store, with a line drawn directly down the middle. She was using Mom's natural tendency to Martha Stewart everything to make it happen in the projected colorways of next spring.

This was all part of a bigger plan. The Camptown Ladies idea had grown into co-ed venture one night while Lisa held us hostage to brainstorm over a bottle of wine at the condo. It had taken two bottles to do the job.

"I've got it!" she yelled, knocking her glass over, again.

"Camptown Ladies and—wait for it, waaaaait for it—Camp Camp for the fairies! We'll double our market, plus, while the dykes do the heavy lifting, the gays will pretty up the place!"

I had to admit, the half-baked, half-boy idea wasn't a half-bad idea.

"But wait," I said, "do gay guys camp?" We all hesitated, looking at each other. If we were holding this meeting at camp, the sound of crickets would have been ridiculously appropriate.

Finally Lisa dismissed her own doubts. "I'm pretty sure that's where the saying 'Do *bears* shit in the woods?' comes from. Of course they must camp."

We had been though Lisa's schemes before, and we knew better than to argue. After she had litter box trained her tiny Miniature Doberman, Cindy-Lu (and made her own litter box from a large plastic bin, into which she cut a small dog-size doorway, decorating the front with a welcome matt for Cindy-Lu to wipe her paws, and adding curtains for privacy), she got the idea to market the item. She used an adorable cartoon image of a young Cindy-Lu as mascot and included a booklet called: "Teach Your Dog How To Pee & Poo, Just Like Cindy-Lu!" In the booklet, she described how to train a puppy as small as six weeks old, by using scented puppy pads placed over a bed of sand. Gradually, you use smaller and smaller puppy pads until the puppy is just using the sand. We all thought Lisa was nuts, but she had the last laugh when she partnered with a plastic blow molding company in Massachusetts who made the prototype box shaped like a little doghouse, and then sold it to an online pet company for thousands of dollars. When she would toss this in our face, Vince and I reminded her we were the ones who had talked her out of calling the product: "Litter Box, Doggie-Style."

We had avoided bringing up the real trouble at the campground—the fact that it was way too much work for our family to handle, and that our family was avoiding it by inventing silly jobs we were qualified to tackle, like raking pine needles and clearing dirt roads of the smaller tree limbs, while the decapitated buildings with caved-in roofs remained untouched. That night, when the three of us drank our wine and Lisa got the idea about expanding a camp we already couldn't handle, she clapped her hands as if the meeting was ready to adjourn.

"Attention! Before we do anything official about the camp, I need to ask my hairdresser and Spiritual Advisor about adding boys into the mix."

Vince was shocked.

"Oh, my God. Seriously? You . . . have . . . a . . . *hairdresser?*"

Lisa hit him in the gut and Vince crumpled into a ball to protect himself just a second too late.

Three

Scents & Insensibility

Once Lisa's hairdresser and Spiritual Advisor gave her the OK, Camp Camp was added to her Camptown Ladies plan. Lisa insisted on keeping this from our parents for as long as possible, just like our childhood plot to take over Dad's garden shed as a neighborhood fort. If our childhood fort was any indicator, we couldn't keep secrets from the parents for very long. That secret had lasted only two weeks before Dad went looking for his gardening tools and instead found our beanbag chairs, toys, puzzles, and empty Heineken bottles Lisa used for spin the bottle games. Lisa had convinced the neighborhood girls they must practice before they got real boyfriends, so she did them a "favor" by pretending she was a boy, and did her best to teach them to kiss like experts. (Before her hairdresser, daytime soaps had been Lisa's make-out spiritual guides.)

After our failed coup of his tool shed, Dad was inspired by our efforts to turn his shed into a clubhouse of his own. He still kept his garden tools hanging up, but they got moved to the outside of the shed, where they fashionably turned into shabby sheik-style rusted wall décor. Inside, he rigged a sound system, powered by full electricity and added a mini fridge with a padlock to stock his beer and chilled tequila. Dad had invited me to the shed for my "first" legal drink, so, when I checked out what he had done with the place on my twenty-first birthday, I asked, "Tequila shots without lemons?"

"Lemons are for *fanuks,*" he said. (Fanuks: Dad's affectionate Italian slang for gays.)

"Ahh," I said. "What about salt? Is that a heterosexual condiment?"

"Salt is ok, unless it's on French food," he said, "I wouldn't generalize, but they have more than their share of fanuks over there." I feared the day Dad decided to generalize.

Soon after the Camptown Ladies co-ed decision was approved (by a wide-eyed, protein-starved vegetarian spiritual advisor from a hair salon called "From Hair to Eternity"), Lisa announced we would add another member to our team. "It's not enough just to have Vince here. We need one more gay guy."

"I'm not gay, you big dyke," he managed to yell, despite the huge chunk of pizza hanging from his mouth. To be fair to Vince, his lack of table manners should have proved his point.

How many times had I heard the conversation that was about to take place? It started when Vince was seven years old, so it had to be in the thousands by now. One look at Vince, and you knew he was not a gay man. A sloppy thick crest of black hair well past his forehead, the in-between stage of his beard (not the fashionable kind, the careless kind), plus, the dead giveaway: functional, not fashionable, clothes. His pants and shirts were paired so poorly that I wondered if he had the week laid out in advance to make sure he didn't accidentally match something.

Mom and Dad joined us at the picnic table and Dad happily dove into the food without a word. Mom said, "We could eat indoors like civilized people," but, even as she said it, she too was lured by Lisa's homemade grilled pizza and helped herself.

Something about the way Lisa was studying Vince tipped me off that she was about to launch into a tirade about him. I'd had my fair share of tirades launched my way, so I was sure I wanted out of there, even before she said, "Can I just say something?"

Uh oh.

"Another perfectly good girlfriend with wife potential bites the dust because you think the pussy's always pinker somewhere else."

"Lisa!" Mom said, with her mouth full. Dad cackled with his mouth completely filled yet still managed to stuff two thick slices of sausage and pepperoni.

"That's not what happened," he said, but Vince looked like he didn't have the energy to fight with her today, and typically, Lisa had missed the subtlety of this. I saw it coming, but not before I could stop her with hand signals behind Vince's back. Dad pretended not to notice, and I could see Mom calculating the best moment to jump into the mix.

Lisa leaned across the picnic table and got into Vince's face as she said, "You butthead, you really think you'll find someone better than Erica?"

"No, I don't," Vince said, before getting up from the table and walking away, leaving Lisa quietly defeated, possibly for the first time in her life. Lisa pretended she didn't like the homemade pizza she'd made, which was better than any pizza, except maybe in Italy, and she angrily tossed her slice Frisbee-style into the woods, and left the table to go after Vince.

I could see from Dad's heartbroken and hesitant glance into the woods that if the slice had landed cheese side up, he would have fought the dog for it. Mom clucked her tongue, both at the waste of good food, and a missed opportunity to lecture all three of us at once. She settled for two.

My Aunt Aggie made Uncle Freddie take her to Camptown Ladies every afternoon so she could bathe in what Lisa called the "crispy breeze" that blew through the center of the camp. My Aunt was probably the only Italian woman (besides my sister) that loved the cold, though due more to her large size than her heritage. Aunt Aggie's clothes were perpetually damp, but strangely she always smelled good, like the same salty pasta sauce that scented her house.

It occurred to me that seeing Aunt Aggie at Camptown Ladies was the only time I'd seen her with zero humidity on her upper lip. Possibly because at her home her head was always over a simmering pot on the stove (but just as probably, it could have been the facial hair). When Aunt Aggie greeted you at the door, she always had a wet kiss waiting, and I was about ten years old when I finally realized it wasn't spit but actually sweat that she left behind from her smooches—not that it bothered me less.

Aunt Aggie was a typical older generation Italian, who never let chewing a large bite from a heavy meal delay her from talking. Once, after visiting her, I went to my sister Lisa's, and her Miniature Doberman practically mauled my tits to get at the Aunt Aggie flecks of meatball shrapnel from the front of my shirt. Yet another clothing casualty due to an Aunt Aggie story that just couldn't wait between bites.

Aunt Aggie is my Dad's older sister and despite their mature ages, they still fought like children. Case in point: Several years ago, after Uncle Freddie's brother was diagnosed with Alzheimer's, he had to come to live with Aunt Aggie and Uncle Freddie in their cramped little house. He was in his late eighties and his memory was evaporating quickly. Aunt Aggie warned Dad that Uncle Freddie's brother had started making random phone calls.

"Friggin' annoying," Aunt Aggie said. "That man can't remember his own brother's name, yet he's like a walking phone book. Last week he called the friggin' army, asking for his old sergeant that been dead for over twenty years." Aunt Aggie said she had to keep the phone cord in her housecoat.

One afternoon, Aunt Aggie forgot to unplug the cord and the old man called Dad. Dad picked up the phone and heard an alarming whisper on the other end of the line.

"Sal? . . . Sal Santora, is that you?"

"Hey there, Lou," Dad said. "Is everything alright?"

"No!" he said in a louder whisper, "everything is not alright. For the last few days there has been a strange woman here. She's feeding cats. She's outside in the yard right now!"

Dad heard a thud. "Lou, you OK?"

The old man continued, quieter, "That was her, slamming the door. I have no idea who this woman is. She feeds the strays, you know, which only makes them come back for more. Everyone in the neighborhood acts like it's OK, but then she comes in the house and stays for hours. She's been here for days!"

Dad said to him, "Oh Lou, don't worry. That's probably just your brother's wife. Freddie married Aggie, my sister, remember?"

"But I've never seen this woman before," he said.

Dad answered, "You probably just don't recognize her. Lou, here's what you need to do. After you hang up the phone, go tell the woman to put on some makeup and get her fat ass to the hairdresser. You tell her she needs to put more of an effort into her appearance because she's scaring you. Got it?"

"I guess so," he said.

"Repeat it back to me, soldier," Dad said, and the old man repeated back every word. Dad said, "Now go tell the woman, OK?

"Yes, sir. I do like that man she calls Freddie," the old man said.

"Freddie's your brother. Now go tell the cat lady what I said."

"To put more of an effort into her appearance," the old man repeated.

"Because her ugly face is scaring you," Dad said.

"Yes, sir," the old man said, before hanging up.

As Aunt Aggie retold the story over the years, she said it was the last bit of instruction the old man remembered perfectly, and every time she told the story Dad would end up laughing so hard he would cry and snort until Mom yelled at him to leave the table.

Aunt Aggie and Uncle Freddie arrived at Camptown Ladies every day like clockwork, and Aunt Aggie emerged from the car in a series of dainty groans, the vehicle rising a half a foot as she did. She outstretched each arm to point to a wayward piece of trash she thought Freddie should pick up, but I knew it was actually to release the underside of her heavy arms from her sleeveless housecoat. Her arms would plop out and glisten like the mounds of homemade dough Dad made on Calzone Sundays. In fact, one of Aunt Aggie's most admirable qualities was that her fat arms were the exact matte white sheen of pizza dough before Dad bathed the dough in olive oil.

As a kid I got up early to watch Dad make calzones, and always thought Mom wouldn't approve of him oiling and kneading this stuff that felt exactly like a big booby. I never told this to Mom, since Dad always snapped off a small ball of dough for me to play with, and I was addicted to the feel of it and the delicious doughy scent.

I insisted on getting a drop of olive oil for my little blob of dough so it would feel extra soft and would last longer before drying out and cracking so I had to throw it away or feed it to the dog. To this day, the gentle grasp of a breast (either real or imagined) always brings this memory back, and my mouth waters just the same.

Aunt Aggie stood at the car and surveyed the camp as she had done every day since Lisa bought the place, and said, "Damn, Freddie, you don't get a friggin' breeze like that back in the city."

"We don't live in the city," he snorted.

"Don't be an ass," she said. I noticed Uncle Freddie tilted his head back, pointing his nose toward the trees. He loved to sniff the pines, just like I did.

Doughy arms sufficiently aired out, Aunt Aggie waddled off, shoving her walker ahead of her as if it were a disobedient child, off to go find Mom at her self-imposed post inside the Gays & Girls Camp Store. Uncle Freddie used this opportunity to sneak away to see what Dad was up to. Their visits always started and ended the same way. Peaceful Aunt Aggie would arrive, but after spending any amount of time with Mom (or Lisa, the other female alpha-male in the family) they would start to bicker. Then, holding her tongue until after Lisa whipped up a delicious lunch, Aunt Aggie would make a noise about how Mom had insulted her by not accepting her help, so, she might as well be going. She would go on about this until around 3:00, before finally leaving in an imagined huff, unless Lisa surprised them with a dessert, in which case, the argument could be extended by another half-hour. Uncle Freddie would trail after her with the same serene smile he had upon his arrival and a little more tomato sauce on his shirt, only to return the next day to begin the ritual again, everyone pretending as if none of it had happened the day before.

It was a particularly warm fall day, and we were all looking for outdoor projects. I asked Lisa if she had any plans for the teen recreation hall.

She answered, "Teen recreation hall, my big, shapely, fat ass! This is going to be my five-star Italian restaurant!"

Oddly, even with its gutted bare concrete slab floor and what appeared to be shingled roof that looked eaten by woodland creatures, there was a part of me that could not deny Lisa's genius behind a stove (or hot plate, or grill . . .) or her sheer will to bend the world to do what she wanted.

But then I remembered where we were standing.

Lisa whirled around inside the remains of the teen rec hall like a bull dyke version of Julie Andrews in a baseball hat and camouflage pants, seeing all the possibilities, while Cindy-Lu danced next to her, bouncing off her legs as if it was a new game and she were begging Lisa for the rules. I was trying to ignore the smell of teen boy urine emanating from the corners of the hall, wondering if our baby brother's pee could have stood the test of that many years. Cindy-Lu had been distracted by the scent too, her tiny high-stepping paws stopping every few feet to sniff around the perimeter of the hall, to find the most pungent spot. Dog's noses are supposed to be remarkable, so I laughed to myself as I wondered if the dog was thinking: Uncle Vince, was that you?

I said to Lisa, "A restaurant? It stinks like the old Elephant House at the Roger Williams Zoo." But this didn't seem to trouble my sister.

"I promise you, someday this place will smell just like Grandma and Aunt Aggie's kitchen used to when we were kids. She pointed to the wall that adjoined the rec hall to the Camp Store. "The mess hall cooking area will be right over there," she said. I noticed all the walls for the first time, and there was not an inch on any log without some teen melodrama carved into the wood or brazenly drawn in black Sharpie or laundry markers.

"Stop!" I said, grabbing her as she passed by me. "This has been fun and all, but nobody wants to tell you this, so I will: At some point you have to be realistic."

"What?" she asked, as if she wasn't surrounded by filth and falling down buildings everywhere you looked.

"A restaurant. Really? Lisa, *Wake up!* We don't have the skills or the manpower to handle what has to be done to just have a shitty campground!"

She shook me off her arm. "I know," she said.

I breathed a sigh of relief. She had been just playing a game of what if . . .

"Good. I'm glad you know," Lisa said, "That's why I already put a call in to Erica."

I walked toward her, expecting to see that she had grown an extra head and somehow trained it to talk like an idiot. "Erica, as in *All My Children*? Erica, as in Vince's Erica? Are you crazy?"

"She's the best contractor we know, and I want the best. I want certain things done here that she can do. I have plans, Marie, plans you don't know about—like the rooftops. I want clay tile roofs, like the kind they have in Italy, they're beautiful and fireproof, and they will give Camptown Ladies a distinctive Italian look that no other campground has."

"Because it costs a fortune!"

"I have a fortune! Erica can do it, she's done that kind of work before in California, you showed me the houses you worked on together. I'll make her an offer she can't refuse," Lisa said, like the head of the Lesbian Mafia. "Besides, she just bought you out of her business. Maybe she could use the extra money."

"Erica doesn't need a dyke campground as a client. And why would she come all the way out to the east coast when she has lucrative jobs lined up all across Burbank?"

"Yeah, well, thanks to our dead grandmother, I can afford to hire the best."

Lisa wasn't getting it. "Has it occurred to you that she needs to keep some distance from Vince and our family? She won't take the job."

Lisa said, "What the fuck is wrong with him, anyway? He's let some decent women go before, but this one . . . what a fucking idiot."

"He says it was her—"

"I don't believe him," Lisa said. "He knows we'd think he was an fool to blow it with her."

Lisa attempted to move a rusty oil barrel disguised as a trash can by kicking it. It made a mind-numbing sound but moved only an inch with Cindy-Lu yelping in protest to the noise. "Fuck. Wow! The acoustics are good in here."

I could see her wheels turning, and imagined what she was seeing as she looked up at the vaulted ceilings. Would it be a surround system to pipe in Italian music to match her cuisine, or, maybe, God forbid, karaoke? Within the seconds it took for Teen Rec Hall to morph to Gay Dining Hall, I suspected Lisa already had the menu planned.

"You need a backup plan for another contractor," I said.

Lisa argued, "She might need time away from Vince, but she might need to be around friends, too. This could be a good project for her."

"Bullshit. You're hoping to get them back together," I said.

"Actually, I never really saw the two of them as a match." She was lying, and she knew that I knew it.

We heard the distant, then blaring thud thudding of techno club music, and were then startled by the sound of tires spinning on loose gravel, ending in a short skid, just outside the hall.

"Hiiiiya girlfrieeeeends!" a voice sang outside the rec hall.

Eddie, Lisa's most flaming boy pal, was wearing a thin lemon-colored scarf, sitting high on the back of the front seat of his matching yellow convertible as if he were perched on a float made of daffodils. Knowing Eddie, I suspected he may have found the scarf and opted to shop for a car to match.

He sang out, "Heeeere I come to save the gaaaaays!"

"Eddie's here!" Lisa said, escaping me to gallop outside.

"Snuck right up on us," I said.

I was thinking how much he would love the Camptown Ladies song as he stepped out of his car on the tips of his pristine white athletic shoes with bedazzled details. He looked down at the ground, absolutely puzzled by the sight of a dirt road. He lifted a toe up in disgust as Lisa grabbed him at the waist and, tall as he was, easily picked up his wispy frame and whirled him around. Eddy squealed in delight with his hands in the air and shouted, "Mr. Load's Wild Ride!"

I hugged him next, and he kept his arms raised, disappointed that I didn't attempt to pick him up, too. "Sorry Eddie, not all dykes have Popeye forearms."

"I forgive you, honey, it takes all kinds. If you weren't such a lipstick, your sister wouldn't look so butch and get all the straight girls."

"Fuck you, Eddie," Lisa said, slapping him hard on his little, round ass as he squealed again. "Ooooh, yes! Now that you have me primed, where's that hot brother of yours?"

"Go easy. Vince isn't himself these days," I said. "Recent breakup."

Eddie made a tsk-tsk sound with his tongue. "What a shame," he said, and I knew he'd drop it there. Eddie was not a guy with whom you could discuss the cruelties of life. If you tried, his smile would remain frozen while his eyes glazed over with a protective coating that shielded him from anything not fabulous. Like a shark biting his prey, Eddie had a protective coating which kept out all that didn't glitter or have a pretty shine.

"Well, what do we have here?" he said, trying to pretend the call of the filthy rec hall lured him away from the gloomy Vince story.

"This is the teen rec hall I told you about," Lisa said, "soon to be my dining hall."

He stepped inside, unconsciously curling his fingers and wrists toward his body like a drying starfish, to avoid accidentally touching anything. Even his thumbs were recoiling backward in disgust.

He said, gravely, "Oooh."

"What do you think?" Lisa asked, though the "Oooh" should have said it all.

Eddie's arms began curling inward now and his back slightly arched to give him courage. His voice was pitched high, but it was quiet, almost mystical, as he said, "It's very dirty, but the pee smell is making me horny, so that's a good sign." When Lisa groaned, he chirped back at her, "Now, now, Lisa, one man's piss is another man's perfume." Then his fingers started fluttering in the air, in a more positive way, as if playing the tinkling high notes on an invisible piano.

Lisa whispered to me, "Teen boy piss must be Feng Shui for fairies."

Eddie spun around as if his track shoes had taps on the heels and said, "I'll help you girls out, on one condition—"

"I know, I know, you need total control of the design. You got it," Lisa said. He tried to interrupt her, but she cut him off, "I know you need an unlimited budget. It's yours."

Eddie gave a ridiculous "Yippee!" and scooped up Cindy-Lu as if she were his long lost accessory, and began surveying the hall by flitting along the edge. "Pretty little girls shouldn't get their feet dirty," he cooed at her, while Cindy-Lu enjoyed the graceful ride. Her tiny front legs always bent delicately when she was picked up, but with Eddie holding her, she appeared to be making social commentary on the suppleness of Eddie's wrists, mimicking him, as he sailed around the rec hall with her.

Lisa whispered to me, "This is downright creepy, since my hairdresser and spiritual advisor said this place would need a special woman's touch."

"Good choice," I said, knowing neither of us was up to the job.

Four

Think Inside The Box

"I hung a rainbow flag up for an hour today," Lisa said, "but I had to take it down because everyone kept asking if our family was Portuguese."

Vince and I laughed pretty hard, but it may have been the wine. I filled our glasses again to keep Vince and Lisa both anchored to the table. There would be no brainstorming tonight.

"I've learned that it's so much harder to stand out as a dyke at a campground," Lisa said.

Vince and I both said, "No worries," at exactly the same time and Vince laughed again until Lisa punched him hard in the gut. Luckily, I was out of reach, or she would have tagged the back of my head.

"Oof!" Vince said.

"Dad and Mom seem to be having fun with the camp," I said.

Vince answered, "Their version of fun. They have a whole new batch of stuff to argue about. Yesterday, they had an argument about a hole."

"Do I want to ask?" I said.

Vince told it anyway. "First Mom pointed out a rabbit hole, then Dad insisted it was a badger hole. Mom corrected him and Dad wouldn't let up, saying he saw it on the Discovery channel. Then Mom said he didn't know what he was talking about because he always falls asleep during that show, and Dad kept saying: Badger hole . . . it's a badger hole . . . yup, a badger hole. Then Mom went on and on about how he was wrong, until Dad started called her the badger, and when he wouldn't shut up about that, Mom ended up telling him the hole she was sure she was seeing was an asshole."

I said, "They nearly came to blows over whether the oil barrel trash can should have a liner. There will be a full hearing on this issue tomorrow. At 10:00. Oh, and Mom is really pissed at you."

Lisa said, "What now?"

"She says her only hope for any peace was that Aunt Aggie found getting around the campground a bit challenging, but now that you bought her a scooter, she is going to be there all day long."

We started laughing, and Vince said, "You didn't! Shit. Aunt Aggie is mobile. *Nothing* good will come of that." Then he turned to Lisa and asked, "Hey, I've been meaning to ask you, you never told us what the deciding factor was that made you buy the campground?"

Lisa didn't answer right away and I wondered, Would it be a rare confession of something sentimental? Could she have known the place would pull our parents and aunt back together to bicker on a regular basis after the inheritance had caused real friction between them?

Lisa said, "I bought it because one of the website pictures showed the gate at the entrance. It gave me the whole idea to turn the place into a lesbian camp."

"Huh?" Vince and I said in unison.

"You know the old coin box on the gate that doesn't work?"

We both nodded as we drank, not getting it.

Lisa said, "It's the perfect welcome sign for a lesbo camp. It says:"

Vince and I joined her in saying: "To insert, tap box lightly to open—DO NOT POUND!'"

"Damned fine advice," she said, as Vince cleaned up his dribble from his wine glass. It made perfect sense she would be drawn to this, since Lisa always had Think Inside The Box mentality.

That was how Lisa decided things. When she bought her place in Maine several years ago, she'd decided to purchase the property not because the backyard butted against a stone quarry and Lisa sculpted stone in her spare time from running her illegal restaurant, but because it had three giant V-shaped trees in the backyard. "See, a vagina! Three in a row! How can I not buy it?"

I had no argument. They were three vaginas, all in a row.

Lisa lifted her glass for a toast, and Vince and I joined her in unison with a toasting chant from our junior high school days: "Never drink water, fish fuck in it!" We clinked glasses, careful to look each other in the eyes as we clinked, to avoid the punishment of seven years of no sex if there was no eye contact. At the rate the three of us were going, we shouldn't take any chances, and I wondered if we were all thinking exactly that as we carefully made eye contact and gulped.

"Do you guys know how many times we've all been single at the same time like this?" Vince asked.

"No," I said.

"Five," he said without hesitation, and we didn't laugh. Vince looked miserable again.

It was still too raw for me to ask him, and Erica had been so distant on the phone the last time we spoke, that I dared not ask her, but their breakup didn't make any sense. They seemed fine the last time they were together. Vince loved living in LA, and Erica and I had been having great success in her business, pulling in several big clients. We were doing so well we had to subcontract to our most talented competitor, rather than refuse the work. Vince would join us mid-day, doing what he could to assist Erica's assistant (me), and we would work into the night, smuggling in a few beers after the end of the day and eating designer pizzas on plastic-covered floors in the houses of the latest Emmy or Golden Globe winner. Aside from our work making me see more of Erica than Vince did, all else seemed fine between them.

I remembered one night Erica and I had a laugh at Vince's expense, but he never knew it, since that night he'd insisted we smoke a joint, which ignited a case of belly laughs. Some time before, I'd made the observation to Erica that whenever Vince smoked pot, he would stare down at his leg with a spaced-out smile, as if he had fallen in love with his own knee. That night he did it again, and with the flick of an eye I signaled to Erica and she barely could contain herself as she watched that spaced-out grin on his face, staring down at his leg, and I knew she was remembering me saying he looked like an ass, like someone had left an invisible rose on his knee.

To make her lose it further, I busted out in an old Leo Sayer song, with a minor adjustment: "When I *kneeee* love . . . I just close my eyes and I've got love . . ."

When Vince, clueless and never breaking eye contact with his knee, said dreamily, "I love that song," Erica laughed so hard she rolled backward onto an open box of pizza. When she rolled back upright, there was a slice, complete with pepperoni and green peppers, pasted flat against the side of her hair. That was when I became a traitor and sided with my brother and laughed my ass off at her.

It went like that. There was never any loyalty. Whoever was the idiot of the moment would get gang-goofed on, and some of the best laughs of my life had been with my brother, sister, and Erica. Now, they were apart, and I wondered if we would ever have a moment like that together again.

Lisa broke into my thoughts as she asked him accusingly, "You ever going to tell us what happened with her?"

"She ended it," Vince said as he got up to grab the local newspaper.

Lisa said, "She loved you, you idiot. What the hell did you do?"

I feared she might start a fight, but Vince just shook his head. "Something I never do. I got too serious too fast and I tried to talk to her about marriage and some day having kids. I'm pretty sure that was the beginning of the end."

I jumped in, hoping it would shut Lisa up, "None of us can claim we're good at relationships." But my plan backfired, and now Lisa's crosshairs were on me.

"Still no word from the actress?"

Vince tried to rescue me, "Hey, why don't we have a parade?"

"What the hell is that supposed to mean?" I shot back, misunderstanding him.

Lisa said, "The campground, stupid. We need an annual parade. He's right, for once, it would be great publicity." She clapped her hands in joy at her own idea, not in a girlie way, but more like an inebriated football coach. "Oh, the gay boys will love that! Any excuse for a parade. We need to start promoting July 4th with Camp Camp's First Annual parade! I'll put Eddie right on it."

"But what about Camptown *Ladies*? The girls will need to

have a parade of their own, or the drag queens will completely take over."

Vince offered, "How about a parade where the women can walk their giant Dobermans and vegetarian rescue dogs—or their kids."

Lisa yelled, "The Dykes and Tykes Parade! Or, wait, I've got it: The Million Mullets & Mutts March!"

"Yes!" Vince laughed hard at her names, but I knew he was just happy that Lisa was off his trail.

I was laughing too, but I said, "I know you don't care, Lisa, but not everyone finds that kind of joke funny. More importantly, are you prepared to tell Mom and Dad about this?"

Lisa said, "No way. We'll just send them off on an old fart cruise if we need to."

I found it strange Lisa would suggest this, since we all knew Mom and Dad shouldn't be in any close quarters together, due to their duplex personalities. (They should be living in a duplex.)

Lisa raised her glass. "To being rich!" We clinked glasses while looking dutifully into each other's eyes. Lisa was determined to make Camptown Ladies and Camp Camp a unique experience for her guests, and despite her not having any commitment from a contractor, she was wearing her trademark overconfident smirk that made me believe anything was possible, good or bad.

I saw that same smirk one summer when I was twelve and Lisa was fourteen, and we decided to surprise Mom and Dad by helping around the house while they were working. Lisa explained I'd be inside, cleaning the entire house, while she would work outside, getting to mess around with Dad's lawn mower and weed whacker. I agreed to the idea since Lisa and I worked better when there was space between us, similar to Mom and Dad.

I started with vacuuming, and by the time Lisa was done mowing, I had moved on to dusting. That's when all hell broke loose and a swarm of bees attacked me. Well, it was probably just one bee, but I was in full panic mode. While I never saw the bee or bees, they were dive-bombing very close to my ears. My first order of business was to run out of my parent's bedroom, smacking my own head with the dust rag. My panic grew worse as the swarm followed me to the next room and, to my horror, to the next. I started screaming for my sister, but Lisa couldn't hear me over the weed whacking she was doing outside.

In the end, I managed to get her attention by barreling through the screen door, ripping the screen clean off the doorframe with my hands. I was flailing my arms and still smacking my head violently with the dust rag as I tripped down the front steps, riding the screen door like a boogie board until I twisted around, falling on my ass right next to Lisa.

Busting outside must have confused the shit out of the attacking bees, since the buzzing in my ears suddenly stopped, but I still beat on both my ears with my fists, just to be sure they had not crawled into my ear canal to make honeycombs or lay eggs. I started screaming at the thought, as I pulled off my shirt, convinced that the grass trickling down my back was the bees moving from my ears to my back.

"Now I can't hear them!" I shrieked. Oh, God, I was deaf!

"What the fuck are you doing?" Lisa asked, her huge shadow looming over me.

What was I doing? Wasn't it obvious? I was out of breath with panic, sitting in our front yard, now just in my shorts and bra, my shirt flung into a nearby birch tree. But even in my panic, I knew Lisa would never let me forget how ridiculous I looked, she would learn the sign language for this, even if I could make her realize how I'd been nearly killed.

"I was dusting in Mom and Dad's room, and, out of nowhere, I was attacked by a swarm of bees!"

"A swarm," she said, perfectly calm.

"Or maybe it was just a few, but they could still be on me! I couldn't get away from the buzzing no matter what room I went in!" I said. "They were in my ears!"

I boxed my own ears with another good swat just to make my point.

Lisa came a few steps closer with her weed whacker still in hand as she plucked my shirt from the tree.

"That shirt could be filled with bees!" I screamed as she tossed it at me. I screamed bloody murder all over again, swatting the shirt to the ground, then kicking it away as neighbors ran outside to help.

Lisa waved off the neighbors and moved toward me with that smirk on her face. I'd seen that expression so many times growing up, and I braced myself. Whatever she had coming, it couldn't be as bad as what almost happened to me. I had just survived a killer bee attack.

Lisa pushed the button to start the weed whacker and it made a droning buzz, buzz sound . . . my swarm of bees.

"Put on your shirt, you fucking imbecile," she said.

Five

Allowing Others to Touch Your Wood

Dad, aka Woody, was at his pyramid, making his never-ending adjustments, when Eddie took a break to chat with him while puffing on a cigarette like Greta Garbo. This conversation would be too good to resist, so I took the long way around the Camp Store to stand unnoticed behind the wood pyramid, the plastic wrap glistening in the noonday sun.

I pretended to inspect the shingles on the side of the laundry room, in case Lisa happened by again. Lisa had already been by to tease Dad once already, going off about pyramids and then segueing to ancient predictions about the end of the world: "What makes people think just because it was written a long time ago on some ancient scroll, that it wasn't written by the Mayan equivalent of the *Enquirer*? There were probably tons of reporters around to write what idiots said or did—just like they do for the celebri-tards today." Dad just gave a few uh-huhs and continued to tweak his wood.

I observed that Eddie was dressed like an Oscar hopeful D-list actress portraying a pretty but downtrodden scrubwoman. His golden hair was protectively tucked under a dew rag (black polka dots on pink silk, with black velvet piping), knotted in front. Feminine as he was, no woman would have the balls to publicly wear the floral housecoat he had gotten a hold of, but if anyone did, it might have been Dad's sister, Aunt Aggie.

"This is some fabulous wood you have here, Mr. Santora," Eddie said, "and believe me, I know good wood when I see it."

"Why, thanks Eddie. You're a man of great taste."

Eddie chuckled and I could hear a smile in my father's voice and could tell he was playing with Eddie, who had no idea my father had learned a fair bit of gay slang after our trip to Jamaica last year.

I marveled at my Dad's liberal view of a guy like Eddie. Dad once told me that in the neighborhood where he grew up, the *fanuks* were regularly beaten straight, so they rarely came outdoors, and this was how the term "coming out" came to be. Dad had clarified, "I like the ones that come out. It's the fake straight ones I don't like." Amen to that, I'd later agree. Nobody hates the fake ones more than the recently dumped.

I could see Eddie's hip jutting out in his pronounced way, his trim waist adorned with a Homo Depot tool belt he wore like a mini-skirt. He had taken the time to trim it in matching orange-colored Victorian lace. Only Eddie could make a tool belt into a fashion accessory.

"Your wood is a work of art," Eddie continued, "a monolith, a glorious Easter Island sculpture right here in Foster, Rhode Island."

Dad said wistfully, "If only my daughters could appreciate the beauty of wood like you do."

I heard the sticky sound of Dad lovingly patting his plastic wrap, as Eddie agreed and said, "You said a mouthful, Mr. Santora. What dykes know about art, could fit in my fanny."

They both laughed. *This was my father?*

"Besides, if they really appreciated wood, they wouldn't be lesbos now, would they?" Eddie said.

"I try not to judge," Dad said. I wondered on which day he had tried not to judge?

"You know, Mr. Santora," Eddie said, "if you structured this just a bit differently, when people came to take the wood, we could make sure the pyramid design doesn't get ruined."

"Take . . . the wood?" Dad said, appalled.

Uh-oh.

"Yeah, we could pretty it up even more and have the folks take the wood from one side only, so the bundles would roll down and replenish itself from the tip." I was pretty sure Eddie brought up the whole conversation just to say "replenish itself from the tip" and that he had no idea he was breaking the big news Dad had not considered.

"Oh, I don't know," Dad said, unprepared to commit, still reeling from the shock that people might someday be defiling his creation.

I could hear shouting coming out of the Guys & Girls Camp Store, so I left Eddie to deal with the trauma he'd started. Mom and Aggie were loudly debating color schemes and when I walked in, they were stationed at opposite sides of the store, waving color swatches at each other. It appeared Mom wanted an eggshell white, while Aunt Aggie campaigned for the robin's egg blue swatch in her chubby fist. I saw my chance to direct Mom, while knowing I ran the risk of getting taken out by fight shrapnel, which was quite common in our family.

"Lisa already decided on the colors," I said, and Mom sighed as if I had wasted a year of her life.

Aunt Aggie snapped, "So why are we even here?"

I wanted to ask that very question myself, but I didn't dare.

"So, what are the colors?" Mom asked, followed by a second Darth Vader sigh.

"Pale olive green on one side, and lavender on the other," I answered.

"It'll look ridiculous, but whatever she wants," Mom said. She began rifling though the swatches for the least-offending versions of olive and lavender as Aggie snorted behind her. They shook their heads in unison—a silent agreement that despite each other being wrong, the younger generation didn't have a clue.

Mom walked over to the "Girls" side of the store near the feminine products section, and held the lavender swatch against the wall. It looked good against the blue packaging on the tampon shelf, but I had to correct her.

"Nope," I said, "olive green is for the girls' side and lavender is for the boys'."

"What?" Aggie and Mom said together, as if I had commanded them to strip naked and call a taxi.

"That's what Lisa wants," I said, leaving the store with Mom and Aunt Aggie in amicable agreement that my sister and I were stupid asses, a fact that many couldn't argue. Nothing could bring Aunt Aggie and Mom to a united front more quickly than ganging up on one of the kids.

"They take after their father," I heard Mom hiss, and Aunt Aggie cackled in agreement.

Outside, I found Eddie had convinced Dad to take steps to preserve his art. He had begun structuring a second wall of wood around the base of the pyramid, while Dad stood silently, as if observing a molestation. Eddie continued to plead his case for the changes, and he was as animated as a young mother in a supermarket, trying to keep her spoiled child from losing his shit.

Eddie said, "When people take the wood from this area, the pile will spill from the top to this second protective wall, like a moat. This way, you can just replenish the pyramid from the top. It'll keep the design from getting ruined by people taking wood from wherever the fuck they please. Otherwise they'll ruin this beauty."

This must have convinced Dad, because he spun into action as if he had joined the Red Cross to haul emergency sandbags to shore up a dyke. He was moving so quickly, I was tempted to yell, "We must save the village!" but decided to leave them be.

Two problems solved, I thought, as I wondered where my brother and sister had gone off. I walked the main trail of the camp and noticed it had gotten cold enough to see my breath. Aunt Aggie and Lisa must be in heaven, I thought, wishing I had inherited their tolerance of the cold. California weather had suited me. I had always thought of the cold weather like an enemy encroaching on my camp—this time, literally. I did feel some comfort in the colder weather; it was a reminder that I was far away, from California, and from Lorn.

A few of the year-rounders had opted to leave their trailers for the late fall and winter, despite the sale of the camp. Many were likely to never move again, since the years of occupying the same patch of woods had encapsulated them in the trees. There were dozens of trees that would have to be cut to get the trailers out, but this would prove impossible as well since it was clear the trees were the only things holding some of them together.

There were signs of life, though. Family signs: The Williams, The Homans, The Rileys, The Henrys, and The Sarnos, each announcing their family's presence with a favorite icon or theme. I made a mental list of the most popular: Winnie the Pooh, Mickey Mouse, butterflies, frogs, and the ever-popular Betty Boop squatting (panties showing) over a tiny garden of tulips.

Most signs were handmade, badly drawn cartoon characters sawed roughly out of painted wood. Crafty but deformed renditions of Mickey, Minnie, and Betty stared back at me with creepy, asymmetrical eyes, and peeled painted skin, appearing like radiation burned versions of their more famous counterparts. Some sites had "duplicates" for sale, standing in line like cartoon solders, each attempts at a duplicate of the last, some morphing badly from the more careful first whack of the camper's newly acquired jigsaw. The originals, more carefully cut and painted, proudly sported "This one not for sale" signs.

Some campsites had remnants of past holidays and seasons; July 4th flags as whirligigs, garden stakes made of sawed-out wood tulips, random Halloween characters scattered in trees and on trailers for the holiday weekends, all compacted on a camper's calendar and celebrated between spring and early fall. Christmas in July was the most observed holiday, celebrated with chunky wooden Mr. and Mrs. Claus characters perched on porches, and leaning against children's bikes and skateboards as if on guard duty.

There were more unique sites, revealing a bizarre cottage industry that had taken hold of the camp. People had taken to selling oddball crafts, and advertised them by tacking up signs on the walls of the public toilets, zipped inside clear plastic baggies for protection from the rain. Inside were photos of items for sale, with a site number for easy shopping. There were knitted scarves shaped like giant caterpillars and snakes, crudely painted initials that appeared hacked out by a drunken woodworker set loose on a scroll saw binge, and an odd assortment of giant bugs and figures made from common household items. My favorite was an aluminum soda can, split open, rolled and painted to look like a ladybug, with the words "CLING PEACHES IN LIGHT SYRUP" still visible under the washy red coat of paint. I noted the sun-washed gray polka dots on the wings, which were probably black last summer, but had not weathered through the miscalculated overstock inventory, which made me wonder if things ever got marked down.

One seller specialized in several variations of a Tin Man made of vegetable cans, and a smaller version where the character's "pants can" could be pulled down. Leaving nothing to chance, there was a red arrow pointing down to the tin man's crotch and the word "PULL!" painted on his tomato sauce can belly. If you did as instructed, you were rewarded with the revealing of a stubby penis made of wood and mounted on a spring for movement. There were signs everywhere shouting the prices based on size of the cans, and Polaroid photos of happy buyers trapped in Ziploc bags, their ghosting images fading in the sun as they posed with their new tin friend, all tasteful photos with the pants cans in the up position.

Most of the buyers were men, but there was an occasional woman, and even one grandmother who posed with two younger generations of Tin Man buyers grinning toothlessly at the secret of the spring-loaded penis. Small veggie and soup can Tin Mans went for $10, while larger coffee can Tin Mans went for $15, and the tiny Tin Man went for $8. I noticed the smallest size had to forego the spring movement and thought it a shame. I decided that once the tin can artist opened up shop again I would have to get the large or medium Tin Man as a gift for Eddie.

The owner of the site is Ray, a fact deduced from a sign hung on his tree: "WELCOME TO MY SITE! I AM RAY, MAYOR OF THE CAMP!" The mayor may have loved his self-appointed position, but he didn't trust his constituents; a fact revealed by the way he permanently soldered the feet of the Tin Man samples to an iron railing of his deck. Ray would be a guy I would have to meet. Next door to Ray the Mayor was a sign announcing the Town Sheriff, and two trailers after that was the Tax Collector, who had nailed a bucket to a tree with "Tax Donations" painted on the side and a promise to use the taxes for buying flowers for the shared areas of the campground.

I continued looking for Lisa and Vince, but my distractions had slowed me a bit. The trees were heavily dropping their brittle brick-colored needles and would have to be attended to in order to keep the fire hazard low around the campfires. I decided I might take that project on, since, strangely, Lisa had not assigned me a job.

As I looked up at a particularly tall pine, I wondered if my sister thought I was in too fragile of a state to boss around. That would be a first, I thought, as the pine tree reminded me of a dream I had last night. It had waited for just the right moment to sneak up on me with a memory of a dream about Lorn. Cruel how dreams can do that, lie dormant all day, then sneak attack when you least expect it.

In the dream, I had been in California, looking up at a palm tree, which I noticed was branded PALM TREE along the entire length of the trunk. I looked around and realized every palm tree in sight had been branded this way. It was then in the dream that Lorn approached me, sliding her hand into mine.

"Beautiful, aren't they?" she said.

"I guess," I answered, but I wanted to tell her the branding of the trunks concerned me. Instead, I kept it to myself and tried to admire the perfect palm fronds bursting at the top, each tree identical to the one that stood beside it. This was when I noticed that the underside of the palms looked as if they had been molded from a green plastic and realized in dismay that none of them were real. The trees I had passed by and admired each day on the way up to my house in Hollywood Hills had been fake, and it struck me now that the dream made me feel they were tackier than a penis-popping Tin Can Man.

In the dream, I had looked at Lorn, noticing her hair was not the same stunning auburn red I had loved so much, and wondered if the color had been fake as well. "I love you," she said, interrupting my thoughts. "Not enough," I'd answered in the dream, and her hand slipped out of mine.

A distant banging broke me out of the memory and I walked toward it to find Lisa and Vince attempting to repair a bathhouse. Lisa was in the more dangerous roof position, while Vince was below her, handing her the supplies.

She was yelling down to Vince. "I'm thinking if this particular shitter ends up being on the Camp Camp boys side, I should have glory holes built right into the bathroom stall walls. Sort of a nice perk, don't you think?"

"I guess," Vince answered, paling at the thought.

"In the long run, it'll save us from some hack job, since you know they'll cut the holes anyway. This way, we cut a professional hole, and maybe even line it with some vinyl padding, just to avoid a lawsuit when some horn dog gets a splinter in his dick."

Lisa let go of her toolbox and it slid off the roof, carrying a strip of shingles with it, raining down the other side of the building.

"Whoops," Lisa said, "accidents happen."

Vince said, "Yeah, well it might be a good time for me to tell you about Martina. The neighbor's kid didn't do it." She glared at him. "It was their fucking dog."

I yelled over to them, "You guys really need to wait for the contractor, or someone's going to get hurt!"

Lisa said, "Hey Marie, as long as you are doing nothing, go get Eddie to pick a good color for the vinyl to line the holes in the men's bathrooms. I'll try to figure out a way to advertise it without being tacky. Something like: 'All the men's stalls outfitted for easy toilet paper passing' or something like that."

Six

Campgrounds, Catholics & Curses

Campgrounds practiced strange traditions like cramming all the holidays into the short camping season, and Lisa had plans to do the same. My enthusiasm for scheduling events for Christmas in July made me wonder if my religious past was rearing its ugly head again. My relationship with God had always increased during the lowest points in my life, like whenever I was nursing a breakup, or retching over a toilet. I was a foul-weather Catholic.

I wasn't religious in the homosexuals-are-going-to-hell way, of course. I was more the if-you-steal-something-you-will-pay-for-it-tenfold way. Lisa, Vince, and I all had a similar lack of enthusiasm for religion, amplified by our aunts and uncles, who were old school Italians and reveled in all Roman Catholic traditions. Lisa said once, "You know you were raised by a bunch of fucking Italians when a candle promises a scent of Christmas Eve, and you expect it to smell like fish."

It was one of the many oddities that differed us from our peers. You grow up figuring that everyone does the seven fishes thing on Christmas Eve, sitting around a table eating struffoli and torrone and never daring to eat meat until after midnight. We thought all kids knew the secret of how to lift the Malocci curse, which could be passed along only by the eldest male relative, and only on Christmas Eve. The Malocci is a headache curse caused by someone who is thinking ill thoughts of you, and the curse is lifted by saying a special prayer while running oil down a finger into a bowl of water. Throughout the year, if there is no elderly relative handy, an Italian horn may ward away this curse in a pinch. The blood red horn, usually plastic with a gold crown on the thick end of it, also plastic, was easily found in heavily populated Italian neighborhoods. Gas station convenience stores often had them near the front counter with the Life Savers. As kids we were not swayed by the cheapness of this item. We believed it had special powers because our grandmother wore a small one right alongside her crucifix and her gold Number 13 necklace.

I had always prayed when I was scared at night, or when I needed something, but when I was about ten years old, I convinced myself that God talked to me through the trees. I was sure of this, though I never told anyone. Who would I have told? Lisa? ("What the fuck are you? An idiot? I'm not going to have a nut bag for a sister, so knock it the fuck off.") Vince? He was four years younger than me, and easily spooked, so I would have given him nightmares about birch trees. I couldn't have told my mother, who was only half Italian, and whose concept of anything mystical or religious was for people who had far more free time than she had.

Mom may have been right, since religion came to me for the first time when I was painfully bored. I was in the backyard trying to lay low from Mom, who could hone in on my boredom like a professional bass fisherman, even if I was hiding under the couch like a perch under a sunken log. She would go trolling the house and throw her hook below the couch, then inform me that she needed a hand with the laundry since I was just wasting time. When the weather was good, it was easier to hide my boredom from her, since most of Mom's chores were indoors.

On this particular day I was laying low outside and I remember it was cold and windy, since I was fantasizing about what it would be like to have been born by a mom who was OK with children hanging around the house during a nice day, watching more than three hours of TV. I nearly caved and went back inside due to the cold, but Sundays were floor-washing day and I didn't want to get roped into moving kitchen chairs. Plus, washing floors made Mom particularly grumpy. Lisa always said she was grumpy because none of us had yet mastered the art of floating, and she could not accept the impossibility of three children's feet not touching a floor for a solid hour.

On that day, I did what I always did when I was bored outside; I went across the street into the only entrance to a small patch of woods. I felt lucky we had these woods. It was the only one in the neighborhood and all the kids would have to walk by our house to get to it, and we had it right across the street. This was a safer option than moping around the backyard, where Mom might spot me out the kitchen window.

I watched the wind kick up the leaves into a dance and thought of a game where I asked the trees Yes or No questions. If the trees stayed silent, then the answer was No. If the wind picked up and made them wave, then the answer was Yes. A poor kid's Magic 8 Ball. At first I asked questions that were silly, like, Would I be rich some day. (The trees said yes—and they turned out to be right.) Then I started to ask questions that I already knew the answer to, to test the unsuspecting trees. (Is my house white? Does Danny Gallagher from my English class have a pimple face, etc.) After the trees had answered eight in a row correctly, I got the eerie feeling that I was not just playing a game. I stopped asking questions and the trees stopped too. I remember sitting in the woods for a long time, until the silence got spookier than playing the game. So, I did what I always did when I was scared (and only when I was scared):I talked to God.

"God?"

Just then, the wind picked up the biggest gust yet and swayed the trees back and forth as if they were enthusiastically, or insanely, nodding their heads and the breeze pelted against my widened eyes. 'Yes, of course it's me!' they seemed to be saying.

When the wind died down, I asked softly again, "Really? It's you?" And the wind picked up again, in a rage this time, twisting the trees until they bent in impossible ways, seemingly that only something made of rubber could do. The wind kicked up and up, and when I didn't think it could kick up some more it kicked up again as if all the trees wanted to show me how silly I was to have doubted them.

The leaves were vibrating so fast and furiously that they sparkled like a body of water, cresting in waves that built and fell, then built again. I thought I heard music, I thought I couldn't breath, I definitely couldn't move. I thought I had found God.

I told nobody.

My superstitious mind told me I should not mess with powers like this, and quizzing God could get me in a shitload of trouble, like playing with a Ouija board, so I didn't talk to the trees for a long time after that. But, as the intensity of that first day faded, I began to talk to them again, and this habit followed me into adulthood so gradually that I never had time to analyze if it was a dumb thing to do. I just did it. I still did it—and I still told nobody.

And now I was spending time in a campground, and today I did it instinctively on my walk back through the camp after Lisa shared some news. "She's coming," Lisa had said.

"Who's coming?" I asked.

"Erica. She is taking the job as our contractor."

"You're shitting me. Does Vince know?"

Lisa said, "Not shitting you. You should tell him."

"Hell no! Your idea, you do it."

"You want them back together, too, and you're much closer to Erica. You tell him. It's a good sign that she agreed to come," Lisa said.

Was it a good sign? I silently asked the row of trees looming behind my sister.

Immediately, the wind whipped through the campground, pulling the pines into a frenzied dance on the horizon. Maybe it was.

"Where the fuck did this wind come from?" Lisa said, "It's been still all day."

The trees seemed to be dancing an enthusiastic "Yes!" celebration. Or maybe they were flailing their limbs to warn us about a horrible mistake Lisa had made. Good sign or not, I realized selfishly that I wanted Erica to come. I had missed her, and missing a person like Erica was not the easiest thing to do. To the world, Erica was not the warm and fuzzy type; she was more like the cold and prickly. But toward me she was cool and neutral, and I was flattered by it, since this was Erica's version of warmth. My brother liked this about her too. When Vince first met her, he had interpreted her tossing a few barbed comments his way as a sign that she might like him, and he'd turned out to be right.

I wrangled a job out of Erica and used my new fortune to pay for a distraction. What I had bought myself was a job with a talented and overbearing boss. Over time, I had noticed her critical assessments about my work had slowed to an occasional snide comment, and, with Erica, this was probably the only evidence I would ever have that we had become good friends. No criticism was like someone else saying "Good work!" and I understood the gruffness of her. I was Lisa's sister, after all.

Erica was a dangerous spitfire, who carried just over the safety level limits of butane; an attractive Bic lighter in a stunning fashion color, one that always seemed just shy of torching a person if they irritated her. She cranked hard on that flint when someone had the misfortune to annoy her, but there was something about Erica that stopped her just short of being a bitch. Erica was ridiculously attractive and savvy, and I often thought that had she also been charming, it would have been overkill, and I might not have approved of her being my brother's girlfriend. Too much of a good thing.

It was her cocky and caustic edge that fascinated me from the day we met. I had called her business, looking for a contractor, by checking the Pink Pages to support the gay and lesbian community in my new neighborhood. Somehow, Erica had managed to convince me she was the woman for the job by insulting me over the phone. The balls on this woman, the irritating and unfathomable nerve.

Before I hired her as my contractor, I had one demand of my own: I wanted to work on my house with her. Erica answered with a stipulation of her own: "Will you take orders even though you're paying me?" This would have been a warning sign from anyone else, but, looking back on it now, I realized we had built a friendship as she barked orders at me.

Vince had a crush on her the second they met, and I warned him he was barking up the wrong tree, that while she looked like a straight girl, she was one of my people, but Vince convinced himself he could turn her, as I convinced him he was an idiot. After months of letting both of us think she was gay, I busted her when she showed up one day in a cute sundress. (To her credit, Erica never curtailed her truck driver language while wearing a dress.)

Concerns about Vince aside, having her join our Camptown

Ladies project would be just what we needed, since Lisa was clueless about the larger jobs. I knew from experience that Erica could assemble a crew to whip the place into shape. More importantly, Lisa was in her frequently wrong, never in doubt mode, and this can prove dangerous, especially with nail guns lying around. With so many roofs needing to be replaced, and special roofs at that, and log walls to be replaced and electrical and plumbing to be added or completely updated, we were in dire need of someone we could trust. Truth be told, our greatest building achievement so far had been Dad's woodpile.

Eddie, however, was cruising along just fine, except for the fact that we were doing everything backward and the structure needed to be addressed before the cosmetics. Lisa had the money to burn, so Eddie was doing what he could to prep the rec hall and ready his decorating decisions. Today I was stopping by the rec hall on my way to get the leaf blower take another crack at managing the pine needles in the worst buried sites.

Lisa was standing at the entrance of the rec hall, testing the ice cream inventory of Mom's store by chomping on a vanilla filled-waffle cone thing and beaming at Eddie as if she had sired him. Lisa has a way of doing this; of claiming something with such convincing authority that I knew I would soon have to fight the urge to put my arm around her and offer the proud papa a cigar for the fine job she did raising her son to be a decorator.

I stood next to Lisa at the doorway, marveling at the site of Eddie on all fours. He was humming "It's Raining Men" while he scrubbed the urine-stained corners of the hall as Cindy-Lu sat nearby, hurt and disappointed that Eddie was ruining the urine perfume they had bonded over. She whined and he leaned until he was nose to nose with her.

"I know, my darling. But the world doesn't understand the beauty of these things as we do. Trust me, once the boys start drinking, there will be plenty more where that came from."

Perhaps the only thing gayer than watching a man with a pink boa scrub urine stains while singing "It's Raining Men" is . . . well . . . my sister and I decided there just isn't anything gayer. Eddie cheerfully worked with his nine-pound supervisor at his elbow until the bleach smell drove Cindy-Lu to the farthest corner of the hall, disgusted by his choices.

Lisa said, "I don't like my dog hanging around this filthy floor. She sleeps with me, and a Miniature Doberman is like a heat-seeking missile in bed. I sleep naked, so sometimes I wake up with her so buried in my crotch that she's wearing my labia like a Princess Leia wig."

"Charming," Eddie said.

"Keep singing, Eddie. I love that song. If only it could rain men, huh?"

"Tell me about it, honey!" he said.

Lisa said, "It would be great. The fall would kill most of them." Pleased with herself, she took a dramatic lick from her ice cream.

"What the hell are you eating now?" I asked her.

"It's called a Choco-Taco. Very yummy."

She turned the ice cream taco vertically and shoved it in my face and shouted, "Look, a vagina!"

I pushed it away, but not before she had nailed my nose with vanilla.

"I had Mom order these for the dykes. I got Drumsticks and Bomb Pops for the boys—they're shaped like penises and butt plugs. Oh, and Hoodsie Cups. Despite the boring shape, there is just about nothing gayer than a Hoodsie Cup."

We both looked at Eddie, who was wiggling his ass in time with his scrubbing and humming. I should have known better than to point out when Lisa was wrong, but I tried, and she shoved the Choco-Taco in my face again.

"Licking something taco shaped is the only thing that will cure you," she said.

I pushed it away again, but she shoved it into my face harder; this time, the ice cream entered my nostrils. I tried to push her away but it was pointless, she was too strong, and I was in a weakened state, choking and laughing. Years of different variations of the same struggle flashed before my eyes. The pool fight, the car fight, the beanbag fight, the shopping cart fight. They all ended the same: Lisa wins.

"I'm doing this for your own good!" Lisa said, with such certainty I almost believed her. Still, I managed to bat her hand away.

Eddie yelled over his shoulder at me, "She's right, honey, it's for your own good, just lick it."

"Girls! Stop that out there!" Mom yelled from inside the store.

Eddie giggled, "Your mom called me a girl again."

"There's no window. How the fuck does she do that?" Lisa said, letting me go at the sight of Mom rounding the doorway.

"Language!" Mom yelled.

I wiped the chocolate and vanilla from my mouth onto my sleeve. I whispered, "She can hear through walls."

"Looking good, Eddie!" Lisa shouted, the thunderous echo making Cindy-Lu cower as Lisa stuffed the rest of the ice cream in her mouth, despite my nostril contact. "Work it, boy! Bottoms up, elbows down, you dog!!"

Eddie delicately put a rubber-gloved hand on his hip, "Girl, I just know you're not talking to me like that."

I said, "Lisa, what would you think about hanging an Italian Horn somewhere in here for luck?"

She answered, "I suppose it's less creepy than the string of rosary beads Aunt Aggie wants."

Eddie piped, "You Catholic types are weird."

"Amen," Lisa said.

Eddie said, "I don't get it. The whole drink the wine and eat the host."

"Only if she's hot," Lisa said, before she walking off. She thumped me on the back, hard, and said: "Well, I'm off to stock the pond with some fin-less brown trout."

Eddie waved his rag, "Isn't the pond that way?"

I laughed at him. "She says that whenever she has to go to the bathroom."

Eddie shook his head in disgust. "Dykes," he said as he lovingly scrubbed a petite spot of urine.

It felt good to laugh again, and as I scanned the edge of the campground the trees waved, laughing with me. I would always keep my Tree-as-Magic-8-Ball religion to myself. It was a bizarre part of me and I needed it . . . just like I needed to hear Mom and Aggie snapping at each other over what shelf the plastic tablecloths should be stored on. I needed to see how Eddie would visually transform a smelly teen recreation hall into my sister's dream. I needed to watch my Dad fester, dramatically guarding his wood like the insane man that comes barreling out his screen door when neighborhood kids make the unfortunate choice to cut across his lawn. I needed to hear Lisa barking orders like an insane short-order-cook-football-coach, using insults and sarcasm to motivate her weary and mostly unskilled team. I needed my brother and I to forget two women; one who was coming back too soon, and the one I realized I'd never had.

Seven

Testing For Soft Spots

I knew Vince wanted Erica to come, for all the wrong reasons. He looked like a heartbroken, but hopeful, boy, with dreams of still winning the girl. "This might be our only chance. I would have never gotten her back with Erica in California and me in here in Rhode Island."

It was then I feared the trees had been signaling doom, and I had misread it. "Remember, Erica is coming to help us with the Campground," I said.

"It's a long way to come for a contracting job when she's doing so well out there." He was trying to stifle a grin. It was a grin I hadn't seen in so long.

I tried again, "She's doing it as a favor to Lisa. That's probably all, Vince."

Still, I supposed there was a chance, since it really didn't make any sense for her to take the job. She'd be leaving lucrative clients out west, to come across the company to be closer to someone she just broke up with, yet she had decided she'd be the lead contractor of a campground? Maybe there was still a chance for her and Vince, but I knew better than to encourage him since, by the look on his face, he was already counting on it.

A few days later, Erica and what she called her "scouting" crew of three roared into Camptown Ladies in a rented, flatbed, diesel engine truck, outfitted with ladders and tools and some other heavy gear I could not identify. Since Lisa and Mom had forced me to eat a meatball sandwich for lunch, I did a quick face check in the mirror before heading outside to greet her. It had been over eight months since I had seen Erica at my Uncle Tony's wedding to Lorn's mother. Since then, the phone calls between us had dwindled down to nothing, the last few times with me doing the calling. Erica had been all business over the phone, except for Erica always getting in one cold comment about Lorn, "Dump her before she makes a fool out of you."

"Too late," I would say, and she had been right.

Erica hopped out of the truck, her hair stylishly pulled back from her face by the expensive sunglasses perched on her head. Erica was dwarfed by the doublewide truck, making her look nothing like the mighty woman I knew she was. In strength, her personality was the level of my sister, though her barbed comments were a bit more tasteful than Lisa.

I could see by her hands-on-hips pose she was already accessing the structure of the Camp Store and the tired rec hall with the oddly sparkling cement floor. She dropped her hands from her hips when she spotted me.

"Hey," I said.

Erica just stared at me, as if I were a stranger.

"What's wrong?" I asked, scanning for meatball on my shirt.

"Italian's aren't supposed to be thin," she said, disapprovingly.

"I'm still fatter than you, and I just had a meatball sandwich," I said.

"Well, you look terrible."

Her concern flustered me a bit.

"Well, you look great, as usual, bitch." I said, and she did.

Erica was a gorgeous woman. It was no wonder Vince had fallen for her the first day they met, right after she'd insulted his shirt (and deservedly so). Done deal; he was hooked. I remember thinking back then: Who wouldn't be, poor bastard. I always expected to see a trail of men following behind her like ducklings, and my brother expected this, too. Lisa had warned me back then, "Vince aimed too high this time." When I reached Erica, she surprised me with an awkward hug.

Erica would have shocked me less if she had struck me across the face with the back of her hand. (Which I had seen her do to a worker after he made a suggestive comment about her flawless body. He had been holding a bucket of nails and the contact of her hand across his face sent the bucket flying across the room. She let him apologize for an hour before firing him.) Clearly, Erica had been in pain over this breakup and I felt this in her quick hug, which felt more like a quick body slap, and also in the way she yanked her sunglasses down over her eyes when she parted from me.

Seeing Erica this fragile was not something I had ever considered. Her hug had made me catch my breath and my eyes sting at the corners, threatening unexpected tears. I was reminded of when I returned from college to find that my childhood dog, a regal female Doberman, had gone from a bounding ball of energy, to a fragile old dog, seemingly overnight. When I knelt in front of her, she tried to rear up on her shaking legs. I had cried when I finally hugged her, her third attempt finally landing her paws on my shoulders. We'd done this since she was a puppy and to see a sign of frailty in one of the strongest beasts I had ever known was one of the saddest moments I ever felt. Erica would not have appreciated me comparing her to my Doberman, but there it was.

"You don't hug," I said.

"Let's never speak of this again," she said, flashing a forced version of the smile that had sent my brother over the moon.

"I'm glad you're here," I said, launching into business mode, since I knew this was what she'd want. "If you've already eaten, I can give you a tour of all the buildings, such as they are, so you can assess the crew size you'll need."

"Sounds like a plan." I could hear the relief in her voice. "The guys know what to do here." They were already unloading gear. "Jesus," she said, looking around. "It's so much worse than she said."

"I told Lisa you required full control of the budget, and that you'll quit if she questions you regarding spending."

"Aww, you remember. And she caved without a fight?"

"I vouched for your ability to beat up vendors for the best prices," I said, starting toward the rec hall. Erica caught me by the arm to stop me, surprising me again. Erica was not a touchy person, either.

"How are you holding up?" she asked.

Seeing her had brought freshness to the pain of losing Lorn, and I wondered if she could see that. Erica hadn't exactly been the supportive gal pal, back then. Instead, she was more like the beer buddy that came over to fix your drywall with a silent agreement not to speak about your troubles. (If you had a beer buddy that was ridiculously attractive.)

She had been just what I needed then, and now, here she was again, only this time I was wondering if we both needed each other. What had happened between her and Vince to affect her like this? I took a deep breath and said, "You don't do sensitive chats, either."

"I just brought it up because you look terrible, worse than the last time Lorn left," she said.

"Thanks. Technically, this is the last time Lorn has left. So, you don't look terrible. How the hell do you manage that?"

She let go of my arm. "I didn't look so good after everyone left."

"You mean after Vince moved back."

She nodded. "How is your brother?"

I said, "I know you don't want to hear this, but he's devastated. He won't talk about it. Will you?"

She said nothing, so I said, "Lisa and I assumed he messed things up like he usually does with women, but we finally got it out of him that it was you that wanted out."

Erica looked away at the rec hall again. "I realized right after we were together—I had made a big mistake." She started walking again, so we continued to the rec hall.

"Are you going to tell me more?"

She shook her head. "Just that I wish this was new to me, but it's not. I'm great at the chase, always have been. After that, well, I can't really say what happens, usually nothing. I bail."

"Funny. I'm always the one that always wants to stay."

"You didn't stay," she said.

"I think I can finally recognize a hopeless case. It was over with Lorn before it really began. You told me that, Lisa told me too. I was just too stupid to see it."

"You were in love," she said, not looking at me. "We all want to recognize a hopeless case before diving in. It doesn't really work that way."

I could not believe who I was hearing. "I'm not sure if I can get used to Sensitive Erica," I said.

She wouldn't look at me as we walked, so I put my arm around her and felt her stiffen from the contact. This was the Erica I knew. She moved away to get a closer look at the building. "By the looks of this place, we should get to work. Will you tell Vince I'd like to speak with him?"

Now she sounded like a school principal. "I will. But Erica . . ."

She turned around to me. "Yes?"

"Be gentle with him. This isn't business. He's hurting."

"We're all hurting," she said, surprising me again.

I stayed with Erica as she surveyed the buildings, whipping out a small book out of her back pocket and jotting down some notes. From another pocket she produced a giant tape measure, pulled the end out, and stabbed my middle with it. "Take this. Go over there."

I took it and went over there. And with that, I became her assistant again. She moved like a cat, whipping the tape in and out of its holster, sometimes whipping it at my head and instructing me to go here or there—but the more challenging angles, Erica did herself. Just like old times. The whole time, she was making comments to herself about how we had started this all backward, that Eddy should not have touched a thing without her first shoring up the foundation, and replacing the main structures. I knew she was right.

Erica got an accurate measurement of the large, open barn-style windows by climbing up the 4-foot-high pedestal where teenagers had carved their every desire into the splintered wood. With one hop and a pull of her arms, Erica hoisted herself up to the roof. I stood below and watched her feet disappear past the edge of the roof.

"Jesus," I said.

"They say he was a carpenter," she called down, well out of my view on top of the sagging roof. "But I can't see him yelling down at girls from the top of a roof. Hey, get me that other tool belt from the truck."

"You have a ladder, do you want it?" I asked.

"No need for this, I won't be up here for long, it's not safe," she said.

I was used to the silence that followed and didn't wait for an explanation. By the time I'd returned, I heard the thudding and knew what would happen next. She was within my view on the apex of the roof and was walking heavily in a squatted position.

"Rain dance?" I asked. But I had seen her test for soft spots before, and it always made me cringe. "So we get confirmation if one of your legs caves through, right?"

"Or both of them," she said, and it seemed likely as the thudding got muffled.

"No rain dance . . . the last thing we want is more rain," she said. "Thankfully Lisa wants brand new, since this is completely rotted, and all has to come off."

She said this as casually as if she needed to change a tablecloth. She stopped walking and straightened up. I looked in the direction where she stared, and spotted Vince walking toward the Camp Store. Erica scaled down the side of the roof but didn't jump down to the pedestal. Instead, she sat on a less rotted edge with her legs dangling over the side of the roof and waited for Vince to look up. She looked like a kid on a dock waiting for ducks to swim by—and Vince was the sitting duck.

I pitied Vince. She was quite a sight up there, her highlighted hair shimmering in the sun. Even from the ground you could see the flawlessness of her skin, but I knew the casual position of her hands folded in her lap betrayed her self-consciousness.

Vince stopped short as if he had struck himself with a badly-placed cartoon rake.

"Erica's here," I said, playing Captain Obvious.

I had warned him the night before, because if left up to Lisa, this would have been his first warning: Erica perched on the edge of a roof, looming over him.

Vince walked to the rec hall with his eyes locked on Erica. "Hey," he said. "Marie hid the ladder on you again?"

"Nah," She said. "Climbed it old school. How are you, Vince?"

They both sounded overly formal and I wanted to walk away, but thought it would be more awkward for them if I did, so I stood there, trying to look concerned about the job Erica had ahead of her with the rec hall.

Vince answered, "OK, I guess. Just trying my best not to read into why you took this job."

He was not wasting any time, and I felt my face flush with embarrassment for him. He walked closer to the rec hall as he said, "The rock stars in LA pay a lot more to build their mansions than you're gonna get refurbishing this tired Campground."

Erica said, "Lisa probably has more cash than some of them do; they all snort it up their noses. You OK with me taking the job?"

"Sure," he answered. "So . . . should I be reading into the reasons why you're here?"

Erica looked at me before answering, looking equally heartbreaking and unintentionally cruel. At that point, I couldn't face the look on my brother's face, so I turned away and walked to the Camp Store.

"You shouldn't read into it," I heard Erica say.

Eight

Hanni And My Sister

The first time Lisa made a name for herself in elementary school was during her very first exposure to sex education. It wasn't sex education so much as an introduction to the changes our pre-teen bodies would be going through during puberty. Since she was a year older than me, (she was eleven at the time) and since we were in different parts of the school building, I had to hear about the results after it happened. It was discussed where all important things got sorted out: at the dinner table after Dad got home from work. This is how it went down:

MOM: Lisa, your teacher called us. Your father and I want to discuss what happened today in class.
LISA: It was ridiculous, so unfair, and someone had to say something!
DAD: Lisa, be quiet, and listen to your mother.
MOM: Your teacher said you were disruptive to the class.
LISA: She was the one being disruptive, breaking news like that!
DAD: Still, that's your teacher. It's not her fault. I mean, the news she had to tell.
LISA: Someone had to say something, Dad. Some of the girls were crying.
DAD *(to Mom)*: It is unfair. She does have a point.
MOM: Stan, we discussed this. This is about Lisa being respectful in class.
MARIE: What are we talking about?

LISA: They showed secrets today about how our bodies are going to change.
MARIE *(I laughed and tried to act cool, like I had heard it all before)*: Oh, like getting boobs. So what? *(Vince laughed at the word "boobs.")* You just don't want it to ruin your field hockey game.
LISA: You have no idea, you dummy!
MOM: Lisa, don't—
LISA: You think it's funny because you don't know about the bleeding part! Plus, they told us both the girls and the boys stuff—
MOM: Lisa, stop it.
LISA: They tell the girls you're going to bleed between your legs for five whole days, and it's so disgusting that you have to wear a diaper or stick a piece of cotton up you know where—
MOM: Lisa!
I dropped my fork, Vince's little eyes bulged out of his tiny sockets, and Dad pissed Mom off by trying to hide hold his smirk behind his napkin. We all knew Dad didn't touch his napkin until the very end of the meal.
LISA: Worst of all, *this* is the boys part: 'Look out boys, while you are sleeping you might get an orgasm without having to do a friggin' thing!' We bleed from our crotches, and they get that! *God is outrageous!*

The scene ended with Dad bursting out laughing, sending an explosion of peas past his napkin back onto his plate. In the end, Lisa didn't get punished for speaking out in class that day because Dad convinced Mom that the whole bleeding for five days for the next forty or so years was outrageous, and punishment enough for his girls.

The story about Lisa's outburst became legend at school and solidified my sister's position as a leader, which followed her all through her school years. Whenever she chose to run for a school position, she got it, no campaigning necessary. If she decided she wanted to be the captain of her sports team, she was voted it, unanimously. This was a comfort to me, since, until that time, I believed I was the only one who automatically fell in line to her every command, and it was good to see the rest of the world was going to do it, too.

Years later, when Lisa was in high school, she boldly brought home a stray pet she named Hanni. The original owners called her Hannah, but Lisa wanted her newly acquired pet to have a nickname. This pet came in the form of a high school exchange student from Ireland.

She had been lured to the States under the guise that she would experience America while finishing her senior year of high school. What she got instead was a family who desired a full-time nanny for their cantankerous children, and a maid for their filthy house. Hannah was beautiful, and Lisa, having a weakness for all female things beautiful and unattainable, brought her home one Friday for the weekend.

Lisa planned to work on our mother over the weekend until she had sufficiently pleaded Hannah's case of imprisonment and white slavery. I thought she looked quite healthy for a slave girl, but later we heard stories from Hannah about the way her host family treated her. However, those stories were nothing compared to the version Lisa told our parents over dinner, after Hannah had hugged Lisa goodbye and sadly returned to her host family's house.

My sister painted a Cinderella story, though Hannah dressed not in long layered skirts with chimney sweep stains, but rather short corduroy cut-off shorts and tight t-shirts that fell, oddly, and beautifully, just short of meeting her waistline. Lisa told story after story of how Hannah was brought to this country as an indentured servant, as Mom ate her dinner with a permanent look of skepticism emblazoned on her face. Now, this was Mom's natural state and perhaps Lisa in her effort to get her new pet had misinterpreted this as something out of the ordinary for Mom, and clumsily oversold her case.

Mom finally said, "Well, maybe she is a girl that doesn't like to pitch in. Maybe she thought she was getting a vacation. I'd sure like to hear that family's side of the story."

I had no doubt of that.

Lisa reminded Mom how helpful Hannah had been all weekend, and she wasn't overselling that. Hannah had made us feel obligated to take our plates up to the sink and rinse them off, so we didn't look like animals compared to her. I resented her for that, but my brother did not. He shadowed her every move that weekend and she could scarcely turn around without bumping into him. Mom agreed she'd been very helpful, but she still kept her lips tight together, a sign we knew meant nothing foreign was getting in, least of all, a teenager from Ireland.

Vince broke the silence at the dinner table. "How old is Hannah?"

I was embarrassed for him, since all his life he had never asked about anyone's age. All eyes were now on him, a welcome relief from Lisa's filibustering.

"Same age as me, dumb ass," Lisa said. Mom gave the back of her head a flick with her hand.

"Language," Mom said.

I noticed Vince had lost interest in his dinner. If we hadn't been having his favorite, Uncle Freddie's homemade ravioli, I might not have noticed it, but now he was just rolling his fork over his plate.

Lisa noticed it too, and sensed an opportunity. "Why aren't you eating that? You know, Hannah would love it if her host family fed her a homemade dinner now and then." She paused for a deep sigh. "She has to eat McDonalds and Burger King almost every night, if she gets to eat at all." Well played.

Mom stopped eating, her lips parting slightly. Mom's fork was lowered slowly, laid down on her plate in horror. Lisa had her in her hooks, and now was happily eating the ravioli off Vince's plate. Her work here was done. Lisa and I knew that no Italian mother, no matter how skeptical, could tolerate the idea of withholding food from another human being, especially a growing teenager. Mom had already judged that Hannah was dangerously deprived of food, her trim figure lacking the doughy coating that all American kids had these days, us included. This was an angle that Lisa should have considered earlier.

Hannah confessed to me months later that she had never been so fat in her life. I confessed to her that she was a lunatic, and she must think she'd joined a family of right whales. Hannah, now officially named Hanni by our family, lived with us the entire year she was supposed to be with her host family, and little Vince, always assumed by Lisa and I to be too geeky to take notice of a girl, had fallen deeply in love before the age of twelve.

When Lisa brought Hanni home, she was meant to be a toy for her own amusement. A more improved sister, one who would act more according to how Lisa wished. A sister who happily would ask her questions to learn her way from someone who had been there, done that. As it turned out, Hanni was more of a gift to our baby brother, who taught himself how to make eggs when he found out it was Hanni's favorite, and who wouldn't take her yellow terry cloth robe off ever since she draped it over him one morning while he sat chilled as he watched his cartoons.

The yellow robe became his uniform, the layer of Hanni he could drape over his clothing, and even when the summer came, and it was much too warm for a bulky terry robe, Vince would wear it, still opened in the front, terry belt dragging on the floor, since Hanni was so tall. He made her a fancy card for her birthday, and bought her favorite chocolate with his allowance money. He protected the Sunday crossword puzzle from Dad to save for Hanni by ripping it out of the paper each week, having set his alarm to get up before anyone else in the house.

Lisa and I teased him mercilessly, but, for the first time, Vince took no steps to avoid being teased, his way of not denying his love. He got up on weekends as if he was the new parent of an older adopted child, cracking eggs and hovering over the stove until Hanni smelled the bacon and was lured out of the bedroom she shared with us. Out by the pool, the terry robe converted into his beach towel, making Vince appear so small when he wrapped himself up on one of the lounge chairs. Lisa and I thought he was making a total fool of himself. But the truth was I feared for his heart when Hanni returned to her country once the school year ended in September.

Hanni loved Vince and said he reminded her of her baby brother back home, and I was a little jealous of Vince, who had done what I couldn't do: hijack Lisa's friend right out from under her. Hanni liked me well enough, but who could resist the devotion of little boy Vince? It would be like ignoring a shaggy little puppy that follows you around, appreciative of any scrap of love that fell to the floor.

When it was time for Hanni to go back home, it was difficult for our family. We'd all grown attached to her, but it was nothing compared to what Vince was about to go through. I was still lashing out at him for handing his heart over on his terry sleeve, while I braced myself for his pain. The day she left, Vince said he had a surprise for her in the living room. I wondered what he could have gotten her when he had already spent every penny of his allowance on a ridiculous gift, a red plastic round tablecloth with an umbrella hole cut out of the middle, simply because she said she loved the color red, and it was something he could afford. She had fawned over the tablecloth while Lisa and I shot looks back and forth to each other. Vince had beamed.

Vince had set up a boom box in the living room and told her to sit on the couch, while Lisa and I watched, uninvited, from the kitchen. He was carrying a wooden spoon and pulled two of the sofa cushions to the floor for his stage.

"Oh God," Lisa whispered to me, "the spoon is his microphone."

Vince pressed the play button on the boom box and Lisa and I watched in horror as he did an Elvis impersonation in Hanni's yellow robe, worn out and dingy after a year of dragging on the floor and refusing to let Mom wash it. Vince pumped his arms and used the wooden spoon microphone in spastic, Elvis-like moves.

Why the fuck Elvis? Lisa and I were both thinking this as Hanni clasped her hands together, eyes tearing up with joy, as she shouted, "I love Elvis!" like only a non-American could do. Lisa and I looked at each other, then ducked out of view to snicker from our humiliated embarrassment of him, like two cruel schoolboys.

Vince ended the song by spreading Hanni's tattered robe like giant butterfly wings, then, thrusting the wooden spoon microphone in the air, he bowed his head under imaginary floodlights, to Hanni's thunderous applause. Lisa and I were covering our mouths, laughing our asses off, even as the pit in my stomach widened for Vince. I peeked around the corner in time to see Hanni storming his cushion stage, giving him a giant hug, lifting him off his feet as he shyly looked away from her, smiling as she told him it was the best present she had ever received in her whole entire life.

I remember being angry with Vince, but I know now it was because I was devastated for him. I knew the following day Hanni would be gone from our lives and he would be checking into Heartbreak Hotel. I didn't know it then, but my brother would meet Erica and, so many years later, check right back in.

Nine

Patty & Anne Should Have Done The Nasty

Lisa had planned a dinner at our condo the first Friday night of Erica's arrival. In this case, "planned" meant she had invited everyone over and the rest was up to me, which meant it wasn't going to be a home-cooked meal. Mom and Dad took a pass (Mom said her jammies had been calling out to her since 6:00) but, surprisingly, Erica agreed to come, Eddie was his typical "maybe" (which, in gay man speak, meant no, thanks, he was going to hold out for something better to come along, or go out whoring for a date at last call).

Lisa doubted it had been a good idea once the confirmed crowd turned into just the three of us and Erica, but it was a done deal once Erica accepted. To make matters worse, Vince made my heart ache when he emerged from his room overdressed for the night. It was so obvious that even Lisa resisted the urge to tease him.

I tried to keep things light as Vince and I set the table while Lisa selected her seat at the head of the table and played with her phone.

"Maybe it was sex," Vince said, breaking the silence.

Lisa and I glanced at each other, then back at him.

"Erica," he said. "The sex was hot at first, but it fizzled kind of fast." Then he quietly added, "Well, for her."

I moved away from him and the table to find something to appear busy with near the kitchen sink. It was his profound sadness, not the mention of sex that made me want to jump out the nearest window.

"One question," Lisa asked, "you went south, right?"

"Yeah, it went south," he said.

"No, you idiot. Did *you* go *south,* you know, did you take care of her oral needs?"

I cringed as I re-washed a cup at the sink. Unfortunately, I could still hear them over the faucet and my insane humming.

"Oh! Of course," he said, insulted at the question.

"Well?"

"She said she wasn't really into that," Vince said.

"Uh, oh," Lisa and I both said in unison.

"What does 'uh oh' mean?"

Lisa said, "Vince, write this down. *Every* girl is into that. Repeat with me. *Every girl is into that.* Unless—"

"Unless?" Vince asked.

"Unless the guy doesn't do it right."

I winced, but Vince ignored her and said, "It's just . . . after the chase was over and we finally went to bed—"

Lisa interrupted, "Wait, how long was the chase?"

"Well, we kind of had sex right away, but then not again for about two months."

I dropped the cup, and it shattered on the floor.

"Uh, oh," both Lisa and I said.

Lisa put her phone down and folded her hands in front of her, looking like an angry dyke therapist who was pissed her client didn't follow last week's recommendations. I feared for Vince's very soul.

"Did you at least try a vibrator?" Lisa asked.

Vince said, "What? Of course not."

Lisa Therapist shook her head and rubbed her forehead in frustration as she looked down at her non-existing appointment book. She thought this patient was beyond help. The look on her face: Oh, well, maybe my next patient will have a clue. Next.

Vince defended himself. "I would have done anything to make her happy, but we were so new together I didn't think we needed—besides, I never got the point of those things."

Lisa and I looked at each other again. I was grateful to have the shattered cup to deal with, and I made a small production out of cleaning it up using two magazines, since buying a broom is something wealthy people think of only after something gets smashed.

The therapist said, "It's not for *you,* you idiot. Can you imagine that for even a second?"

I didn't look at them yet I knew Lisa had grabbed Vince by the face. "OK, listen up. I am going to teach you the difference between sex with a vibrator and sex with a man." I braced myself, for Vince's sake, and dared to sneak a glance to see Lisa pluck three grapes from the bowl in the center of the table. Uh-oh. There would be a lecture, with props.

Lisa began, "Sex with a vibrator is like having somebody peel grapes and place a bunch directly onto your tongue, one right after another." She plopped the grapes onto her tongue and savored each one as she chewed them with deliberate slowness. "Mmmm," she moaned, "yummy and oh, how easy that was. Each grape landed where it was supposed to, *deee*-lecious!"

Vince wanted to run, but I could see he also wanted to hear the ending since he was getting secret lesbo information about pleasing women.

"Now," Lisa said "sex with a man is like being told you *might* get one grape if you're lucky, but it's certainly not going to be peeled, and might not land in the right spot. In it fact, it might be way over here." With that, she picked up a grape and with her state champion softball pitcher's arm, she hurled it across the room to splatter against the far wall.

Lisa's 'Licker Is Quicker' talk—it had been only a matter of time before he got it. She had given it to me on my sixteenth birthday. I remembered it well.

The doorbell rang, so Lisa was forced to release Vince's baffled face from the vise grip of her non-pitching arm and he looked at me with helpless confusion, which only magnified when Lisa opened the door for Erica. Poor Vince. He was the best of any of the guys on the planet, but (from what I had heard my straight friends complain about) what most men knew about pleasing a woman in bed evaporated after the first six months of dating. I flash-backed to overhearing Aunt Aggie saying: "I'd like to kick the balls of the man that convinced the rest of them if they just stick that thing in, we'll hear angels sing. Most often it's like hearing a drunk on karaoke with the microphone not on."

I felt better about Vince being overdressed when I saw Erica, but

I heard Vince let out a little groan, though it may not have been him. My sister took a step back to leer at the whole Erica package from dress to girly shoes. "Wow. Don't walk too close to me dressed like that," Lisa said.

"Like what?" Erica said.

"Like a girl that wants to be fucked by me."

"Lisa!" I yelled.

Erica laughed, but Vince was too busy having his feet melt onto the kitchen floor to force a laugh.

"Hi, Vince," Erica said.

"Hey," he said casually, sounding like a boy in a high school gym pretending his prom date hadn't dumped him in front of all of his friends.

Erica looked away from him a bit too soon. "Thanks for inviting me, Marie," she said, and I wondered if she had ever used my first name more than a handful of times. Despite her feminine appearance, Erica was more of a last name kind of girl. I could only imagine how it must have pained my brother to look at her. As I was admitting to myself how stunning she was, I heard a wet "splat" sound as the wet hunk of grape dropped from the wall behind her. Erica turned to see a dribble of grape from the spattered wall.

"Come on in," Lisa said. "We were just making wine the old fashioned way, and talking about . . . grapes."

Vince shot Lisa a look that could kill. I was thinking tonight was a huge mistake, when Lisa said, "I know just how to get this party started."

She popped on some music and rushed to prepare a tray with eight generous shots of tequila. I wondered what it said about us that we didn't have a broom or a laundry basket, but we did have a full set of twelve shot glasses. The four of us gratefully downed our two shots each and I excused myself to pull the Mexican food from the oven. Vince tried to make small talk, and before the shots did the job, I was cringing for him again, pretending it was the heat from the stove.

"So, what have you been up to since, um, how's business?" he asked Erica.

"I've been busy," she said. "Which is good."

I missed working with Erica and said, "I remember. It was fun while it lasted." It sounded a bit more sentimental than I would have liked. She smiled, and I felt another deep pang in my gut for my brother. That smile had to be hard to give up. One glance at my brother's face and I knew I'd been right. He reached a little too quickly for his next shot.

"I have a new assistant," Erica said.

This time, the pang in my gut was for me, but as Vince poured another round of shots, I said, "My Homo-Depot skills were that easy to replace?"

"Real, easy," she taunted me, but then threw me a bone and said, "not really." Then she asked Vince, "Do you still have your camper?"

"I do," he said, "It still needs work, but it's sitting for now since Campground Ladies has taken over our lives."

"It will be taking over mine soon enough," she said.

"We're all glad you're here," he said, and it sounded so awkward that after a few seconds of silence, we all laughed at him, and Vince laughed too.

"So, how are Mom and Dad doing with all this?" Erica asked.

I said, "They're the same. They don't change."

Lisa said, "I give them shit to do, but never enough to keep them entirely off our friggin' backs. I have to admit the camp store is coming along pretty good, if Mom doesn't kill Aunt Aggie." Erica nodded as she laughed. She'd witnessed more than a few scuffles and enjoyed the show.

"I've been enjoying that," she said quietly, and again I thought about how she seemed so different. Softer. If my brother noticed it, then we both hoped the softer side meant she might still be in love with him.

Later, many drinks later, we were between laughs and stunned silent when Lisa said, "Last night I was too tired to change the channel on the TV. The remote was across the room so I watched the movie classics channel. Seriously, I know I'm not the only one who thought Patty Duke and Anne Bancroft should have done the nasty in *The Miracle Worker.*"

Vince said, "The one about Helen Keller and her teacher?"

Lisa said dreamily, "I had such a crush on Patty Duke when I was younger. She may have been wearing a dress, but she looked like a second baseman to me. Anne was hot, too. They should have banged in that movie. I'm just saying what everyone else was thinking."

I turned to Erica and said, "Actually, that has never, ever happened."

Erica laughed her head off and it was so infectious that I joined her until we were both snorting over our food. Lisa and Vince just stared at us, wondering what was so funny, and that just made us laugh harder.

Our laughter was followed by an awkward silence, until Erica lifted her glass of wine to the three of us. "Thanks for including me. And, I mean, not just for tonight."

As we clinked our wine glasses with hers, I wondered why Erica's eyes looked a bit watery, since of all the things Erica was not, she was definitely not a crying girl. She took her last swig and said, "I've missed this, you fucking crazy Italians."

We drank to that, and although Vince looked happy for the first time in a long while, I knew he would have preferred she'd said she missed him.

Ten

Sticks Or Stones

"Attention Happy Campers! Good morning to all!" Erica was barking sarcasm at her crew—a small group of men, but smart (they feared her). At an alarming speed, they were tearing off the Camp Store roof, and shards of rotted roofing shingles were flung like nail-filled Frisbees from every corner of the building.

"Did I hire a bunch of friggin' pansies? It's almost ten and I can't believe that roof is still on!"

They appeared to be working at breakneck speed to me, until she yelled at them, and they moved in double time. I noted once again that knowing how to motivate a work crew was an essential part of being a great contractor. The tiles spewed off the roof and I took a few steps back after a roofing nail flew by my head.

"Looks like it's going well," I said to Erica.

"If this were the only building, maybe, but after this office building, we have the camp store, six bathroom houses, and last but not least, a rec hall to be turned into a restaurant." Now didn't feel like the right time to warn her my sister was considering building a dozen individual log cabins to bring up the caliber of the campers. Less tents equals less drunken college kids, she had said.

Erica continued, "Not to mention all the other buildings that need minor structural work, which is all of them. What a flipping mess. Good thing I didn't know the extent of this on the phone, or I never would have taken this job. As it is, we need to line up a second crew of workers to handle the specialty Italian clay roofs; these guys here are strictly demolition. We'll switch them out as needed."

I bent down to grab some nails and one of the crewmen let out a short whistle. When he turned back around, Erica flung a roof tile at him and hit him on the back of the head, but she never stopped talking. God, I missed her. She said, "Lisa considers the rec hall to be the heart of the camp, so I need to make sure my best guys work on that building. Not these bozos."

We'll switch them out, she'd said. So maybe it wasn't just my hopeful imagination that she considered us a team again. "What can I do?" I asked.

"We should call the dumpster delivery place to see what the holdup is. This is going to be one huge mess to clean up since they didn't have the dumpster ready this morning."

"I'll get on them," I said, knowing Erica hated to repeat an order, and when she said "we" she really meant "you." I noticed a burst of excitement coursing through my veins, which I hadn't felt in a long time; I was a part of Erica's crew again. I headed to my phone and when I turned back to see if she had anything to add, I was surprised to see her eyes not on the crew, but on me.

"Hurry up," she snapped, "before we make a bigger mess here."

No, we wouldn't want that.

I had the dumpster guys on speed dial and was harassing them within seconds of Erica's harassing of me. That was why we had made a great team. I finished the call and was thinking this and smiling when I saw Uncle Freddie across the road, watching the roof progress from under the pines. He was sitting in one of the rocking lawn chairs Lisa had given him and Aunt Aggie. Despite the fact I should have been asking for Erica's next order, I walked over to him.

"Hey there," I said.

"Marie, my *Marieooche,*" he said, exaggerating his Italian accent.

"I see you found the chair."

"This is where the supervisor sits," he announced.

I put my hand on his shoulder and turned to see the supervisor's view. Erica had jumped on the railing and hoisted herself onto the roof to get a better view of how her crew was failing her. She kicked a lunch bag off the roof when no worker cared to claim it, sending a half-eaten sandwich and potato chips exploding in the air as Uncle Freddie chuckled.

"They're afraid of her," he said. That girl has a nice kick."

"She does," I agreed.

"You sure pay a lot of attention to that crew. You after my supervisor job?" he asked.

"I never did roofs, but I miss being a part of a crew," I said. "Just keeping an eye on the help. Don't tell Erica I called her that, she'll kick my ass."

Uncle Freddie chuckled and said, "Want to know a secret, *Marieooche*?"

I crouched down next to his chair as his eyes returned to Erica and her crew. "I'd love to know a secret," I said.

"My Papa was a stone mason in Italy from the time he was a very little boy." He smiled, remembering his father. "Nobody in our village was as strong as my papa was. I could hardly lift some of the tools he used all day. When we was young, he could walk me and my brothers, all three of us, on his shoulders."

Uncle Freddie put both hands out to show me how wide his father was. "I was always on his left shoulder and my two smaller brothers rode together on his right. We thought if we stayed still he would forget we were up there and ride on his shoulders all day, and a few times we did."

I sat on Aunt Aggie's chair, as we watched the crew, and like clockwork, seconds later, Aunt Aggie buzzed by on her scooter, yelling over her shoulder to me, "Don't get too comfortable in my fucking chair!" Then she beeped and was gone, a blur of red scooter and flapping floral housecoat, no doubt off to harass my mother at the camp store.

Erica was working side by side with the crew now, pulling up the rotted roof tiles and hacking away at the soft beams underneath to see what needed to be replaced. She looked over at us once, and surprised me by refraining from asking for a report on the dumpster.

Uncle Freddie said, "My papa always said, 'In life there are only two things: *In o fuori?* Are you in or are you out? Because in life, either you're in—or you're out." I'd heard Uncle Freddie say this a million times, but I loved hearing it every time.

"My father never did anything halfway, always he made beautiful work. The most beautiful stone walkways and walls, and entire houses, all from stone, and his work was so fine that wherever he went, he was treated as a fine artist."

I had often thought Erica's work was that of an artist. Though the flying shards of rotted roof lacked the beauty of the interior work we had done in the multi-million dollar houses in LA, there was still finesse to the way she did everything. She used the back of her hammer to gouge the underside of the tiles and pry them up and pitchfork them in one motion, spearing them, and spewing them over the side of the roof in a flow that for some of the men took two, sometimes three moves.

Uncle Freddie continued, "You know, in Italy you're an artist if you do something very, very well. There was no such thing as blue-collar workers out in the country; because we all had blue collars, most times we had no collars at all. What do you kids call those white T-shirts with no sleeves, housemaker slappers?"

"Wife beaters," I said.

"That's mainly what we wore, still wear them as my skivvies, but as far as wife beaters go, I don't kid myself. Your Aunt Aggie could kick my ass." I laughed with him and he was quiet for a while before he continued.

"I loved working with my dad, and because he was a stonemason, this meant me and my brothers were apprentices from the day I could walk. Some people said I became an artist, too, but I was never as good as my Papa. Everyday I tried to get up before him, but no matter how early I was, he was already up, eating his bread and cheese for breakfast in the dark kitchen, waiting for me. On the day of my birthday it was the one day I got up before him and beat him to the kitchen. I was so excited to be the one to put out the bread and cheese on the table. I was so excited to do it that my hands were trembling. I knew he would be so proud of me. I had just turned twelve years old . . . and that was the morning he passed on."

There was a painful lump in my throat as I pictured Uncle Freddie as a little Italian boy, sitting at a dark breakfast table, bread and cheese laid out, trying not to eat a tiny bite before his papa got up. I wondered how long he'd waited, and if he'd got dressed to go out to work with his shock of curly black hair tucked under the tiny wool cap, a smaller version of the cap he still wore today, holding down his thick, gray hair. I had never heard this story, and I wondered, since he said it was a secret, if he had ever told it. Uncle Freddie was silent now, the corner of his eyes glinting with tears, but he was still smiling when he finally spoke again.

"It was good that I was a skilled stonemason by then, so I could help take care of my family. My brothers tried to help, but they were younger than me, and they needed to go to school. Do you know your dad's sister didn't go to high school?"

I nodded. I knew that about Aunt Aggie. She was much older than her brother, my father, and my dad had told me the girls needed to stay at home. Such a different world now, I thought, as Erica scolded a worker for something she deemed careless.

After a long pause, Uncle Freddie said, "When I grew up, I wondered if my Papa had known he was sick and maybe this was why he taught me everything so young. Later, after helping to support my mother and brothers, I was able to make a life for your Aunt Aggie and your cousin Frederica, who still lives in Italy. My father had saved two families by teaching me everything he knew." He gave a little chuckle. "Your Aunt Aggie never considered me an artist. She mostly complained about how my clothes were always dirty and my hands were the same sandpaper as my chin, but she always cleaned my clothes for me, and always packed me a homemade lunch so I had good food at work."

He watched as Erica's men moved swiftly along the top of the rec hall, hurling boards over the edge of the roof. I wondered if he was thinking about how it looked like they worked with wild abandon, not like artists at all. I also remembered the time Erica confessed to me how different her family was from mine, that it was only her and her parents. I couldn't imagine not growing up with a brother, a sister, an eccentric grandmother, two sweet uncles, and our lunatic Aunt Aggie.

I was still watching Erica as I said to him, "Your secret was that nobody knew you had been up waiting for your papa the day he died."

He smiled, watching the crew, as he said, "No. My secret was nobody ever knew what I really wanted was to be a carpenter."

Eleven

Lisa, Unleashed

Unlike my Uncle Freddie, nobody ever had to guess about what my sister wanted in life. Anyone who knew her for longer than a few minutes sensed that the best approach with this woman was to step back, smile, and do things her way.

When Lisa became enthralled with an Emmy-winning soap actress, she decided she would go to NYC to meet her, and she did. She had dragged me with her, and the three of us ended up talking the actress into going to a lesbian bar (the actress was straight, married, mother of twin girls), drinking vodka shots until we were kicked out at two-thirty in the morning. How does a gorgeous soap actress get kicked out of a lesbian bar, you might ask? This happens after Lisa coached the actress on all the best moves a pole dancer should treat the crowd to, improvising a stripper pole with a hallway coat rack.

All was well at first, and there was a brief and riotous show, right up until we learned the coat rack had also been a load-bearing structure, and half the hallway collapsed because Lisa yanked the pole out of the wall. The collapsing took place during Lisa's somewhat graphic demo of the next move she wanted the actress to do for the crowd. The bar owner was pissed, but the lesbian crowd cheered in protest (except for the bar people still trapped in the hallway) as the three of us were escorted to the door.

The bouncer wasn't as big as my sister, so Lisa got the idea to whip out a Sharpie marker (from God knows where) so the gay-friendly actress could cheerfully sign breast autographs on her slow parade out the door. The soap actress said it was the best night out she could remember in years and when she finally parted ways with us on the street corner, she gave my sister a steamy kiss in front of the screaming crowd. Lisa says they still chat often.

What was it with the Santora girls and actresses?

I had been anxious to see how Erica would work with Lisa since, next to my sister, Erica was second on my list of most strong-willed people, worldwide. They proved to be a good team, since their paths didn't cross often, except when Erica wanted to up the budget for one reason or another. Camptown Ladies was her baby, so, for the first time in my life, I watched as Lisa said yes to everything suggested to her.

Erica and I worked together almost everyday and I noticed she was less prone to yell when I was around, and the workers noticed it too. If I left to make a homo-depo run for Erica, the workers would ask me to hurry back. "She thinks we're much more stupid when you aren't here," one of them said. I didn't understand this, but I did notice she yelled at them more when I was not on the project. As I approached or left on a mission, I'd hear her barking orders, insults flying like a drill sergeant as I headed out to grab more supplies or came back with lunch for Erica and me if Lisa wasn't whipping up an Italian treat for all the camp workers to enjoy.

On this day, Erica and I'd worked for hours non-stop, and the smell of doughboys wafted up to the roof, paralyzing all the workers. Even Erica stopped her signature hammering bang-bang-tap rhythm as she checked, re-checked all the beams herself. They were all to be replaced.

"What the hell is that?" she said, sniffing the air.

"Dad and Lisa are making doughboys," I said.

"Whatever the hell that it is, I have to have two," she said.

"Fried homemade pizza dough, usually with powdered sugar."

Erica said, "Let's go, before these animals beat us to the line."

We hustled to the ladder. With every step the smell got stronger, and without even looking I knew Lisa and Dad had two stations to pick from, one for powered sugar, and one for eating the doughboy in a bowl with Lisa's mouthwatering tomato sauce drizzled all over it. I waited for Erica at the bottom of the ladder, planning to convince her that she needed to try a sauce-topped one for lunch, then split a powder sugar doughboy with me for dessert. I was at the bottom of the ladder, looking up, licking my lips at the thought.

Lisa yelled out from the rec hall, "That must be some hot ass coming down that ladder with you looking up and drooling like that!" I glared at her, but she had already walked away to taunt Vince about the sugar all over his face.

Erica had skipped the ladder and hopped down from the roof to the porch rail, in her gymnast move, so it was a male worker who was next down the ladder. Of course he heard my sister. He gave me a cocky smile and brushed his beginner beer gut a bit too close as he confidently swaggered passed me. He turned back to give me a wink, in case the gut was not encouragement enough to keep on admiring the big, dusty ass butt crack showing from the weight of his tool belt. Erica was laughing at the scene as she hopped down off the porch rail. The difference between the vision of his hairy body and hers, made my stomach jolt. (It could also have been the guy's greasy smell, which lingered and competed nastily with the doughboys, temporarily ruining my appetite.) I got in line behind Erica anyway, noticing the guy waited off to the side so he could get in line behind me.

Erica pushed me ahead of her so she was between the guy and me and said, "You show me how to assemble this thing. I'm not a damned wop like the rest of you."

The way my sister's mouth still could throw me after so many years of being victim to it, was a tribute to her craft. All of my most embarrassing moments have been by my sister's side. Occasionally my screw-ups were caused by my paranoia of future ball-busting, so it became a self-fulfilling prophecy. However, most of the time Lisa could take full credit for the trouble her mouth got her into—or us.

I cringed as I remembered a trip to the mall my sister and I took (even though Lisa was missing some girl DNA and hated to shop). Everything was going fine, aside from her leering at any attractive woman that passed, and we were both getting into the spirit of window shopping when I spotted a woman ahead of us, walking her toddler on a leash.

"Holy shit," I muttered under my breath, instantly regretted calling Lisa's attention to it.

"Holy shit," she said back, not in a whisper.

We were at least thirty paces behind the woman, but I opted to start my begging early. "Please, Lisa . . . Please. Just let it go."

My warning did nothing to stop Lisa's inevitable rant; in fact, it encouraged it. She started the rant quietly, at first. "Is that really necessary? That kid seems perfectly well behaved. For fuck's sake, he's just learning to walk."

"Lisa, please. Don't." I said.

The flow of the mall crowd kept us moving toward the woman and her leashed child. I started taking baby steps, hoping we wouldn't catch up, but changed my strategy to quicken my pace so Lisa and I might pass by her quickly, limiting the damage to more of a drive-by assault.

Lisa was getting louder. "I don't understand parents today. Mom and Dad would never have to worry about us kids being out of control."

"You're out of control right now." I said.

"Seriously, if your kid needs extreme discipline, it's better to give a spank on the bottom like in the old days, than to do this," Lisa said.

I tired distracting her again. "Not everyone likes to give spankings, you should leave your personal kicks aside."

She ignored me, "And that kid is behaving just fine! Why the fuck would you treat any child like a dog?"

"Lisa, please, you treat your dog like a child," I said in a very low voice, not believing she would follow suit. We were gaining on the woman and her wobbly toddler, and I was starting to sweat.

The baby's hands were innocently outstretched as if he were doing a bad impression of Frankenstein, stiffly walking side to side and reaching out as if he wanted to touch the clothes of the people who passed by. I didn't want to agree with Lisa (nothing good would come of that), but the child was walking right by his mother's side, not fussing a bit, and I had seen so many others who were more leash-worthy. My sister, for instance.

Lisa was rapidly catching up to the mother and child, raising her voice in righteous indignation as she walked right behind the woman doing her diatribe of "what the hell is this world coming to when parents can't control their toddlers." I fantasized doing an about-face on my sister, but was blocked by a group of shoppers behind me. I'd lived through my share of scoldings by Lisa, and along with my sweat, pity flooded me for this woman and the inevitable scolding that was about to take place.

If I stayed, maybe I could at least try to control Lisa. Maybe some extra harsh shushing, or grabbing her arm to physically redirect her. (OK, I wouldn't have the guts to do something *that* rash.) Or maybe I would get lucky and the mother would punch Lisa in the mouth, silencing her for a moment or two, while I dragged my sister's unconscious body across the food court. (As if I could move the most determined woman on the face of earth even for a second, unconscious or otherwise.)

Lisa was yelling now, "You know, it is a sad thing when a parent has to resort to tying their child up, rather then friggin' teaching them!"

The woman pretended not to hear her as we walked past, but my sister would not let it go, calling over her shoulder as I pretended to window shop at a blinding speed, "I mean really, that is *so* Not Right, using a leash on a child!"

The woman called ahead to us in a weary voice, "It's OK, everyone thinks that."

Her answer made Lisa and I turn back in unison at the woman and child. What we saw made us both turn away and quicken our pace, almost to a run.

"Oh my God. I want to die," I whispered.

"How the fuck was I supposed to know the kid was on an oxygen tube?" Lisa said.

Twelve

Mobsters For Lobsters

"Please pay attention to an important announcement!" Lisa bellowed over the loud speaker.

Eddie stopped his work and waved his hand over at her with a wrist that seemed barely hinged. "Let me guess, they fucked up another dyke storyline on network TV."

Lisa ignored him while we all gathered near the speaker.

Vince pointed at Lisa and said to Eddie, "Note the hands on the dyke hips, the gym teacher stance, this is going to be big. It may involve illegal activities. Eddie, sit and protect your favorite asset."

Lisa yelled into the speaker, "Everyone stop talking! Eddie, sit the fuck down."

We did, and he did.

"Language," Mom muttered as she joined us.

Lisa said, "I had the greatest idea last night. We have all been working so hard, I think it's time I treated everyone to a little P-Break!"

"Yipeeee!" Eddie yelled.

Dad said, "Thanks, but I just went."

"Not that kind of pee, Dad," I said. Mom headed back to the camp store doorway while we assembled an impromptu meeting in front of Eddie's over-the-top 80s-inspired dining hall. He flicked on the switch for the rotating disco balls to show off his decorating and Erica's supreme wiring skills.

Lisa blasted into the loudspeaker, "Mom, you need to come here and listen too!"

"I'm not your father. I don't like bathroom humor," she said, folding her arms.

"It's a P-Break, Mom. As in P-town. We're all taking a trip to Provincetown, Massachusetts. As a thank you, I thought it would be fun to go to Provincetown for a long weekend to rest before we have our opening in a few weeks."

Aunt Aggie joined Mom. "That's all the way up on the Cape Cod," she said, as though she would have to swim to get there.

"Yes," Lisa said. "All the way up on *the* Cape Cod."

Dad and Eddie slapped each other five. "Eddie and I are in!"

Lisa smirked, "See, Eddie already has a date. Mom, Auntie Aggie, Uncle Freddie, we'll just talk about you behind your backs, if you don't come."

"Why do we have to go so far?" Mom asked.

"It's not far. Plus, it's research," Lisa said, winking at Vince and I.

Aunt Aggie asked Uncle Freddie, "Are there a lot of campers up on the Cape Cod?" Uncle Freddie shrugged.

"You'll also have the best damned lobster dinner you have ever had in your life!" Lisa said.

Uncle Freddie stood up. "Well, I'm in! Aggie, if you girls want to stay and hold down the fort here at camp, I'll eat your lobster."

"Oh no you won't," she said, then she turned to Mom. "You know if we don't go, our husbands will dive face-first into bowls of butter and have heart attacks right at the table."

"The Italians go to the Cape Cod!" Dad yelled, now hitting Uncle Freddie with a high five.

Vince said to Erica, "I'll make a sign for the van: Mobsters For Lobsters." When Erica laughed with him, Vince looked a little too hopeful.

Erica asked Vince, "Why do they keep calling it *The* Cape Cod?"

Vince said, "Old people put 'The' or 'My' in front of everything. 'I've got to go to *the* Stop and Shop to pick up *my* tea.' Or, 'Something is wrong with *the* Comcast.'"

When he stepped closer to her, Erica said, "Maybe I shouldn't go?"

"*Maybe* you shouldn't go? That's ridiculous," Vince said. "Of course you shouldn't go. We did break up and being around me must be unbelievably tempting. You are only human, after all."

He moved his face close to her and batted his eyelashes. Erica playfully shoved his face away, "Don't be an ass. I just don't want there to be any mixed signals."

Vince said, "No worries. If there were any, you just unmixed them."

Erica was anxious to change the subject. "Your folks have no idea it's a gay town, do they?"

"Not so much."

"Well, I think I want to see this," she said, and her decision mixed Vince's signals again.

Lisa got off the microphone and looked worried, as if a bad idea just hit her, "Mare, the last time our family vacationed together was in Jamaica, it got kind of crazy."

"I could write a book," I said.

"On the plus side, lots of lesbos in P-town. Maybe on this trip you'll find the real love of your life."

"Not looking, thanks," I said.

Lisa turned back to her audience, "So, like Uncle Freddie always says, there are only two things in life: 'Are you in, or are you out?'"

"In!" most of us shouted.

"In," Mom and Aggie grumbled.

Of course, Lisa had a bigger plan. Marketing printed materials about Camptown Ladies in Provincetown was really the point of the trip, and Lisa was determined to make this work for her. It was disguised as a vacation, but I knew Lisa would be working this trip like a Rhode Island politician, pressing flyers about the opening of her campground into the hands and bars and restaurants of *everyone* she talked to—and my sister talked to everyone. She had an irresistible, abrasive charm, and the balls to use it to her advantage.

On the way up to Cape Cod, Lisa stopped so she could pick up some salty snacks. As she got out of the rented mini van (Aunt Aggie insisted we strap her scooter to the roof), Lisa stopped off for gas. "Ten bucks should do it," she said, walking toward the store.

Then she pulled a twenty-dollar bill out of her pocket and balled it up so she could toss it through the passenger window at me. "Don't go over ten, I don't want a bunch of fucking small bills."

Lisa may have been a millionaire, like the rest of us in the van, but, being so new at it, she forgot that twenty dollars was not really considered a big bill. She was remembering all those childhood years of us pooling our change to buy a bag of potato chips or a sleeve of Oreos. I was distracted thinking of this when Lisa headed back to the van. I looked at the pump in a panic, but I hadn't gone over the ten-dollar amount, or I'd hear about it for the entire three-hour drive. I carefully squeezed the handle to choke out small bits of gas, as I felt her hovering behind me.

When Lisa was judging me, I could feel it deep in my bones. It made me paranoid, clumsy, prone to mistakes, and it made her delighted. I squeezed the pump carefully so I would not go over: $9.53 . . . $9.56 . . . $9.58 . . . I must hit that ten-dollar mark or suffer the wrath of Lisa for not following her instructions . . . $9.60. I breathed a sigh of relief, until Lisa tagged me with an affectionate slap on the back of my head. She followed with the helpful explanation, "It's dollars, not hours and minutes, you fucking tool."

Lisa was pulling out of the parking lot when a guy with a "GO GREEN" protest sign yelled: "Enjoy your gas guzzler, you jerks!"

Lisa didn't warn anyone to hang on and I winced for the sake of the protester as she threw the van into reverse and careened right toward him. Aunt Aggie and Uncle Freddie collided in the back seat and Aunt Aggie slapped Uncle Freddie on the arm as if it was his fault. "Ow!" he howled, and he laughed at her annoyance.

The protester's eyes widened as the minivan skidded just inches from his feet. The scrawny guy's back was pressed against a fence to avoid being run over. Lisa leaned out the car window and looked like she might grab his neck, which was within reach. He was petrified, and appeared ready to pee himself from fear.

Lisa shouted louder than was necessary, "Hey, little douche bag, if you wanna do something green, stop killing trees with your stupid signs. Go mow my lawn since you need a fucking job!" Mom and

Aunt Aggie gasped as Uncle Freddie wheezed with laughter in the back of the van.

Except for one fight between Mom and Aunt Aggie, the rest of the ride was uneventful. Dad was the first one out of the van when we reached the town, dramatically taking a deep breath of salt air as he asked, "Where are the Margaritas?"

"Dad, this isn't the Caribbean," I said.

"It's the Cape Cod," Vince said.

The owners of Gabriel's Guest House, who are known to us frequent visitors as The Two Elizabeths, greeted us as if they had been anticipating our arrival all year. Our disorderly group spilled out from the van directly into their tiny lobby, shattering the peaceful quiet of the beautiful inn. We drowned out the soothing jazz from the adjoining Great Room.

There would be no soothing sounds while the Santoras were in town, and I tried to think of a gentle way to break it to the Elizabeths as they scrambled to address the questions we fired at them. They were barraged with a sea of ridiculous questions from every direction. I wanted to offer the option that we could get by with one spare towel each if they felt they wanted to leave town during our invasion.

The questions ranged from "What is the population of this town?" to "Any good Italian restaurants around here?"

When she could get a word in, the one my sister and I called Sweet Elizabeth did the talking while Quiet Elizabeth (a woman I rarely ever saw indoors, unless there was an internet problem) was more serious as she helped lug all the suitcases out of the van, placing them in an orderly row along the cobblestone driveway, as if they were the critical sandbags needed to hold back a dam. Or a dyke, as the case might be.

Dad spotted the movie library. "Hey, does this mean we can rent movies here?" he asked.

Sweet Elizabeth said, "Actually, you can't. They're free."

"Free?" Dad pushed Eddie out of his way to get to the movie alcove and Eddie announced, "Mr. Santora is too shy to ask where the gay porn section is." Dad snorted a laugh from the corner.

"Those you have to ask for," Sweet Elizabeth said, adding, "He'll need to show ID that he's over twenty-one."

Dad laughed and told Sweet Elizabeth to ignore Eddie. "That Eddie's such a card."

"Eddie The Card," Vince said, and I knew my brother well enough to know when another nickname was born. "Sounds like a gay gangster."

I was thinking that maybe we wouldn't be quite the shock to the town I feared, when my sister asked Sweet Elizabeth, "So, where are all the white women at?"

I apologized to Elizabeth. "Sorry. That's a Mel Brooks quote—*Blazing Saddles.* She really isn't the total ass she appears to be, just really close." Then Lisa proved me wrong by taking the baseball cap she kept folded in her back pocket and slapping it on her head. The cap advertised Titleist golf balls, which would have been fine, if she hadn't ripped off a few of the embroidered letters so it now read: "Tit."

"What's all that noise about?" Aunt Aggie asked, irritated.

"I'm sure it's us," I said.

"No, that constant chiming," she said with a face that more accurately described squealing brakes or nails on a chalkboard, rather than the charming sound of the town clock tower.

Sweet Elizabeth answered, "Isn't it lovely? It's the clock bell from the town hall. After you've been here a month or so, you won't even notice it." She winked at me as my Aunt Aggie visibly turned her festering up a notch.

Aunt Aggie said, "They better turn it off after eight o'clock so I can get my beauty sleep."

"It's already at the critical stage," Dad muttered from the video corner.

"Shut the fuck up, Sal," Aunt Aggie said, as I winced an apology to Sweet Elizabeth, who was kind enough to pretend to be looking at the check-in book.

Vince asked, "Are the bars still open in the off-season?"

"Of course," Eddie answered for Sweet Elizabeth. "I can't wait to bring you to my favorite club. All the boys will just eat you up al-live!" he gushed, as Vince's face lightened a shade. Even in the dead of winter, no Italian should be that color.

Since it was still off-season, Lisa was able to book some of the best rooms in the inn and, taking advantage of the pet-friendly policy, she'd brought along Cindy-Lu. Lisa, Cindy-Lu, and I would share a large guest suite called Ariel, which was on the highest level and overlooked the Pilgrim Monument. It was a great room with a stained-glass, sea turtle-themed bathroom door and a Jacuzzi that made me wish I wasn't sharing the room with my sister and a dog. Erica had the room right below us, named Willow, while Eddie and Vince were sharing a room (despite Vince's protest) closest to the health club so they could work out each morning. We put the older folks in two rooms at the front of the compound so Aggie wouldn't have to navigate many stairs with her walker, and the Two Elizabeths arranged for special parking for Aggie's scooter inside the pet gate leading to the garden.

On the night of our arrival, we accommodated Aunt Aggie and Uncle Freddie's early bird feeding schedule and ate at Napi's, a restaurant made popular by locals and tourists alike, and one of the few places large enough to accommodate a family of our imposing size. The interior had an odd ethereal glow from the backlit cathedral-sized stained glass wall over the bar. Years ago, the stained glass had shown Jesus, Mary, and what appeared to be some cute Asian girl with words above her head that read "Hot Stuff," oddly cut in traditional stained glass craftsmanship. (The inappropriateness of it reminded me of the Korean girl I once worked with who, whenever she didn't know the answer to something, would say, "Beat Me.") The "Hot Stuff" quote had disappeared—not, I hoped, due to political correctness (Provincetown is not known for this)—now replaced by plain chunks of stained glass. It was better suited for my Aunt Aggie to be dining under, but I felt something was missing.

One side of the restaurant was a wall of bricks, which appeared structured by molten lava instead of mortar. They tumbled in a circular pattern before the bricks sobered up, and solidified into straight lines again. There were marvelously peculiar antiques, which covered every inch of the walls, and an Indian War Mask shaped like a giant warthog perched directly over our table, keeping a watchful eye on both Jesus and Aunt Aggie.

The older folks didn't notice that the place was filled with gays, but Lisa, Eddie, and I signaled each other with happy nods of approval. While surrounded by tables of boy-with-boy and girl-with-girl pairings, I amused myself by picturing the diners as the older folks did, smirking when I realized that many tables had a female couple dining opposite a male couple, and so, from my aunt and uncle's point of view, all must have seemed right with the world. Mom commented there must be a theater nearby, since there were so many well-dressed young men, but that was the closest anyone got to figuring out they had landed squarely in the center of Gaytown, USA.

They hadn't figured it out earlier, either, during the short walk to the restaurant when Eddie made Vince take a photo of him standing near a sign on Commercial Street that read, "All Deliveries In Rear." During the picture-taking, a man who made Eddie appear straight galloped up to him and squealed, "Oooh, honey, are you advertising? Cuz I'm buying!" We all waited patiently on the cobblestone street while they exchanged numbers and made plans to exchange God knows what else, God knows where.

Mom asked, "Does Eddie know that boy?"

"He will," Lisa said. Then she whispered to me in her best Obi Wan voice, "There's been a power shift with the Dark Lord Vulva in favor of the Fairies; do you feel it? Anything with a vagina may be lost."

Right now, in the warm comfort of Napi's Restaurant, surrounded by fairies who were surrounded by fairy lights, we were being served obese lobsters, each sitting on a La-Z-Boy mound of mashed potatoes, claws high in the air in a final gesture of *What the fuck?* The Mobsters With Lobsters were happy—except for Lisa, who expressed her dislike for seafood with the delicate statement "It smells like my nose is stuck up a fish's cunt."

Mom scolded Lisa, and Aunt Aggie laughed until she had to

wipe away tears. She scurried off to the restroom, threatening the diners she clunked by with her walker that she was going to "wet the friggin' floor." My siblings and I attracted the attention of the rest of the place with our peals of laughter.

Thirteen

Wonder Woman Attacks!

The next morning, long after Aunt Aggie, Uncle Freddie, and Mom and Dad had eaten the fabulous breakfast in the Great Room at Gabriel's Inn, Vince, Lisa, Erica, and I realized we'd slept through the breakfast hour and needed to venture out for food. Erica was completely overdressed, in high contrast to Lisa's hand-cropped yoga pants and t-shirt, which thankfully was covered beyond readability (I knew it had a trashy saying on it).

I said, "After that huge dinner last night, I almost called Aunt Aggie to tell her I had something of hers—her ass."

"You're eating with us, so don't even start," Vince said.

Eddie cheerfully greeted us in Gabriel's courtyard gardens as he came in from the night, just as we were heading out to the Post Office Café for our very late breakfast. Lisa yelled across the quiet garden, "Eddie! Good morning. Are we walking a little funny today?"

He smiled, "I had a great night and I walk more ladylike than you, like a truck driver with a cross-country hemorrhoid flare-up." Lisa giggled, a little bit like a girl. We braced ourselves for Eddie's details, but, when none came, Lisa said, "Tramp. Come with us."

Eddie happily rolled his eyes and said, "Oh, no, honey, I can't come with anyone right now." We couldn't argue with that, so we set off without him.

The Post Office Diner is a small restaurant jammed into the bottom corner of a larger building that was converted eons ago from the original town post office. It's still lined along the interior walls with metal post office boxes with decorative skeleton key keyholes. We entered a door that sat inches from the main street, and were rewarded by the aromas of fresh baked waffles, ham, maple, and fresh brewed coffee.

A waiter waving a dishrag shouted across the room, "Hey dolls, sit on anything you like. Hell knows, I do!" I loved this place.

Lisa smiled like a kid in a candy store, and we took the booth by the window so we could watch people walk by on Commercial Street.

"You've all been here before?" Erica asked us.

"Not me," Vince said. "It's my first time in Provincetown, but Lisa's practically a local."

"Obviously, you've never been," Lisa said to Erica.

"Why do you say that?"

Lisa answered, "Because in this town, only the boys wear heels. You're going to fall flat on your fucking face on those cobblestone sidewalks. And when you do, the dykes will pounce on you like a fumbled football on Thanksgiving day."

I was thinking Erica did look dressed way too fancy for the cobblestones, as Lisa illustrated her point, gesturing to an imaginary fallen woman on the street and yelling in her deepest voice, "Vagina down! Vagina down!" Then (in a deeper voice) "I'm starving!" She made loud submarine siren alarm sounds, and did a fair impersonation of a dyke leaping on top of the fallen victim, by straddling Erica who was laughing too hard to push her away. Several of the fluffy gay male wait staff were alerted to our presence and waved their perky figure-eight hellos to Lisa.

After much sighing and theatrics, Jay, the lead male waiter, floated over to our table without the slightest hint of urgency. He looked at us and said, "Hello, lovelies." Then he turned to Vince and Lisa and nodded a greeting, "And gentlemen." Lisa slugged him in the arm, hard, as he yelped like a girl and laughed.

"Your sister knows everyone," Erica said.

"Don't assume she knows someone just because she hits them," I said.

"So, how long have you two been together?" Jay asked under his arched eyebrow as he checked out Erica and me from head to her well-heeled toes.

"Ha. They're not together," Vince said, as he and I both laughed a little too hard. Erica silently studied her menu.

The waiter clasped his hands in delight, "Ooooh, I sense drama! I'll get you kids some waters and be right back. I don't want to miss a damned thing."

"You alright?" Vince asked Erica.

"I'm fine, why?" she said, coolly before going back to her menu. Vince, Lisa, and I exchanged looks but were soon distracted by a commotion at the door as our waiter shouted with a snide tone, "Oh, no, no, no, no, no! Not in here, you don't!"

All the diners turned to the door to see the egregious offense; it was a straight couple with a toddler jammed into a baby stroller. "Outside, outside!" Jay said as he made shooing motions with wild jazz hands, "That thing *must* stay outside!"

The couple looked horrified. They must have been wondering if he meant for them to leave their baby, or possibly their straightness. The husband had the freaked-out look you see on straight males who stray into P-town, brought by wives who are lured by the shopping. The straight guys have no clue how to act, and since the gay men act more like women, it follows that even if they are insulted, straight men can't get too aggressive with gay men. Mix that with not wanting to risk anything beyond a half-polite nod of the head in case a gay man might think that they are leading them on, and that they also take it up the pooper.

The straight couple still didn't get the commotion, and the whole place was watching the floorshow as if the couple had tried to bring in a wheelbarrow rumbling with grenades. As Lisa liked to point out, you just don't get to witness this kind of reverse discrimination anywhere else in the world, and, wrong as it may be, it sure was fun to watch.

"Didn't you see the sign?" the Jay the waiter asked. "All strollers are to be left outside. It's much too small in here for that *thing!*"

The husband looked aggravated, as a man might after being scolded by his boss's wife, and took the walk of shame out to the curb with the stroller. The wife, an attractive woman in her mid-thirties, shouted back across the restaurant, "Can the child stay, or should I park him on the street, too?"

The waiter giggled with delight that the straight girl was sassing him back, and Lisa watched with rapt interest. Jay shouted back to her, "Oh, honey, you and the kid can stay, but if that cute and clueless husband comes back in, you risk me serving him for dessert!"

The place broke out in laughter, along with the woman, and Jay galloped over to her and gave her a flamboyant hug. She was thrilled, as many straight girls get when a man bothers to hug or pays attention to her yet has no interest in fucking her. (Note: This was how the Fag-Hag Syndrome was born. Women feel valued by gay men because their friendship has nothing to do with their vaginas—or, I'd say, breasts, but the truth is, many gay men are just as obsessed with breasts as straight men.)

As Jay sauntered away after making nice, he yelled over his shoulder, "Love your boots, darling." The woman laughed in such solid camaraderie with him as though she would have locked her husband outside on the street if this girlie waiter had just asked her too. They were life-long girlfriends now; he was just her husband.

The husband came in from parking the stroller, saw his wife was busy with his child, and immediately fixed his stare on Erica, as happens with every man who sees her, especially when we are not in the gayest place on Planet Earth. Erica seemed oblivious, but Vince was watching the guy with daggers in his eyes.

"Only in P-town," Lisa said, then proved the point by leering at the attractive mom as she bent over the child to get the kid's toy as it fell to the floor, while her husband was still leering over at Erica. Jay the waiter returned to leer at the husband's clueless ass. I could see the look on Erica's face; she was fascinated, this was an amazing place. Welcome to Provincetown.

Lisa said, "Marie, doesn't she kind of look like you-know-who?"

"A little," I said.

Erica asked, "Who's you-know-who?"

Vince answered, "A ex-girlfriend Lisa embarrassed the hell out of, then got dumped by at a Christmas party. She doesn't remember her name, and she didn't that night, either."

Lisa said, "Can you believe she dumped me just because I called her a nickname?"

"Lisa. It was in front of her boss, and you called her Retro-Bush."

Lisa snorted, "Oh, for Christ sakes, women are so fucking sensitive! If she hated the nickname, she should have taken a weed-whacker to that thing. It never would have worked out otherwise. You know, that woman with the kid over there is hot. Should I go talk to her?"

"Her husband just went to the restroom!" I said, while Erica and Vince laughed.

"Exactly," she said getting up. "That geek will be festering over how to be in a gay bathroom without touching anything except his own dick. I could get a lot done in six minutes."

I pulled her back down and asked, "Seriously, Lisa. Are you a man? I'm asking the question."

She ignored me as Vince and Erica laughed, and said, "Where is that fairy waitress with our fucking drinks?"

After brunch, which included pancakes, waffles, and a side dish of the best spicy French fries in town, Vince stepped outside for a smoke from a ridiculous glass pipe he bought at one of the head shops, and Lisa joined him, to "scope out the hot chicks."

Erica and I waited for the bill as we watched them from the window. She seemed visibly nervous now that Vince was away from the table.

"How is it, being here with him?" I asked her.

Since Erica and I were not deep talkers, and this might have been the most personal question I had ever asked her, she didn't answer right away. Then, finally, she said, "It's OK. Some things are much harder than I expected; others, a bit easier."

"How do you mean?"

"Well, sitting here with all of you feels, well, natural. It feels good for us to be together again . . . in certain ways. It's just that—"

"He looks at you with those puppy dog eyes and you wonder if you made a mistake leaving him."

She looked at me, sadly. "No. That's not what I'm wondering."

"Oh," I said.

"I realize now I hoped that would happen. It would be so much simpler," she said, drifting off.

"What's more simple than realizing you don't love someone anymore?"

I didn't expect an answer, but she said, "Realizing I never did."

She looked at me so sadly then, that the pit of my stomach flipped uncomfortably for her. Or maybe it was for Vince; he had no chance. She was not ever going to be with him, and he had no idea. I felt my face and hands get hot, so I took a sloppy, forceful gulp of water to avoid looking at her, and a lemon wedge slid forward, nearly plugging my nostril. Thankfully, she wasn't looking.

We watched out the window as streams of gay boys paraded by. The streets were pretty busy for the off-season. Nearly all the men were taking notice of Vince. Some nodded at him, some winked, one yelled something we couldn't hear, then Lisa yelled back and waved to the guy to come back as Vince grabbed her arm in a lock hold behind her back. Erica and I laughed as we watched Vince smoke the rest of his pipe with his eyes on the pavement so he wouldn't make accidental eye contact.

Down the street, I could see trouble coming in patriotic flashes of fire engine red and white stars on royal blue, and Lisa saw it, too. Vince was too busy with snuffing out his pipe to see trouble brewing. I had no idea what Lisa would do, but I did know she'd try to make the most of it.

"Watch this," I said to Erica.

An extraordinarily tall drag queen, dressed in full Wonder Woman garb with bright red roller-skates, was heading right toward them, and Wonder Woman had spotted Vince. Lisa signaled from behind Vince a big thumbs-up for Wonder Woman to approach, and the six-foot superhero made a beeline for him.

"Uh, oh," Erica said, and she gripped my arm as if we'd just turned a bend and the biggest drop on the rollercoaster had appeared out of nowhere.

Erica's grip was tight on me and I could feel the side of her start to pulse as she began to laugh, and I flashed to one other time she had grabbed my arm like that. It was just before she told me she was ending our business partnership and I was about to take a header as I slipped on a paper bag of nails I'd carelessly left on the floor. I had laughed, but she'd not found it funny and had let go of my arm without comment, going back to work, looking pissed I left the nail bag in our path. It felt good to hear the sound of her laugh again.

With his natural gift for detecting impending drama, Jay the waiter flitted over to the window to watch the show with us. Even the straight couple with the stroller-less child turned their chairs to watch when they saw the flash of color zoom past the window.

Vince was the only one not looking when Wonder Woman made full impact.

She grabbed Vince by the waist and picked him off his feet in a bear hug as she did a perfect spin on her rollerblades before setting him back down, but she didn't let him go. Through the window we heard Vince give a loud girlish shriek, which further encouraged Wonder Woman that he was fair game. Lisa roared with laughter as Wonder Woman tried to get Vince to dance with her in the street. All Vince could do was hold on for his life, shocked, laughing, and once again turning a P-town-straight-guy shade of non-Italian pale.

Jay started hooting and clapping, which alerted the rest of the diners to watch the show unfold. Lisa was doubled over laughing, watching Vince's confusion and embarrassment. He hadn't been manhandled by a female superhero since we were kids at Halloween and Lisa abused him when she dressed as Batman. ("You're the Penguin," she would shout, whipping the cord from mom's old vacuum cleaner around him, tying him up rodeo style, then beating him with a black, spray-painted Wiffle ball bat.)

"Well, if you change your mind and you want him back, you'd better move quickly," I advised Erica.

"I wouldn't dare get between them," she said, and now we were laughing so hard we had to hold each other up in our seats. Vince tried to dodge Wonder Woman and once nearly broke free from her grip, but she was skilled with her bright blue boa, and snapped it around his neck like a leash. Vince was laughing, but there was a growing look of panic in his eyes. When Wonder Woman almost pantsed him in the street, Lisa at last took pity and placed herself between Wonder Woman and her brother, but the superhero would not give up that easily. As any good performing tranny, she was very aware of her audience in the diner and on the street, so she chased Vince, *Tom and Jerry*-style, in a circle around Lisa, whose eyes kept flicking back to me to make sure we weren't missing the show, her face contorting with laughter. Vince yelped every time Wonder Woman got a hold of him, holding on for protection to the same dyke sister who had served him up to the six-foot superhero. Finally, Lisa shoved him back through the restaurant door and the people inside clapped in appreciation for the show and Vince, relieved to be safe, and red-faced under his beard, took his bows like the good sport that he was while the place cheered for him.

By the time the show was over, Erica and I were exhausted from laughing and she had cried off a good amount of mascara. I helped clean her face with a napkin, while she fought another wave of laughter, which brought fresh tears. I smiled at her and said, "Not helping. But, you look pretty good without makeup." I was lying, and worried she would see it in my face. The reality was she looked *gorgeous* without makeup.

Erica took the napkin and turned back to the window. We watched Wonder Woman wave and bow to the crowd, reminding everyone that she was performing that night, down the street at the Crown & Anchor, before roller-skating down Commercial Street.

Erica didn't turn back toward me, but she quietly said to my reflection in the window, "I'm so glad I came."

"Good. Me too," I said, and it bothered me how glad I was that she was here, knowing my brother could get hurt all over again. I wished they still had a chance. She was perfect for him and I wanted to see Vince happy again. Selfishly, I also didn't want to lose her again. When I turned back to the window, Lisa was watching me with a raised eyebrow. I looked for Vince, but he had disappeared from inside the doorway.

Vince seized the rare opportunity to grab Lisa when she wasn't on guard, and pinned her against the glass window to administer a favorite childhood move, the Revenge-Wedgie. When he succeeded, the whole restaurant applauded again for the encore, but since Vince had boa feathers stuck in his hair, Erica and I agreed that the well-executed wedgie did very little to restore his dignity. This was especially true when a well-meaning passerby grabbed Vince by the scruff of his neck because it looked like he was attacking a woman. This was not Vince's day.

Vince ended up yelling, "But that's my sister, that's my sister!" and Lisa, of course, shook her head no and shrugged her shoulders like she didn't know him and walked back inside the restaurant, hanging Vince out to dry, pleading for his life from one of the rare straight guys wondering Commercial Street in a Patriots jersey.

Much later, we were laughing about this as we walked through the center of town toward the live music. We knew it had to be Gertie, our favorite 70-something singing transvestite. Her identity was given away by her choice of music that was more Aunt Aggie and Uncle Freddie's speed, and by her crackling karaoke sound system. She was a big woman in a tight mini skirt, whose specialty was a blend of Frank Sinatra and Judy Garland tunes. But while she dressed as a woman, she made no effort to disguise her deep, yet pleasant, male voice. As we approached, we saw Aunt Aggie leading Uncle Freddie, Mom, and Dad through the crowd to secure the bench closest to Gertie.

Lisa signaled to them like a soldier using hand signals. We held up, fanned out, waited, and watched. Gertie was blasting out a beautiful version of "My Way" as Aunt Aggie sang along and swayed her large body to the music, clueless that she was enjoying a transvestite performer. I could tell that she disapproved of the shortness of Gertie's skirt (which barely covered her ass and other unmentionables) and was puzzled about her deep voice, but Aggie had been known to generously give "creative types" a pass.

She had done it for Eddie and she had done it for Liberace (though this may have been because Liberace was half-Italian) and I could see the struggle as she tried to do this for Gertie. Still, her expression ranged between pleasure and puzzlement and occasionally a brief wave of disgust that she beat back with an awkward smile.

Dad and Mom appeared to know the deal—not really to their credit, as you would have to be well over 70 or legally blind to miss the tranny angle—and Mom was wearing her best "I can play along with the best of them" frozen smile.

My sister and I both keyed in on a flatbed truck loaded with college boys as they rolled down the street with a video camera. They slowed the truck for as long as possible before the traffic behind them started beeping. Once they spotted Gertie, they began whooping and hollering like a bunch of escapees from the movie *Footloose,* just let out of their cornfields for a tour of New England gays in the wild.

Erica's attention drifted away from Gertie to the boys in the truck, who were now making catcalls. "Obviously, she wants an audience, but she doesn't want to be treated like that."

I said. "Imagine if those boys were yelling at people of another race like that, what this crowd would do . . ."

"Gay is the new black," Erica said under her breath. Smart and beautiful, I thought, feeling pity rise up for my brother once again. How does a person get over a woman like her?

When the boys on the truck spotted Erica, they turned their whistles in her direction and one of them yelled over to her, "That's more like it, a real woman!"

Just then, Lisa barreled over to Erica and put her arm protectively around her and yelled to them, "Hey boys, you are you saying you want this young guy right here?" The boys looked stunned as some of the crowd laughed. Erica held her lips together so she wouldn't laugh, but her true test was when Lisa yelled, "If you think he's pretty, you should see his package!" She followed that by grabbing Erica by the crotch and adding, "You guys have great taste in boys!"

Erica was the superhero now. She stood, Lisa's hand at her crotch, and simply nodded her head like her package was legendary in these parts, and it was perfectly normal to have someone acknowledge it with a public grab.

What a woman!

This proved to be effective since the boy with the camera lowered it, and the truckload of them look sickened as they thought they had been yelling sexual offers to a man. "That ain't a guy," one of them said, but he didn't sound completely convinced, and when Erica took a step toward the truck, the boy pounded on the top of the truck, which must have been a signal to get out of Dodge since the truck lurched forward.

As the truck started to roll off, Lisa grabbed the guy's arm and said, "Oh, don't go, stay for your mother's next song." There was legitimate fear in his eyes as he pounded the roof of the cab again and the truck sped off.

There was an interruption to the song when Gertie said into the microphone, "Thanks Lisa," and Lisa gave a chivalrous bow as a smattering of applause broke out around her.

As we turned our focus back to the Gertie, Erica asked, "Your Aunt and Uncle don't have a clue about the whole transsexual thing, do they?"

"Nope," I said.

"But when Aunt Aggie figures it out," Lisa said, "we need to be there."

That moment came when Gertie's song ended, and she bent down very low to change the song on her karaoke machine. This was when she revealed her ample nut sack under her mini-skirt; a special treat to the folks lucky enough to secure prime seats on the bench right behind Gertie's Karaoke machine. Since Dad had inherited the need to grab the best seats for an event, the senior Santora family was lucky enough to be seated in the best view in the house.

Not that we needed the explanation, but Lisa narrated the scene. "So here you are, an elderly Italian couple, here to visit a quaint, sleepy, East Coast fishing village, delighted to hear a lady singer belting out the oldies, only to be hit in broad daylight with a view of a nut sac the size of a Saint Bernard."

Vince was losing it, trying to hold back, the guaranteed recipe for tears to start streaming down his face. It was ironic; after our indignation at the college boys, Erica and I could barely hold ourselves upright as the crowd attempted to trace the source of the laughter. Of course, we weren't laughing at Gertie, we were laughing at our relatives. The laughing only got worse when Aunt Aggie went from frozen dumbstruck by the ball sac unfurling before her, to pure reason when she seemed to be bargaining that surely this nut sac would be gone in a second, but no, Gertie needed to select just the right song . . . and this took some time.

The crowd was forced to part when Vince doubled over in an explosion of snorting fits, which made the rest of us lose it, but only Lisa fell backward through an opening in the bushes to roll onto the town hall lawn, in hysterical fits of laughter. Her jacket opened as she rolled back and forth, which of course revealed the slogan on her extra-large t-shirt: "Unless You're a Pretty Girl, Stop Looking At My Tits."

Fourteen

Would You Rather Be a Clueless Fruit Or a Blind Date?

"There must be a circus or a theater troop in town," Aunt Aggie announced. "I just saw some very large clowns riding down the street in makeup and feather boas."

Uncle Freddie declared, "Those were the sexiest clowns I've ever seen," and Aunt Aggie swatted him with her purse as he giggled.

"Another great dinner!" Dad said, as we left the Front Street restaurant. "So, what are you kids up to tonight?"

Lisa quickly answered for us. "Ah, nothing much, we're just meeting some friends at a charity thing I got roped into." This was the first any of us had heard of it, but we knew better than not to play along.

"Sounds like fun," Dad said.

"I only have four tickets, or I would force you guys to come with us," she said, shooting me a look for backup.

"Yeah," I said, "she roped us into it without even asking, and now we all have to go."

"What's the charity?"

With impeccable timing, Lisa answered "AIDS" and I answered "Cancer." We looked at each other. Lisa said, "It's for people with cancer caused by AIDS."

"Right," I said.

"Well, have fun, kids," Mom said sarcastically as she hauled Dad away by his elbow.

We were surprised to hear that Lisa really did have tickets to an AIDS event at The Vixen, a lesbian bar toward the gallery section of Commercial Street. Normally, this time of year it would be quiet without the summer crowd. Tonight, though, the bar was hopping from the benefit.

"Can we just make an appearance and go?" I asked Lisa. "You know I'll be happy to make a donation, I just hate these things."

"Don't worry, you'll make a donation," Lisa said.

"Why didn't Eddie come with us?" I asked.

Lisa said, "He had a party to go to, where they were playing his favorite party games."

"I'm not asking," I said to Vince.

Lisa answered anyway, "The games were, 'Who's in My Mouth?' and 'Attached By A Dick.'" Erica and I laughed, but for the third time today, Vince's olive skin turned a sickening Caucasian white.

We entered the bar and every head turned to look at Erica, who remained oblivious as she surveyed the building, turning her nose up at the décor of a typical old New England dark wood bar and four beat-up pool tables with tasseled corners. Lisa disappeared immediately into the crowd, so I stuck close by Erica's side to hold back the wolves.

Vince whispered to me, "This is the one time I'm glad I'm not with Erica. Most of these girls could kick the shit out of me."

Erica looked at the staircase leading to the hotel rooms upstairs, "I could suggest a little updating . . ."

"Don't even. You have your hands full at the camp," I said.

We found an abandoned cocktail table close to the bar and Lisa showed up with a round of drinks. "This is going to be fun," she said.

Vince and I exchanged worried looks. Crazier nights had happened without her announcing there would be "fun." Lisa's definition of "fun" differed from the rest of the world's.

Erica finally noticed that so many women were looking in our direction. "Why is everyone staring at us?" she asked.

"Oh, this happens every time I come here," Lisa answered.

Someone announced a raffle was about to begin and Lisa grabbed my arm and pulled me out of my seat, toward the front of the room. "Where are we going?" I said, looking back at Vince for help.

"Just trying to give Vince and Erica a little time alone," she said, once we were away from them.

Lisa plowed her way through the crowds, toward the woman on the microphone. The lady running the show nodded at Lisa, but before I could anticipate what was happening, Lisa gave some sort of hand signal and the woman announced into the microphone, "Ladies, this is our first date for raffle. Let's hear it for Marie Santora!" The room erupted into applause as I glared at my sister, who was in her glory.

I whispered harshly, "What did you do?"

"Only one way to get back onto the horse," she said. "In your case, I guessed it might make sense to speed things up a bit and let the ladies bid for you."

"I'm not ready to start dating!" I said, but she ignored me and forced me to turn around.

"It's for charity," she said. "Now face the crowd so they can see your goods." Thankfully, at least the crowd approved.

I grabbed my sister by the arm and hissed, "No way, not doing this. Tell the dyke with the mic it was all a mistake!"

"It's for a great cause," Lisa said. "Don't be such a pussy!"

The woman with the microphone indicated a large bucket near the stage and said, "Place your bids in here, ladies! The highest bid wins a dinner date, and maybe even a kiss at the end of the evening! She's a pretty one, huh, ladies? Come on, it's for a great cause, so don't be cheap!"

Lisa abruptly left my side and, to my horror, grabbed the mic and shouted, "Come on, that's my sister over there. Get those bids in! Ladies only, of course. You can be anonymous if you want. Let's hear it, who's in the mood for a little Italian?" The crowd cheered and laughed as I felt my face turn the shade of a thick ragu.

I wanted to run. I wanted to die—but only after killing my sister. Since there were not too many males in the room, I could easily pick out Vince's laughter toward the back and thought I was pretty sure I could hear Erica's laughter coming from that direction as well. Someone handed me a shot and I tossed it back, deciding I had no choice but to go along. So I gave a dainty twirl before grabbing the mic from my sister and yelling: "I'll never hear the end of it from my friggin' sister if I don't fetch a big bid. So give it up, BITCHES!"

The woman took the mic back and said, "Remember, ladies, mark your bids that you want Blind Date Number One!"

One especially tough-looking woman in the crowd moved forward to deposit her bid into the bucket. She winked lecherously at me and licked her lips. I glared at my sister and whispered in her ear, "What the fuck were you thinking?"

"Oh come on, I would have done it, but they said the femmes always fetch bigger bids," Lisa said.

"You should have told me!"

"You wouldn't have come."

"Exactly!" I said.

She slugged me hard on the arm. "You're being ridiculous. You'll do your good deed tomorrow night and then get over it. Let's find Vince and Erica and let's drink!"

We found Vince at the bar, talking to a trio of attractive young women. One was grabbing his face and saying, "You are so adorable. If only I dated men, I would be all over you." Vince was loving it.

"Where's Erica?" I asked, and for a second I thought he would answer, "Erica who?" I wondered if it was stupid to hope he'd get over his heartbreak due to some lesbian admiration.

"Ladies room?" he guessed.

Lisa and I said in unison: "You let her go alone?"

When we at last found Erica, she was surrounded by a group of five butchy women trying to get her to play pool. Erica was politely declining, but the women were insisting, begging her over and over, "All you have to do is grab a stick. Come on, just grab a stick—"

"Kind of ironic," I said to Lisa, and she snickered.

Lisa said, "I'll distract the big one by talking shit about her pool skills, while you grab Erica and run for it."

"What could possibly go wrong?" I said.

Lisa moved in like a shark, targeting the largest of the girls, just like you would in a jail yard. She put her arm around the big girl, who made Lisa appear petite, not an easy thing to do. The larger woman bristled at being touched, and straightened up as she turned to face Lisa. I assume that Lisa also noticed that the top of her head was even with the woman's chin. The other girls turned to watch Lisa and the big girl. The big girl was speaking and had easily pulled away from Lisa's buddy grip, but then the big girl made the mistake of putting her finger too close to Lisa's face. (Lisa hated that; I had done that *once.*) I saw the opportunity and lunged for Erica's hand, yanking her out of the pool table area like a rag doll.

I didn't have to turn around to know what happened next. In seconds, the big girl would have to choose either to back down and play nice, or be on her knees to avoid the near breaking of a finger. Been there, played that, and lost.

The big woman yelled after Erica and I, "Hey, fuck youse!"

I could hear Lisa say back, "Youse must be from Rhode Island!" as I pushed Erica along ahead of me.

Erica said, "I thought they just wanted me to play pool."

I looked back to see the big girl had made the wise choice, since she was still standing as Lisa walked away, and her friends were all making various versions of a *What the fuck* face. As I pulled Erica across the room, they were finishing up the last contestant and I realized I had forgotten about the bidding, so the announcement over the mic surprised me.

"The woman who got the largest bid for dinner *plus* a kiss goodnight is Marie Santora!"

I heard Lisa shout from somewhere in the room, "Yes!" like she just coached her team to the Super Bowl.

"Oh, Jesus," I said.

"Congratulations," Erica said. She scanned the room at the clientele, "Aren't you curious who it might be?"

"Curious, no."

Erica said, "Maybe it's that woman over there, she's pretty and she sure is staring."

"At you," I said.

Lisa and Vince joined us, and I noticed Lisa was a little out of breath. Lisa said, "I heard the announcement. I hope it's some big diesel dyke!" and Vince made a valiant effort not to laugh at my expense.

The announcer said, "Sorry girls, the bidder wants to remain anonymous, and with the amount of money she donated, we have to respect her wishes. Would Marie Santora come up to the front please?"

I reluctantly walked up and was handed a piece of paper with a restaurant name and time noted on it. I looked into the crowd and a large woman wearing a Celtics jersey winked at me and pointed to two of her friends. "I can't do this," I said to the woman at the mic, and I tried to hand the paper back to her.

"If you don't go through with it, we'll have to give the money back, and it was quite the donation."

"I'd be happy to replace it," I said.

"It was three thousand dollars."

"What?"

"Someone wants that date real bad," she said.

I could have paid. I had the money. But three thousand dollars? Not exactly a small amount of money and I had planned to donate over triple that to a breast cancer foundation. I took the slip of paper from the woman and walked back to Vince, Erica, and Lisa. "I have to go," I said.

"Of course you have to go," Lisa said, smirking at me. "It's for a great cause."

I said, "No, I have to go because somebody paid three thousand dollars!"

Erica gasped and said, "Holy shit, lesbians are crazy! Straight girls complain when they have to buy their own drinks!"

Fifteen

Why Throwing Poop Is Sometimes The Best Choice

I refused to tell Vince and Lisa where my charity date was so they couldn't show up to enjoy the show. I'd been through that experience before when our family had traveled to Jamaica and my siblings figured out where my first date with Lorn was after we met at the resort. As uncomfortable as meeting a stranger for dinner would be, it would be nothing compared to having the whole family along for a ride.

Fanizzi's restaurant was where I was to meet my date, and although I had not eaten there, the Elizabeths had told me it had some of the best food around. It was in the east end of town (so I told Lisa I was heading toward the west end) and I wore my "Just in case we eat at a fancy restaurant dress." I knew the choice of outfit would make Lisa's teasing so much worse, but I was grateful Vince was doing some evening fishing with Dad and Erica had stayed in town to shop, so I had to deal with teasing from only one of them.

Lisa laughed when she saw me. "You're going dressed like that? Your date will probably show up in Nikes and a fanny pack!"

The truth was, I was thinking that very thought as I entered the restaurant, looking to see if anyone appeared to be waiting for someone, but everyone was seated in pairs. Pairs of men far outnumbered the women and a quick survey showed that I was not the only woman in a dress, as there was an attractive woman in a blue dress sitting at the bar. When a man returned to the seat next to her, I cursed to myself. Of course I couldn't be that lucky.

A moment later, a woman approached me as I waited for the host. She was a short, plump woman in her mid-to-late 50s, smiling up at me with a pleasing face. "Are you waiting for your date?"

"Yes," I said, relieved that she seemed awfully friendly, though Lisa was right, she was wearing Nikes. She seemed non-aggressive and perfect since I was nowhere near ready to be on a real date.

"I'm Marie," I said, not intending to sound as relieved as I did. The woman was quite a bit older than me and looked like she could be one of my mother's younger friends. This is good, I thought, I would know how to talk to this lady.

"I'm Brenda, nice to meet you. I saw you at The Vixen last night."

"Right, well, shall we sit?"

Brenda laughed said, "Well, you can join us if you wish, but I think your date will be disappointed."

"So you're not—"

Brenda said, "No, no, honey, I just recognized you from last night. I've been with the love of my life for over twenty years." She flashed a warming smile. Of course she has, I thought. "My partner would love to meet you, too, since she was with me at the Vixen. She always says I could talk to a wall and I'm always picking up strays."

"I am feeling very much like a stray at the moment," I said, laughing with her.

"Well, I would invite you over, but I don't think you should keep your date waiting. Hell, I know I wouldn't! You two have a great evening," she said, and I turned to follow her gaze to see the lady in the blue dress standing right behind me. I was startled at how the lady took my breath away.

I was more startled that the lady was Erica.

"What are you doing here?" I asked her.

"I have a date," she said.

"You have a date. Let me guess. You're here with my brother to goof on me?" I said, scanning the room behind her.

"Hey, I paid good money to be here," she said seriously.

I finally got it. Oh no. No, no, no. My brother loves this woman.

"Why did you do this?" I asked.

"It was for a good cause," she said. "I would have donated anyway, business is good, so why not give back? It's a good tax break, and I may have saved your ass from some biker chick."

I laughed at her. Then, more serious, I said, "That's a long list of reasons, right there."

The host brought us to our table, which was in the center of the window with the best view of the ocean. "Our best table was reserved for you by the Vixen."

Erica smirked at me. "Money can buy some things, right?"

"You're right," I said. "I almost paid three thousand dollars to get out of this date."

"Glad you didn't?" she said. Erica's playfulness was foreign to me, but it also seemed weirdly familiar. Then I remembered that I had witnessed Erica flirt with my brother, and it looked . . . oddly . . . a little . . . like . . . this.

My face must have betrayed me, because she asked me what was wrong.

"Forgive me for being blunt, but you're still not a—you're still straight, right?"

"Right."

I laughed. "Thank God. Or this would've been one awkward dinner!"

"Agreed. So, is this place any good?" she asked, and picked up her menu and started reading.

"I hear it's great," I said. What an idiot I was to think she was flirting with me. Clearly, being alone for the last few months had taken its toll and I was damaged and in need of some attention, some small victory with a woman well out of my league.

Oddly, this made me remember something I had read about rescue dogs. After too many bad experiences of not finding the living, rescue dogs need encouraging. So once in a while, one of the handlers hide. The dogs find a live body and regain their hope, and then carry on looking for victims. Otherwise, they'd stop; apparently, even rescue dogs can't cope with too many lost causes. Lorn was my latest lost cause, and for a second I wondered if Erica had been my fake taste of victory, staged not by rescuers but by a lesbian bar, and unknowingly, my sister, who had no idea it was Erica I'd be meeting. Too funny.

We both relaxed and ordered our drinks and dinner and our

conversation turned to family, as it usually did, though she carefully avoided talking about Vince. "Has Lisa ever been in a long relationship?" she asked.

"Lisa acts like a womanizer, but don't let her kid you. She is the fussiest person I know when it comes to women."

"Really?"

"Really. Once she broke up with a woman because of a bad cold," I said.

"Do tell," Erica said, sipping on her red wine, holding the glass up. "This is amazing."

"Glad you like it. Blackstone merlot. Anyway, Lisa went to bed that night, and when the poor woman woke up, she had a snot rag stuck to her left tit."

Erica started laughing, and I felt like I always did when this happened, lucky.

"So there she was, in the bed, naked, except for this snotty Kleenex, which had cemented itself to her boob, poor thing. She carried on a whole conversation with Lisa about how she was feeling much better, and the whole time, the Kleenex chunk was stuck to her. The worst part is, when Lisa tells the story, she says, if it had just stuck to the smaller tit, she might have stayed with her."

Erica had to spit her sip of wine back into her glass to laugh without choking.

I laughed at her. "Nice . . . very pretty," I said, but I wanted to see her laugh like that again, so I kept going. I had a million Lisa stories, I could go all night.

"Another time, Lisa broke up with a girl on a first date, while they were sharing their first drink. It was at a Chinese restaurant, the drink was a scorpion bowl."

"Why?" Erica said, still chuckling from the last story.

"In her defense, Lisa discovered the girl was dumb as a rock."

Erica said, "During the first drink?"

I told Erica how Lisa described the girl stabbing herself in the eye three times on the extra-long straw. "Lisa said it was just one too many times, but what had really sealed the deal was when the girl whipped out a nail clipper at the table and clipped her straw to a normal size to stop stabbing herself and Lisa dumped her on the spot. She said she couldn't stop staring at the end of the straw, cut curved like a tiny toenail, and the way the girl had to lean way over it now since it was so short. Dumped her before the dumplings."

Erica was laughing again, and the sound of it, along with the wine, was making me feel content for the first time in months. There was no place I longed to be, and no breakup conversation with Lorn replaying in my head.

Erica said, "So, the final straw, so to speak, was that she used a nail clipper at the table? That is amazing."

"Well, she had a point, if the girl knew she had to clip the straw or she would keep stabbing herself in the eye. I mean, that is a level of dumb that is pretty frightening. Who the hell knows, maybe Lisa really liked the dumplings."

We both laughed and then talked about Dad and Mom. Later in the meal, Erica said, "So, you plan on living with Vince and Lisa forever?"

I said no. Then I confessed to her a fantasy that I had not even told my brother and sister. When Lisa bought Camptown Ladies, she had deeded Vince and I each a large plot of land on the outskirts of the campground, mainly to stop anyone else from building near the camp, and I'd been thinking about building an authentic log cabin in the woods. After my confession, Erica studied me seriously, feigning interest, before she said, totally deadpan: "Dyke."

Then we broke into more laughter, which ended when she stole something from my plate I had been looking forward to eating. I knocked it out of her chopsticks and popped it into my mouth in an impressive defensive counter move—rookie mistake on her part: gloat after you eat the stolen food, not before.

I learned a lot of trivial stuff about Erica that night, but she wouldn't talk about Vince. No matter how many times I tried to steer her that way, she would veer off to avoid talking about him and ask me a random question about Lisa, Mom, Dad, or books or movies.

She asked, "Favorite movie?"

I answered, "Meryl Streep."

"That's not a movie," she said.

"It should be," I said. "Now, you are gonna really laugh at me, but one of my favorite movies is *The Bridges of Madison County.*"

Erica put down her glass, outraged. "You have got to be kidding me."

"You wouldn't understand. Straight girls see it as a sappy romance, but lesbians love it because they know the entire first hour is entirely about Meryl getting wet." Erica nearly spewed her wine again. I continued, "Sure, they don't actually *show* this, and Clint Eastwood looks old enough to be her father, or at least a scary uncle, but still, Meryl is playing the part of a woman squirming to get boned the entire first hour of the movie. Good fucking times for us lesbos." I sighed.

Erica laughed and shook her head at me, "Sometimes I do see a bit of Lisa in you."

"Watch out! Lisa would like to see a bit of her in you."

Erica just shook her head at me. "You Santoras are crazy."

"Lisa and I are so different. She was born a parade-marcher; I'm more a parade-watcher. You wouldn't think this was possible, but one time, Lisa went off on a political tirade while watching a dog show."

Erica didn't believe me, so I explained.

"We were watching the Westminster dog show on TV with a couple of friends and Lisa went to the kitchen to grab a beer. While she was in there, she heard the announcer say: 'The thirteen-inch Beagle is no fan of gay men.' She came tearing out of the kitchen swearing up a blue streak, screaming, 'How could they say that, someone better get fired for this!' and on and on about how she was going to write friggin' letters to the network, and on and on—"

Erica interrupted, "Well that is an odd thing to say, I mean, how could they say that a certain dog breed—"

"Oh, I let her go on and on in front of our friends. Lisa loves a good fight, and wants the world to say Fuck you to her so she can fuck them back ten-fold. Just for fun, I even let her call the network before I told her that the announcer actually said: "The thirteen inch Beagle is no fan of game hen.'"

This time, Erica doubled over as she laughed. I could have been so caught up in the joy of making fun of my sister without the fear of getting pummeled, or maybe it was the bottle of wine that caused my guard to be completely down, but that was the moment I looked at her and thought: *I've never been attracted to someone who wasn't older than me. Lorn's power over me was so controlling, while Erica's power is so much—*

Whoa.

It had been the tiniest voice, like a distant trumpet on the farthest, tallest mountain in Whoville, yet I somehow heard it loud and clear. I gulped the last of my wine and stared at her. Of course I was attracted to her, the entire world was attracted to her, who could blame me for that? There. Now that I'd acknowledged it, I could throw it back over the fence. Like scooping your dog's poop and throwing it into a nasty neighbor's yard: I had put that shit back where it belonged, and I needed to forget I ever thought it.

I was staring at Erica, no doubt with a freaked-out look, and she was staring back, completely baffled by my expression. The silence grew between us, and I was thrown into a word association panic and started blithering.

"I had a dog growing up," I said.

"OK."

I said, "He was a Rottweiler named Bear. I got in big trouble when my neighbor told my parents I had been throwing his poop over the fence into her yard."

There was a long pause while Erica considered if she had missed something in the conversation.

"And, you had been doing that?" she finally said.

"Yes."

"Feel better?" she asked, looking at me for quite some time, unblinking. When I didn't answer, she said, "Good story."

We both laughed our asses off again, even with me knowing the secret about my attachment to her laughter, and her rare and dazzling smile. I realized all my attachment had not all been in the hope my brother would win her back. For the rest of the night, everything was suspect: the thudding in my chest, the heat in my face, the stalling for more time together, the pleasure of seeing her again, of spending time alone with her, all of which had happened before, all of which I had never questioned until now.

But the damned distant voice had now named it, and I had heard it, so I spent the rest of the evening wondering how long I could ignore it, before everything would be ruined from what I should have known so long ago. How long would it be before she would know it? Or worse, how long would it be before my brother did?

Sixteen

Going Out With The Parents Is Such A Drag

I walked into the breakfast room at Gabriel's Inn and Lisa said, "What the fuck is wrong with you?"

"I'm fine," I said, and stupidly asked, "Why?"

Lisa answered, "How was your date last night? You look as white as a ghost. Holy crap, did somebody bleed you dry last night?"

Mom scolded her while I glanced over at Erica, who had a twinkle of mischief in her eyes as Lisa grilled me for details. I glanced over at Erica, and damned if she wasn't enjoying watching me squirm. Last night, we had agreed to not tell them she had bid on me because it would be more "fun" to taunt them. This seemed a great plan to Erica, who didn't have anything to hide.

In desperation, I took a different tack and covered a quick smirk at my sister as if I did have something to hide, and that maybe last night I had gotten the complete opposite of unlucky. This worked.

Lisa yelled, "Details!"

Happy to have dodged a bullet, I playfully ignored her and sat down at the table. Slowly, elegantly, I unfolded my napkin and placed it on my lap as if the world were watching me, which didn't feel far from the truth.

"Come on," Lisa pleaded, before she turned on Vince. "Do you know anything about this date?"

He put his hands up in surrender, looking like Uncle Freddie. "I've got nothing," he said.

Lisa said, "I don't think for a second that you got laid—"

"Girls!" Mom said, "This isn't proper breakfast conversation."

"You're right Mom," Lisa said. "Can someone pass Marie the hot, creamy butter."

"Lisa!" Mom said, as we all laughed at her, especially Dad. Dad loved nothing better than inappropriate talk at the table. When Aunt Aggie finished devouring the last bite of her pancake tower breakfast, she cracked with her mouthful, "These children have terrible table manners."

This was pretty much true, but when she said "terrible table" pieces of pancake flew out of her mouth and landed on the white tablecloth. Being part of a generation that never wasted food, she scooped them up with a two-finger dip and licked them back into her mouth. Uncle Freddie caught my eye and covered his peaceful smile by sipping on his coffee. Only one gentle "hee-hee" escaped and Aunt Aggie thudded him in the side, making him laugh harder.

Lisa was still studying me, so I risked a glance at Erica but regretted it when our eyes met and my stomach took a diving leap under the breakfast table. I could almost hear it land with a loud splat on the floor. When Erica winked at me playfully, it made me feel worse, yet I couldn't help smirking. While I smeared butter on my pancake, my sister continued to taunt me for details, and when I chose to say nothing, I realized that might have been a mistake.

Lisa let her fork drop loudly to the center of her empty plate. Everyone looked at her and the feeling in the pit of my stomach was replaced with fear. I knew that look. And, apparently, she knew the look on my face as well.

"Shit!" Lisa said, "You liked her! Whoever it was, you liked her!"

I felt my eyes widen and this time I forced myself not to look at Erica. Then a perfect way to deflect Lisa occurred to me, and I gave her the "hubba-hubba" eyebrow action followed by a not-so-subtle wipe of the corners of my mouth, as a queen might do—if the queen had just chowed on a beautiful woman. Vince, gullible as always, gave a congratulatory slap on my back, and my reaction had the desired effect on Lisa.

"I call bullshit!" Lisa said, and Mom yelled at us again as I kicked the gloating up a notch with an over-the-top cocky look, even blowing a puff of air on my fingernails. I looked around and I noticed our family had yet again taken over the Great Room and not another guest had dared to venture near the breakfast table with all the noise we were making. I saw Sweet Elizabeth poke her head in from the front desk room as if to remind herself that we were still just a bunch of rowdy Italians and there was nothing to be alarmed about, that yelling and profanity was happening in her usually peaceful breakfast room. I apologized a smile to her as she went back to her desk with a cheerful wave.

Finally, I felt confident enough to chance a sneak look at Erica, who was smiling that dazzling smile, and even though the smile was directed at her plate of pancakes, there was yet another leaping fall in the pit of my stomach. When I looked back across the table to my sister, I feared Lisa might not believe my story was bullshit after all. She was watching me, with that powerful older sister look that could make you confess things you didn't even dream of doing—but what scared me most was that she didn't call me on any of it.

On our last evening in P-town, I made the mistake of telling Lisa that since I had negotiated dinner plans with Aunt Aggie and Mom for nearly an hour, she would be in charge of finding something fun for us all to do after we had dinner. Of course, Lisa decided nothing would be more fun than to take everyone to a drag show at The Crown & Anchor. Thankfully, Aunt Aggie and Uncle Freddie had pooped out shortly after supper, since I suspected Aunt Aggie would have rallied for this one, had she known. (My second mistake? That would be not poking my eyes out so I wouldn't have to see Erica in her outfit, another drop dead number, too dressy for a seaside town. I braced myself for a long night.)

When we got to the theater, I was suspicious when all the front seats were still available, but Dad was so excited that he nearly knocked over a couple of girlish men to claim the seats, and one guy let out a high-pitched shriek that rivaled Vince's when he lost his battle with Wonder Woman. As Dad commandeered the entire front row for us (including a seat for Eddie, who had been MIA for the last two days), Lisa wouldn't let me tell Dad why the regular visitors to P-town knew those seats were dreadfully undesirable.

Mom and Dad wanted the seats on the end so Mom had an easy to exit to the bathroom, and Dad could "sneak out for a smoke if some fanuk started to sing one too many Liza songs." Lisa and Vince took the next two seats, which left the only open seat for me, right next to Erica. When I took the seat beside her, I was alarmed when she leaned in closer to me to whisper, "Something tells me we're taking a big risk."

"Why would you say that?" I said, my voice an horrific impersonation of my mother.

"The front row of a drag comedy show," she answered, looking at me like I the idiot I was.

I had spent the better part of the day going over our blind date, finding her only suspicious move had been buying the date in the first place. We'd both fallen uncharacteristically quiet as we rode the taxi back to the hotel. It was strange since we'd left the restaurant laughing about how withholding any information about the date would make Lisa's imagination run hog wild, and yet, when the taxi door closed, I could smell her perfume and we both got strangely quiet.

My biggest fear last night was enjoying every second with her. My biggest fear tonight was that I might look like a bit like my brother, who was uncomfortably sitting next to the woman he thought was the most gorgeous woman on the face of the earth. Poor guy, I thought, as I sat drowning in the nearness of her; by the look of Erica this evening, Vince had to be suffering terribly at the sight of her.

The show started and the first act wasted no time exploiting the front row. It was hysterical, but Lisa and I had been to enough of these to know that we were screwed. The first performer wore a dress that appeared to be fabric made of purple and pink glitter on a milky glue backdrop. She strutted back and forth on the stage and within the first thirty seconds she had targeted Mom and Dad.

"Hey there, Pops," she boomed down from the stage in answer to my father's ridiculously wide smile. The crowd laughed and Dad looked like a guy about to be hit with a cartoon rake—if a cartoon rake would ever consider wearing a purple and pink feather boa.

The performer, billed on the poster outside as Glady Ateher (pronounced *Glad-He-Ate-Her*), turned to the crowd and said, "Who's gonna tell the old people there isn't a dinner special?" The crowd laughed and the performer and audience was hooked on a steady diet of Santora family ball-busting. My father was in heaven, and Mom had a look we had seen many times: equal parts forced good humor and constrained horror.

Glady Ateher asked, "So Pops, who's the lesbian to your right?"

When Dad finished splitting a gut laughing, he answered into Glady Ateher's mic, "That's my wife."

Glady Ateher put her hand on her hip as she looked Mom up and down while the crowd laughed. "Denial ain't just a river in Egypt, folks." Somewhere off in the distance, I heard Mom's tires squealing as she departed Good Humor Town. Glady Ateher inched closer and said, "I ain't buying it. How long you been married?"

Dad said, "Over 30 years. If I had killed her when I first married her, I would've been out of jail by now!" The crowd laughed in encouragement and Dad beamed at them.

Glady Ateher's eyes gleamed, "Oooo, a comedian! Don't ya think it's kinda late to start a new career there, Pops!"

Under the hot lights, I could see Glady Ateher's makeup crack and melt, which, up close, gave her the appearance of a murderous clown. It added to the humor of her giant body looking like it was crammed into a glitter pen. Glady Ateher turned and said to Mom, "He thinks you're not a lesbian," and put the microphone in her face.

Mom answered, deadpan, "I'm aware of that."

Erica and Vince simultaneously grabbed both my arms as we laughed with the crowd while Glady Ateher surveyed the rest of our crew. The performer stopped at Lisa and gave a long dramatic pause as the crowd howled in anticipation. Lisa beamed like a shorter, more masculine version of Dad. Her eyes flashed and said: Bring it on.

Glady Ateher waved her supple wrist at Lisa as if she was shooing a fly. "Too easy," she said, and she moved down to Erica as the crowd went wild. "Hmmm," she said, but instead of taking a shot at Erica, she sidestepped back to Lisa and the crowd roared again. Then she slid over once more to Mom and asked in an accusing voice, as she pointed to Lisa, "Did you make that?"

Mom's affirmative answer was lost in the hysterical crowd's cheers.

Glady Ateher slid back to Dad and yelled into the microphone to be heard over the laughter. "Pops, we need to talk. Here's the thing: Unless this is some elaborate ruse to hide the fact that you are actually dating the cute fairy on the end," she said as he pointed to Vince, "none of this makes any fucking sense."

Dad thought it was really funny to nod his head and pretend that he was really dating Vince behind Mom's back, until Glady Ateher shoved her microphone under her armpit and pulled Dad out of his seat with his giant ham-sized hand. Then she walked Dad over to Vince, dwarfing him with her height magnified by towering heels, and grabbed Vince too, hoisting them both effortlessly onto the stage. She ignored their protests, feeding off of the cheering crowd, as she dragged them both and yelled into his armpit microphone, "This is why it's called a Drag Show, folks!"

The place erupted into full applause and Erica nearly fell into my lap laughing her head off. On stage, Glady Ateher grabbed them both by the back of the head and made them kiss her on either side of her cheeks just as a giant camera flash went off. Then the performer gave Dad and Vince two choices: "Either I use that picture we just took for my next poster, which means it will get plastered all over the web. Or . . . one of you has to get in a bikini top while the other one gets spanked."

Before Dad had time to thoroughly weigh all his options, Vince yelled with his hand raised up like a kindergartner with a weak bladder, "Bikini!!"

Glady Ateher said pointing to Vince, "Candy Ass over here knows a good deal when he hears it!" Then she yanked a bikini top she had kept stuffed inside her own bra, and threw it into Vince's face. The crowd was encouraging as Glady Ateher said, "Shirt off, Candy Ass . . . Sugar Pops needs to get some pleasure out of this when he's getting his spanking." Dad was laughing, but not nearly as hard as we were, especially when somebody off stage handed

Glady Ateher a ping-pong bedazzled paddle with the word BITCH spelled out in sparkling pink rhinestones.

I could read Dad's lips mouth the words "Holy shit" as Erica fumbled for her camera, but she was laughing so hard she could barely see straight and eventually had to give up on the idea of capturing the moment. Lisa was holding her stomach and rolling side to side in her seat, every once in a while re-charging her laughter by looking at Mom sitting perfectly still with her frozen smile, like a teacher attending a really bad elementary school play.

Dad was shaking his head no, and as Glady Ateher directed him to kneel, Dad finally grabbed the microphone in a moment of panic and said, "No, wait! That's my son!"

Glady Ateher said, "Listen, Sugar Pops, just because a Candy Ass calls you Daddy, don't mean he's your son!" The crowd roared again as Glady Ateher placed a beefy hand on Dad's shoulder and I could see in that moment he was torn between spanking his son and hitting a man dressed as a woman.

Dad dropped to his knees just as Vince got his bikini top adjusted over his hairy Italian chest and grinned sheepishly to the crowd. Vince was humiliated, but I knew he was thinking about the years of laughter we would get out of this night when it was all over. He was dying up there, and his sisters were loving it.

Glady Ateher handed Vince the ping-pong paddle, tipped the mic toward Dad, and asked, "Any last words?"

Dad said, "Yes! This is my son, and that's my wife!" There was a tone of desperation in his voice that made the crowd more rowdy. Glady Ateher stopped Candy Ass Vince with his BITCH paddle poised to strike.

Glady Ateher said, "I don't know, folks. Should we release him?" The crowd started booing, insisting on the full floorshow. "Aww, come on. I'll tell you what, Sugar Pops, if you can prove you are married to that lesbian over there, I'll set you free."

Dad yelled into the mic, "Honey, tell him!"

Glady Ateher glared down at him and said, "Tell him? Sugar Pops, I know you ain't calling me a *him,* not after two hours getting in this dress! I think you want to rephrase—quickly."

Dad was confused until the crowd started yelling, "Her! Her!"

Dad said, "I meant tell *her*!"

"OK, Pops, lets see if the governess just called to save your ass," Glady Ateher said as she pulled out a pair of handcuffs and attached Dad to a stool on stage. "Stay put." Then she lumbered down the stage steps and over to Mom with the microphone and Mom paused dramatically for a moment before saying in a deadpan voice, "I have never seen that man before in my life."

Lisa fell off her chair laughing as the crowd went bananas, and I could tell by the way my sister was crossing her legs as she rolled back and forth, that she was dangerously close to pissing herself. So dangerously close, that when Vince paddled his father's ass, she couldn't risk watching.

Seventeen

Be Careful What You Fish For

The official opening weekend in May was still a month away, so there were barely any campers at camp. Probably for the best since that didn't stop Lisa from testing out her idea of making what she planned was the first of many regular announcements over the crackling loudspeaker:

> *"Attention, Happy Campers! Good morning to all! Since the Camp is under new ownership, allow me to introduce myself: I'm Lisa Santora, your lord and master of all things Camptown Ladies. You can call me Camptown Conquistador, or Lisa, whichever you prefer. Joining me is my brother, Vince Santora, otherwise known as Candy Ass, or the little ones can call him Candy Butt. Please see him for any and all complaints about the bathrooms; this is his specialty. My Mom, Mrs. Santora, will be running the store, and my Dad, Sal Santora will be in charge of selling wood. Hurry, though: On a chilly morning Mom says his morning wood will go very quickly, if there is any at all.*
>
> *"My Aunt Aggie and Uncle Freddie are strictly here for your amusement, and ours. Nothing like having a couple of old folks around if you need to borrow an extra cranky old person. I don't want to say which one is the cranky one, but her name rhymes with "Taunt Raggy," or "Haunt Baggy." And kids, don't be shy! Be sure to ask for a ride on her scooter, since Aunt Aggie is a big fan of the little ones, but first, go ask your parents what sarcasm means.*
>
> *My Uncle Freddie can be counted on for an Italian joke whenever you need one, but if you can't speak Italian, just assume the*

punch line has to do with eggplant, grape vines, or the stone mason trade, and the guy'll have you rolling.

The really tall looking girl you may have seen flitting about is actually our decorator, a boy named Eddie. He's only here three days a week, so those are the perfect days to sign up your teenage sons for Little League across town. Remember, safety first! Eddie has been working tirelessly planning all the decorating of all our renovated buildings.

You may be wondering why there are no roofs on any of our buildings, or why our decorating is only happening under tarps and tents. We can only decorate after we get all the authentic Italian clay tile roofs in place, and this has been a challenge, since, leave it to a gay man, Eddie thought the first shipment was a tad off in the shade of terracotta, and sent the entire shipment back, and re-ordered instead from a cute little company from Italy that forms each clay tile the old-fashioned way, by taking the wet clay and bending it against the workers legs to create the nice U shape. Sexy, yes, but Eddie did this all without consulting with our contractor, Erica. If you heard the sound of two wild cats fighting a while back, that was Erica and Eddie, though it could have easily been mistaken for Mom and Aunt Aggie in the Camp Store.

This has caused a huge delay in the roofing, which of course means we can't work on the guts of the buildings until that is done. My dream was to have Camptown Ladies look unlike any other campground—this part has come true! We now have more than a dozen log buildings with no roofs, but the clay tiles are due to arrive today, along with our specialty crew from Italy to get all the roofing jobs done right. I know what you all are thinking! Yay, more Italians!

Rest assured, we are pig-scrambling to get the old recreation hall converted into a dining hall, to realize my plans of having the best Italian restaurant in Rhode Island right here in Camptown Ladies. I have been working with my favorite chefs on Federal Hill in Providence to secure an amazing menu. All I need is a building and some campers. Oh, and if anyone knows anybody who can get a restaurant permit or two pushed through, that would help too.

So, in order to get you the best restaurant in town, if you see any signs of slacking off by our lovely contractor, Erica, as in All My Children, *please report this to me immediately. I understand the value of a dollar, so when I purchase a woman, I expect her to be working her pretty tail off 24/7. Also, feel free to ask her any questions about her work, and Erica just loves questions about her job, and if you have any suggestions, or any thoughts on how she might do her job better, please speak up and let her know—especially from the men. She loves this!*

We also have lots of activities planned for the upcoming year, and at the end of the camp season, we'll be having an annual bonfire that I invite you all to return for, even if you're not a season camper. Immediately following the bonfire, there will be an auction of any children that are left unclaimed, so please stick around for that. A reminder that at Camptown Ladies, leashes of all kinds are welcomed, we don't judge.

That's all for now, and if you have any suggestions, please take a walk right by the suggestion box hanging outside the camp office. Seriously, walk right by it, since there is no place in the box to put suggestions. Have a great day."

The weather had started to lose some of its chill and we were all taking a break in the middle of the day. Although Camptown Ladies was officially open, it was so early in the season that only a few of the diehard regulars had come back to their trailers, and there was not one gay camper in sight.

Aside from the contracting issues that sat squarely on Erica's shoulders, we discovered the regulars needed nothing from us except for us to switch the electricity on, and take their payments for the season. Since we had never turned the electricity off, and we certainly didn't need their money, this left an Italian family too well prepared with too much time on their hands after officially opening the camp gates for the very first time. (The gates were always open.)

To address the critical issue of our boredom—and, more importantly, to comfort each other with drinks—Lisa had called a meeting at the end of the work week at the condo. We had to face the fact that the expected caravans of gays had not arrived on glitter-filled buses named Priscilla, or dyke-filled Subarus named Argo (after Xena The Warrior Princess's horse). The evening would also signal the end of my avoidance of both Vince and Erica and my stomach churned at the thought of sitting around a table with both of them, one in particular. Then, luckily, Erica took a pass on the meeting.

Then, later, not so luckily, I felt cheated that she wasn't coming.

But now it was midweek, and I'd decided to avoid Erica's construction crew by sitting in a lawn chair I had dragged over by the fishing pond and watching Lisa expertly fly-fishing on the other side. I comforted myself with the knowledge that the less I was around Erica, the less my thoughts about her in P-town seemed an issue. But there were two things that bothered me. Why did I feel the need to avoid her, and why had I almost completely stopped thinking of Lorn?

Lisa had chosen fly-fishing as a way to spend her downtime since the few regulars at camp were merely scattered trailers of retired folks who barely did more than sit on their trailer porches and flee at the first sign of a nip in the evening air. Since schools were still in session, we had to face the fact that Camptown Ladies might remain quiet for another month or two.

I had been distracted by the rhythmic whoosh-whip sound of Lisa's fly-fishing line and hadn't noticed right away that behind her, at the edge of a campsite, a little boy had been secretly watching her. When Lisa looked over at me, I nodded toward the patch of trees behind her and she spotted him as he ducked behind the trunk of a terribly skinny tree. He thought she couldn't see him but the width of the tree barely covered the width of his head.

Lisa called out gently to him without turning around. "I have taught so many boys to fish, if you want to learn."

She was being truthful. While we were growing up in our middle-class neighborhood, both the dads and the moms had to work several jobs to keep their houses in a town were taxes were getting out of control. Our dad was the only one who taught his kid to fish, and right after that, Lisa taught all the boys in our neighborhood. She worked as a busgirl at an ice cream shop to earn the money to buy herself a fishing pole that summer, and later she got so good that the adult fisherman would sometimes ask her what she was using on her lines. She had a great casting arm, but her real secret had been to dip her flies in Mom's meat marinades overnight, and sneak them out at the crack of dawn to hit the pond.

The little boy stayed behind the skinny tree, his body exposed on both sides. She kept fishing as he peeked at her and she called out, "If you change your mind, I'll be happy to teach you," but he was attacked by shyness and ran back into his campsite.

Since my mission in life was avoiding Erica, I got to witness this for the next two days, until the little boy called back a confession that he didn't have a fishing pole. The third day, Lisa stood a child's fishing pole next to his tree, and when the little boy showed up, he stopped short at the tree, in shock. Lisa called out to him, "That's your pole if your mom and dad say it's ok."

"My Dad doesn't live with us," the boy said, as he grabbed the pole. He crept toward the water's edge, holding the pole as if it were a gun about to go off. Lisa didn't waste any time and began teaching him. He was shy at first, but he so badly wanted to fish that he got over it and asked a million questions; I was sure he knew the answers to some of them. They stayed fishing side by side for some time until a panic-stricken young mother came running out of the woods.

"Buddy! I've been looking everywhere for you."

"The boy lady is teaching me to fish!" He said as Lisa chuckled under her baseball hat and adjusted her football jersey so the mom could see she had breasts.

Lisa said, "It's my fault. He's been watching me fish for a few days, so I coaxed him out with this extra pole I had kicking around." Lisa had bought that pole at a local bait shop, and the price tag was waving from a string on the grip like a tail.

"That's very nice of you, but Buddy knows he's not supposed to leave the campsite without telling me, and is never to come to the pond by himself."

Lisa said, "Yeah, Buddy, you shouldn't do that."

The woman said, "Say goodbye to the nice lady, your lunch is ready."

Buddy tried twice to put down the pole, but couldn't do it. Finally he said to Lisa, "Can I keep it?"

"Buddy, that's not polite," his mother said.

Lisa said, "If your mom says its ok."

Buddy looked up at his mom like his very life depended on her answer, and Lisa said to her, "There's no hooks on his, it's completely safe."

The woman said, "Buddy, what do you say to the nice lady?"

"Thank you!" And with that, he ran off, clutching the pole in hand, in case the boy-lady changed her mind.

"Thank you," the woman said, and Lisa nodded at her before setting another perfect cast whipping in the air just inches above the surface of the pond. A fish made a dive for the fly and missed. The woman watched a few more casts before she followed her son toward their campsite. The woman turned around, hesitated, then asked, "Would you like some lunch? It's only peanut butter and jelly, but I have some ice cold beer."

Lisa smiled in my direction, her back still toward the woman. "Got any Fritos?"

"I have a kid. Of course," the woman said, laughing at her.

Lisa packed up her fishing things and I watched her head toward the trailer, wondering why she stopped short before going in. She gave a victory fist in the air, looked over at me, and pointed to something at the back of the trailer. There was a sign indicating the woman was a past Hilary Clinton supporter. This sign would not have meant much to anyone else, but to Lisa, this meant she should make a lewd motion as if she was spanking an invisible woman's ass over her knee. Then she took off her cap, folded it in her back pocket, and disappeared inside the trailer to attempt fishing on dry land.

Later, I busied myself by helping Eddie finish the last of the interior sanding on the logs on the recreation hall. Lisa's dog, Cindy-Lu, was hanging with us, as if she instinctively sensed that this would be the place where food would be served, so she needed to make this her territory. Eddie, Cindy-Lu, and I were all cast in a creepy blue color from the draped blue tarps over the roof, and

Eddie's constant whining was being drowned out by Erica's scolding voice in my head telling us about how we were doing everything backward. But even Erica knew that at this point we had no choice. If we waited for the roofs to pull everything together, it would be down to the wire if our promotional handouts in P-town worked and campers arrived with the warm weather.

Erica was not around since the clay roofing tile shipment had finally arrived. Although Lisa wanted the crew to start on the rec hall, Erica finally convinced Lisa it was more important to get at least a few of the bathroom houses in shape first, which meant she was deep into the camp, working her way to the front with her new Italian crew.

Lisa showed up about an hour later. Since she wasn't gloating, I knew she had struck out, but she was grinning.

"How was lunch?" I asked.

"Delightful," Lisa answered, "but, she's in the middle of a divorce—to a man, no less, not that there is anything less. My gaydar must be on the fritz. I can't figure this woman out." Lisa liked to figure people out in ten seconds or less, and if she couldn't, it irritated the crap out of her.

"What else did you find out?" I asked.

Lisa said, "That she was so hot I left a slug trail all the way from her campsite."

Eddie moaned, put his hand to his stomach, and gagged to show his offense. In case we still didn't get how much it grossed him out, he clarified, "I feel like I just barfed, ate it, and barfed again."

Lisa said, "Like that isn't a regular Friday for you."

Later, at the condo, Lisa was updating Vince on the events of the day as we prepped for our evening festivities.

"So then she made me a cute little peanut butter and jelly sandwich with a side of Fritos, and looked damn hot doing it, too—even though peanut butter was not what I wanted her spreading. If you get my meaning."

Vince said, "No, Lisa, I didn't get your meaning."

"Enough," I said, as the doorbell rang. "Mom and Dad are here."

If I could have pressed the rewind button after opening the door, I would have. Then maybe Erica would not have heard me gasp like a total ass. She was dressed casually, but somehow managed to make jeans and a simple T-shirt gasp-worthy.

"Oh. Did I scare you? I rang the bell," she said.

"You said you weren't able to make it." I answered.

"I decided I could come. Is it OK?"

This might have been the only time I ever heard Erica ask if something was OK, and it puzzled me. Erica was of the taking variety, not the asking variety.

"Of course," I said and stepped aside, since she was not making her way inside until I did.

Erica greeted Vince and he seemed happy to see her until she walked past him to the kitchen and his sad puppy face flashed back. This was a face I needed to remember when I did something dumb, like gasp at the sight of her. I thought for the hundredth time, how did this damned switch get flipped, and, more importantly, how do I switch it back off?

Mom and Dad arrived next and we all assembled at the kitchen table. Lisa had fixed a tray of assorted olives and chunks of extra sharp provolone cheese and opened a bottle of dry red wine. There were several backup bottles lined up on the counter like doomed prisoners waiting to get their corks popped. A bottle of red wine never fares well when there are more than two Italians gathered.

"Mmm. That's some strong-smelling cheese," Dad said, and dug in to the pile.

Lisa said, "You know what they say . . ."

"Don't," I warned, with little hope.

"If she smells like trout, eat her out. If she smells like provolone, leave her alone."

"Lisa!" Mom yelled, spanking her hand, but Dad laughed and threw two chunks of cheese and an olive into his mouth. Vince and Erica laughed too, and I knew if Erica looked at all embarrassed, it was only because of Mom's reaction.

I called the meeting to order. "So, let's get down to business."

"Yes, please," Mom said.

"We have to find a way to drive more business into the camp. Who has ideas?"

Mom raised her hand. "Yes, Mom? You don't have to raise your hand."

"No need to be disorderly," she said, lowering her hand. "My first idea is to put up notices at all the sporting goods and outdoor stores where people go to buy camping things."

Lisa said, "Not bad, but I was thinking we put notices at all the local bars and colleges and promote how Camptown Ladies and Camp Camp will be catering to a special clientele."

Mom and Dad said in unison, "It will?"

"Yup," Lisa answered, while I winced. "We are catering to . . . creative people," she said.

Mom liked this. "Theater people, like Eddie?"

"Yes," Lisa said, "exactly like Eddie. Theater people, dog and cat people, people who wear distressed leather with metal rivets, women who like to cut and stack their own wood—"

"Hey, wait on that," Dad protested.

"Are there that many people who wear leather with rivets?" Mom asked.

"Depends on the bar," Lisa said.

Dad popped another olive in his mouth to stop himself from grinning.

Erica pulled a list out of her notebook and slid it over to me. "I pulled together a database of all the magazines, websites, and blogs that we need to get the word out to, plus a service that will do a massive email blast for a small fee. I'm thinking we could also get a lot of free PR for, uh, specializing."

Lisa and I looked at the list, both impressed, and I wondered if I was the only one smelling her scent on the notebook as we flipped the pages. "Perfect," I said, not looking at her, "Thanks for doing this."

"It was nothing. It's the same basic list I used when I launched my contracting business," she said.

We looked at each other then, and I was sure she was remembering the same thing I was, and we were both back in LA, and she was trying to fake a gay-owned business when she was no gayer than my brother, who was blatantly staring at her as he sipped his wine. I looked away from them both.

Lisa said, "We did some marketing with handouts in P-town, but until the season kicks in up there, not much will happen. Hey, maybe we should raffle off another date with Marie! We don't need the money, but it sure brought a lot of attention."

"No, thanks," I said, keeping my eyes on the list. Mom and Dad pretended not to listen, as Mom sipped her wine.

Vince chimed in, "Yeah, Mare, we never got the details on that date."

"You're right, you didn't," I said.

There was silence until Erica spoke up, "I bet she was a real hottie."

Erica was smirking at me. "She was OK, I guess," I said. "It was her personality that was the problem."

Erica tried Dad's tactic of hiding her smile with an olive, but my stomach still did a triple flip when her lips parted to eat the olive, and she flipped it into her mouth with the tip of her tongue. I reminded myself there was nothing about this I should be smiling about. Nothing funny about this at all.

Since Erica had done all the heavy lifting with plenty of ideas, the evening turned from a work session to a drinking fest, and after the third bottle of wine was opened, we had long since forgotten the mission, and Lisa was telling stories for Erica's benefit which our family had heard a hundred times.

Lisa said, "So, I once had this beautiful Rottweiler. His name was Bear."

"I heard about this dog," Erica interrupted, "he liked to poop in your neighbor's yard. Great story." Erica caught my eye with a ball-busting twinkle as she sipped her drink.

Lisa continued, "Huh? Well, anyway he was my favorite dog—"

I interrupted, "Worse than that. She was in love with him."

Vince jumped in, "She was totally attracted to him. Borderline, sick."

"What made it weirder was that it was a boy dog," I said, faking a shiver.

Lisa said, "Well, he was a stud. What a handsome guy, the best looking man I had ever laid my eyes on: big, fat head, nice heavy coat, strong shoulders," she sighed. "If a human man could look that good, I might have gone in a different direction."

Erica's eyebrows were raised, and she was equally freaked out and amused, typical when people were around Lisa. "That's just wrong," she said to Vince. "Is this story supposed to be creepy, because it's creepy."

Lisa continued, undaunted. "So anyways, he had this one flaw about him, though I didn't really see it as a flaw. He had this mole on the side of his face, pretty big, like the size of a grape, only wrinkly, like a small scrotum. I called it his raisin."

Erica looked at me with concern, so I assured her, "Don't worry, Bear didn't seem to mind it. I think a part of him accepted that it really did look like a giant raisin." She started laughing, and wine was making the pounding in my chest start to feel good. Or maybe it was hearing her laugh again.

Lisa said, "So anyways, one night while I was watching TV, I was petting Bear with my bare feet, like I always did."

"He probably minded that a bit," Vince said.

Lisa continued, "And I started playing with his raisin, between my toes, you know, just twirling it around between my big toe, and my next toe."

I said to Erica, who was starting to lose it, "Yeah, you know, as you would normally."

"Which was fine," Lisa said, "until I felt something sticky between my toes and looked down to see that my toes had blood all over them."

Erica covered her eyes and said, "Oh, God! That. Is. So. Disgusting!"

Lisa said, "Freaked me out too, I thought I had ripped his little raisin nub off, you know, playing with it too hard."

"Every man's nightmare," Vince said.

I was trying like hell not to laugh, and chimed in as seriously, "Yeah, raisin-play always seems like a good idea, until there's blood."

Erica clutched her face harder, trying to make the images go away, but Lisa continued, "So, I scream, of course, which upsets Bear, who shakes his head, sending his raisin flying right at me, hitting me on the throat and bouncing right down the front of my shirt, and it sticks between my tits."

Erica exploded with laughter, putting her hand up to stop Lisa.

"But wait, here's the damnedest thing," Lisa said.

"That *wasn't* the damnedest thing?" Erica asked me.

Lisa said, "I reach down my shirt for it, and using two fingers, like a scissor, peel it off between my boobs, but when I pulled it out, I saw it was a giant, swollen, bloody tick!"

Erica shrieked in horror, and Vince and I couldn't stop laughing, pounding the table and rolling off our chairs, despite having heard the story so many times. Erica screamed, "Bear's raisin was a tick?"

Lisa answered, "No, no, silly. The raisin was fine, thank God. I just had been playing with a tick with my toes and *thought* it was his raisin."

Erica said, "Well, thank God you still had the raisin, that makes the story so less crazy." Although Erica was shaking her head in complete disgust, she was laughing and Vince and I knew it was the first time we had seen her looking so happy since she had come back to us.

Eighteen

Be Careful What You Curse For

Mom and Aggie were at it again. They were so loud that people gathered near the Camp store to see the show. Mom and Aggie were arguing over which side the pop-up tents should go in, and Lisa was telling them why they were both wrong.

Despite their constant bickering, the camp store was shaping up nicely and it was the one building besides the office that had not been stripped of its roof due to the inventory, such as it was. Mom had followed Lisa's orders and kept the inventory for women and men on separate sides, and it gave the store the appearance of an adult toy store, which my sister said the gays would love. Mom displayed all the girly tablecloths and pretty awnings together on the boys' side, while the green mosquito coils and hand hatchets were on the opposite side of the store. The problem came when Mom insisted on grouping the tents together, and Aunt Aggie was fighting her on it.

Aunt Aggie widened her stance in front of Mom, "You're not going according to the plan."

Mom yelled back, "Plans need to change when they're not any good!"

Aggie spat, "And who ever heard of a home décor lighting department in a camp store?"

Mom slammed down a box of mauve candlesticks on the counter and the old cash register answered with a "ping!" Eddie yelled from the adjoining rec hall, "Every time a bell rings, a fairy gets his wings!"

Mom hissed, "Of course you wouldn't know a thing about home décor! You have a bleeding Jesus on every wall of your house!"

Aunt Aggie crossed her heart and looked up to the camp store ceiling as she said, "Ooooh, deee. What woman did my brother marry?"

Mom answered, "You're asking the ceiling this question? Your brother probably married the first one he met, to get out of your house!"

Aunt Aggie roared. "That's the most sense you have made all day!"

Lisa tried again to get between them, but Aunt Aggie cock-blocked her with a long tent pole and said to Mom, "You know, there are no gays on the Santora side of the family. It's not a 'thing' in Italy like it is here."

Lisa fought back a laugh, but had to chime in, "Yeah, Michelangelo was into pussy. Also, who do you guess designed your stunning floral housecoats back in the old country?"

Mom snapped at Lisa, "Don't be fresh to your Aunt."

Aunt Aggie turned to Lisa with a smug smile. "Yes, listen to your mother."

I stepped in the middle and said the only thing I could think of.

"I have an idea, let's all just all get in a circle, hold hands, and do a nice Kiegel wave. What do you say? It's easy, empowering, and keeps our bladders strong."

Lisa laughed and said to Aunt Aggie, "Unless you're already on the Depends, in which case don't waste burning the calories."

Aunt Aggie turned to Lisa, slowly, and said, "Lisa, honey, not to change the subject away from your potty humor, but I've always wanted to ask: that pretty young man Andrew that you dated in high school, was he the one that made you gay?"

Lisa answered, "That was second grade. And no. Everyone knows that *men* don't make women gay. Men's *balls* make women gay."

Aunt Aggie roared at this, and even Mom had to stifle a laugh.

Mom regained her composure, though, and returned to her frown and said, "I am just saying that between the two of us, my opinion should outweigh hers. It's not like your family is known for their smarts."

Aunt Aggie fumed. She knew Mom was referring to Aunt Aggie's identical twin and nearly departed sister, Etta. Etta Santora was the spitting image of Aunt Aggie, and family legend had it that Etta once attended a party at a friend of a friend's house. She hadn't seen her sister for a while and was stunned to see her across the room. "Aggie!" she screamed, "I didn't know you were coming!" Etta yelled this in Italian, as she came barrel-assing across the room, as the sea of people parted let the large woman run past them. The partygoers watched in disbelief as she slammed into a mirrored wall. It was Mom's favorite story. Mom had to pretend not to enjoy the story too much, since Etta had slammed into one too many things in her life and had been left in a permanent coma for as long as we kids could remember. Aunt Aggie still visited their sister twice a week to read to her. (Aunt Etta was fascinated by books, since she never could grasp how to read English—or Italian for that matter.) Dad had visited his sister daily for years and years, but when he married Mom, she made him stop since it was taking its toll on him. Mom said he couldn't stand to see any sister of his in such a state not fitting of a Santora: silent.

"Now what is the issue with the tents?" Lisa asked as if she could possibly regain control of the situation.

Aunt Aggie explained Mom wanted to keep all the tents together and not sort them into boy and girl colors the way she wanted.

Lisa said to Mom, "As much as it kills me to agree with her, Aunt Aggie is right. Red, purple, and orange tents here, and all the army green, brown, and beige tents over here. Here is the deal: My way or the highway. Any questions?"

Mom had a question. "Who the fuck do you think you're talking to, young lady?"

Like a smart sibling, I slipped out the back door, walking backward. It was every man for himself now, and I knew Lisa and Vince would have left me to fend for myself if they had been the fortunate ones to be near a viable escape route.

I heard Aunt Aggie say to Mom, "And who do you think you are talking to my niece like that? I told my brother you were rude and you had a potty mouth the day he met you—"

"Drop dead!" Mom screamed at her.

Nineteen

A Farewell To (Doughy) Arms

"Do you really think Mom believes Aunt Aggie kicked it because of her?" I asked Lisa.

Lisa answered, "You know Mom has always been weird about death. Remember after we were punished and sent to bed without supper, she would sneak in cookies because she was convinced we'd starve to death overnight?"

She was also convinced the song "Wake Up Little Susie" is about trying to wake a dead girl. "Poor Mom," I said, watching her as she moved guiltily through the crowd, pretending to be straightening the chairs that already looked like the military had aligned them.

Aunt Aggie's funeral was planned, as enthusiastically as these things can be planned, by Eddie, who fancied himself a budding party planner and thought this might be a way to break into the biz. Several of his friends attended to give moral support to his floral arrangements and helped artfully arrange the tiny mesh bags of black and purple jellybeans (the morbid equivalent of Jordan almond wedding favors), which he labeled: "Parting Gifts." Although several people muttered about the inappropriateness of it all, not one mesh baggie was left on the table by the middle of the funeral, with several people still left in line, growing anxious as the pile dwindled while they waited for a viewing.

Eddie's new boy toy had made the ride down from The Cape Cod, and gasped like a girl when he saw the massive laid-out body of Aunt Aggie. It was probably the shock of seeing the heavily applied eyeliner, bright blue eye shadow (perfectly replicated from a recent photo), and black helmet hair against the white satin coffin pillow. Or maybe it was just the way she appeared wedged into a coffin that was a wee bit too small for her. When questioned about this, Uncle Freddie said he had not seen the point of upgrading when Aunt Aggie preferred sleeping in a twin-size bed. Uncle Freddie had pulled the death equivalent of shopping at Gap Kids when you don't have a child: instead of shopping at a regular Gap store, you buy your clothes in X-Large sizes in the kids side of the store, where the clothes are a lot cheaper, but the arms are a just a bit short.

When my sister heard one of the boy toy's friends coo, "Mmm-mmm, that is one big *girl*," Lisa leaned over to Eddie and said, "Make sure your boy toy's friend knows she's actually a woman and not a tranny." Eddie did, and the boy toy's friend raised a well-plucked eyebrow, accusing him of joking. I smiled as the boy toy self-consciously touched his trim abs to assure himself that being around a group of people who frequently abused calorie intake had not made him fat by proximity.

There is nothing like the funeral of a fairly unlikable woman to bring out the crowds of elderly Italians. Going to a funeral that is guaranteed to not be sad was basically an exercise of paying your respects for the free buffet. The buffet, in this case, would be held after the service, at our condo. Erica had volunteered to take care of the food arrangements so we could focus on the funeral service and whatever else Uncle Freddie needed, but Lisa wouldn't hear of it. She had laid out a spread of homemade lasagna, stuffed artichokes, and two vats of simmering meatballs, and had put together three trays of stunningly arranged antipasto that could have fed twice the people attending. Vince and I had already carefully raided the sharp provolone chunks and rearranged as needed.

The flowers were amazing, and Eddie was able to fill an entire row of guests with his overdressed friends, their ultra-conservative suits and ties contrasting with tastefully applied makeup—if you can ever consider makeup on men tasteful. I walked through a crowd of people who were marveling at how Eddie managed to make floral arrangements with birds of paradise somehow work with the somber décor of the funeral home, but Lisa and I knew that making the unexpected thing work was one of Eddie's many gifts. Vince and I both glanced at Uncle Freddie, who was having a conversation with Dad.

Vince whispered in my ear, "I shouldn't say it, but it's not at all like when Uncle Tony lost Auntie Celia."

I had just been thinking the same thing. "Don't forget that while Uncle Freddie lived under her iron fist for all of his adult life, it's still going to be a big adjustment for him."

Vince agreed, "Yeah, like how some lifers don't want to leave jail when their time comes up."

"They get attached to the beatings," I whispered back, as we both stifled a soft chuckle. "Could have been the great Italian food that kept him."

"Gotta give Aunt Aggie credit there," I agreed.

"Remember at Grandma's funeral, when Aunt Aggie tried to throw herself in the grave?"

I sighed. "Good times."

Vince said, "Well, if it happens again, there'll be no waiting."

We were unable to get Uncle Freddie's favorite priest, so the eulogy was so benign it sounded like the priest was working off *Mad Libs: The Eulogy Edition.* It was shaping up to be a very uneventful wake and funeral, a rare thing in our family. I had been so busy with the camp that the droning of the priest got to me and I nodded off to sleep a few times, waking up when Vince elbowed me as Uncle Freddie stepped in front of the gathering to say a few words.

Mom was still wincing with her I-killed-someone-with-my-evil-powers face, and I watched it twist it up a notch as Uncle Freddie began to speak. "Thank you all for coming," he said with his Italian accent and sweet smile. "My wife and I were together for over fifty-seven years, and there was not a single day where we didn't look into each other's eyes . . . and have an argument." The crowd let out a relieved chuckle, hoping they'd dodged a tear-jerking speech.

Uncle Freddie continued, "I had no idea all I had to say was 'drop dead' and I could have lived my whole life in peace!" Everyone chuckled again, as Mom shook her head and covered her face in embarrassment.

"But seriously, my wife and I argued, but we had a lot of laughs, too. Nobody could energize a room like my Aggie, you could never deny her that. I used to tell her she was a tough lady to love . . . but she was my tough lady."

The room took on a tense silence, noted by shifting bodies and creaking chairs and a few uncomfortable coughs. "When we were first dating, Aggie used to tell me I was the only man strong enough to love her. But I don't feel very strong today . . . Maybe this is what I will be—a little less strong without her."

I caught the eyes of my sister and brother, who both looked like I must have looked: We were all hit by the realization that, despite all the yelling she did and complaining he did, Uncle Freddie had lost his best friend.

"We didn't expect her to leave us this suddenly, and she sure would have wanted to stretch it out a bit. Aggie loved to be the center of attention, so she had talked about what she wanted for her funeral. I was surprised when she asked me to do only two things. The first was to ask a favor of all of you, and I promise you, she really asked this. She asked that you all forgive her for the way she was sometimes. She loved you all, but she couldn't help it. She said it was too much fun to be a bitch."

There were a few small laughs, but now people were tearing up, and the row of stout female cousins and Eddie and his friends began sniffing into Kleenex's. One of our cousins, the one that Lisa called "Buff," was putting on the best show of grief I had seen since Grandma's funeral when Aunt Aggie eclipsed the competition, even though Aunt Aggie had not spoken to Grandma in years. Like Aunt Aggie, Buff was quite the character, equal parts sweet and bitchy, and she was equally wide as she was tall, which this was the reason Lisa called her Buff. (Her real name was Faye—as in, Buff-Faye.)

Uncle Freddie continued, "The second thing she asked me to do is a little harder . . . but I have to do what she wanted since it is her last request." His voice cracked and I could feel my eyes burning with the threat of tears. "So now, I am going to ask that my Lisa, Marie, and Vince and my brother-in-law Sal come with me into a private room." There was a hush to the crowd again, but Uncle Freddie lightened his voice and said, "Please join us back at the house to enjoy the lovely buffet Lisa has prepared, and thank you so much for coming. See you back out here in a few moments."

We followed Uncle Freddie into a back room of the funeral home, where a man had been standing at the doorway. The man nodded at him as we passed and opened the door for him and before he closed it behind us, I could see Mom's face scrunched with concern for what was happening without her, the assassin of Uncle Freddie's wife.

When the door was closed, Uncle Freddie walked silently around to the other side of a long table in the middle of the odd-looking room lined with plastic on the floor (for the hard-core criers?). He leaned on the table with both of his hands. The table was covered with a bland tablecloth that reached to the floor and had a floral arrangement on it that was attractive but not offensively pretty for the occasion of death. He paused and didn't say a word for a long time while we stared at him, not knowing what to do.

Dad finally asked, "Freddie, are you alright?"

Uncle Freddie took a deep and serious breath. "Aggie asked me to do is this, because she said keeping the kids' traditions are important, and, you know, she knew you kids always did this at funerals . . . and she couldn't leave this earth without getting in one last shot . . ."

Just then, Uncle Freddie dipped under the table and whipped out two large, bright fluorescent plastic objects, and pointed them at us: "She said none of you would dare shoot back at the bereaved!"

Even as it was happening I knew later the scene would be remembered and retold in slow motion in classic war-movie style like a scene from *Full Metal Jacket* and *Saving Private Ryan,* only we would be laughing our asses off.

Vince, Lisa, and I all mouthed in slow motion the word "Noooooooooo!" as Uncle Freddie blasted us with two giant water pistols, outfitted with automatic trigger-action, light, and blaster sound effects. Uncle Freddie had skimped on the coffin, but had gotten the deluxe Super Soakers. Good choice, I thought, as I dove for the floor, despite my tight black skirt.

My siblings and I all hit the deck at once, and I knew my brother and sister would be thinking what I was, that for years we'd thought our discreet shooting of each other with water pistols at family death-related events had gone unnoticed by the older folks. I realized now as I shamefully crouched down behind the table Uncle Freddie was shooting us from, that I would have used a row of elderly relatives as human shields.

Sprawled out on the floor, I looked to Vince in desperation and hope. "Do you?" I asked. He nodded, then I turned to Lisa, "Do you?" and she nodded back with a sinister grin.

While Dad was getting nailed by the water pistols for not reacting quickly enough, I called out, "On three! One . . . two . . . THREE!"

The three of us jumped up, pulling out our own water pistols (sadly, not the type to do battle, just the tiny, easy to hide, snub-nosed variety, the twin bed of the water pistol industry—perfect for drive-bys, but not for a battle like this) and we laughed our asses off as we fired back our pathetic weapons at Uncle Freddie in our perfect policeman stances, legs far apart, eyes on the barrel of our yellow, pink, and purple guns with bright orange safety plugs at the end of the barrels. The thought struck me, What does this sound like from the other side of the doorway, but there was a battle going on, and a guard at the door, and I couldn't concern myself with that.

Then, in a stunning act of betrayal, Dad finally got his act together and pulled out his water pistol and chose to jump to the side with the heavy artillery. He sidled up to Uncle Freddie and helped him soak us as he and Dad laughed like hyenas. Collectively, we turned our guns on Dad, but even the three of us were no match for the Super Soakers, especially since Dad yelled to Uncle Freddie to play dirty and aim for the eyes and ears.

Uncle Freddie was heading closer, in slow motion (his usual speed), and my one thought was if my shirt got much wetter it would be completely see-through, so I backed out of the room, laughing and shooting, like the last action hero left on an alien-infested starship. When Lisa and Vince realized I was leaving, they turned their guns on me, Lisa's last stream—tiny, but a direct hit to the eye—made my vision blurry when I emerged from the room soggy and stupid, unfocused on my Uncle Tony and his new wife Katherine who had entered the funeral home.

My heart stopped beating as what I feared would happen, did: a beautiful red-headed woman entered the room right behind them. Lorn Elaine, closeted actress, ex-love of my life, the woman who had dumped me three times (or was it four?), was now standing just a water pistol stream away. The door to the war room was still open, so my siblings naturally took advantage of my shock and nailed me repeatedly in the face, and everything went back into slow motion, the water pelting me in the head doing nothing to revive me from my state of shock.

"Oh shit," Lisa said, as she halted her shooting.

"Oh shit," Vince echoed.

"Oh perfect," Erica said, somewhere behind me.

As Lorn moved toward me, I wiped a wet chunk of hair stuck to my face, feeling the sting of running mascara burning my eyes. A shallow thought pushed to the very front of my brain: Why is it when you look your worst, you see the person you wanted to see when you look your best? My body was frozen, but my heart was thudding loudly in my ears . . . or maybe it was the contents of Vince's emptied water pistol sloshing around in my sinuses.

Katherine and Uncle Tony stepped back to let Lorn approach me first, her eyes boring into mine. Of course she looked amazing. I dropped my full pistol on my foot and stared down at it, as confused by the pain as if my foot had been hit with a steaming meatball. Meatballs would come later, along with some fresh grief from seeing Lorn again.

"It's good to see you," she said, and my body betrayed me by reacting naughtily to her voice. When I didn't answer, she moved closer and said, "I'm so sorry about your Aunt Aggie."

I could smell her, and instantly my senses came alive like someone had switched me on. A neon sign that had been turned off and cool to the touch, now raged hot and blinking: OPEN TO SERVE YOU. When I at last found my voice, I was thankful it remained ice cold. "You didn't have to come all this way. You hardly knew her."

Lorn's eyes searched for some sign of the woman she knew before. I hoped she saw none.

She said softly so only I could hear, "I came for you."

I could feel my brother and sister drifting away from the door behind me, leaving a sinking ship, and the ship was me. "You didn't have to," I said, "Aunt Aggie didn't like a lot of people, including me, I think."

Lorn took another step closer and I could see the tiny flecks of gold in her green eyes, the detail I could see only when we were close enough to touch. I could also see she was fighting back tears. Actress, I thought.

"Marie. I said I came for you," she said again.

I felt a drop of water release from my chin. "You said a lot of things. I'm saying you wasted a trip."

Twenty

Punch To The Gut, And I'm To Blame

Lisa was yelling a barrage of questions at me in the car, but I heard only a few: *Why didn't you tell her off?; Why didn't you smack her across her pretty face?; Why didn't you let me smack her pretty face?; etc., etc.*

"Lisa—" Vince tried to shush her, but she was not having it.

"I don't know," I said as something hot tumbled down my cheek. A tear splashed on my pants and I looked at it, puzzled, as if it were a leak in the car roof. I turned my head to look out the window, hoping they didn't notice. Lisa's questions kept coming as I watched the cemetery trees whip by. Another tear rolled down my other cheek, which really pissed me off because I had made the decision not to cry.

As Vince tried to shush Lisa, I felt a hand gently press the middle of my back. It was Erica. Her touch made the floodgates burst open further. Lorn was not supposed to be here, I was not supposed to still hurt this much, and Erica was not supposed to behave sweetly to me. Erica felt the shudder in my back and thought her hand upset me, and took her hand away. It didn't matter, of course, because I could still feel her there. She had left a scorching mark on me—and I worried if everyone else would see it, too.

We arrived at the cemetery, for which I was grateful, since it's the only place besides the movies where you can cry in public without anyone asking what's wrong. Specifically, I was grateful I could cry out of a maddening confusion about Erica, which my siblings would assume was about Lorn.

Lorn was there, but she kept her distance, or, more likely, Vince and Lisa kept me distant from her, since I had been led from the car by both my elbows as if I could lose the use of both my legs at any moment. I glanced over to Uncle Freddie, who looked sad but also quite strong for a man who had just lost his mate, and I stared at him, using him to will myself to get my frigging act together. I could not appear to be the most shattered person at a funeral for my famously cantankerous Aunt Aggie . . . it was fucking ridiculous.

I took a deep breath and scanned the crowd. Lorn was directly across the grave, her gaze fixed on me. I felt a punch to my gut. The distance gave me courage to risk staring back at her and ignore my inner voice telling me that the more sane option would be to poke my own eyes out and flick them into Aunt Aggie's new digs. I was scanning the ground for pointy sticks to help me do just that, as I felt Vince's arm slide around my shoulder.

It was Vince who understood best what Lorn had done to me, and what she still could do to me, if I let her, but it occurred to me that Erica also knew. I looked at Erica and saw that her eyes were also on me, but she shot her gaze away as if I had caught her pitying me. Instead, she turned her attention to Lorn and glared at her across the grave. I saw some hate there, and if Lorn knew Erica as I did, she would best be served by yelping like a wounded dog and running her pretty actress ass back to California.

Erica looked back at me and sadly, almost imperceptibly, shook her head no at me, a Charades-style warning to watch my step around that woman who had hurt me before. I stupidly looked back at Lorn and felt the punch to my gut for the third time. That is not how you should feel when you look at someone, right? I looked back to Erica to acknowledge that her silent warning was likely good, solid advice, but Erica had already left and was walking toward the car. The feeling in my gut was an unexpectedly stronger kick to the stomach.

I was grateful that Lorn didn't come back to our condo after the funeral. My Uncle Tony and Lorn's mother Katherine did, however, and although I really liked Katherine, I tried to avoid her until she cornered me in the kitchen and completely disarmed me with a warm hug.

"I've missed seeing you," she said. "You know my daughter still loves you." Katherine's directness was the last thing I needed to hear as my heart pounded with the confirmation that Lorn was still mine, in some small way.

"I can't do it again," I said.

"Good," she said, surprising me. "As much as she needs you, it really wouldn't be best."

I was disgusted by the regret that roiled up inside me. Maybe I was secretly hoping her daughter had changed and she could somehow guarantee she would not run from me again. But I knew this wasn't true.

Katherine gently held my chin until I looked her in the eyes. It didn't help that her eyes were an exact match of Lorn's. "You need to do what's best for you. I told Lorn she shouldn't come, but you know how my daughter doesn't listen to her mother."

"What daughter does?" I said.

Katherine looked at me with concern. "Protect yourself."

"She could never be with me, not in the way I wanted."

It occurred to me that I was finally speaking in the past tense, the first time ever when it came to Lorn. Katherine hugged me again and over her shoulder I looked for Erica, but she had disappeared again. When our hug ended, I asked her, "How's life as a newlywed?"

"Marrying your Uncle Tony was the smartest thing I ever did," she said, and her bright smile and voice reminded me so much of Lorn, but, luckily, by then, my gut had gone numb and I could no longer feel the punches.

Lisa, Vince, and I returned to the camp just in time to see a trail of cars arriving, a fully decorated truck leading three other cars, with five gay boys in the back of the flatbed, shrieking like puppies, happily exaggerating the danger every time they hit a small bump, and fabulously presenting themselves as if they were in the Macy's Day Parade instead of on a dirt road leading to a campground. I heard a high-pitched voice sing out: "The Camptown Laaaaadies are heeeeere!" They went on to chant the classic version of Camptown Ladies, minus Lisa's original dildo refrain, which I knew Lisa would be teaching them, ASAP.

Eddie heard the approaching tribe too, and bounced out of the rec hall, where he had been installing sets of gauzy bug-proof curtains he had custom-sewn. Eddie squealed, and I worried for all the glass in the camp lanterns. Two of the boys were in full drag, and one was wearing an extra long colorful boa flitting out behind him, making it appear as if the flatbed truck was wearing a scarf. One of the young men was Eddie's new boyfriend from P-town.

I watched the campers they passed, nobody willing to stand near the road, instead watching from the safety of their sites and inside their dark trailers. Always one to sense a party, Lisa joined me outside the office as the boys waved and squealed.

Lisa said, "The girls! They're here at last!"

Dad poked his head out of the office. "I have this feeling Aunt Aggie is with us right now."

I was rather touched. "Really, Dad?"

He said, "Sure. That screeching would have woken the dead." He disappeared back inside just as Mom came out with her clipboard, looking like an army sergeant dressed by Ann Taylor's poorest cousin.

The boys whooped and cackled when the truck came to a stop in front of the office, and shoved each other like high school boys (in prettier clothes) to be the first ones out of the truck. Mom greeted them and began giving them what seemed a well-rehearsed speech about store hours, check-out time, and quiet hours, as if they were checking into a Marriot. I saw several of the boys' eyes glazing over, so I stepped in front of Mom.

"Welcome boys!" I said. "Since you won the award for Best Arrival, we'd like to show our gratitude by asking you to join us as our guests for best Italian dinner of your lives at the rec hall tonight, or as soon as it's finished." There was more whooping and cheering as Eddie made his way around to inappropriately hug each of the boys. When they were done hugging Eddie hello, I suggested, "Why don't you all pile back into the flatbed so we can give you a tour."

"Hey, where are you from?" Lisa yelled at the beautiful caramel-skinned young man with the pretty accent.

"I'm from Jordan," he said, his voice revealing that he was instinctively a little afraid of her. A smart man for his young years.

"That's in the Middle East. That's alright," Mom assured the young man.

"I'm sure he appreciates that, Mom," Lisa said as she moved to take a closer look at him. "Jordan, huh? What a coincidence, that's where Italian people get all our wedding candy from." He looked confused, but didn't ask.

Lisa turned to me, "Hey, Marie, remember when I found a sack of insect eggs in a spider web and I told you they were mini-Jordan almonds?" I remembered. "That was a fun day," she said with a sigh as my stomach lurched. I'd always hoped she'd been kidding, though the historical odds were stacked against me.

As I wondered if you could throw up from something you ate twenty-five years ago, the boys insisted I give them a tour and they pig-scrambled back into the truck, spanking each other's asses and fighting as if there were amazing and horrible seats to be won in the back of a pickup truck. Several hands reached for me at once and hoisted me into the truck, propelling me, crowd-surfing style, across the pack of them. I felt hands everywhere as they carried me into the truck. "Nice tits," one of them said politely as I laughed, "Momma like."

"Why, thanks," I said, meaning it.

We took a tour and there was much squealing, although the boys quieted and turned up their noses at the pond, but when we cruised by the built-in pool, the squealing reached a crescendo that threatened the ears of several dogs at camp. One of the older boys made a proclamation as if he had just moved his gay army across a battlefield, "Ladies, our Home Base . . . WE shall break camp here!"

There was cheering as I tried to advise them over the commotion, "Someone is setting up right over there, so you won't have much privacy." He told me not to worry, that those people would not be staying there long, and he was right. Even as we circled the pool area to satisfy their demand of a full 3D view, I could see the family of four had already slowed in the unpacking of their Volvo, and were pretending to be checking the number posted on the tree, as if they had landed at the wrong site.

One of the older men pointed at a patch of grass near the pool entrance, "We can set up a gas grill over here to cook our steaks!"

"Is there a pool or cabana boy?" one of them asked.

"Of course," I said, "his name is Vince, and he gives the best massages." They squealed again. "He's shy, so you'll have to insist."

When we cruised by one of the shower houses, the boys gave some ooo's and aaaah's and even a few moans when I described many of the toilets had been outfitted with a discreet way to pass emergency rolls of toilet paper, or what-have-you.

"We love you," one of them said with great emotion, forcing his bottom lip to tremble with emotion, and then he hugged me, twice.

One of them said, "Can we touch your boobs again to show our appreciation? We just love boobs, don't we, girls?" I laughed along with the truckload of them, correcting my tone to be a bit more high-pitched, so as not to be the least ladylike of the pack. It didn't really work.

Oddly enough, our first group of lesbians arrived soon after, on the very same day. They entered camp in a precise row of dangerously silent Honda and Toyota hybrids, weaving their way through the camp, actually observing the 5-miles-an-hour posted speed limit that made you feel as if you were driving backward.

We got business-like hellos from a few of the women, who had already figured out what each one owed for the campsites, to the penny, before they had even reached the office. (By contrast, the gay boys had emptied their pockets and decided whoever had the most cash leftover from the drunken debauchery of the night before, would pay for the sites. Anything left over, would buy more booze.)

When the lesbians saw Dad's pile of firewood, one of the stockier ladies asked if there was a hatchet around to further split any wood they might buy. In a panic, I looked around, but, thankfully, Dad was out of earshot, and he missed the dyke threat to his pile. I assured the woman we could work something out, and arranged for her to come back when Dad usually took his hammock siesta.

I gave the women the same tour I gave the boys, which commenced in a bitter silence I knew not to analyze. While they turned up their noses at the convenience of a camp store and the absurdness of a sparkling swimming pool when there was a perfectly fine pond, they applied a sensible strategy to spend their days fishing by the murky, weed-fringed pond, and firmed up plans for which night each person was responsible for cooking their vegetarian dinners over an open fire.

When I got back to the office, another car was parked near the entrance, but since it was devoid of camp gear, it seemed the occupant was not waiting to be checked in. As I walked over to the car, Lorn got out, and I stupidly considered running for it.

"I hope you don't mind that I came," she said, her auburn hair pissing me off as it caught the sunlight, gently moving in the breeze.

"Of course not," I said.

She shut the car door and walked toward me.

"It's beautiful here," she said. It sure was, I thought.

Lorn feigned interest in seeing more of the camp and, without me agreeing to, we started walking. "I thought it was best not to come back to the condo after the funeral," she said.

"Probably was," I agreed. In fact, she'd stayed away a few days, and I had assumed she'd gone back to California with Uncle Tony and her mother Katherine. We fell silent, and Lorn walked closer to me, a few times our arms brushing against mine until I moved farther from her.

Lorn said, "I didn't just come to pay my respects to you and your family about your aunt. I also came to say I'm sorry."

"Long way to travel for that," I said.

"And to tell you I know I made a big mistake."

I stopped walking. "No," I said. "I made the mistake. It took a long time, but I did eventually realize you won't ever let yourself live the way you want to."

"Marie—"

I held my hand up to stop her. "No. Did you hear me? I finally accepted that it was me who made the mistake. The same mistake, many times."

Lorn moved closer to me, and I thought, Why were mistakes often so tempting? I took a step back from her and she reached for my arm.

"I love you. I made the mistake," she said.

"It's too late," I said. She let go of my arm and studied my face for a different answer, but when I didn't give her one, she said, "There's someone else."

"What?" I said, a bit louder than I should have, "No."

"I know I kept you waiting for so long, but I thought, you couldn't have—"

"Waiting? Is that what you think I was doing? It wasn't waiting. It was . . . suffering."

She moved closer again. "Marie, please. I know I don't deserve to ask, but give me another chance. I promise you, I don't care if the press finds out. In fact, I'll do what my manager has said I should have done all along. I'll have him manage it. I'll make a statement and come out. It will be my story that way."

"Your story."

She said, "Our story. But I wouldn't use your name if you didn't want. Or, better yet, my manager says it would be even better to say I was bi-sexual, if you didn't mind—"

"Why would I mind what you say," I said. "I won't be taking another risk."

We stood not saying anything for a long few minutes, before I finally said, "You know, Lorn, you'd have made a stronger case if you had already come out to the press, before asking me to take you back."

"But why would I take a chance if I wasn't sure you'd be mine?"

"Exactly. And why should I?" I said to her. This time, it was Lorn that looked punched in the gut.

I was neither sad nor angry as I left her standing there to walk back to the office, where Uncle Freddie was talking with Erica. They had been leaning over building plans on the ground, and I warmed at the idea that Erica had been trying to keep Uncle Freddie busy after losing Aunt Aggie. It appeared to be working, as he was animatedly talking to her, but as Erica was listening to him, she was looking over his shoulder, disapprovingly watching Lorn's car making a U-turn as she pulled out of camp.

Twenty-One

The Soundproof Insulation Of Large Boobs

When we were kids, Lisa started speaking in an English accent after becoming obsessed with a couple of Louisa May Alcott novels. She had been convinced (maybe tricked) into reading them by my mother (who didn't bother to tell her Alcott was American, not English), and she kept one by her bed for almost a year. I kept asking her when she planned to read it, since it had become dusty and the pages were starting to turn yellow. The book was *Little Women,* and she insisted she was saving the best one for last.

One Saturday, I came home from a friend's house and headed to my room, passing by my mother, whose odd and hopeful expression did not make sense until I opened the bedroom door to find Lisa lounging on her bed, dressed in her First Communion dress, which was now much too small for her. *Little Women* was carefully laid out on her lap, and a cup brimming with Nestlé iced tea was perched elegantly on her nightstand in a Boston Bruins hockey mug. I was shocked to observe there was even a doily under the mug and I thought it would have been less embarrassing if had I caught my sister masturbating.

"What the fuck are you doing?" I asked, in a gentle voice, on the chance my older sister had just suffered a stroke.

"Today I shall be reading my literature book," she said in her full-blown Hallmark movie English accent.

"Your literature book."

"And . . . I love it already. I know this book shall change my life."

"Is it making you say the word 'shall'?'

To truly understand the sight I was witnessing, you have to

remember that Lisa was born with a street hockey stick in her thick baby fists. My childhood memories of Lisa had been filled with episodes like: her insistence at age seven that she wanted a crew cut to match the neighborhood boys; how she loved the Patriots football jersey she wore almost daily from age eleven to thirteen (the last year, she had to operate on the thing with wide scissor cuts in order to still fit it over her growing body); and how occasionally she slept with her softball trophies dangerously tucked in her bed, until the day she rolled over wrong, proved Mom right, and got four stitches on her ass cheek. I laughed, telling her the trophy was for being Number One Dumb Ass, just seconds before receiving a nasty punch to my arm, which left a bruise the size and shape of two conjoined plums.

She clutched the Louisa May Alcott book to her breast, and sighed, "I was just introduced to Jo," she said. My sister had been talking about Jo for months. Mom had said there was a girl named Jo in the book and Lisa would relate to her, so Lisa had convinced herself that Jo must be the carbon copy of Jo on the TV show *The Facts of Life.* I stayed planted in the doorway, not daring to get the Social Studies book on my bed, and deciding it would be much safer to risk not finishing my homework on the bus. I took a step backward out of the room, and she went back to her reading.

Later that afternoon I saw, much to my mother's heartbreak, Lisa had returned to her scrappy football jersey, and wrapped the book in her communion dress, then tossed it into the trash. It seems that *Little Women* was not the tale of awakening lesbianism for which she had hoped.

I had never seen Lisa fret before, so it was a little disconcerting. She darted about the rec hall, Eddie occasionally swatting and shooing her as if she were a fly whizzing by him as he arranged his beautiful centerpieces on all of the tables. The rec hall was completely transformed, and as dusk approached, the tiny twinkle lights threaded in the rafters made the rec hall appear roofless with a billion stars out. If only the rec hall, now a restaurant, could remain roofless. Despite all the progress, there was still much to be done to have the exterior ready by tomorrow when Lisa planned to debut her restaurant.

I could hear Erica barking at her crew, but I knew that her annoyance had transferred from Eddie (and what she called his decorator-playing-contractor-clay-tile-fuck-up) to my sister, who instead of letting Erica replace the group of damaged rafters, had asked that Erica keep some of the older rafters for a more authentic look. After much work had been done, it became clear that many of the exposed rafters had been eaten by termites in ways that were not immediately visible, and her crew had roofed over several rafters that would now need to be replaced, and this could not be done after the new roof was on, or they would risk cracking the clay tiles. This meant the crew was stripping parts of the roof, instead of replacing it—and going backward was something that did not make Erica a happy camper.

"You can knock off for the night if you want, but don't bother coming back," she yelled across the rooftop. Along with the constant hammering, I could hear the heavy feet of the men, followed by her lighter, quicker steps as she led them about. "There are soft gaps over here!" She pounded her foot on the roof. "And who did this area?" There was silence. "Do not step where the clay tiles are. Only the Italian crew goes there, got it?"

I came out of the camp store to see two of her crew unwrapping a sign and leaning it against the outer wall. I remembered Lisa's first choice for a name, and how we had to talk her out of it. She was pushing for "Does a Bear Eat In The Woods?" Although Bear Week would surely bring in a crowd of hairy men to appreciate her joke, we convinced her that most campers wouldn't. She ended up opting for a sign colored with the green and red of the Italian flag and with a beautiful white dove sculpted in the wood. "Dove Gaio Mangia," or, as we called it, the Dove.

It pleased Lisa to think of all the hillbilly campers that would be eating under this sign before returning to their trailers adorned with confederate flag stickers. Lisa told the campers the sign said: "Where happy people eat," but only Uncle Freddie had been able to translate the name on the sign, which actually read, "Where Gays Eat."

Erica was on top of the roof with her arms folded in front of her as she chastised a worker who was on his knees on the roof. "I feel bad for your wife. You call that hammering?" Then she whirled around to bust on an older guy I hadn't seen before. He had been chuckling at her comments as he hammered and she said, "What the fuck are you laughing at? Not enough work to do here?"

There was something about this man, but he was not part of her regular crew; too old, I thought. He quickened his hammering to double time, and something about the way he hammered, his "bang-bang-tap," sounded like he had been trained well by Erica.

Erica shouted out, "At least the old man knows how to hammer, not like the rest of you pussies." The old man turned his head toward me to hide his smirking, and I realized the man looking down from the roof was Uncle Freddie. Our eyes met and he stopped hammering for just a second, before happily winking at me and turning back to his work. Erica followed his gaze down to me.

"You're not going to interfere with my crew, right?" she said.

"Never," I answered, feeling a powerful warmth spread within me, which I dearly hoped was Uncle Freddie's happiness. I thought I saw Erica let out a small smile before she turned her back on me, and I felt the alarming warmth again.

Later that evening, after Mom and Dad and Uncle Freddie had gone home, Vince, Lisa, and I realized we had been working all by ourselves for quite a while when the lights at the Dove Gaio Mangia shut off by automatic timer, leaving all of us in the dark, except for the moonlight.

Lisa said, "Well, I'll take that as a sign from God. Let's go home and get some sleep."

Vince loaded up some extra kitchen things in a box Lisa she said she didn't need and said, "I'll leave these by your car. I'm done."

"You done here, Mare?" Lisa asked me.

"Almost," I said, wanting to finish up the last preparations on the buffet area. When my eyes adjusted to the loss of light, I saw how beautiful the atmosphere had become in the hall, even without the tiny lights on. The campfire light and heavy smoke just outside the hall had mixed with heavy fog and created a thick orange glow that held low in the air, pooling inside the hall. The path of the fog was moving, gently swirling as if someone had been drawing patterns into it with a giant stick.

"Wow," Lisa said, "fog by campfire light is amazing! It needs to look like this every night. I'm going to pick up a dry ice machine in time for the Dove Gaio Mangia opening. It'll be fantastic!" As crazy as it sounded, I had to admit it would be beautiful if she could re-create the effect.

Lisa left and I finished covering the buffet tables with new blue tarps to keep the dampness from settling on the plates and flatware. When I finished, I was struck by the silence of the campground. All voices had fallen to a distant hush, even the gay boys had stopped hooting, and all that could be heard was the pop and crackle of the campfire just outside the hall. It had been smart of Lisa to build a large fire pit within full view of the tables in the hall. I thought, if I were the type of person that allowed myself to stop and enjoy a moment, I would chill out in front of the Dove Gaio Mangia right now, just to feel some time pass.

Before I could change my mind, I walked to the bench outside the hall near the camp store to sit and enjoy the sounds and smells of the camp. There was a chill in the air, but it was not uncomfortable, especially since the fire had warmed the wood bench seat. I breathed in the smell of pine and sweet wet smoke as I made a conscious effort not to think about Lorn or Erica. It was impossible.

I heard footsteps to the side of the hall and checked my watch, and was surprised to see it was only ten-thirty.

"Hey."

It was Erica.

"Hey," I said back. "What are you still doing here?"

Erica said, "I don't want to face your sister if this hall isn't ready for her opening night. I secured a tarp over the last weak spot in the roof, but there's a storm coming in."

"I heard," I said. "Want to sit?" I slid over to one side of the bench, feeling the warm wood from the fire once again. She hesitated before joining me. She was dressed too well for someone who had climbed roofs to supervise men all day and I looked away, but not before I thought how campfire light was indeed her best friend. As she pulled her hair band out to shake her hair down, I could smell fresh air and the scent of her shampoo, so I got up to throw another shard of wood on the fire, now making an effort to think about Lorn.

As if she had been reading my mind Erica said, "It was hard seeing her today."

"It was," I agreed, then repeated what she said in my head as I thought, Had she meant me? The pounding in my chest seemed audible to my ears. I thanked God for the soundproof insulation of my large boobs, fairly certain they would stifle the loud thuds that were bellowing deep within my chest. Thank you, my boobs. Thank you.

This wasn't the first time I have thanked my boobs. I thanked them a lot, and to distract my thoughts of Erica, I began recounting the many times—ending with the time I caught my shoe heel in a parking lot pothole, sending me splatting to the pavement—that my boobs hit everything first and saved me from breaking my nose, or my jaw. "Bumbles Bounce," I thought each time, one of many Rudolph quotes that ran through my head at regular and inappropriate intervals.

I grabbed a few more pieces of wood and threw them into the struggling fire and stood watching the fire an extra moment before I turned to look at her. How long had she been staring back at me? Erica's serious expression brought the thudding back—or was it just the nearness of her? I heard Rudolph's thrilled and nasal voice, "She thinks I'm cuuuuuuute!" while I sat stewing in hatred of the part of me that was so thrilled to hope, the part of my idiotic heart that was galloping wildly out of control.

When I walked back to the bench, Erica looked away from me, staring hypnotically at the campfire as I heard the distance voice again, although this time it was warning me: Of course Vince loves her, look at her. Vince will always love her. Don't forget that. Ever. And don't forget the person I used to be, the person that chased

Lorn Elaine like a lunatic from one side of the country to another, dragging her out of the closet kicking and screaming in total fear of what it would do to her career—all because it was what I had wanted. Well, not this time. Not with this woman. Not to my brother. Not ever. Not that I even had a chance.

Erica looked back up at me as if she'd somehow heard, and I quickly sat back down.

I felt her arm graze against mine as she reached deep into her jacket pocket. She handed me a flask.

"What's this?" I asked.

"Your Dad left it on a table back there. Tequila."

"Of course," I said.

"Let's give it back to him empty. That'll teach him to leave things lying around."

I smiled at her. "I wondered why he was so generous with the wood today," and she laughed.

Note to self: Don't make her laugh. She is ridiculously beautiful when she laughs. I remembered working so hard to make her laugh before. Before, when I was clueless.

I spun the plastic top open and took a long swig and passed it to Erica as she said, "For his birthday, you should get him a real flask. What's with this Tupperware version? It looks like something truckers pee in on long hauls."

I laughed. "Airplane proof. He bought that to take on the Jamaica trip a while back."

"Your dad is crazy."

"And this is news?" I said.

She took a long swallow and we sat side by side, both feeling the warmth of the hot liquid slide into our bellies. A symphony of crickets drowned out the fat croaking bass note of a nearby bullfrog.

"Jamaica is where you met her," Erica said, and I didn't answer.

I was thinking about how so much had changed. How Erica had joined us in Jamaica for Lorn's mother's wedding to my Uncle Tony, and how she had been in love with my brother, and how it didn't seem that long ago.

"You should stay away from her," Erica said in a low voice I didn't recognize. She took another sip from the flask before handing it to me.

I nodded and said, "I learned who I need to stay away from."

I said this knowing that not once in my life had my dim-witted heart ever listened to a word I said. I pulled another long swallow from the flask, and half-closed my eyes. There was warmth spreading on my face from the tequila and the fire, but it was nothing compared to the side of my body that was nearest to her.

There was a long silence, then Erica took two sips in a row, and coughed a little from the strength of it. When she finally spoke, her voice was soft.

"Marie. I've been wanting to talk to you about something."

I didn't know this voice, either. This voice could say anything. The voice that said my name like that could change everything. I pretended I didn't hear her, stood up and started talking.

"I know the schedule has been tight and there's still a lot of work to do, but Lisa is hell bent on opening the restaurant tomorrow night."

I was rambling, and by the look on her face, she thought I was rambling, too.

"So, I guess I'll head out so tomorrow I can start out early." She nodded at me, and the look on her face was heartbreaking. My stomach turned as I wondered if maybe I was wrong and she wanted to talk about Vince. Maybe she wanted me to help get him back for her. Maybe the look on my face was already revealing I didn't want this. Maybe I needed to follow my instincts and just get the hell out of there.

I asked her, "You OK with putting out this fire?"

There was a long pause as her eyes met mine, as if she was searching for another choice from me, before she finally said, "Yes, if you need me to, I'll put it out."

There was no mistaking that tone in her voice, but I tried to tell me I had not heard it, and I wished I had left right then instead of braving one more glance at her. She was no longer the Erica I knew, and I supposed, might never be again. The old Erica was cool, confident, and unreadable. People understood this at her first firm handshake, as I had. But this new Erica—she seemed unsure, and worse, much worse, she looked scared and . . . sadly hopeful, just like Vince had looked so many times after she came to the campground.

She said she was OK with putting out the fire, so I left her there.

"Goodnight," I said, and I walked away into a night that had turned unexpectedly cold.

Vince was yelling at me. "Tell me it's not true!"

My mind raced. I needed to lie to him. But how could he already know, when I just learned it tonight? Had he seen us sitting together on the bench? Or, maybe he had seen it long before I did. Maybe Lisa had suspected and told him.

He knew me well enough to suspect how I looked at her, and more suspicious, how I avoided looking at her. Why had Lisa asked her to come? Why couldn't that damned tiny voice have shouted out sooner what I should have known all along? When Lorn left me, it was Erica I had craved seeing. For comfort, I had told myself. Ridiculous, I told myself now. Erica was not a person you look to for comfort. I had wanted something I wouldn't let myself admit.

And now, somehow, Vince knew.

I felt a violent crack across my face, the sound ringing loudly in my ears. Had he hit me? My baby brother whom I loved more than anything in the world? Even in childhood when we fought as siblings do, we never conceived of raising a hand to each other. My jaw throbbed like it does when I clench my teeth at night, and tears stung my cheeks as if he had caused an open wound. It burned. Had he been wearing a ring when he struck me? I glanced at his hands and saw his wedding ring, the edges glinting sharply in flashes of light. Why was he wearing his old yellow terry cloth robe? Had he married Erica? Please tell me he hadn't married Erica—and why couldn't my boobs insulate my chest from this pain? Everyone could hear the loud thudding now, it sounded like thunder. Another violent clap of pain in my ears, this time with a blinding flash of light. I deserved it, but he couldn't have hit me.

Of course Vince had not hit me. I sat up in my bed and thunder cracked above the roof again. I had been asleep for only two hours, yet it felt like I had destroyed several lives within that tiny space of time. It had been a terrible dream, but before I could sort it out, another crack of thunder released a heavy deluge of rain. I could hear the gutters outside my window overflowing and I flew out of bed to throw on whatever clothes I could find. I had one thought: the roof of Dove Gaio Mangia. I had to go check on what my sister thought was the heart of Camptown Ladies. Maybe it was knowing what a big day it would be for Lisa tomorrow, or maybe it was the freshness of the dream that made me want to avoid my brother, but I decided to let them sleep and head back out to the campground alone.

Twenty-Two

Stormy, Stormy Night

I told myself I was overreacting to the severity of the storm, since I didn't want to believe it was my dream that made me not want to wake my brother. My heart was still pounding from the memory of it, yet as I drove through the night, I told myself it was the storm that seemed to be building in strength. I knew better than to ask the trees a friggin' thing, since the pines were bending as if they were made of rubber, so I would not like their dramatic answers.

It seemed to take a ridiculous time to get to the camp as mini flash floods covered some of the dirt roads, and I had to push through very slowly or risk the car stalling out. It turned out I had not overreacted, and now that I had arrived, I thought it was stupid not to wake Lisa and Vince. I was reaching for my phone when I saw Erica's truck was already there.

I wasn't surprised. Of course Erica would be there. I saw the white of her jacket moving back and forth from her truck to the Dove dining hall, and the huge flash of blue from the largest tarp being pulled off the buffet table. I was no sooner out of my car and into the thick mud when she started barking orders at me.

"Help me hoist this onto the roof!" she screamed, but I could barely hear her over the storm.

I saw the source of her panic. A leak had started from the roof and was bleeding a steady stream of water into the main seating area of Dove Gaio Mangia. Erica had already moved the tables away and constructed a makeshift trough from a piece of half pipe lined with a tarp to direct the water off the floor and safely away from the building. Remarkably, under some protection of the nearby pine boughs, our campfire was still smoldering, but now it emitted the sickening odor of a burned-out building.

With the main floor and tables protected, Erica's concern now shifted to the roof. "Hold this," she said, stuffing the folded wet tarp into my arms as she grabbed one of the columns and hoisted herself up onto the railing before I could protest. I knew it was no use trying to talk her out of it, despite the danger of the storm. For a moment, I was paralyzed with fear, imagining her slipping off the wet roof or, worse, getting struck by the lightning that lashed dangerously close at the woods surrounding us.

Erica leaned dangerously over the side of the roof and extended both arms. "Toss it!" I threw the heavy tarp and she caught it, and as I feared, the weight of it nearly pulled her over the edge. She regained her balance and disappeared with the tarp, and I, with a lot more effort than her, hoisted myself onto the railing and tried to pull myself up to the roof to help her.

Erica yelled, "What the fuck are you doing?"

"You need help, now give me a hand, will you?" I yelled back.

She grabbed my hand and, with great effort, helped to pull me up, but directed me to stay clear from the new clay tiles, which would be very slick in the rain and likely to break under my unskilled footing—though she didn't phrase it quite like that.

Erica had her tool belt on, and hammered down the original tarp to the old roof shingles until it was secured, and even in the madness of the storm, I noticed she still kept her distinctive nail-tapping pattern, only at a faster pace. Then we laid the larger tarp over the first one, the pelting sound of the pouring leak immediately slowing beneath us, then stopping all together.

"It's working!" I yelled. She smiled over at me, and my stomach flipped over as if I had tumbled off the roof, and at the next loud clap of thunder, I treated myself by mumbling an "Oh, fuck" that only I could hear.

Erica nailed down the second tarp, pulling up a few shingles and using those to trap the tarp at each corner and nail them both to the roof to stop the wind from pulling it up like a sail. Before she secured the last corner, it whipped up in the wind as the storm charged closer.

Without thinking, I quickly headed for it and slipped, which sent my foot crashing through a soft spot on the roof—so noiselessly compared with the thunder clapping over our heads, that Erica never looked up. Before I could think about what a bad idea it was, I had yanked my foot out violently out from the hole, which sent me flying down the side of the roof, the clay shingles too slick for me to stop sliding, until I got to the very edge. I pictured myself as Wile E. Coyote, having failed at one of his harebrained schemes, my legs flailing over the side of the roof like I was peddling an invisible bike.

"Erica!" I shouted, but the thunder droned me out, "Erica!" I yelled again, weaker this time, but the thunder had paused, so she heard me and whipped her head around.

She dove at me in an instant, grabbing both my arms with no fear that I would pull her over the side with me, though it seemed likely this would happen. Her face was pressed against mine and I said into her ear, "I think the fall won't kill me, but I could break both legs."

"You're not going to fall!" she shouted into my face, her voice straining from the weight of me. "And don't bother looking down. That's not where you're going!"

I was petrified, but somehow I managed to say against her face, "I'll just look down your shirt, OK?"

"Yes, do that," she said. Then she scared me with the panic in her voice, "Just don't let go of me!"

Maybe the fall could actually kill me with a juicy head injury, I thought, the terror making my legs go numb so that I could no longer pedal into thin air, trying to catch the edge of the roof. Erica dug her fingers painfully into both my arms like the claws of an animal, and I held as tightly as I could to her jacket, slick from the rain and threatening to tear right off her from the heaviness of my grip.

"Don't let go of me," she said again, but this time her voice was soft in my ear.

I shivered, I hoped from fear. Then I said, "This *Grinch* re-enactment sucks." Then the fear found my voice, and I said in a ragged breath, "Please don't let me go!"

"No, never," she groaned between her teeth. I could see over her head that Erica was using every bit of strength she had in her legs to create traction against the shingles so we both didn't go hurtling over the edge.

I clung to her. "Every woman has, so far."

This time, Erica pulled me hard enough to stop me from slipping farther, then several times more, and with each pull she said one word, "I'm . . . not . . . every . . . woman."

She was right about that.

She managed to pull me forward a few inches away from the edge before having to adjust her grip. When she let go of my arms, I felt the pain where her fingers had dug into my skin, right through my shirt. Regretfully, I launched a scream into her ear, "Fuck!", and I could feel myself start to slip backward again. I said, "If I go, don't you dare fall with me. I don't need you falling on top of me!"

Erica said, "I won't fall for you. Fucking just hold on!"

I won't fall for you?

I fucking just held on. It was then that I thought, Of course it's her. Who else could it ever be for me? Was I in love with Erica? Had my world really tipped upside down and was I really left hanging by my fingernails like this? I was not only hanging from the edge of this roof. I could *not* feel this for her. I would not continue feeling this. But what else could I do? The crazy thought occurred to me, Could I let go?

Maybe for my brother? Judging by the way I was fighting, No, I couldn't do that. I wasn't enough of a hero to give up on life for anyone, even Vince. So, I hung on like that stupid old poster with the orange kitty that says: "Hang On, Friday is Coming!"—only I was dangling from a roof instead of a tree limb, desperate to have a life that could never be mine.

As I was dangling there, I wasn't just desperate to live. I thought, Even if I get off this roof in once piece, there will be no way home from this, there will only be running away—and I doubted I had the strength to even do that. I would be dangling from this roof forever, now that I knew this. Even if I was saved, I was lost. And yet, I was fighting to live, as hard as she was fighting to save me.

Erica gave a gut-wrenching scream and yanked me up far enough so I finally could hook one foot onto the edge of the roof, then I kicked wildly with the other as she pulled once more, and somehow she managed to pull me over the edge.

I had been pulled over the edge, for sure.

I kept kicking and she kept pulling me long after she needed to, until I finally said, "I'm up, I'm up! You can stop!" and Erica released both of my arms and embraced me hard and I held on to her as if my life still depended on it.

We were both breathing against each other, ragged, deeply, and in exactly matched gasps, so I could barely hear her whisper as she rocked me back and forth in the rain, "I won't lose you. I can't lose you."

I loved her. This time it wasn't a voice inside telling me. It was just me admitting it: I loved Erica. I felt a deep tremble in her body against me, and I reminded myself her nerves had to be more shot than mine; she had done the heavy lifting, after all.

I tried to pull away from her, but even after saving me, she still had the strength to hold on, hard, and I relented. Just for another second, I thought, I'll hold on to her for just another second; she may have saved me from a broken neck, or even saved my life. I could have been dead. And then my next thought: Never to have felt this way again, never to feel her again. And then the selfish thought: Just let me have a few more seconds of her warmth and strength before I pull away. I had almost fallen off a roof, after all.

I felt Erica unwrap her arms from me and move her hands to my face, pulling me away just far enough to look me in the eyes. She opened her mouth to speak, but the invitation of this made me want to kiss her, so I tried to look away, but she was holding both sides of my face now, so I was unable to avoid looking anywhere else.

"Do you think about me?" she asked. What a question. Such an odd thing to ask on top of a roof during a powerful storm. A very powerful storm.

I couldn't lie; she had me by the face. And in one breath I said, "Of course I do."

I had planned for my answer to come out as a casual dismissal of her question, but it didn't. It came out as I felt it. From the gut. Of course I think about you. Of course I do.

Erica pulled my face toward her and I managed to say "No, don't," just before she kissed me. We kissed just once, and for only a few seconds, but the heat of it made the lightning bolt that followed seem a weak little echo. I came to my senses and pulled myself from her warm mouth, but now I was fighting her strength, instead of being saved by it.

I said what we both knew, "Vince loves you, and I love my brother."

"What about who I love?" she asked, her words creating an infuriating hope flooding into my stupid heart. Could it please be true? Then, oh no, it can't be true. I can't want this, she can't also feel this.

Erica said, "This thing with you, with us, it's been happening for so long, maybe even before I was with Vince, back when it was just us."

Even through the rain, I could see that her eyes were filling, and I wanted to stop her pain. And I wanted to kiss her again. But there was one thing I wanted more than this, and that was *not* to break my brother's heart.

"But it isn't just us," I said, and I remembered my dream, my brother's hurt still so vividly clear. I pulled back to let a sheet of water rain between us, doing absolutely nothing to cool the heat. We were both breathing as heavily from her revelation as from exhaustion. I wanted her. I could never have her. And now I knew she wanted me.

Erica said, "Back then, I didn't understand what I was feeling, I was so confused by it—"

"Maybe you're still confused."

"No," she said, and she had me by both sides of my face again, pulling me so close to her face again. "Marie, you have no idea how sure I am." Then she slowly closed the space between us, the curtain of rain thinning as I braced for the electric current to hit my lips again, hoping the lightning would hit me at the same time, taking me out, since I was powerless to stop this.

"Mare!"

The shout came from directly below us. I couldn't see him, but it was Vince. His voice made us both jerk back from each other, though our eyes never parted. I was staring at Erica as I shouted back to him, "We're up here, we're OK! Everything's OK now!" I backed away from Erica like a crab who had been given a chance to escape from a trap, and my heart broke as she watched me with the most wounded expression I had ever seen.

Vince yelled up, "Jesus, somebody's cooler just floated by! Mare, Erica! You guys need to forget the roof and get down here before you get struck by lightning!"

Erica said just loud enough for me to hear, "I said I wouldn't let you go."

"You have to," I said.

Erica didn't ask for things she didn't get, she didn't try for things she didn't win, she didn't want things she couldn't have. She was not that kind of woman. She took what she wanted and she probably could have taken me if I hadn't lied to her right then.

"I'm sorry, Erica. I was scared. I almost fell off the damned roof and you saved me. It's not just my brother. I . . . don't want this."

Erica studied my face as I heard Vince moving tables down below us. To make sure she understood me, I pounded it home as my gut twisted in knots, "I'm already in love with someone I can't have." And of course Erica thought I meant Lorn, and so I didn't have to lie, since I really didn't want this (because of Vince) and I really was in love with someone I couldn't have (her).

I really was so screwed.

I imagined Erica was not a woman who had ever heard anyone didn't want her before, so I feared she would guess how ridiculous this was. She had to know how impossible it was for this to be true. Who wouldn't want her? Yet, the shattered look on her face, the one that was *killing* me, said she believed it, and I was left feeling like I was falling off the roof again. And what I really wanted was to take it all back. I wanted to tell her, Of course it isn't true. I wished I could tell her that I wanted her more than anything in the world. Anything in the world, except hurting my brother.

Vince called back up to us once more, his voice finding a break in the storm. "You both need to get down here, now!" Erica finally looked away from me, so I could find the strength to crawl the rest of the distance away from her.

Twenty-Three

MILF's, Meatballs & Mistakes

It was opening night, and while Dove Gaio Mangia wasn't due to open for another hour, the smell of Lisa's giant vat of meatballs and half-dozen trays of lasagna were filling the hall. People were waiting patiently, the smell keeping them happy with the promise of an amazing feast. They were grateful to be occupying any table at all, since there was already a line forming for Seating Two.

I had asked Lisa what she would do about switching from Seating One to Seating Two: "What if someone isn't done with dinner?" Lisa said she'd toss a To-Go box at their heads and wish them a pleasant walk back to their campsites. This seemed a reasonable solution for the price.

Vince and Uncle Freddie were looking handsome in their suits for the opening night, which clashed with the bulk of the clientele, who came to dinner in typical camp garb of shorts and t-shirts. Except for a stray feather boa or two on a few of Eddie's friends, Vince and Uncle Freddie were the most dapper of the evening. (Lisa had insisted they be, even though she wore her signature army green cargo shorts with multi pockets and her favorite "My Girlfriend Is Hotter Than Your Honor Student" T-shirt.) Erica was nowhere to be seen, and I assumed, miserably, she wanted to avoid me, too.

Lisa was a master in the kitchen, and anyone who went into the kitchen looking to help, was told to stand back and not get in her way. It was an unspoken agreement that we handled everything else but the food was entirely my sister's territory. I was convinced she had a kitchen timer built in her head, and I thought of this again as

I watched her jump from giant vat to pot to pan to skillet to oven, just at the right moment.

I stood a safe distance from the entryway, watching her start another pan of tomato sauce—or gravy, as Uncle Freddie called it. She held a long row of pepperoni slices like a stack of poker chips and flicked them into the pan like a casino dealer, starting at the outer edge and working her way in to the center, the disks just barely overlapping, each one placed exactly the same distance as the one before it.

When we were kids we watched our Aunt Aggie do this, and we said she was doing *The Wizard of Oz* since the pepperoni pattern looked like the perfect yellow brick spiral. Lisa let the pepperoni simmer, scenting the partially open-air kitchen with its spicy steam, before moving on to prepare another dish.

"Remember when Lisa got dumped by that girl Rhonda?" Vince asked.

He was right behind me, and I hadn't meant to jump when hearing his voice. I was relieved he sounded normal. He seemed to have no idea my world had cracked in two: the side with Vince on it, and the side with Erica, and a treacherous chasm with a weak tarp pouch overfilled with stormy water stretched dangerously in between. With the earth still cracking beneath my feet, I had an idea how wide that chasm would get.

"I remember," I said, laughing too enthusiastically. Oddly, I had been thinking of that just a few minutes ago when Lisa was readying the main buffet table.

Lisa had thrown a surprise shower for her former girlfriend, Rhonda, who unfortunately had gained a sudden 40 pounds over the winter she dated Lisa. For some reason, Lisa thought inviting everyone over to a surprise buffet dinner and calling it "Rhonda's Food-Baby Shower" was a good idea.

Rhonda was always reasonable when it came to not wasting food, so she stayed for the dinner and a double helping of dessert, but then she dumped Lisa with the smell of Lisa's delectable anise egg biscuits still on her breath.

Vince asked, "Where's Erica?"

"I haven't seen her," I said, my heart pounding like a convict who was about to have her escape hole discovered behind a bathing suit poster of Farrah Fawcett.

He said, "So, listen, I think there's something going on."

I spun around to him, "What?" I said, panic rising in my voice, "Don't be ridiculous."

Vince looked at me, totally confused, then pointed to the table closest to the kitchen, where a woman was seated with her son. They were both waving at Lisa, who had not missed this. She was the same woman who had found her little boy, Buddy, fishing with Lisa, and who had invited Lisa to her trailer for lunch.

Vince said, "Lisa is trying to score with someone that doesn't play for her team."

"She loves a challenge," I said, feeling relieved and guilty.

Vince mumbled, "I hate challenges."

When he patted me on the back, I said, "Ditto."

Lisa rushed a small dish of spaghetti and two meatballs over to us, fanning it to cool it a bit before handing it to Vince.

"Who's that for?" Vince and I asked at the same time.

Lisa answered, "Give it to the little boy with the hot MILF at table two."

Vince said, "I thought everything was buffet-style?" but Lisa ignored him, shoving the steaming dish into his hands. "Warn the MILF it's very hot."

He grinned, "I should definitely warn her."

"I'll kick your ass," Lisa said. Then she noticed the stacks of small plates had not been moved to the buffet table and yelled over to Eddie, "You forgot the dessert plates, you little fruit." He cheerfully flitted by her as if she had asked perfectly nicely and she yelled after him, "When you're done, help us get ready in the back!" Then she snorted to me, "I can't imagine how many times he's been told that."

Lisa went back to her stove to unload the first steaming trays of lasagna as I watched Vince introduce himself to the MILF. He crouched down next to the boy and put the plate in front of him, but the boy looked troubled. Without missing a beat, Vince took his fork and cleared off a large amount of sauce to the side of his plate, then tossed the spaghetti a few times until it was just barely sauced, the only way he used to eat spaghetti when he was a boy. The boy smiled, reached for the fork, and Vince smiled at him as the little guy dug in.

The MILF thanked Vince and appeared to ask him if he would like to sit, but Vince politely refused, and pointed out that the dish was from his sister the chef, and the MILF thanked Lisa with another enthused wave. Lisa said under her breath so I could hear, "Oh, honey, stop waving, rest those pretty hands, you'll need them later."

Dinner was a huge success, the gay boys moaning orgasmic appreciation over each delicate bite they took. Their plates were scarcely filled, so as not to risk their tiny waistlines. By contrast, the lesbians asked for extra To Go boxes and several hit the buffet for refills before reluctantly abandoning their tables to the anxious Seating Two campers. The line was now wrapped around the hall, indicating that Seating Two would be another full house.

Erica was still nowhere to be seen. Thankfully, signs of the near catastrophe from the storm last night were barely visible: a few drying tarps out by the campfire, and my shaking hands every time I let my mind wander.

After the second round of dinner was completed, Erica finally came in as we began to transform the dining hall for the rest of the evening so the gay boys could have their fun and put on a G-rated show. I looked away as Erica greeted everyone and busied myself moving tables. Could I get away with not looking at her all night? I attempted to move a large table one side at a time and didn't notice it was Erica who grabbed the other end, so when I finally looked up, I made an audible gasp.

"Did I scare you?" she asked.

Why, yes, you did, I wanted to say . . . very, very much.

There was a long pause before I could say, "I'm fine." But I wasn't. She looked at me as if I should have more to say, but I had nothing. "This table needs to be against the wall." We moved the table together and when I released my end so I could get some distance from her, I noticed she still had her end raised from the ground.

"You should let it go now," I said.

She stayed still, looking hurt. Specifically, she looked like I was hurting her. She also looked beautiful, which hurt me. Touché, I thought.

She finally lowered her end of the table and walked away. I watched her safely from a distance as she did a final check on the wiring for the sound system, while all I could do was lean heavily on the table we had just moved, exhausted. I looked across the room in time to see that Vince was also leaning on a table, also looking at Erica, also looking hurt. I left the hall and was relieved by the coolness and privacy of night, content to be swallowed up by the darkness. I rested my head against the side of the rec hall and closed my eyes.

How would I ever get myself out of this one?

Sadly, this was one of those times when you ask the universe a question and the universe answers you. Not the best answer, certainly, but that universe was pretty fucking funny sometimes. When I opened my eyes, Lorn Elaine was standing in front of me. Very close.

Lorn said, "I saw Erica and she said you just slipped out back. Are you OK?"

I had forgotten how her voice used to affect me, and my exhausted heart started pounding. I felt relieved by it, hoping it was for Lorn, but fearing it was more likely from the mention of Erica's name—and the fact that she had been watching me.

"I just needed to take a moment. Lisa works us to death," I said, but I could see she doubted this was the reason I was faking a horizontal snooze against a spider-covered wall. "Why did you come back?" I asked her.

"I never really left. I just gave you some time. I'm here so we can talk about this . . . huge mistake I made."

I sighed. "Oh, there have been so many mistakes since then," I said coldly. "A few months ago, I would have been thrilled to hear you say that."

"What's happened since then?"

"Nothing," I said, defensive, "nothing at all. I'm still the same."

"Still in love with me?" she asked.

When I didn't answer, she studied my face and said, "Am I too late? You said there wasn't anyone else?"

My head spun a little, then I shook it emphatically, No. "Of course there's nobody else," I said, and I held her gaze just to prove it. She was beautiful. But she wasn't Erica.

Lorn took this as a sign she should move closer, "You don't know how sorry I am. Please tell me it's not too late."

It was way, way, too late. Not only had that ship sailed, it had wrecked into a dock and taken out a deck hand—namely, me. And that was why grabbed I both sides of her face and kissed her. Hard. She was surprised at first, but recovered, returning a passionate kiss, which felt familiar and good. My head spun again, maybe with the memory of loving her, or maybe it was my desperate wish that I still could. Lorn was beautiful, that had not changed, so why was it I held my eyes so tightly closed?

Maybe this was exactly what I needed now.

When our kiss ended, we were left staring at each other. Lorn had the same look on her face I must have had the whole time we were together. It said: Is this for real? I was grateful she didn't ask. "I should go back inside," I said.

"I know," she said. She reached into her purse and handed me a plastic card. "I'm in room two sixty-seven. Right up the street at the Radisson. Will you please come when you're done here?"

Would I ever be done here?

She left then, and I watched her go, her beautiful auburn hair shifting in the moonlight, wishing it still affected me as it once did. I attempted to regroup by taking deep breaths going back into the hall, but all was lost when I walked through the doorway to find Erica waiting for me, her hurt expression hardening. I didn't know what to say, but she did.

"She'll leave you again."

"I know," I said stupidly, our eyes locked like angry neighbors over a much-needed fence.

Erica walked away, and I fought the powerful urge to follow her as I thought of my sister throwing *Little Women* into her trashcan. This evening may not have been the tale of awakening lesbianism for which Erica may have hoped. I imagined myself running after her, and spinning her around to kiss her, my body weakening at the thought. How could the mere thought of kissing her eclipse a real-life kiss with Lorn, the person I once thought was the love of my life? The bigger question was how could I even imagine ever hurting my brother?

I reassessed the dining hall and saw that Uncle Freddie had appointed himself doorman to keep the crowd from re-entering until Lisa got the dining hall converted to a dance hall. Soon the music was underway and the gay boys took turns singing respectful renditions of "Dancing Queen" and other Abba delights, as children slid on the new weatherproof floor, comparing their dance moves. Adults gathered around the edges of the room, well armed with coolers of beer substituting as barstools.

As low-brow as this scene may have been, I found myself marveling at the mix of people gathered happily under the wounded roof, lulled into cheerful camaraderie by the best food they may have ever tasted. The twinkle lights in the rafters became a star-filled sky, and with Lisa's dry ice machine cranking, the floor filled with a low-hanging cloud of thick white mist, moving in magical swirls the entire rest of the evening, every time Erica walked through it.

Twenty-Four

Greg Brady Learns His Limits

It was late and I was driving away from the camp like a fugitive. I saw Erica leave without saying goodbye to anyone except Lisa, and I had done the same. The Dove was still in high swing when I made my escape, telling Lisa I wasn't feeling well and that I needed to go to bed. I had not lied. Minutes before, I had allowed myself a long glance at Erica, and was scared to death that Vince saw me do it, though he didn't act differently toward me when I said goodnight. Soon after, I approached Lisa to let her know I was leaving.

She was surrounded by an enthusiastic crowd of campers, mostly straight, mostly drunk, and all die-hard fans of her cooking. I waited patiently to talk with her, forgetting my troubles for a few minutes as I took pleasure in my sister's success. One by one they took turns telling her that she could be the chef of a five-star restaurant (to this, Lisa answered that Camptown Ladies *was* a five-star restaurant) and they tried not to insult her while finding out why she was "wasting her talents cooking at a campground."

An elderly lady—who liked to be called Grandma Mitzy by everyone except her grandchildren (they were only allowed to call her Grandma)—grabbed Lisa by the arm as only an old person is allowed to do. "This was the best meal I have ever had in my all my seventy-eight years," she said, in a frail but cheerful voice. The crowd nodded their heads and several lifted their cans of beer in agreement.

Lisa beamed and said, "Why thank you," and she gave a gentlemanly bow.

Grandma Mitzy said, "If you could do anything, what would your next goal be? Do you want to find a nice fellow and get married? You gotta have goals in life," the old lady schooled. "Otherwise, life just happens to you."

Eddie was always one to join a drinking crowd and he called out from the back of the group, "Yeah, Lisa, do tell us your goals," he said, smirking at her.

Lisa said, "Well, I have this one fantasy . . ."

I braced myself as Grandma Mitzy said, "Oh please tell us, dear."

Lisa said, "I want to cook dinner for Meryl Streep and Dana Delany. But that's not all, I want to eat with them too." Eddie chuckled, but Mitzy listened with rapt interest, as I tried to catch her eye to warn her to be polite.

Lisa created an invisible diagram before them. "Meryl will be right sitting here," she indicated close to her right, "and Dana will be sitting right here," close to her left side, "and we'll be sitting at this tiny, tiny table. Almost not a table at all, it's so small. Actually, it might just be the pole that the tabletop is supposed to sit on . . ."

Grandma Mitzy was perplexed, "But how would the food fit on a table that small?" she asked.

"Not sure, I just know the table would be so very tiny that our elbows and knees would have to rub against each other . . . and maybe even our vulvas."

Eddie slapped his hand over his mouth, but not before a tiny shriek slipped out. He turned away and doubled over to finish his girlie chortling into the privacy of his own crotch. A few people chuckled with him, and one bearded guy shouted "Yeah!" Only one woman walked her child away in disgust, so, all in all, it could have been worse. Grandma Mitzy glanced down at Lisa's T-shirt, then patted Lisa on the arm and said, "That's nice, dear. If those two girls have any friggin' taste at all, it'll happen for you."

Lisa started toward the kitchen, but Mom walked over in a little panic just before I could catch her alone. Mom said in a hushed voice, "There are two cars out there with Massachusetts license plates."

Lisa said, "Mom, a Massachusetts plate doesn't necessarily mean we have drug runners. Rhode Island is the size of a postage stamp, we're bound to have some out-of-towners." Mom let out a clucking sound with her tongue to indicate Lisa still had so much to learn; she really had no idea how her children had survived this long.

When Lisa broke free into the kitchen, I followed her.

"Listen, I'm not feeling well. I need to go to bed," I said.

Lisa glanced at me sideways. "Bed, huh?"

She had me. I pig-scrambled to be more convincing.

"I think I'm coming down with something."

Lisa said, "I think you're going down on something. Lorn's pussy."

I breathed a sigh of relief that I turned into a sigh of exasperation. "Don't be an asshole."

"Have fun," she said sarcastically as I left the kitchen. "But remember, Einstein's definition of insanity is fucking the same woman again and again, and expecting a different result."

I don't remember the drive there, but it wasn't because I was drunk. I actually drank safely in my car just before I knocked on her door. When she opened the door, I thought it best to launch at her like a misfired rocket and kiss her, before I thought about what I should or shouldn't do, or before I thought about my brother. Erica responded, and her kiss was warm and wild, as we both clutched at each other, tearing off each other's clothes before I could get fully through her door.

"Are you sure? You've been drinking."

"Yes, I'm sure I've been drinking."

I wanted to look at her, but kept my eyes tightly closed, so I could pretend it was all happening to me, and not because of me. This just happened, it's not that I ran to her. I didn't drive over here, I didn't have the criminal intent to pack some liquid courage to swill in the car before attacking her in her doorway. I wouldn't think of Vince. I would think only of her.

As I unbuttoned her pants, she whispered within our kiss, "Yes, please." So, I shoved my hand down and she moved her hips up toward me so I could get inside. Perfect. Women are so perfect, I thought, as she moved against my hand, moaning my name in my ear, and I felt myself responding as she was. "I love you, Marie," she said.

I rammed into her harder, not my usual style (unless specifically requested, of course), which made her words melt into senseless sounds, which was exactly what I was going for. I didn't want to hear that she loved me. I didn't want her to make any sense at all. It was all so very wrong, and I fought to keep thoughts of my brother's love for Erica out of my head as I moved her away from the door. Since she was impaled on me, she had no choice but to comply, and I may have even lifted her a little.

"I want you," I said, a bit of a redundant declaration when you have a woman attached to your hand, walking her backward down a hallway like a bowling ball.

She said, "I need you," and I shut her up by angrily kissing her again.

We reached the bed. I need you too, I thought. More than anything, more than everything . . . obviously. Why else would I do such a thing as this?

Vince would move on eventually, I thought. He would find someone else and be happy again. This happens all the time, right? Erica had fallen for me and there was nothing he could do to change that. I had realized there was nothing I could do either. When Erica left the campground tonight, she had ripped my heart out of my chest, flinging it across Lisa's restaurant, possibly landing undetected into one of Lisa's vat of meatballs, and now that my heart had been broken free, it was likely devoured by some Budweiser-drinking camper in a dirty John Deer baseball hat.

Erica was the most beautiful woman I had ever seen, and it crossed my mind as I desperately was having my way with her, that I had once thought that of Lorn. What the hell made me think Erica could love me forever? I fucked her harder and forgot the question for a moment.

But it came roaring back.

Erica had lived a straight life, much like Lorn had. Would she run from me as Lorn had done so many times? Maybe after the excitement wore off she'd go back to the much more sensible choice—the male version of me, my brother Vince. Not a bad choice, really. No other guy I would more highly recommend, if you didn't want me.

I pulled her bra up over her breasts, and did a face plant on her as she writhed beneath me, my sucking pushing her into a corkscrew motion to get away at the same time that her hands were grabbing my head to pull me harder against her, as if she couldn't make up her mind—was she having trouble deciding what she wanted? I knew this: she would not get away while my mouth was attached to her nipple like an oxygen leash.

Maybe I could keep her attached to me like this forever. It's not like she could get away and lead a normal life with me dangling from her left tit, right? How would you show up for work with another woman attached to your nipple like a large mouth bass latched to the head of a succulent worm? Not likely you'll get far, my dear, and people will stop inviting you places, lessening the chance at a party for someone to say, "You know, Erica, you were way more normal when you were straight, before you had that Italian woman constantly hanging from your left nipple. Could you pass me the olives, and perhaps a cracker?"

I fucked her harder, curling my fingers deep inside her with each thrust and she screamed out as the combination of this and my best bass moves made her come. I couldn't see her since my face was completely buried in her chest, but I could easily imagine her, so beautiful: Erica's mouth slightly open with intense pleasure, now going into a silent scream as she writhed beneath me, her breath catching in surprise as a second wave of orgasm hit her when I refused to stop, even when she clutched my wrist, even when she tried to stop me with words, I simply covered her mouth with my other hand. Nope. There would be no discussion, because there would be no stopping. No stopping.

Hearing her, feeling her body responding from inside, a wave came over me. Sadly this was not an orgasm-type wave but one of those giant Hawaiian waves, the kind that curl up twenty feet or more, exciting, beautiful—but as the wave crested, there came a dark shadow inside and Greg was now trapped inside the wave. Greg Brady, gangly teen, inexperienced surfer, illusions of grandeur shattering under the fierce power of the giant wave. We all saw that *Brady Bunch* episode, we all know what happens.

Greg was completely out of his league and the massive wave overtook him, and now he was somersaulting as the wave crashed over him again and again. It might have felt good to be out of control, if it weren't for the unlucky tiki necklace that pelted him repeatedly in the face, reminding him that this was all bad, nothing good would come of this—and I was now being dragged out to deeper waters, into deeper trouble.

When the first hint of a wave curled over me, I had not cared, since the intense excitement and pleasure has a way of blinding even the most experienced surfers, and I had needed Erica that badly. Except that now, after having her, and after her breathing was returning to normal and the wave of excitement melted into the beach sand along with the once mighty wave, it wasn't until she was *talking* to me . . . that I could finally admit to myself that this wasn't Erica. I opened my eyes and my vision cleared.

Not Erica.

Lorn's orgasm had ended, and she was holding on to me tightly, and I could feel her chest heaving and she was crying as she whispered, "I'm so sorry for what I did to you; I thought I'd lost you forever."

I whispered flatly, "I did, too."

Lorn said, "But, you seemed angry, and you wouldn't look at me. You wouldn't let me slow you down. We never made love like that before." Then she stopped and I could feel her hold her breath as she asked, "Please tell me there isn't anyone else."

"There isn't anyone else." I wasn't lying. There was no one else.

I could never have Erica.

Twenty-Five

People With Dyke Sisters Shouldn't Throw Stones

The next day I arrived at camp to find that Erica was already on the roof, instructing Uncle Freddie to hustle as if the men he was working alongside were not a third of his age. She was on a tear about the water damage and they were bowed low, albeit to pound nails, each looking as if they feared to raise their head higher than their ass.

Erica saw me approach the hall and busied herself with re-nailing the areas where the men had already been. She didn't look up from her hammering, a steady rhythmic sound: Bang-bang-tap, bang-bang-tap, that unmistakable steady rhythm against the rest. I walked my burning and twisting stomach past the hall.

Lisa bounded out of the camp store and startled me, "Hey, slut. Aww you changed your clothes, that's cheating. I was looking forward to the walk of shame."

The rhythmic sound stopped on the roof as I felt as if a nail had settled deep into the pit of my chest.

"Shut it, Lisa," I hissed.

"Seriously, what the fuck were you thinking?"

She had a point, what was I thinking? Right now I was thinking Lisa had The Voice on, probably the same one that got her fired at her first restaurant job.

They had given Lisa a trial as a cook, and she confessed to me she liked to pretend the entire wait staff was her team of personal servants. She had been teasing a pretty Latino girl from Day One, who (according to Lisa) had been flirting with her mercilessly, telling Lisa that she would never go back to "dry white girls" again after her, etc. Of course I wondered how much of this was in my sister's head.

On Lisa's second day, before the restaurant opened, the owner had slipped into the kitchen unannounced just as Lisa had admitted to her kitchen assistant that she was bored and a bored Lisa is a recipe for disaster. She raised her eyebrows and tossed her head in the direction of the Latino girl, who was prepping the tables for the lunch crowd with one of the Irish girls. Lisa, not seeing the boss behind her, slammed her chopping knife down, clapped her hands twice at her assistant, pointed at the Latino girl, and bellowed in her best Henry the Eighth voice, "Bring me the brown one. She *amuses* me!" The girl thought it was hysterical and laughed her ass off, but Lisa was fired on the spot. (That night, Lisa claims she banged the hot Latino girl and got to use the line again, only changing it to "Bring me one of the *white* ones," when the girl brought two Caucasian girlfriends along.)

I walked away from Lisa, fearing I might smack her for pointing out I never came home last night in front of Erica, but this would repeat a pre-pubescent mistake. I had learned the hard way: I was a fly swatter; Lisa was a bazooka gun with a backup round of ammo.

Lisa yelled after me, "Seriously, I think you've lost your mind!"

I hated when she was right, and wished I would hear the bang-bang-tap hammering begin again, but as I walked toward the center of the camp, all I could hear was the unsteady tapping of Uncle Freddie and the crew as they pretended not to listen to the Santora sisters squabble. The quiet from Erica's hammer was chilling. I knew when she was not yelling at the crew or not hammering, she was pissed off beyond measure.

Or worse, she was hurt.

I wondered how all this had gotten so out of control so quickly. It had started so tiny at first, that occasional odd feeling in my stomach, a faint tickle, then building to a steady state of euphoric fluttering, which promises something wonderful is about to happen. However, when something wonderful can't happen, because you've fallen in love with the woman your brother loved first, it starts to feel like a stomach flu. A pleasantly fluttering stomach evolves into a churning, acid-filled pit, and the waves of excitement turn to nausea, until you are left walking across a campground with the constant feeling that something terrible is about to happen. And worse, that you very badly want it to.

I circled the camp and wound up back in front of the camp store, and ducked inside to avoid the view of the construction crew. Mom and Lisa were going at it, while Dad pretended to be restocking the candy shelves. Lisa and I both knew he came into the camp store only to steal black licorice. We ordered extra boxes for him and kept it off the inventory list, and secret from Mom.

Mom was trying not to shout, which meant she was shouting. "Why the hell would I put the girl's sign over the boy's stuff and the boy's sign over the girl's stuff?"

Lisa was laughing at her. "Mom. Don't you get it yet? Camptown Ladies and Camp Camp attracts a certain clientele. And that clientele has girls that wouldn't be caught dead buying pink picnic tablecloths and boys that would squeal at the sight of them."

Mom snapped, "You're not making any sense."

This fight was a relief compared to the one going on inside my head. Lisa got up on the ladder to hang the Camp Camp Supplies sign over the matching rainbow umbrellas and plastic tumblers. The Camptown Ladies sign was already perched high over the sea of army green merchandise. Mom placed both hands on her hips and sighed a Darth Vader breath. Darth's appearance was a sign things could end badly.

Lisa saw me as she came down the ladder and said, "Let's ask Marie, she's great at making decisions. She'll probably want to hang a sign that already fell on her head and hurt her several times, a sign that will no doubt hit her in the friggin' head again."

I glared at her.

Mom turned to me and said, "Don't tell me this makes any sense to you," and she waited for my reply.

"I don't have an opinion," I finally said, deathly afraid to have the crosshairs turned my way.

Lisa said, "Oh come on, Marie. Make a decision and stick with it. You know, dive in or not, but stick with your decision."

I narrowed my eyes at her to tell her to back off, but this never worked, and I knew this time would be no different. Just then, Vince hopped into the store, yelling, "Hey campers!" and his cheerfulness was so bizarre that we all just stared at him. "What?" he said, checking his face in one of the small hand mirrors hanging on the wall. "What are you all staring at?"

Lisa said, "Those strange little white things in your mouth called teeth. What's the shit-eating grin about?"

"Would you mind if I ordered another truckload of beach sand for around the pond?" he asked Lisa.

"I said, what's the shit-eating grin about?" Lisa said.

"Nothing. I want to put some beach sand over near the pond by Katie's trailer. Can I do it?"

"Who the fuck is Katie?" she asked.

"It's for Buddy," he answered.

Lisa said, "OK, who the fuck is Buddy? Are we talking about your dead dog from ten years ago? Tell me you didn't keep have him stuffed, you were always such a weird kid." Mom nodded. Even her argument with Lisa could not make her disagree about something that obvious.

"Buddy is Katie's son," he said. "The kid's favorite thing was to go to the beach with his father, even though he only took him once. Buddy doesn't stop talking about it, so I thought we could make the pond look more like a beach for when he goes fishing."

Dad popped up from the candy aisle as I waited for Lisa to take a crack at Vince. Some kind of joke about Katie, about how notoriously bad Vince's gaydar was, about—worse, from Lisa's perspective—how Vince's horrible fishing technique could cripple a child's talents before he ever had a chance. But all she said was, "Sure, go ahead."

Vince bolted out the door. "Great. I'll go find Erica so she can negotiate the price for the sand," he said over his shoulder, and our hopes were dashed that Vince was showing the first sign of a distraction from his heartbreak.

The distraction of Vince did lead Mom and Lisa into an unspoken truce. Lisa signaled for Mom to hand her a bracket for the sign, and she did so with no comment. Peace at last.

"So," Lisa said, "Marie banged Lorn last night."

"Lisa, what the fuck!" I yelled, and I punched her in the arm as hard as I could before she got me in a headlock vise grip. In seconds my nose was touching the floor. From that angle, I could see the piles of Dad's secret candy wrappers that he had shoved under the shelves.

"Girls!" Mom yelled, and I heard Dad's licorice-muffled laugh. Mom heard it too, and even with my face to the floor, I recognized the sound of Mom giving him a gentle smack on his arm. "Stan! Stop stealing candy!" and Dad laughed again. It was so awkward for us kids when the parents were flirting.

Later I saw Vince hanging by the pond, looking more like his angst-filled self, and I summoned the nerve to approach him.

"Hey," he said.

"Hey. What's going on?"

"I have a date tonight," he said.

I put my arm around him, casually, like he was an ottoman to my arm. "That's great," I said, gently, not wanting him to think it was a big deal and chicken out. "Katie asked you?"

"Nope," he said, "I asked her, and she said yes." Then he tossed a flat stone across the pond. Six perfect skips, though it seemed his throw was less to skip the rock than to relieve an irritation.

"Maybe you could teach Buddy. You were always good at skipping rocks."

"Not like Lisa," he said miserably.

"Well, no," I said.

"Lisa used to say I should leave my skipping to hopscotch."

"Well, you were pretty good."

Vince attempted a small laugh, but it came out as a cough. "The thing is, Katie said yes, which surprised me, since technically, she's still married. She wants a divorce, but the guy won't sign because then he'll have to pay child support."

"But they're separated, right?"

He nodded.

"Well, then just see where it goes," I said. "It's just one date."

Vince looked at me. "I'm not going."

He threw another stone into the pond, but this time the stone plummeted without a skip. I was confused and said, "You said you had a date tonight."

"Right after I asked Katie, Erica asked to see me tonight. I have to see where that goes first."

Though I was standing right there on solid ground next to my brother, my stomach convinced me I had just fallen off the roof again.

Twenty-Six

Every Day Is Gay Day

I waited a few minutes so Vince wouldn't get suspicious, then stormed over to where Erica had obviously returned back to her usual self and was shouting up at her crew, who was still working on the Dove Gaio Mangia roof. "Never in my life have I ever seen such a crew of women! Three days on a goddamned roof!" Even at a distance I could hear the wheezing laugh of my Uncle Freddie as he threw some shingles down, just a few feet away from hitting Erica. "Freddie, you throw like a friggin' girl! Did you follow the Red Sox back in the day?"

Uncle Freddie looked over the roof edge at her, "Yes," he said.

"Remember Fred Lynn? Well, I'm just gonna call you Lynn to remind you how you throw like a girl!"

My uncle laughed again, but he also had the good sense to go back to his work. She yelled up at him again, "Lynn and crew, I don't have all night, I have dinner plans, so move it! You guys, on the other hand, are gonna be eating shit on shingles for dinner if you don't get going! There will *not* be a tarp on this friggin' roof tonight!"

I approached her and Erica started a bit when she saw me, but quickly recovered, turning her eyes back to the roof as she snapped at me, "Your uncle is part of my crew, don't ask me to treat him differently."

I said, "Why would I ask you to treat a man in his seventies differently than men in their thirties? I need to talk to you about something else."

My heart was beating wildly from standing near her and I lied to myself it was my anger.

"So, talk," she said, with the same disinterested tone in her voice she reserved for vendors she prefers not to do business with, letting them go through their spiel before handily rejecting them.

"Not here," I said, with a tone just angry enough for her to take me seriously.

I walked ahead so I couldn't smell the scent of her hair, and she followed me at a distance until we reached the secluded parking lot where she had left her truck. I walked around to the other side of it for more privacy, and when she came around the truck, she completely disarmed me when I saw the pain in her eyes. I told myself that it didn't matter, what she planned to do with Vince was wrong. If anyone knew that, it was me. I took a deep breath and spoke in a low voice.

"What do you think you're doing?" I asked her.

"My answer depends on what you're attacking me for."

"I think you know," I said, my voice rising.

"What, Marie? What on earth do you think you have the right to school me about? My attitude? My crew? Or is it my date with your brother?"

"Don't do this to him," I said. "He was just starting to get better and you're pulling him back in!"

"You were getting better too. How was your reunion with the actress last night?"

Erica's venom dissolved at once into sadness. She turned away from me, and my heart felt trapped in a cold metal vise. No, Erica, I thought, please stay angry with me. This was so much harder.

She asked quietly, without turning around, "Was being with her everything you hoped it would be?" Her words barely got out, getting caught in her throat. When she turned back to me then, and I saw her eyes were filled to the brim, the vise tightened around my chest. Erica would sooner die than have somebody see her cry, so witnessing this was worse than if she had struck me hard across the face. My own eyes now burned at the corners, threatening tears, while Erica's anger spiked out of nowhere again.

"I have to accept you feel nothing for me, and I will! I have to accept that and forget about this, and what a fool I'm making of myself. But I shouldn't be standing here, wasting my time, letting you tell me who I should and shouldn't spend my time with!"

I lowered my voice to a gentle tone, hoping she would follow. "Just please don't give him hope. You'll hurt him all over again," I said. "If anyone knows what a brainless thing it is to get back with someone you don't love, it's me."

As soon as I said it, I realized, I had probably blown my cover about Lorn. She now knew I didn't love her anymore.

Erica studied me, then asked, "Are you sure this is all about protecting him?"

"I'm sure," I said quickly, and I took a step back from her. I knew I didn't sound sure, and Erica knew it too. She took a step closer and held my face, as she had on the roof, only her eyes were blazing with pain and anger. Hit me, I thought, I deserve it. But then, her gaze moved to my lips and I saw her face soften and this terrified me so much more than her anger. I tried to shake my head no, but she had a good grip on me.

"Erica, please," I said, but my voice betrayed me and sounded as if I was begging her to do exactly what she was thinking. Then, she kissed me, and my entire world was tossed upside down again.

Just one kiss, I thought, I'll stop after this.

She held my face tightly against hers, and I lied to myself that that was why I couldn't pull back from her. It wasn't at all because her mouth, so hungry and warm, made me weak, and drowning in her until I was Greg Brady on his wave again, only the wave was lifting me up high, maybe miles above earth, lifting us both so high that I was safe from Vince witnessing that I was taking her for myself. He could not see us from way up here on this wave. We were so high up he could never get to her. She was all mine.

Why shouldn't she be mine? She wanted me, the grip on my face and then the back of my neck told me I was right about that. Erica cried in a whisper against my mouth, "I can't stand that you were with her," then she kissed me harder. "I hate that, I hate it." This is the moment I learned there may be nothing more passionate than an angry kiss.

If she had let me pull back an inch from her mouth, I might have told her I had not been with Lorn; it had been her, it was my need for her that made me take Lorn last night. But who would believe a line like that? Though it had been completely true.

I had run away from Lorn the second I could no longer pretend she wasn't Erica. And now all I wanted was for Erica to know that she owned me, completely, even though I couldn't have her. My brother loved her, so I couldn't. And we were outside where we could be seen by anyone who happened to come walking around the side of her truck.

I was going to tell her all this, all this as I brought my hands to her face to pull her mouth off me, to stop the insane bliss that was her body pressed against me, soft and strong as I knew it would be. But my hands disobeyed me, and instead, I slid my fingers into her hair to press her mouth harder, still against mine to continue the mind-numbing kiss, angry, passionate, sad—and so hungry. How many times had I thought about touching her hair? Hundreds, likely thousands without me consciously knowing it. And now, knowing what it felt like, would I ever think of anything else?

Then I felt the tip of Erica's tongue touch mine, Greg Brady got completely knocked off his board once more, the ridiculous heat between us so intense that it made my head spin. By some miracle, the world righted itself again, and I was reminded by the sudden quiet of the campground that we could be seen, and she was definitely not mine. As wrong as it was for me to take Lorn when I knew I didn't love her anymore, this was much more wicked. My brother loves this woman. Vince, who'd had dozens of women before her and had never come close to marriage, had fallen for this woman the moment he met her. He had wanted to marry her.

I pulled myself from her, and put up both my hands against her shoulders to keep her back from me. I spoke in a wobbly voice that sounded anything but decisive, "No, Erica, I can't. Not ever."

The tears of pleasure that had streaked down her cheeks when I had responded to her kiss were now changing to pain as I held her apart from me. I was vaguely aware I might be crying as well, but all I could feel was her pain, and I fully understood all the hurting I was causing her. I had been on the other side of it with Lorn, riding the rollercoaster of her push and pull. The difference here was that Erica knew where I stood, and where I could never stand. I knew from the look in her eyes that she had guessed the depths of what I felt for her, and what I couldn't feel for her—and they were exactly the same damned thing.

"Erica, I can't."

Erica unlocked her eyes from me and finally looked down, sending a fresh pair of tears down to her boots, and I felt her strength sap away as she stopped fighting me. My hands were no longer keeping her apart from me, but instead, they were now resting, exhausted, on her shoulders. Finally, she backed away from me.

"Vince reminded me so much of you," she confessed in a raw whisper, as if, right now, she was just figuring this out. "He did right from the beginning. I know understand why I thought I loved him, what my connection was to him. I know why I hated Lorn back then, too. I told myself I hated her because she would hurt you."

Erica had hated Lorn. Why hadn't I seen that?

She leaned against her truck, defeated. She said, "When I met your brother, I thought everything I felt for you I could maybe feel for him. He's so much like you. He even looks like you." Then, in a desperate, childlike voice she asked, "If I can't have you—and he is so *much* like you—you think someday I could love him, too?"

I waited a long time before I whispered, "I don't know. I hope so, for his sake." But my heart was aching excruciatingly at the thought. My body was still saying: mine. I want her. She's mine.

Erica wiped her eyes with her sleeve as she said, "I've never not taken whatever—"

"I know," I said.

But her determination withered as she said, "But I don't want to hurt him again. This is going to sound awful. I sometimes think if I can't have what I want, my best chance of falling in love ever again is with Vince. If I could learn to love him, maybe I could feel like this again, someday."

"Please don't," I said, before I could stop myself. I hoped I sounded as protective of my brother as I felt, and not like I was begging her not to be with anyone but me. At that very moment, I was not sure which

I meant. I took a deep breath and said, "Please don't risk hurting him."

She looked at me with a flicker of hope in her eyes, searching mine for a different answer as she said, "I'm sorry that I can't love him more than you."

"And I'm sorry, but I do," I said.

At that, Erica backed off, just as I had needed her to. She nodded her head slightly before opening the door to her truck, and got inside. When the door shut and she pulled away, I fought the urge to chase the truck like a wild dog, biting at the tires to stop her from going. And now that she was moving away from me, I wanted to tell her how I feared my heart might stop beating if I gave her up, and I knew that my brother wouldn't want that, so could she please come back?

My other choice beyond chasing the truck like a junkyard dog was to let myself cry, but since I was no longer hidden by Erica's truck, this was as impractical an option as chasing a flatbed down a dirt road. Greg Brady's monster wave was long gone and it was me washed up on the shore, beached with a mouthful of sand, bathing suit ripped and spun around backward, and a crusty starfish stuck to my left boob (the big one), like an aquatic version of a Janet Jackson wardrobe malfunction.

What a mess. When I looked up, I realized I had been seen long before the truck drove away, since Uncle Freddie had a bird's eye view from the roof. Since he was alone up there, I wondered if he'd cleared the workers off the roof to spare his niece an audience for what may have been her worst day in her life. Before he leaned back over his spot on the roof, he looked down at me and nodded as if he had heard my thoughts, and said, *"Abbiamo can't scegliere chi amiamo."* I repeated this phrase over and over so I would remember it, and later, when I was home and could cry alone, I looked up the translation and found nothing was ever so true:

"We can't choose who we love."

The Dove Gaio Mangia was proving to be a continued success, especially after one of the first gay boys to visit the camp (who sported a porn name) turned out to be a freelance journalist, and wrote an article for Out And About Travel. As Lisa's luck would have it, the article was picked up by the Associated Press and spread to at least a dozen newspapers.

If a Lesbian Builds It, Will They Come?
By Johnnie Rocket

Camptown Ladies and its "sister" campground, Camp Camp, is probably the last place you would expect to find a four-star Italian restaurant, but that is exactly what I stumbled upon after joining friends at a campground that openly caters to a gay clientele. The campground's owner, Lisa Santora, self-described "dykecoon," runs the camp along with the rest of her colorful Italian family.

Santora's idea was simple: "I wanted to create a campground that was plush enough for the gay boys, while remaining rustic enough for us more hardy gals." Add to this, all the warmth (and volume) you would expect from an Italian family welcoming their guests—Santora has come through on her promises.

Upon arrival, Santora took us on a tour to show off the amenities. For the boys of Camp Camp, this includes bathrooms with marble sinks, a never-ending supply of plush, Ralph Lauren towels, and complimentary facial products. There is even a shower area large enough to host four of your closest friends. Lisa laughs when I ask about this and says, "I wanted to remind the boys of their high school gym days, when you had to pretend you weren't looking."

Camptown Ladies women's bathrooms feature a more rustic approach; with water-saver toilets and empty towel bars curtly labeled "Camptown Ladies is an eco-friendly Camp. Please provide your own towels." Among the other charming oddities, there stands a Jenga-like tower of wood and beside it is a plaque dedicated to an aunt's recent passing. Santora's father stands guard over the wood and cheerfully admits to a rumor that his sister, known to the camp as Aunt Aggie, was "taken out" by the woodpile, which makes campers hesitant to buy the wood, and encourages them to bring their own.

He also explained that his sister's widower (affectionately called Uncle Freddie, by everyone at camp) has recently joined the construction crew, despite being in his seventies. Uncle Freddie can usually be found teaching Italian songs to the other crew members on the rooftops. The crew is lead by a female contractor—hired, according to Lisa Santora, not for her talent but strictly as "eye candy."

Other amenities include a Camp Store, which is comically segregated with a boy side and a girl side, and a built-in pool where the boys gather to gossip and work on their fabulous tans, and some of the ladies meet to do early-morning laps. Most of the women prefer to hang out at the weed-fringed pond, where you will find pairs of mommies closely monitoring their children's every move, a place that Lisa Santora has dubbed Micro-Management Beach.

Every Saturday morning there is a fly-fishing tournament, mostly for the ladies. It's called "A Rottweiler Runs Through It," because the women are encouraged to bring their dogs but asked to leave the children back at the campsite. Lisa Santora holds all the fly-fishing records, and she teases her brother Vince: "Despite his supple wrist, he never could get the hang of it, even though he's forced to fly fish because he's petrified of worms. Go figure."

The boys have made the refurbished teen rec hall the It place to go summer clubbing when the restaurant magically transforms from food to frolic. The gay boys, some in drag, have been known to put on impromptu shows, laden with Abba and Bette Midler songs. The lesbians (and a fair amount of straight folks) are lured here by the food but stay to watch the show, hauling beer coolers on wheels, with small children hitching rides. Teenagers watch the show from the safety of the woods.

Lisa Santora offers a pass for non-camping visitors to experience her restaurant, Dove Gaio Mangia (Italian slang for: "Where Gays Eat"). If camping is not your thing, I strongly suggest purchasing a One Gay Pass, as the restaurant should not be missed. Authentic Italian cooking is served up in a beautifully decorated dining hall—the work of flamboyant friend, and self-appointed event coordinator, Eddie Stella. The food is so heavenly, and seconds and leftovers so strongly encouraged, that you will quickly forgive the lesbian-style customer service. There is none; it's strictly buffet-style and clean up after yourself, or be chastised openly by chef Lisa.)

*Be advised to get there early, as the restaurant has two sittings every evening and word has leaked out in town that this is the best place in the tri-state area to get an all-you-can-eat, four-star Italian dinner for $8.00 (or whatever you chose to donate)—and kids always eat free. Santora offers a Double-Dyke-Discount for any family sporting two mommies. Nobody seems to mind the discrimination, and she says she does it because most male heads of household have higher incomes. Lisa's answer to anyone who may brave a rare complaint? "I tell them they should go to f***ing Disney World, where it's straight except for once a year, and that here, every day is Gay Day. Next year I'm considering having a straight week, with a parade where the straight couples can pull their kids on their Coleman coolers, and the gays can stand and wave at them from the sidewalks. It'll be awesome."*

The morning after his date with Erica, I watched Vince as he sat at the kitchen table reading the newspaper. He was laughing his way through the Camptown Ladies article; grateful he only got hit with the worm comment. When he finished reading it, he looked at me and said, "You look like crap ever since you spent that night with Lorn."

"And you kind of look happy."

He put down the paper. "Don't worry, I'm being realistic. I know this may not work."

"Knowing that doesn't stop you from being crushed," I said, and Vince nodded and we both sat in silence.

Finally, he asked me, "What's going on with you and Lorn?"

"I ended it. Being with her was just sad."

"Because you still love her," he said.

"Because I don't." I excused myself from the table, before he had a chance to give me details about his date with Erica.

Twenty-Seven

She Shoots, She Scores!

The next few weeks, Erica and Vince were scarcely seen at camp. When Lisa would ask Vince how things were going, he would decline to answer. But I saw the old, cheerful Vince was gradually coming back and I was both worried and happy for him, despite the fact that I had barreled through the same turnstile to Depression-land just as he was exiting, and all because of the same woman.

When Vince was not off the campsite with Erica, he was spending time with Katie's little boy, Buddy. Vince had become fascinated by the shy little kid and would trek once a day to the far side of the camp to Katie's trailer to see if he could borrow her son.

Vince would invent goofy games that reminded me of the games we used to play in our backyard when we were kids. Vince circled the entire camp with the child riding in the back of his red wagon while Buddy pretended Vince was a horse. I recognized this one particular game as Lisa's since Vince's bad coaching of an English accent had Buddy yelling out warnings to the campers that a bubonic plague had hit camp, and that after a fortnight they would be allowed to line up for rations of beans and towels. To Buddy's delight, a few of the campers played along and shouted back to them, "When will this plague be over?" and "Tell me sir, how can a guy get some extra beans?" Vince coached Buddy to yell back to the Mayor, "No extra beans! Your wife says you eat too much!" On Buddy's second pass by the camp store, Lisa ran over to hand the boy a long, thin tree branch with instructions to use it on his Vince as a horse whip, but Katie put an end to that after the third lap.

Since Vince and Erica were never at camp together, I worried if Vince sensed there had been something between us. If they were avoiding camp, I was pathetically hopeful it was Erica that was controlling this, that maybe she knew I wasn't strong enough to face seeing them together. Every morning I braced myself to see them together, and was grateful for every day that I was spared the sight.

I tried to find joy in the return of my brother's boyish smile and the bounce that was back in his step, and most days I could. But I would also get up in the middle of the night and wander down the hallway at the condo to see if my brother had come home. I usually found his door left open and that his bed had not been slept in, and my heart would ache at the thought of them together. I was grateful they never stayed together at the condo, but that didn't stop me from staying awake night after night, staring at the ceiling, knowing they were together. She was his first, I would remind myself. But then the thought would creep in as I slept: was she, really?

While I was no longer assisting Erica with any construction projects, my Uncle Freddie was becoming a roofing expert. It was common to see him do Erica's signature moonwalk and he had gotten so skilled at it that she even let him walk along the new clay tile roofs, when she never let me do that. When I watched him, I had no idea if the pit in my stomach was worry that a man in his seventies was walking high on top roofs, or simply that the roof walking reminded me of her. Everything reminded me of her. Just reading a random reference to California in the newspaper would send me into a funk, as I remembered all the celebrity house projects we'd worked on together.

Several mornings I would see her truck slow, then pass by the entrance of the campground, as if she had decided at the last minute not to come. Later in the day, she would show up, but only to check on her crew or to move a piece of equipment to work in another part of the camp—whichever part I was not in, it seemed. Other mornings, my heart would lurch into my chest when I saw her truck parked in the camp, but often she would arrive just to bark a few orders or check the work of her crew from the previous afternoon before she was pulling out of the camp again, sometimes not coming back for several days.

Today I especially hated myself. Vince had stopped by to say he was taking off for several days for a bachelor party in Vegas with some college friends. I sighed with relief and then hated myself for it. I hated that his being away from Erica made me feel stupidly hopeful, like she would somehow be mine in some small way while he wasn't around. More evil than that, most of my relief came from knowing he would not be around to hold and touch her, if only for a few days.

I hated myself.

Lisa knew there was something wrong with me, and while she couldn't put her finger on it, that didn't stop her from guessing every chance she got. Was I sick of the campground? Was I secretly back with Lorn? To all of this I would say no, and offer no more. She gave me a little space, but she would still be observing me, that damned eyebrow of hers lifted in constant suspicion, and I knew it was only a matter of time before she'd find out. I even toyed with telling her, but I knew I couldn't. How could I tell her I was the sibling who had broken the trust between the three of us? Our entire lives, it had always been the three of us; we'd been able to count on each other for as long as I could remember, and I now would do anything to keep up the charade that I had not breached this.

Vince's Vegas trip was bad timing for the camp, since it came over the long Labor Day weekend, which would start with the parade and end with a bonfire to signal the official end of the camping season. Camptown Ladies and Camp Camp would stay open until the end of September, but already some of the full season campers had started to winterize their trailers and pack away their less hardy decorations. Vince was gone and when I arrived Friday morning at camp, I saw that Erica's truck was already there, but aside from Uncle Freddie, there was no sign of her or her crew.

Lisa caught me staring at Erica's truck, as my brain reenacted the kiss I'd had with Erica, and I started when she spoke. "Since Vince is away, I asked Erica if she and her crew could stay for the weekend to help us run the bonfire."

I didn't know if my gut reaction was panic or pure joy. I could no longer tell the difference. All I knew was that I felt alive for the first time in weeks, knowing Erica would be again spending her time here. My blood beat in my veins again at last, and I may have even smiled, before it occurred to me to turn away from Lisa, who was studying my face. I pretended to search the trees for new signs of Gypsy Moth invasions.

"What the fuck is going on with you and her?" Lisa said, grabbing my arm to stop me from walking. I had to look at her then, and in that second, I knew that she knew.

"Nothing," I said, and even if my voice hadn't cracked, I knew I was fucked.

"Oh my God!" Lisa said, then she lowered her voice, "Is something going on with you and Erica?"

I shook my head no, but my eyes had filled and I knew that Lisa would never be convinced otherwise.

She interrogated me, "What happened between the two of you?"

"Nothing. Nothing is happening . . . now," I said.

Lisa was stunned, and I realized then she had made a wild guess, and was reeling from the shock that she had been right. Horrified, she said, "You can't be that stupid."

"And cruel," I said.

Lisa muttered to herself, "Vince obviously has no idea, since he sneaks off to see her every minute. Is this why he's afraid to tell us he's seeing her again?"

"He doesn't know, he won't know—not ever," I said. "I stopped it from happening, it won't ever happen."

Lisa's eyes bulged from her head. "Are you telling me she feels the same way about you?"

"I'm sure she doesn't anymore," I said. "Not after I told her I still loved Lorn. Look, Vince is happy, so whatever she thought she wanted from me, she found it again with him. She realized this wasn't real for her."

"But it's real for you," Lisa said. "You're in love with her."

"No." I shook my head, but then stopped, hopeless to deny it. "I'll get over it. I got over Lorn, I'll get over this."

Lisa surprised me by saying, "That was different. Lorn was wrong for you." We stood together for a long time, letting that sink in. Then she said, "I know I don't have to tell you this would destroy him."

She didn't have to tell me.

The parade on Saturday was a big hit and a welcome distraction for Lisa and me. The gay boys all dressed up, Mardi Gras style, while the lesbians opted instead to dress up their dogs and march them through the camp, following the flowing feather boas of the gay boys. Lisa, of course, led the parade. She'd bought an authentic English military uniform from the Army Navy store in Provincetown (the uniform still smelled like the store) and she carried a large baton, which she raised up and down with moves less like a baton and more like a barbell, keeping everyone marching in time. There were so many lively sights to see—the gays, the colors, the children on decorated bikes, the dogs in costume—that I was able to forget myself for a while. That, plus, as usual, Erica was nowhere to be found.

Hours later, just as I began to wonder if she had possibly joined Vince in Vegas, Erica showed up with a small crew, including Uncle Freddie, to begin the difficult negotiations with Dad over the wood for the bonfire. I could see by Dad's conflicted body language that his instincts were to throw himself onto his tower to protect it. At the same time, he knew it made no sense. Thanks to Dad's rumor that a tumbling woodpile was the cause of Aunt Aggie's demise, the tower had hardly been touched all season. In fact, parents made children take a wide path around it to get to the camp store. Dad was pleased he'd kept his tower relatively intact, but now he looked like he was circled by a pack of vultures. They were closing in, and this was Woody's last stand.

Erica spotted me approaching, but she continued her campaign for the wood, talking to my father as if he was a special needs child, a tactic that occasionally worked. "Mr. Santora, it's a beautiful tower, but I know you could build an even better one next season," she said.

Dad answered, "It would be fine with me, but how would Freddie feel? We dedicated the tower to his wife, my sister Aggie, and I wouldn't dream of—"

"Torch it!" Uncle Freddie interrupted from behind him, "Aggie would have loved to see a bonfire. I would like to think if we build it right, she'll see it from up there."

I was not completely convinced Aunt Aggie didn't have a long layover before heading "up there," but I agreed with Uncle Freddie and said, "Dad, we can take off the plaque and dedicate the camp store to her memory instead. Makes sense since she spent a lot of time in the store."

I heard Lisa whisper behind me, "She friggin' croaked in there."

Dad showed signs of weakening but would not give up without a fight. He said, "What if I ordered more wood for the bonfire, and left this tower intact, then we would be all set for next year." Then he smiled as if it was all settled.

Gentle was not Erica's natural state, but she was nothing if not savvy. She paced around the tower and Dad watched her as if she was a giant alien termite, circling his nest of helpless wood babies. Erica turned to me and said, "Even if we did use the wood from this tower, I still haven't decided the best way to build the biggest bonfire, while still keeping it as safe as possible."

Though she didn't look at me, it was the first time she had talked to me in weeks, and I was thrown by it, but I recovered to help her bait Dad. I said, "Don't look at me. You're the Bobbi The Builder. I have no idea how to make a bonfire."

Erica and I both saw a fire ignite in Dad's eyes. "Airflow is the key," Dad said. He paused to make a pompous stride forward, closer to the tower. "It's simple enough, but you still have to do it just right, so the structure doesn't collapse while it's burning. If it collapses, that would create a lot of smoke, which can snuff it out entirely." Dad studied the tower and said, "We'll need to use a basic tee-pee construction of birch bark for the inner heart of the fire, since that's the best wood we have here on the East Coast for igniting. Then we'll surround it with an overlapping square log structure. That's the safest way to build it high, with the minimum danger of collapsing."

It did not occur to Dad that he was surrounded by expert builders and Erica let him think he was directing the whole thing, from selecting the perfect spot for the fire to the method in which they would move the tower. Before long, Dad was tearing into that tower like he had been dying to get rid of it, shouting out instructions to Erica's men, who had been instructed by Erica to do whatever Dad said. The crew sprang into action as if they were in boot camp.

When Dad clumsily stumbled over some wood in his haste to scout out the best location for the fire, Erica turned to Uncle Freddie and said, "I'm counting on you to be second in command on this project. And by second, I really mean first."

Uncle Freddie laughed his wheezy laugh. "You got it, boss." And with that, he trailed after Dad, directing him away from the trees to suggest the more open field. Dad put his arm around Freddie and said, "You sure you're OK with us using Aggie's tower?" Uncle Freddie nodded and said, "You sure you're OK?" I heard Dad laugh at him.

Lisa had hurried off to The Dove and Erica and I were left standing alone. "Well done," I said. "Thanks for handling Dad."

Erica wouldn't look at me, but she gave a small smile and said, "I've worked with men long enough to know when you want them to do something, best to make them think it's their idea," she said. We both fell silent then, and she finally looked at me as my stomach flipped over and over under her stare. Good Lord. Nobody should be that beautiful.

I started walking as I said, "So, Vince is off to Vegas for a bachelor party." Erica followed at my side. "Worried?"

"Why would I be worried?" she asked.

I thought, Of course she shouldn't be worried. What man in his right mind would think there was any woman more spectacular than her? It was likely that anyone who ever fell for her still loved her today, and always would. She had no worries about that. I was the one with the worries.

I blurted out, "Lisa knows something happened between us."

Erica stopped walking, but she didn't look at me. She stared straight ahead and said, "You told her it was over."

"Yes," I said, with the ridiculous hope she would fight me on this. How could it be over? How could she start over so soon after that last kiss? It was a kiss that haunted me, and I was convinced it always would. This is how I wanted it to go, I reminded myself. This is how it had to go.

She turned toward her truck and called over her shoulder, "I have some things to do off site, but I'll be back late afternoon to check the crew."

When she walked away, I felt a hard lump settle in my throat as I often did these days. Clearly, she was using any excuse to be away from camp to avoid being around me. When Erica turned back to look at me as she was driving off, I realized I had been frozen there, staring after her truck. Lisa was beside me again, and, feeling caught, I stupidly waved to Erica's truck. For a moment, I thought Erica saw me in her rearview mirror and that she had waved back, but I realized instead that she was wiping her hands across both of her cheeks. Had I made her cry again? My stomach turned.

Lisa grabbed my waving hand and pulled it down to my side. She was not angry, and instead pity filled her eyes. She held on to my wrist and said, "We now officially have cable in the store. Come see."

"Don't drag me in there to see a friggin' football game."

"No, much better! Hurry, before a stupid kid comes in to buy candy or something."

She dragged me by my arm into the store, which was empty. Mom had made a Wal-mart run for supplies as we were out of black licorice again. I saw the cause of my sister's excitement. The installation of the widescreen TV had been completed high on the wall in the back of the store, and as luck would have it, Lisa had found the movie *Desert Hearts* on cable. Except for the danger of someone walking into the store, it might have been the perfect distraction, but I'd watched this movie before with my sister, and she watched it like a football sport announcer—if a football announcer narrated a sex scene. As Lisa's luck would have it, the famous sex scene was about to begin, and off she went:

LISA: Oh, Lordy! Helen Shaver in that sherbet-colored robe. Raspberry, yummy, my favorite. Just makes me want to lick her silly. You think the director chose that color for this reason?
MARIE: Oh, sure.
LISA: Oh fuck, the dark-haired one is hot, too. Which one do I want? Which one do I want?
MARIE: You may not have to decide right now.
LISA: Woo-ho! Here's where Helen peeks around the corner of the room and the dark-haired girl surprises her by getting naked.
MARIE: You know Helen is the *actress's* name.
LISA: Wait for it. Waaaaaait for it—boom! Naaaaakid!
MARIE: You're ruining this movie for me. Again. Forever.
LISA: Now, Helen hesitates.
MARIE: Vivian hesitates.
LISA: She tries to make the dark-haired one take her clothes . . . but, then, lowers her hand . . . she doesn't hand them to her! Oh no! She does *not* want her to put the clothes on . . .
MARIE: I have eyes. I can see all this happening.
LISA: Helen wants it, she wants it so bad! Oh! Here is where she nervously tucks that piece of hair behind her ear. And it falls out, and she tucks it back again. Oh, she is *soooo* uncomfortable with this.
MARIE: Well, you should have your hair out of your face at a time like this.
LISA: So, what's up with the messy hair, anyway?
MARIE: I don't know, you brought it up.
LISA: I'd still fuck the crap out of her, even with that rat's nest hair.
MARIE: You should call her agent. She'll be so relieved.
(Lisa hits my arm, hard.)
LISA: Uh-oh, she's locking the hotel room door. Here's where

they are gonna make out! Look how much they want it. *Look at that.* Don't tell me that ain't real!

MARIE: It's not real. It's a movie.

LISA: Bullshit! That scene earlier, when Helen watches the dark-haired girl with that guy on the dance floor? You could practically see her get wet right on screen! Nobody acts that well. Bold choice wearing those tight cowboy jeans when you really think about it.

MARIE: You're disgusting.

LISA: Oh, God. Listen to the make-out noises!

MARIE *(I am starting to laugh now)*: I can't hear a thing over the pig commentary.

LISA: *Oh my god Jesus!* . . . The nip to nip touch is coming soon . . . but first the little string of spit during the make-out . . . there it is! *Boom! She crushes it!*

MARIE: Lisa, seriously, shut up. The whole camp can probably hear you—

LISA: The nips, the nips! Touchdown! Yessss!

(Lisa was now jumping up and down with both fists in the air as if she herself had pulled the woman across a finish line made of tits.)

MARIE: Really? Jumping? You have watched this a million—

LISA: Holy shit! Here's the quick cutaway to the pussy, *right there,* got that one by the sensors, then Helen's gonna come, right on top of her! That's *so hot!*

MARIE: Usually, but right now, it isn't.

LISA: Hey, can you do that? So economical, no fingers, no toys, just the rubbing. I need to learn to do that. Good option, easy clean-up. Respect, Helen, respect.

MARIE: There's something wrong with you.

LISA: Whooo-hoo! Here it comes! *Boom!!! Yessss—Score!*

Just then, we hear a man outside rushing toward the camp store with two very young kids in tow as he says to them, "I have to stop in and check the score!"

This sends Lisa diving for the remote, desperate to shut off the

TV before the kids get an eyeful of tits, just as the guy runs into the store, looking totally confused to find the TV shut down.

Lisa flings the remote back onto the counter as she says, "Damn! Cable went out just as there was a touch down. But it looks like there'll be a big spread."

I lose myself in a belly laugh that doubles me over the counter.

Twenty-Eight

If a Lesbian Falls In The Woods, Does She Make a Sound?

Erica came back as promised to check on the crew. She had changed into a thick cream-colored sweater in anticipation of the cool night air. The light color set off the warm hue of her skin and the light shade of her eyes. I was working with Lisa at the Dove Gaio Mangia, when Erica scanned the hall before spotting me. I looked away from her and busied myself with the buffet table, but Lisa had witnessed the exchange.

Lisa was not someone who ever looked worried. She was too strong an influence on the world around her to have irrational fears that she could not make anything bend to her wishes. But even from the distance from the buffet table to the kitchen I could plainly see the worry on her face.

Without Vince around to help, and Mom convinced she would be needed to supervise Dad (we agreed, a wise choice), it took Lisa and I until nightfall before we had the restaurant shut down for the evening. Tonight, with the impending bonfire, there would be no amateur drag show, and the silence of the hall when we closed down was eerie. I shut down the fog machine and watched as the white cloud lowered closer to the floor until it crawled along the floor, spilling off the edges and dissolving into the damp grass and gravel around the hall.

The rest of the campground was quiet too. Most of the campers had already gathered in the field and set up lawn chairs and blankets, so the campsites were dark without the usual dotting of small camp-fires. Lisa was unusually quiet, and that was the most eerie of all.

Even Lisa's little Min Pin, Cindy-Lu, trotted along without once reminding the chipmunks who was boss in these here parts. Lisa's silence seemed to be rattling her as well.

Finally, Lisa broke the silence. "You know, even if it doesn't work out with them—"

"I know," I said.

Still, she cautioned me needlessly, "Remember Hanni," she said, futilely. I remembered that every day. "Except maybe for that little boy, Buddy, Vince has only loved two people outside of his family."

"I know."

The open field was alive with everyone at the camp. Erica was instructing the crew to make last-minute adjustments to the woodpile, which towered majestically in the moonlight. Dad, aka Woody, stood closest to the tower, looking prouder than he had at his kids' college graduations. I knew my sister and I were both hoping that he wouldn't have second thoughts as the lighter approached.

"Why don't we stay on this side," Lisa said. We were on the opposite side of the field that Erica was on. Not waiting for an answer, Lisa laid a blanket on the cool, dewy grass, and Cindy-Lu immediately claimed it as her own, ready to watch the show. Lisa and I joined her, and Cindy-Lu opted to sit on the end of Lisa's knee instead, looking like a little bird perched on a building.

With the preparations for the fire, Erica had not yet spotted us directly across from her. Lisa had given her instructions to light the fire at 8:30 sharp, regardless of whether we had finished closing the restaurant, and the crew prepared under Erica's instructions to do just that. She made a group of campers move back a few feet before passing the lighter to Dad to do the honors. Dad stepped a few feet closer, then stopped. Lisa and I both held our breath, but were both relieved when he handed the torch to Uncle Freddie instead of Dad.

Lisa snorted, "Whew, I thought he was going to take the lighter and run for it."

When Uncle Freddie lit the wood and the flames quickly licked up the tower, I got more mileage over the joke about Dad forever hearing the Screaming Of The Limbs, and Lisa snorted with laughter, slapping hard at my knee. I wondered if Erica would hear Lisa laughing, but the crowd was cheering and clapping as the bonfire climbed to its full height, and she had not spotted us yet.

Erica was looking past the crowd for us, and I could see she was disappointed, believing she had to light the fire without us. She had a blanket laid out, and she stayed on one edge, leaving the rest of it open as she stared over the fire and the crowd. I saw her look over to the Dove, where the tiny white lights cast a twinkling glow in the blackness of the night. I thought Erica looked distressed now, and I wondered if she too was thinking about our kiss on that roof. Warmth spread within me, aided by the blazing bonfire. I saw her eyes lower to the large empty side of the blanket next to her, and she shifted herself to the middle. She looked up then, across the bonfire, and her eyes finally met my stare.

Lisa was saying something to me, but I couldn't hear her over the pounding in my ears, so I just said, "Uh, huh."

Across the fire, I could see Erica's breathing quicken, her sweater rising and falling as she stared at me, unblinking, unsmiling. Someone in her crew broke her stare by directing her attention to a piece of the fire that had crumbled out of the stone formation, but people were seated safely back and she assessed no danger, so she waved him away. Her eyes snapped back and stayed fixed on me.

Despite witnessing her breathing, there was a coolness in her gaze, an indifference that hurt as much as not having her, and when she finally looked away, I felt a sharp stab in my chest, and the pain increased with each minute she chose not to look back at me. This was worse. Much worse. What did I expect? Isn't this what I wanted her to do? I had asked her to leave this alone and move on, but with every second I felt her trying, the heat of the fire was suffocating me.

My eyes burned in fair warning, and I knew I couldn't fall apart here. I stood up, and lied to my sister, "The smoke's getting to me."

"You wimp, it's not that bad, but we can move back if you want," she said, starting to get up.

I put my hand on her shoulder to make her stay put. "I just have to go," I said, knowing my voice betrayed me as I walked away.

I was comforted by the darkness that swallowed me, relieved by the blindness of the black night as I bolted from the fire in the fastest walk I thought I could get away with that would not cause attention from others, beyond my sister. I didn't want to walk in the direction of the camp where there might be a few latecomers strolling to the bonfire, so I turned toward the woods. I glanced back only once, and told myself that nobody could see me over the brilliance of the bonfire, and walked on. Maybe I even ran a little.

When I reached the edge of the woods, I felt tears chilling my cheeks, wiped them on my sleeve, and saw that away from the fire the moonlight had lit up my white sweatshirt to a luminous neon blue. I wondered again if I could be seen by the campers, but was comforted by how blinded I was when I left the light of the fire. When I was at last convinced I was completely under the cover of darkness, I let myself think of Erica, of her with my brother, of how much I loved them both, of how selfishly I did not want them together—and I let myself cry as I could not have done anywhere else in the world. Not at the campground, not in my bed at night at the condo. I cried violently, a long and indulgent cry, until I was left struggling for air. But as quickly as I let myself go, I had to stop myself so I could breathe.

I was leaning against a tree, bent over slightly, making ridiculous sounds trying to regain my breath, when I heard footsteps. Against the backdrop of the bonfire, I saw the distinctive silhouette of Erica, who had gotten extremely close without me hearing her over my gasping. I tried to recover, straighten myself up, but seeing her made me cry harder, and instead of standing, I caved into my shame and covered my face with my hands and dropped to my knees like a total fool.

She came closer, and I thought any impact would crash against me as if she were a demon in the night (she was, after all, the one person I could not have in the entire world), but when she knelt down in front of me and took me in her arms, I was astonished by her softness, and I could do nothing but bury my face against her shoulder. She only held me and said nothing. She waited for me to calm myself, and it took a terribly long time.

While she waited, she talked to me.

"I'm in such trouble," she said, "I thought it was bad enough when I was confused, when you left California and I couldn't figure out why I was so unhappy without you, why Vince couldn't make me happy. But the confusion, that was easy. This, this is hard. Knowing what I want is hard. All I want is to look at you, be near you—all I want is you."

When I found enough air to lie, I said, "And all I want is you to be happy with him."

"That's not what you want," she said, then, when I tried to pull away, she locked on to me tighter, and then pulled her face back to cover my lips with hers, and I was gone. I was a little girl completely lost in the woods.

I didn't have the strength to fight it, I told myself this. I told myself I was too weak from the crying, too weak from wanting her, too weak from losing her to fight this anymore—or, did I just make the evil decision not to? Could someone this weak be returning her kisses this hard? I wondered this as her hands moved to the front of my sweatshirt. She unzipped it, and in a brief moment of sanity, I grabbed her wrists, but not before she had already landed both hands on my breasts and set my chest blazing like a satellite bonfire, in a very dangerous location. Bonfires in woods cause forest fires—bad idea, very, very, very bad idea.

I knew all this, and yet, instead of peeling her hands off, I kissed her harder as I slid my hands from her wrists to let her grab me as hard as she wanted to—and this woman was so much stronger than she looked. The groan that escaped me (which I didn't recognize as mine) gave her permission to kiss me more deeply, leaving me wondering how something so insanely soft could press so fucking hard against my lips.

Then, just as I was thinking it, she said: "I am *yours.*" And, if it is possible to whisper a command, that is what Erica did, right into my ear.

"You. Are. Mine."

Since she had possession of both my breasts, with such a remarkable grip, a bizarre thought occurred to me, something that I'd learned when I was quite young: Possession is nine-tenths of the law.

I. Was. Hers.

I blocked out everything but the feel of her, otherwise I could never have reached under her sweater, then under her bra to climb along the front of her like a teenage boy in the back seat of a car. I was racing the clock, expecting to get a flashlight in eyes from some cop at a make-out spot. There were moments I was in total denial of what I was doing, and it made my mind spin off into bizarre directions. My mind raced from being grateful I had a ridiculously large rack of boob to offer a woman as spectacularly attractive as Erica—and, oddly, like I often do at the most inappropriate moments, I escaped to a vivid memory of my last trip to a department store to buy bras.

I was in the lingerie department and asked a size question to the young woman working there. She took one look at my giant jugs (with a half angry/half frightened look that said: *Hell, no, if I am working overtime, bitch*) then she said, in a voice that could only be described as terrified, "I have to call my boss." Minutes later, after placing the call for help over a Madonna-style headset, the lingerie boss arrived with such an air of importance, hair fashionably disheveled, that I wondered if they had flown her in via a helipad on the Macy's department store roof.

The boss was a fantastically attractive, tall, rail-thin African American woman who strode toward me confidently, with a practiced look of *You don't scare me* arranged on her face, like that of a doctor who has to face (with no detectible alarm) the worst cases of skin disease, giant tumors, or alarmingly giant jugs that need measuring. I watched her eyes for changes as my boobs came into alarmingly clearer view. Oh, this woman was good at hiding fear. The lingerie boss's ridiculously long cloth tape measure was draped around her neck with the fashion sense of an orange scarf but the importance of a stethoscope, the ends fluttering behind her armpits as she strode toward me. If she had been my height, that tape measure would have dragged on the floor.

Was this really necessary?

She directed me to go in the fitting room, where she proceeded to take three lightning fast measurements, with knuckles boob-grazing me in a professional carelessness that I didn't doubt, while I babbled how I knew the Wal-Mart bra I was wearing was probably incorrect at a size D, and that I might actually a be a double or (giggle) possibly a triple D—she interrupted my pre-teen banter to diagnose me a "G."

My response: "Um, as in A, B, C, D, E, F, G?"

She said, "Yup. Small frame, but *very* big ones."

But I dyke-gress.

I was pleased about my big ones now, as I was ripped from my Macy's lingerie memory by Erica's stirring responses as she attempted to get her hands around my most pronounced feature. Good luck, honey.

Meanwhile, I only thought I was lost in the woods before, because I had her breasts in my hands too, and Erica's nipples were hard and pressed against the center of my palms as I held on, a feeling so distracting it was nearly impossible to touch her and kiss her at the same time.

"Please," Erica said against my lips, "you have no idea how much I need you."

If I could have spoken, I might have said she was the one that had no friggin' idea, since the woods were spinning around me and I felt I was plunging through this delicious hell I had chosen to dive into.

"Please, take me," she said against my mouth, and when I didn't move right then, shocked from her words, she grabbed one of my hands and pushed it down the front of her jeans. If that had not been instruction enough (and it may not have been, since I was in the middle of having my mind completely blown), she whispered into my ear, "I need you. Now," and I thought, Erica was always at her best when was she was telling me what to do.

If I had been weak from crying, her words erased this now, and I wrapped my other arm around her, leaning against her until I pushed her flat onto the ground. Something, maybe a button, tore off her jeans as I slid my hand inside her. She cried out, I think, but

I was a total animal by now, and, actually, the cry might have been mine. When she whispered hoarsely, "Yes, more of you, please—" I once again did what I was told, but then she said "Oh fuck" as if it had not been her idea at all, and this is when I found out that three was Erica's lucky number.

So this was what it was like to be with a contractor. Take this, put it there, now. More. Harder. Yes. No. Yes. Just like that . . . faster, please, yes, right now. She may have cried out when she came, and this time it really may have been her, because I was watching her face, and in the dim moonlight I could see her cheeks flood with color, and her mouth open as I heard a cry. Or maybe it was me, because when you were doing something perfectly, the beautiful contractor says nothing at all.

Her orgasm served only to make us more desperate, so I roughly pulled her sweater off so my mouth could feast on her breast (why had I waited?), sucking and opening wider until I had most of her in my mouth. When I released her nipple, she clutched me so I wouldn't let her go, and she let me apart only enough to trail my mouth across her chest to feed on her from the other side. The whole time I kept my hand buried inside her and she kept pushing against me, getting so insanely wet that I could barely feel her. Stupidly, I thought: No going back now. It was stupid because I knew that point had come at our first kiss, on top of a roof.

I felt Erica dig her nails into my back as I put my mouth against her ear and informed her in great detail about how very wet she was, in case she wasn't aware. I told her if I could bear to pull my hand out of her, ever, I would rather die than never get the chance to taste her. While I was doing all the talking, continuing to say much more dirty things, Erica took me by surprise. Whatever I said, had excited her so that she put her hand on mine and joined her fingers with mine to push me deeper and take her harder, just in case it didn't occur to me to do so. She came with a series of unfeminine growls behind clenched teeth, and I was certain I couldn't have lived a lifetime long enough to imagine anything hotter than this—except that we kept intense eye contact the whole time, and while it is thrilling to see a woman's eyes roll back in her head from pleasure, the eye contact with her during all of this was almost too much to bear.

When she finally asked me stop, I did as directed, but we continued to kiss, more slowly and deeply. Erica rolled out from under me, and got me laying on my side next to her, our mouths never leaving each other, except when she told me her plans for me. I wondered if two such very dirty girls actually got together, could they survive the explosion? I was betting no, and it seemed such a perfect solution, the two of us fucking each other to death in the woods. Could anyone blame us if we were dead from it? Everyone would see it couldn't have been helped, and that in the end (pardon the pun) we got what we deserved: fucking death.

Erica got me off this track by whispering against my mouth, "I'm completely in love with you. You know this, right?"

I nodded my head. I knew this.

But her saying it made me think of why we couldn't be together, and I would have gotten stuck on this thought if only she hadn't touched me then, slipping inside, to fuck away the last of my thoughts with her unreasonably strong hand. (There are such advantages to a woman's hand, to be able to go where no man could ever reach. Oh, yes, size does matter.) And, I was thinking now for the first time, there are advantages to a woman who can pound nails with a beautiful rhythm. And if she hadn't done it just right, taken me just that way, making me come so hard, just like that, I might not have lost my mind and said, "Erica . . . I love you. Of course I love you." And if I hadn't said that, then she might not have kissed me harder, still, and I might not have had to take her once again.

After, when we had both come back down to the earth that noticeably prickled with pine needles beneath us, I noticed the bonfire flickering far behind her had grown much smaller. I also had my first sane thought since she found me here, falling apart in the woods. I was so much saner then.

The bonfire was fading, but would this fire between us ever go out? Never. Not for me. Especially not now, not after this. Erica searched my eyes, and I could tell she was reading my thoughts. We would not die here, we would live, and in our lives was my brother, who I loved as much as life, easily as much as I loved Erica.

Oh fuck.

When she saw the flicker of fresh tears in my eyes and then I saw them on hers, I wondered if she had read all my thoughts. Erica proved she had by whispering, "I can't love anyone else. It will always be you." If she did read my thoughts, she would have known how thrilled this made me feel—but she would also have known how it didn't matter, not at all.

Twenty-Nine

Nobody Wants To Talk About The Pink Labia In The Room

When Lisa was in college, she saw a demonstration happening on the campus grounds. About seventy students, mostly female, were enthusiastically wielding protest signs and chanting, "Spread the word to end the word!" Not one to miss an opportunity to skip class (and possibly pick up a cute co-ed with perky breasts that bounced lightly in protest as she marched) Lisa worked the perimeter of the crowd like a Boarder Collie with an over-achievement complex.

Lisa's first move was to select what she deemed to be the weakest link and lure a blond girl away from her pack of friends. Who would expect a well-fed Border Collie with a big smile to be any kind of threat?

The girl, happy to have gained a new recruit, stepped aside to speak to Lisa, but not before Lisa showed her commitment by bellowing at the top of her lungs: "Spread the word to end the word! Spread the word to end the word!" Lisa was convinced her commitment to a cause, any cause, would be foreplay to do-gooder chicks. She poured on the charm with a fake-shy chuckle as she asked the girl, "I'm sorry, I'm going to sound retarded, but what's the word we're trying to end?"

The girl's smile faded as she said, "We are trying to end the word retarded."

Another time, when I made the tragic mistake of inviting Lisa to meet some of my work friends for a drink, she launched into a full-scale anatomy lesson with one of my older co-workers. The evening started out innocent enough. We were all enjoying our cocktails and getting a little loose, and of course Lisa had targeted the best looking of my straight co-workers: Sharon, a married lady, Catholic, with three children. At first I wasn't too worried, since I had taken the proper precautions and warned all the women before we ever got to the bar. They'd heard stories about Vince and Lisa, and encouraged me to invite them both. In fact, the women seemed to get a kick out of being openly flirted with by a potty-mouth butchy lesbian who knew no boundaries. It seemed innocent enough, but I kept an ear to Lisa's conversations, just in case she went to far.

The following is how the evening unraveled:

LISA: So, Sharon, tell me, ever experiment with women?
MARIE: Lisa . . .
SHARON *(laughing)*: Can't say that I have. Might be too late for me.
LISA: It's only eight-thirty.
MARIE: Lisa.
SHARON *(squirming in her seat, laughing)*: It's OK, Marie, I think your sister's a riot.
LISA: I'm dead serious. Why are you squirming like that, Sharon?
SHARON: I . . . didn't know I was.
LISA: Well, either you're getting all excited by the question, or you have something under your hood.
MARIE: Lisa!
SHARON: Under my, what?
MARIE: Lisa, shut it! Sharon, don't ask, I'm begging you.
LISA: Well, you should know when you get something trapped under your hood.
SHARON: Under my hood? I don't get it.
MARIE: Lisa, I swear, I'll kill you.
LISA: She needs to know this in order to avert a medical emergency.
VINCE: Oh God, you're not talking about—
LISA: Vince, don't you think Sharon needs to know?

VINCE: It won't make any difference what I think.
SHARON: My hood? You mean like, on my car?
MARIE: Lisa, seriously, I'm warning you.
SHARON: Or, like, a sweatshirt?
LISA: No, silly. Under your hood, where your clit lives.
MARIE: Lisa!
VINCE: I don't feel well. I want out.
SHARON *(horrified)*: Can that happen?
LISA: Maybe you have a super-tight hood. Good for you. You sure that hasn't happened to you?
SHARON: Would I know?
LISA: Oh, you'd know. *(Lisa elbows me and nods, as if we are drinking buddies in total agreement to get plastered and cheat on our wives.)* How old is she?
MARIE: Lisa, I swear to God . . .
SHARON *(faintly)*: I'm thirty-three . . .
LISA: It can happen when a pube goes rogue. So painful! Though I know most of you straight girls go completely shaved, so maybe you don't ever—
SHARON: I don't—
LISA: I'm glad to hear that, Sharon. Kind of creepy that little girl shaved look, if you ask me. That was started by the porn industry, you know. I think a woman is supposed to have a bit of hair down there.
MARIE: Lisa, I'm really gonna kill you.
LISA: Look, Sharon, I like you, and I can tell you're confused, so, I'll explain: A pube can get trapped under your hood and at first it might just make you squirm, like you're doing now, but then: Ouchie.
MARIE: Lisa, I work with these people!
LISA: It's kind of like how a clam makes a pearl, which is friggin' irritating to the poor clam. *(Lisa laughs.)* The worst is when you have to go clam digging to get it out.
SHARON *(more horrified)* : Clam digging?
LISA: It might be the only thing women don't ever talk about with each other.

VINCE: Not anymore.

LISA: Nobody wants to talk about the pink labia in the room . . .

MARIE: Lisa, you're leaving—*now!*

LISA: Sharon, you just give me a call if you ever need any help—

MARIE: Vince, get her out of here!

Lisa couldn't help herself. Inappropriate comments flew freely from her filter-free mouth, never failing to reach impact against the most damaging targets. That's why I avoided my sister after my confession about Erica. To limit the risk of running into her the next morning, I avoided the Dove restaurant by taking a long walk around the campground to get a count of still-occupied campsites.

It was early morning, and the thick mist was crawling low to the ground, imitating Lisa's mist machine after the last dinner seating. When I turned the corner near the safari field, I saw Erica and Uncle Freddie on a distant roof. Instead of approaching, I sat down at the base of a tree so I could watch them undetected. By her pose, hand on her hip, head cocked to the side, I could tell Erica was evaluating Uncle Freddie's roofing shingles, and by his pose, curled back, head lowered, arm pounding nails with a growing, steady rhythm, I could see he was trying to impress her. He finished and looked up at her, more like the silhouette of an awkward teenage boy than that of an elderly uncle. Erica crouched down to inspect his work. A shiver ran up my back as I imagined the view from above her as she crouched.

For a few tense seconds, my Uncle's frozen and hopeful pose stayed motionless. She popped back up and gave a quick nod of her head as Uncle Freddie slapped his leg in attaboy recognition of his own accomplishment. By Erica's tone, I knew she was warning him not to get cocky, and this was confirmed when Uncle Freddie's wheezy laugh floated across the field.

They talked a bit more and Uncle Freddie said something that made Erica laugh, and I wished I was closer, to hear the sound more clearly. When she affectionately slapped him on the back and left her hand on his shoulder, my throat tightened with the (lately, familiar) feeling I might burst into tears. Images of last night flooded over me again, leaving me too weak to be on my way, so I leaned back against the base of the tree and let the sight of her pull me further apart.

After Uncle Freddie climbed down from the rooftop, I waited for Erica to do the same. I wondered if she would bother with the ladder at all, as was her habit if at all possible. But Erica didn't leave the roof. Instead she stood, silhouetted in the early sun, looking over the horizon at the woods surrounding the camp, and then she looked down. I wondered if she thought of our kiss when she was on a roof, but dismissed this, knowing she was on many roofs. Then I wondered if she was checking Uncle Freddie's work again, but when she crouched low, finally sitting on the roof with her back still to me, she was not checking the roof. She hung her head lower, then cradled her face in her knees. From a distance I could see her back moving sharply and my heart ached, knowing she was crying. Tears filled my eyes, turning her silhouette into a shimmering watercolor painting, against the red sunrise. More than anything, I wanted to go to her.

I wanted to climb the ladder, walk across the rooftop, and lift her face to kiss her until all her tears were gone. But I didn't allow myself to move a muscle, not even to brush the tears that rolled down my cheeks. I sat on the ground, pulling my legs up just as she was, hugging them tightly with my knees under my chin. Erica, please stop crying, I begged her silently, please. Then Erica lifted her head, as if someone had called out to her. She slowly twisted her body around, until she was turned toward me. Had she felt me? Now she saw me, but neither of us moved. All that space between us, but we didn't move because there was nowhere for us to go. I stayed watching her, my heart pounding loudly in my chest, screaming at me to get closer to her, until a member of her crew called her away, leaving an empty roof, and my empty heart.

When my brother came back from his weekend, he disappeared shortly after, and I didn't see him or Erica again for the next few days. The sickening pain of it took residence in my stomach as I constantly weighed which was worse: seeing her and not being able to have her, or not seeing her, knowing she was with my brother, trying to make a go of it with him—as I had asked. After a while, I decided that not seeing her was far worse, since what I imagined she was doing nearly choked the life out of me.

The camp season was winding down, and everyday another few trailers would be buttoned up for the winter or hauled past the Tap Box Lightly sign at the gate, the drivers giving a series of waves and polite short beeps, which promised they would be back the following spring. Mom and Dad came by only once on the weekends, mainly just for the drive. Uncle Freddie talked about visiting Italy this winter, and possibly staying until there was more work to be done at the camp in the spring.

It was a particularly chilly day and I saw Lisa standing at the gate, talking to one of the year-round renters. She saw me and gave a quick goodbye to the man as he was heading out, and turned away from me toward the guard shack. I was baffled, since there was never any real camp business to do in the guard shack since she'd gotten to know the town and abandoned the idea of posting any security detail.

I realized that Lisa, like Erica, was avoiding me. I called out and she stopped as if she had been caught. She turned and reluctantly walked over to me. She knew by the *what the fuck* look on my face that I wanted an explanation, and when we reached each other, she gave me one.

"I don't want to know what I know," she said.

I said, fearfully, "Me either."

"I know you don't want to hear this, but Vince is happy. Maybe happier than I've ever seen him," she said.

"Don't you think I want that for him?" I asked. "That's why I stopped it. For him."

I tried to remember when I had ever seen Lisa look so serious for so long, but I came up with nothing. And it was more than that: she looked angry. Our eyes locked and she had the same look she had when we'd fought in a pool as pre-teens and both ended up with ripped bathing suits down to our waists, each with our adolescent boobs in full view of our neighbors, who came out to witness the screaming. It would have made the perfect poster for teaching the importance of going for a win/win in an argument.

"It's not going to work with them," she said.

I said, "It might. You said yourself Vince is happy."

"It's not going to work. Erica just hasn't told him yet," she said. "He's going to be crushed. Again."

"She wants to love him," I said, but even as I said it I realized how ridiculous it sounded. Nobody in love ever has to say they *want* to love somebody.

Lisa unleashed her anger at me. "Really? Did she want to love him the night of the bonfire?"

Oh, God.

I looked at the ground between my feet, wishing it would open up and swallow me as Lisa yelled at me. "I hate this! I hate that I know it's over between them and he has no friggin' idea!"

"Listen, I made a mistake that night, but I told her I couldn't be with her, and we haven't talked since. She probably hates me, and I deserve it." I took a breath, then blurted, "Please don't tell Vince. I couldn't stand it if he knew."

"He'll know soon enough. She's gone."

"What?" I said, now feeling the ground actually opening up at my feet to swallow me up.

"She said she needed to go back to California to tie up loose ends with her business, and she told me to tell Vince. The saddest part is, he's not the least bit worried about her not coming back. He has no clue she is gone for good."

My head was spinning. "Maybe she just needs some time," I said, actually hopeful, forgetting everything I wanted, knowing, as Lisa did, that it would destroy Vince when she didn't return, just like I was being destroyed. On top of it all, I didn't want my little brother to go through what I was.

Lisa shook her head at me. Finally she said, "She's in love with you. I should have known when she first came back here. She didn't come back for Vince, and she sure as shit didn't come back for this job."

"There's nothing between us now."

She shook her head again. "There is. Go take a walk on the piece of land I gave you, you'll see. Erica insisted—" Lisa slapped her forehead with her hand. "God, how the fuck did I not know? It should have been so obvious!"

"What? What did she do?"

Lisa raised her voice again, "I can forget about what she did. What I can't forget about is what *you* did! The three of us have screwed up a lot of relationships, but we never, ever did something like this to each other!"

I stood paralyzed as Lisa turned and walked away from me, mumbling to herself, "I fucking hate knowing this."

"I hate knowing it too," I said, but Lisa had already gone.

I stayed standing in the middle of the street like an idiot, until a group of teenagers used the camp entrance to turn their car around and nearly ran me over. After the car screeched off, leaving me unpunished for my sins, I regretted the car had not made me a hood ornament by plowing into me. And worse, I regretted being so much more irritating and painful to my sister than a rogue pube.

Thirty

Why Some Things Are Wrapped In Plastic

It was getting much too late for a long walk in the woods, but I went anyway. I'd seen the piece of land Lisa had given me only on the first day we'd toured the camp, so, on top of all my other worries, I was concerned that even if I could find my way there, I might not find my way back. The light was fading quickly, so I tried to comfort myself by whispering stupid questions up to the trees.

"Will I find my way back?" I asked. The trees swayed yes in a heavy breezy. I pushed my luck, "Will Vince and Erica stay together?" The trees stilled to a negative, creepy silence. "Will Vince be happy again?" My heart lifted as the wind kicked up above me and the treetops swayed gently back and forth, in a definite, cheerful yes. He would be happy again, I told myself; of course he would be.

I walked farther, working up the courage to ask, "Will Erica and I ever find love again?" The wind picked up in the distance, and as it approached, the sky above me filled with the sound of trees celebrating an emphatic yes. It made me feel better, just as it used to when I was a kid. And, just as I did when I was a kid, I hedged my bets and stopped asking questions for fear I wouldn't like the next answer. Except for my choices with women, quitting while I was ahead was something I understood, and, as I trudged through the woods, I wondered if, had I not inherited money, I could have made a good living playing cards.

I was still looking up at the trees, considering other questions worth gambling on, so when I saw it, it took me completely by surprise, and I stopped dead in my tracks. Off in the distance, where just a few months ago it had been only wilderness, there stood a perfect little log cabin in the woods. Even from the obstructed view in the trees where I stood, I could see it was built in my favorite style, with high loft ceilings and a low area of the roof that overhang the front door. The dark logs were filled in-between with a white sealant I had told Erica I loved long ago because it reminded me of a gingerbread house from a childhood book my dad used to read to Lisa and me. This was something I confessed over drinks one night. She had at the time acted aloof, in the cool Erica-way she had when you shared something a bit too personal. I assumed she was too preoccupied with budgets, client billing, my brother, or maybe the wine we were sharing to really hear me.

She had heard me. Slowly it sank in.

Erica had built me a perfect log cabin home in the woods.

I couldn't ignore my body getting the best of me as I walked toward it, as I noticed all the details she'd added, all the details for which I had complimented during our time together looking over photos in her portfolio. Other details I had revealed closer to the end of our business partnership, and one, she revealed to me one night over several glasses of Brunello wine. Erica had been lit enough to say something warm and fuzzy, shocking me at the time. She said her dream was simple: to build the perfect home for the person she loved. At the time, I had been a bit drunk on the wine as well, and I laughed at her, but I had been so happy for my brother. At the time, I had no idea that I was the one in her heart. Maybe she didn't realize it then, either.

She had built me my dream house, complete with a small front porch, built with the sole purpose of having a place to put the two identical antique rocking chairs, bookends on either side of the porch, facing the brook.

I quickened my pace, but my wild heartbeat was not from the walk. I loved Erica, and she loved me. She was not a woman who expressed her thoughts well in words, but she had built this beautiful home as a monument to what she felt—right down to hollowing out the small window box logs and filling them only with warm colored mums. Not a dreaded purple-colored flower among the group. I hated purple. She'd heard that too. I was amazed by modern skylights set beautifully in a roof with a charming rustic design, the front door the exact warm wood stain she knew I preferred (the one I always wanted to use, despite what her client wanted) and except for a sweet little pathway, the landscaping was left raw and natural, to blend with the woods, just as I would have wanted.

And this was when I knew the trees had been wrong. We would both never find a love like this again; a love that could inspire and build something as perfect as this.

I walked up the steps onto the porch. The wood made a soft creaking sound like music beneath my feet. (Had she orchestrated that too? I imagined her doing her roof walk, only this time on a porch, instructing the workers to nail and loosen boards to create just the right sounds, since I had told her a porch should make creaks as you walk on it.) I knew the door would be locked, and I knew where the key would be. Erica and I had worked on many houses together, and when there was an actual key to share, and not just a code, we would always leave it under the closest shiny object nearest to the front door.

In the corner of the porch was a small grouping of decorative tin milk jugs, and I lifted the shiniest one to find two keys on an oversized ring. The standard key was for the contemporary deadbolt, but the other, a beautiful antique pewter skeleton key, was for the keyhole under the antique doorknob. She knew I loved skeleton keys.

I released the deadbolt first, and then slid the skeleton key into the door, and it made the most perfect trio of clicks as it released the lock. And when I pushed open the door, a shiver ran through my body as the smell of the place washed over me. It smelled like a well-kept library. The combination of the logs, knotty pine, and other woods made my head feel like I had just pleasantly huffed some varnish.

I flicked on the light switch by the door, which illuminated beautiful light fixtures, with thick glass hurricanes shielding light bulbs that flickered like candles. I drank in the sight of the place with watery vision. A stone fireplace took up one entire wall of the living room, the stones left natural and uncut, a stark contrast to the wood floor, which gleamed with fresh varnish. Erica had created a built-in table against the wall under a large set of multi-paned windows. My eyes burned and my throat tightened at the sight of this perfect spot to share meals with her—if she were mine, if this were our place to share, and if I could actually share a meal with her instead of devouring her.

There was a pair of hammered pewter candlesticks on the table, the kind Scrooge would have, with a cradle for your thumb for easy carrying, holding cream-colored taper candles, already burned to achieve dripping on the sides. I touched the tip of the blackened wick where Erica had lit the candles and saw next to them a box of long wooden matches. (She told me once that her grandmother believed it was poor taste to display candles with unburned wicks, and our last tradition as we finished a house was to burn the tips of all the new candles we bought for any new house we had finished.)

I walked across the room to an expansive kitchen with a center island with six burners and a black wrought-iron pot rack hanging from the ceiling above it. There were several old heavy cast-iron pans hanging on the pot rack, as if many meals had already been prepared in the warm kitchen, and I was passing through someone's happy home like a sad little ghost, padding around the rooms in my socks. (I had slipped off my muddy shoes at the sight of that perfect floor.)

I walked through the kitchen as if in a dream and found a second back staircase leading to the loft. I touched the smooth hand railing and the tongue in grove knotty pine boards that lined both sides of the stairwell. Erica knew how much I loved knotty pine—and teased me about how lumberjack-dykey it was. When I reached the upstairs, the sight took my breath away. The loft-style master bedroom had vaulted ceilings with exposed beams between each skylight, offering a perfect view of the starry evening sky and the tops of the surrounding trees. But, worse than that, much worse, was that there was already a bed.

Not just any bed, but an antique four-poster bed, centered under the highest point of the slanted ceilings. White gauzy curtains hung from the frame between the posts, around a mattress still sealed in plastic, and a plush blanket at the foot of the bed. Had Erica guessed

I would love the house so much that I would need to sleep there the first time I saw it?

I took off my jacket and balled it up before sitting on the bed. I realized I was crying for her again, and my exhaustion shoved me down on the bed—a bed I knew I would never share with her. Grateful for plastic-covered mattress, I pulled the blanket over me, laid my head down, and drifted as I felt the tears pool around my face, unabsorbed by the plastic.

Seconds later, I heard my sister downstairs. The thought occurred to me that Lisa may have been here a dozen times without me knowing; the house was so far away from the main trails of Camptown Ladies that you would never stumble upon it unless you went looking. After seeing the log cabin, Lisa knew what Erica felt for me, and had I seen it, or her plans for it, I would have known too. I heard Lisa drop her keys on the table before climbing the stairs. I braced myself for disappointing her again, but couldn't find the strength to wipe the tears from my eyes as I sat up.

Just as I thought Lisa's footsteps sounded too quick, too light, and I wondered if an intruder had slipped into the place, Erica appeared in the dim light of the hallway, and I gasped at the sight of her. She had grabbed the metal poker from the fire and had it raised above her head, ready to bash in the head of what she thought might be an intruder.

We both wore the same expression—alarm and panic, which turned to raw emotion. The sight of her brought overwhelming joy and sadness in equal parts. I let out a breath, not sure for a moment if I had been dreaming, not sure if she was really there. As she dropped the fire poker, the clang of it hitting the floor was a loud confirmation; she was really there. She walked into the bedroom and came toward me as I drank in the smell of her, even from the doorway, and the perfect little log cabin disappeared around me as it only could in it's creator's company.

I'd thought of nothing but her since our night in the woods, and Lisa had just convinced me hours ago that I might never see her again. And, finally, I had convinced myself that it was for the best. And now, she was here.

Maybe if she had walked over and grabbed me, I might have been able to resist her. I might have had a chance of pushing her away, remembering how hard it was to regain my sanity after being so close to her, after having her. But she didn't touch me. Instead, she came over to the bed and knelt down in front of me, her worried expression like that of a child who lost her puppy, and she said, fearfully, "Do you love it? I want so much for you to love it, even though I can't be with you here." Then her eyes filled as she searched my eyes, my silence distressing her as she asked again, "Do you love it? I need for you to love it."

She wasn't asking to be with me, not fighting what she knew we couldn't have, only asking if I loved what she had built for me. It would have been downright diabolical, if she had not been so tragically and completely sincere.

And there was nothing for me to do but to reach for her then, pulling her up off her knees, feeling her hesitate and make a tiny whimper (a sound that was so unlike any sound that should come from this woman) as my face came close to hers. Then, knowing I was so completely lost, my mouth had nowhere to go but to sink into her lips, and the blinding warmth and softness of her stripped away what remained, if anything, of my sanity, and all I could think of was having her again.

Somewhere in our long and frenzied kiss, I told her, "I love it here, I love you," and I tried to warn her with a whisper, "We just . . ." but she covered my mouth with hers and swallowed my words, and I didn't try to warn her again. Then, when my breathing was so heavy and she knew I couldn't speak, she pulled away to whisper into my ear, "I'm leaving tomorrow. I can't be near you anymore."

My stomach was falling into a pit a mile below earth, and I wanted to hang on to her. I wanted to stop her. I kissed her, hard, and this time she pulled away.

"I told your sister," she said, "and I should have told Vince, but I couldn't. I can't love him. Not with you here. Maybe if I leave, someday I'll be able to love someone—" She stopped, maybe seeing how the words crushed me. Love someone else?

She seemed to register the pain I was feeling and she kissed me back, harder than before. I took her face in my hands and in desperation, mixed with a senseless passion, I kept hold of her and considered telling her not to leave. But what would I say? *Please stay so we can continue to torture each other? Or worse, Stay so my brother will be led on to greater pain when he finally found out about us? It would be crazy to think we could hide this—especially now, with this house.*

But Erica stopped my thoughts with the heat of her mouth as it trailed from my lips to my ear, then to my neck, and I realized where I wanted her to go next. I realized, too, there must be no proper place for me other than hell, and if I was going to hell, then I might as well be totally fucked. I loved this woman. I didn't care anymore. I didn't care what happened after this. I pulled her onto the bed with me.

I found myself in two places at once. I was back with her the first time in the woods, and with her now, the perfect scent of her coming back to me in full detail (how had I forgotten so much?), remembering the feel of her skin and the sounds she made. I was remembering what it had been like to have her then, and the sublime feeling of what it felt to have her now. It was too much. It was just right. It was not enough. It would never be.

I was so lost in kissing her and the feel of her body once again under mine, that I wasn't aware she had slid her hand down the back of my pants until she was digging her nails into my backside, deftly sliding one hand around my hip to land between my legs. She snaked her fingers under my underwear then, and when she reached me, I let out what sounded like a cry for help. *Nobody is going to help you now, Marie.* Erica gasped as well when she realized how ridiculously hungry I was for her, and she managed to pull me up higher so she could get her hand inside, and I heard my zipper buzz and bust wide open from the strain (or I hoped it was that.) Oh. My. God.

I imagined a switch being flipped on Willy Wonka's candy machine, causing an automated motion of movement of only two speeds: zero or one hundred. I was immediately at one hundred, lacking no buildup at all, the electric current of her touch sending me into a rage of pushing against her, until she had completely filled me. I cried out, and she cried with me, telling me to come for her, that she would not stop taking me like that until I came again, and she kept her word.

Finally, I had to arch my back to pull her hand from inside me (her experience too new at this lesbo sex thing to know that my last two cries were delirious pleas for her to stop before she might kill me with pleasure). It was maddening, but this made me more starved for her, and I roughly tore her clothes from her body as she looked up at me, breathing marathon style, as I exposed first one breast, than the other. Her chest rose toward and away from me with breathing. It was everything I could do to keep my concentration so I could completely undress her, and when I had, I had no patience left to undress myself. So, this was how I took her, with me fully clothed (only my zipper sprung) totally getting off on the erotic contrast of the complete nakedness of her, against the fully dressed-ness of me.

I wrapped my lips around her nipple, all the while watching her face, seeing the color rush to the light skin of her face, and noticed the harder I kissed her there, the wider she parted her mouth. By the time I had settled into a rhythm between tracing her nipple with my tongue like it was a circular racetrack, digging in extra hard between every third lap, her lips had opened wide to form that silent and perfect "O" shape And I was getting off on the sexual Erica, the Erica that could look surprised and out of control like that, the woman I hardly knew, and might never fully know. Although her lips formed the perfect "O," instead she said, "I love you," as her head tossed from left to right, and I dragged my lips across her chest like a starved animal with an inexplicable sweet tooth that could not chose between two of the most tantalizing cupcakes served on the most beautiful buffet laid out before me.

What was the point of holding back now, I thought, as I said, "And I love you," and I indelicately showed her this by grabbing both her hands and pinning them to the bed as if she had been resisting. Something about being fully dressed made me want to hold her down like that, and I saw a flash in her eyes that told me this made her more desperate for me. So I kissed down from her breasts, across the length of her body, and I never let go of her wrists, bringing them with me, as she softly cried out in frantic anticipation. She needn't have worried, since I had no intention or willpower to tease her slowly once arriving at the center of her.

My plan was to latch on to her *there,* and feed on her until her mouth formed that "O" again, but this time I would make sure the "O" would not be silent. I coached myself to take her, hard at first, but just for a second, like announcing your presence by slamming a fucking door. *I am here.* But then, since I owned the equipment myself (and isn't that just the huge advantage of being a lesbo?), I backed off and sucked on her so softly, almost not sucking at all, but just keeping my lips around her to make her insanely want it, need it, but Erica's hands somehow broke free from my grip and now were on the back of my head, pushing me harder against her; I should have known it was ridiculous to think I could direct this entire job. The contractor was ready. I took her the way she needed me to.

"Don't stop," she commanded. Not if I ever wanted to work here again, I thought. Once again, the thought entered my mind that I wanted to die right here.

First a stillness came over her, then came the tidal wave of her coming as she let go of my head to slam the mattress with both hands in a loud, open slaps against the plastic, as if she was now announcing *her* presence. *I am fucking, here!*

It would have been easier if I had died right then, at the moment of pure heaven, or pure hell, whichever was the case. Besides, I had no other logical plans for my life after what we were doing. But then I imagined my mother's horrified reaction, not of my death but of the newspaper photo of my face planted in the crotch of the gorgeous Camptown Ladies' contractor, and the headline: "Lesbian Dies While Eating In Log Cabin."

Gradually, I felt Erica's body coming back down to earth, but she wasn't relaxing. I could feel an uneasy stiffness settle within her body. I crawled up so I could hold on to the middle of her, the side of my face pressed tightly to her stomach, still able to breathe in the delicious scent of her, and then I felt her belly tighten, and I knew without looking up that she was crying. What have I done to this woman? I was thinking this as I tightened my hold on her. Besides my sister, this is the strongest woman I had ever known and I had reduced her to tears more times in the last few months than I could count. She's supposed to be mine, I thought. Mine. I needed to stop this. I needed to fix this.

"I'm going with you," I said, but this just made her stomach tense harder. I tightened my arms around her, but I didn't look up at her so she couldn't see the fear in my eyes. "I mean it. I'm going with you. We'll disappear together."

The trees had been right in their leafy Magic 8 Ball prediction. Erica and I had both found happiness again. But the damned trees hadn't been specific about how long this happiness would last. When I woke up, she was gone, and I was left disoriented from the fresh memory of her. I wanted to go back to my dreams—to before that time, where the betrayal of my brother didn't exist at all, and all my memories were buried by the blinding pleasure of being with her.

I found a note she'd left for me on the bed, written on the back of a torn envelope. It was not Erica's style to overstate what we already covered, so she wrote only two sentences:

I love you, but not more than you should love your family and I only wish you will consider living here, since I loved building this home for you. Erica

I sat on the edge of the bed, wanting more than anything to be able to tell her at least one of her wishes had come true: from the moment I saw the cabin in the woods, I knew it would be my home.

Thirty-One

Guess Who's Coming To Dinner

Lisa found me at the log cabin the following day. It was late afternoon and I was starving, but I had been unwilling to leave for fear the memories would fade, though they showed no signs. Lisa didn't question why I was at the cabin. She just informed me, like I was being served papers from a criminal court, that Vince had left a message at the condo to ask if we could get the whole family together tonight for dinner.

"He says he has something important to talk to us about," Lisa said.

I winced. "If he doesn't think we know they're seeing each other again, why would he call us together to tell us Erica left?"

She studied me, and I saw that she was no longer angry. It was far worse. I saw pity in her eyes. She spoke so gently that I braced myself for what was next, but it turned out bracing myself was not enough. Lisa said, "It's not that. He said he and Erica would be at our place by 7:00." I had to sit down, and since there were no chairs, I sat on the floor.

Lisa sat down next to me and did just the right thing. She said nothing.

Mom and Dad arrived early as usual, and Lisa and I busied ourselves with arranging the table with take-out Chinese food. Lisa saw my hands shaking as I opened the carton of rice and she took it from me before I could spill any more of it. It was almost 7:00 and my stomach was queasy from the smell of food, but it wasn't until mom wondered if Erica was pregnant that I had to excuse myself to the bathroom to throw up what Lisa had forced me to eat for lunch. I came back, pale and sweaty, but relieved that Mom and Dad were too busy sampling the food to notice I was a quarter of a pound lighter than when I was last in the room.

A few minutes later, we heard Vince pull into the driveway. A small yelp may have escaped me, but luckily it was identical to one Cindy-Lu let out, so everyone looked at the dog, except Lisa, who was watching me. Mom and Dad went to greet them at the door and as soon as they were out of earshot, Lisa leaned over to me to coo a bit of sisterly advice into my ear, "Erica found a way to handle this, so you need to fucking chill!"

I nodded at her numbly, feeling another wave of nausea pass over me.

"Go wash your face again, you look like you're gonna puke again," she said, and I gladly took my escape from the kitchen to the bathroom.

I locked the bathroom door behind me and leaned against it. How could Erica think coming here was a good idea right after we had been together? Worse, how could I sit across a table from my brother and her?

Then, a more horrifying thought occurred to me. Maybe this was Erica's way of blowing the whole thing wide open? Maybe it was Vince who didn't know what he was walking into. I tried to talk myself off the ledge. No, Erica understood how much I loved Vince, and she wouldn't do that to me or to him.

Another thought raced across my mind, which seemed more plausible. Maybe Erica wanted me to see them together. Erica holding my brother's hand, talking about their future, Vince giving her a kiss as he affectionately touches her hair. I felt my stomach lurch again and took some deep breaths. Maybe Erica thought that if I saw him with his arm wrapped possessively around the woman I loved, it would make me have to do something. Then came the worst dread of all: the way my heart was pounding with fierce jealousy, that crazy plan just might work.

I washed my face and took more deep breaths as I tried my best to repair the makeup that had smeared under my eyes. When I opened the bathroom door, I could hear voices getting animated out in the living room as I walked unsteadily down the hallway. Before I turned the corner, I heard Vince's voice, "As soon as we clear up this other big mess, next year, we're going to get married."

My legs went weak. I couldn't go in. I braced myself against the wall where no one could see me.

Vince yelled out, "Marie, where are you? You're missing this!"

I held on to the wall with my sweaty hand as I turned the corner. I saw Vince's face, happy as I have ever seen him, Mom and Dad blocking Erica from my view as they hugged him, then Lisa's face, turning to me, her eyes bulging out of her head, totally freaking out. Mom and Dad stepped away so I was face to face with Katie looking back at me.

Vince had his arm wrapped affectionately around Katie, Buddy's mother, while Buddy was playing on the floor with a toy truck. I blinked hard, yet Katie still wasn't turning into Erica. I stupidly looked around for her.

Lisa walked over to me, inches from my face so she was blocking my expression from the view of the room. She talked to me as if I was totally stoned or had just failed kindergarten or had failed kindergarten because I was totally stoned.

"Marie, I told you there was something going on with Vince and Katie, didn't I?" Lisa was nodding her head as a signal for me to agree with her, but even her subtle-as-a-sledgehammer way could not ease me through my shock.

"Where's Erica?" I mumbled.

Vince looked at me with raised eyebrows. "Well, that's awkward, Mare. Thanks, for bringing up an ex-girlfriend in front of my beautiful fiancé." He gave Katie an apologetic hug as she smiled affably at him.

I still wasn't getting it, and Lisa was losing patience with me, which put us all in great danger of Lisa making it all crystal clear as only she can do. I said to Vince, "But, you said you were bringing—"

Lisa interrupted "He said he was bringing a girl he's been secretly dating," Lisa interrupted, "and Vince has been dating Katie."

"But, why did you hide this from us?" I said.

More confusing than this, while Katie seemed lovely, how could anyone on earth ever love another woman after Erica?

Vince lowered his voice so Buddy couldn't hear him, "Katie is trying to get her husband to sign some papers, so we were keeping this quiet. You all assumed I was seeing Erica, so it was easy, especially with Erica avoiding me like the plague."

It was sinking in at last. Vince wasn't with Erica. He hadn't been with her all this time. Before I could think about how it would sound in front of Katie, I blurted out, "You're not in love with Erica?"

Vince said, "Sorry about this, Katie, my sister is a little retarded today."

"Spread the word to end the word," Lisa said.

Then Vince walked over to me and hissed, "What the hell is wrong with you?"

Where would I even begin to answer that question? When I didn't answer him, Vince said, "I've barely seen Erica in months. I assumed she was seeing someone else."

I said in a shrill and shaking voice, "And we assumed she was seeing you."

Vince laughed at me.

"What the hell is so funny?" I asked, still stunned.

Vince said, "When you didn't get back with Lorn, I wondered if it was because of Erica. She obviously didn't come back for me, so I backed off. Lucky I did, so I could fall in love with Katie, and this little guy too." At that, he smiled down at Buddy.

Lisa looked back and forth from me to Vince and back again and yelled, "Holy shit! You both backed off from Erica for each other—how *fucking romantic!* This is just like the *Gift of the Magi*—only with pussy!"

The world had almost righted itself, my brother was in love, I was in love, and it was not with the same person. One day all was lost, and now there was hope. There was only one problem: Erica had closed up her apartment and she was not answering any calls. She had left, and because money was no object (and I was so in love I couldn't see straight) I booked the first available flight to California to find her.

Lisa thought I was crazy, but she helped me pack a bag anyway, and drove like a madwoman to get me to the airport for a flight time that was a bit ambitious. As my sister careened us across town toward the airport, with me wincing and covering my eyes from several near-missed collisions, Lisa revealed she had concocted a plan to get Katie free of her ex-husband so Vince could marry her.

"Oh, God," I said, both from another near miss and from whatever her next crazy plan could be. "What are you going to do, have him put in a dumpster?"

"That would be stupid," she said, staring at the road as if it were a video game. "Always better to use several dumpsters."

"Ah," I said.

"Tempting idea, but I'm working on a plan that's much simpler."

There was no use arguing with Lisa. After all, this was a woman who'd bought an unprofitable campground after looking at a few photographs and was now getting write-ups on her restaurant from the most respected food blogs all over the web. While her idea had seemed crazy at the time, next year we would either have to either turn campers away or expand the campground.

We arrived in time for my flight and Lisa pulled up in front of the airport with a screech. She grabbed my arm before I could hop out of the car. "Hey, I'm sorry about before. You know, for being so pissed with you."

I smacked her hand hard on the back of her knuckles, like when we were kids, and said, "I get it. You were just protecting our wimpy little brother."

She smiled and said, "He's not tough like us." Then we hugged with our tradition of slapping each other hard ridiculously hard on the back (until I yelped) and then I hurried off. Lisa yelled over the crowds, "Good luck bagging our brother's ex-girlfriend!" Then she yelled, "Ew! Have you ever thought that the two of you have both—"

"Shut it!" I yelled back, but I couldn't help laughing as I ran with my bag toward the door.

I drifted in and out of sleep on the plane, waking every time I remembered names of people or clients she had mentioned, or that I had met. Since most of her clients had been well-known actors, I knew there were very few I would be able to contact. "Excuse me, Mr. Nicholson, have you seen your contractor this week? I drifted off again after counting Hollywood sheep outfitted with fake tans, teeth, and, most horribly, tits.

What seemed like just minutes later, I awoke on the plane. Only it had been hours, and I was not on my way to LA as I had dreamt. I had already spent a full week searching for Erica, only to come up with nothing. I had been dreaming of how hopeful I was when I had first flown out to find her. Now I was on my way back home with the full realization that Erica was not a woman who wanted to be found.

Thirty-Two

Sometimes Your Best Insurance Is In Your Bra

"I'm sick of you moping around. You're coming with me," Lisa announced, as she grabbed my arm and walked me to her car like a criminal. Who was I to argue? With winter coming and so little to do at Camptown Ladies, I had been moping around for weeks.

"Where are we going?"

She didn't answer until she had backed up and pulled out of the Camp and her car doors had clicked with their automatic locks. I hoped it was just a creepy coincidence, but my Spidey senses were rarely wrong, so I looked back longingly at the safety of the campground as Lisa pulled away with me, leaving a cloud of dust and gravel, *Thelma and Louise*-style.

I asked again, "Hello? I asked where are we going?"

Lisa was grinning like a twelve-year-old boy who's just typed the word "boobies" on his computer. She said, "We're going to get Katie's ex-husband to sign some divorce papers, then I thought we'd grab some lunch."

"Oh, no, we aren't!" I said.

"OK. If you already ate, we could just get a drink after," she said.

"Sure, after we stick our noses where they don't belong and get our asses kicked by some lunatic ex-husband. How do you plan to pull this off, and does Vince know?"

"I got the papers from Katie," she said, "Vince doesn't need to know until after it's done."

"Excellent," I said, following with the most rhetorical question you could ever ask my sister: "Are you fucking crazy?"

Lisa said, "We were just hanging out last night and Katie left the papers out on her counter. She's still probably sleeping off the tequila shots I gave her and I'm betting she won't miss them before I can bring them back signed."

My mouth dropped open. "You stole the papers from her trailer."

When she didn't deny it, I slapped my own forehead. "Jesus, Lisa! Katie told Vince this guy has a temper—he's not going to sign, and how do you know he won't do something more crazy than what you did?"

"Who would do something more crazy than me?"

She had a point. Lisa looked over at me with her cocky smile and winked as she said, "Don't worry, I have a secret weapon. He'll sign."

When Lisa says, "Don't worry," anyone within the tri-state area should do exactly the opposite. As she drove into the next town, I was worried—very worried, and her unusual silence as she drove made me more so. She looked serious, and I especially got concerned when another car cut her off and she didn't pound her steering wheel and scream out her usual: "Cock in your ass, douchebag!" Was she feeling fragile? I was worried for my sister, but, truth be told, I was more worried for myself.

When she pulled into a large parking lot in the center of town, Lisa had a huge smile on her face again, and she laughed as I realized we were parking in front of a police station. I grabbed her arm, "Oh, my God. You're going to report him to the police? What the hell do you have on this guy?"

She pulled a large envelope from under her car seat. "You'll see."

Then she slid out of the car and I followed as I asked, "Did you hire a private investigator? Does he have a criminal record? Wait! Do you have pictures of him with a donkey? Did you hire the donkey?" She laughed and didn't answer me, and instead, she made a beeline for the door.

As I followed her, I thought about how my sister could be hazardously impulsive. Of course there were more times when she acted down right outrageous, but there were also times when she handled things with such authority that the world just stepped in line for her, or, more smartly, cleared the fuck out of her way. I hoped this was one of those times.

Lisa marched across the station lobby to the front desk and I imagined if there were a crowd, she would have parted them with her sheer will, like a dyke Moses—if Moses wore a Boston Red Sox hat and blue Nike sandals in the New England cold. Behind the desk a large-busted woman with big hair and a kind smile asked how she could help us, and Lisa removed her baseball cap in chivalrous tribute to the woman's ample jugs.

"I called ahead," Lisa said, as if she were picking up a pizza. "Officer Williams is expecting us." When the woman leaned down to dial the switchboard, I saw Lisa help herself to a long look down the front of her shirt.

In just a few minutes, a meticulously groomed police officer popped his head around the corner. "Ms. Santora?" We both answered yes.

"I'm Lisa Santora," my sister said, sticking her hand out over the counter. She shook his hand in her usual hard grip and I saw the mildly intimidated expression I had seen in a thousand straight guys when they first met Lisa. Typically, this ended when she bonded with them by analyzing every detail of the offense of any given New England sports team. Lisa could non-sexually charm the balls off of most men this way, and you could see them thinking, *If only I'd had a sister like* this *growing up.*

"I'm Officer Williams. Come right this way," he said, buzzing us in. Lisa paused to wink at the woman behind the desk before following him. The woman looked concerned, as if Lisa had something caught in her eye. (She had no idea it was her breasts.)

"I'll wait out here," I said, hanging back.

The police officer said to me, "You can join us if you want." Then he turned to Lisa and said, "Unless Ms. Santora prefers we meet in private."

"This is Marie, my sister, and she's coming with us," Lisa said, grabbing my elbow. The police officer led us to his office, and, on his way, turned to ask me, "Traffic still bad out there?"

"Not bad at all," I said, put at ease by the way he smiled, like he might be interested in more than my traffic report. When a guy flirts, I always feel it levels the playing field. He may be a handsome cop in a position of authority, but I had the mighty vagina—and the added power (often intoxicating to men) that I didn't give a flying shit if he noticed me or not. I didn't know shit about football, but it's a known fact that boobs and vay-jay-jay could be just as effective as knowing New England Patriots offense when bonding with men.

Lisa didn't miss this and raised her eyebrows at me behind his back. When we turned the corner, she said into my ear, "What a cutie—why don't you give the dick a try!" I was able to pinch her tit before we entered his office, and was surprised to feel she was actually wearing a bra. Wow, this was serious.

He offered us seats in his office and sat behind his desk, folding his hands like a first-year teacher as he flashed a smile my way again. My first impression was he was charming and likable, and it might have been worth a date if I didn't so faithfully stick to my rule to avoid any penis I can't pack in a carry-on suitcase. I also reminded myself that my first impressions about men were often wrong, but he had a lot of pictures on his desk, which likely meant he was a family man who was harmlessly flexing his flirting skills.

"So, what can I help you with, Ms. Santora," he said to Lisa, glancing down at his notebook. "You mentioned on your initial call that you were concerned about a friend who is being threatened by her husband?"

"That's correct, and please, call me Lisa," she said, with a smugness that made me worry again.

"OK, Lisa, would this friend be willing to come in and file a report?"

"Oh, I doubt that," Lisa said. "It's kind of messy. There's a kid involved, and this guy is a real—can I say asshole in here?" Officer Williams smirked at her, and Lisa took that as a yes, so she launched into more involved description. "He also has a bitch of a temper. A real douchebag by all accounts."

When the police officer asked if she had been a witness to any of his threats, Lisa answered, "Oh no, he's a fairly smart douchebag."

"Well, I'd like to help, but unless your friend is willing to come in and fill out a report, there isn't much we can do."

"But, he *threatened* her," Lisa said, and her serious tone got his attention. He pulled a pad of forms from his desk and made a few notes.

"Exactly what type of threat did he make?"

Lisa answered, "He doesn't want to pay child support, so he threatened never, ever to divorce her."

Officer Williams looked up at her. "Well, that's not the kind of threat we can do anything about—"

"That's why I brought something he would not want showing up at a police station." With that, she slid the envelope across his desk while I tried to imagine what dirt she'd managed to get on Katie's husband.

While he opened the envelope, Lisa plucked one of the photos off his desk and said, "I see you have a lovely family."

"I do," he answered, glancing at me with a look of apology that he was a family man, assuming I was heartbroken and disappointed that I wouldn't be sampling his dick anytime soon. Cocky, I thought, deciding that I had been wrong about him, that he was not that likeable after all.

Lisa reached for another photo on his desk. "May I?" she said, not waiting for him to answer. "Can you imagine a man not wanting to pay their fair share for his child? I can't understand because money doesn't mean anything to me, which happens when you have too much of it. But, I guess to some people, money means everything."

Lisa glanced down at the picture frame in her hands and said, "Oh, wow, your wife is very pretty."

Officer William forced a polite smile as he pulled out a stack of legal papers from the envelope. I watched as his smile quickly faded.

Lisa said, "You may already be familiar with this guy. In the second envelope, there are exactly fifty thousand reasons why we need to get this jerk to leave my friend alone and grant her a divorce. Just don't open that envelope in front of my sister, she shocks so easily."

I shot Lisa a look, but she was ignoring me. Officer Williams reached in and pulled out the second envelope, tore it open behind his desk, looked inside, but did not reach in.

Lisa said, "With all the scumbags like this you have to deal with, I bet they don't pay you enough for this job."

"I do fine," he said, clearly insulted. He looked down at the envelope again.

Lisa said, "Shocking, right?"

When he looked up again, his expression had iced over and there was a dead look in his eyes that chilled me. "Nothing shocks me anymore," he said. "It's the nature of the job."

Despite him saying that, I thought he'd seemed rattled by what he saw and I wondered what kind of monster had Katie been involved with that would freak out a cop? I wasn't sure I wanted to know.

Lisa said, "The funny thing is, my brother wants to marry this woman, so the scum wouldn't end up paying any alimony anyway. I think what I have there is enough to convince him. If you think so too, maybe you could verify that the police took note of it."

He thought it over while still looking at Lisa. He was calm, but I saw an irritation boil under his surface. Maybe he was the type of guy who got pissed when ordinary citizens tried to do his job for him, especially when it was a woman. Lisa handed me the picture frame she had taken from his desk. "Marie, take a look. Officer Williams has a very pretty wife."

Though I was used to Lisa checking out men's wives, since it was a game she played to make me laugh, I had no idea why she would do this now. Her favorite part of the game was seeing how sexual she could get with her comments while still keeping the guy clueless that she wanted to bang his wife. The game would start with, "Oh, she's pretty," but it deteriorated to, "I'd like to have me some of that" with alarming speed. I was pretty sure she wasn't stupid enough to play the game with a cop, but you never know.

Officer Williams put the smaller envelope in his drawer and picked up his pen. He wrote something on the papers before putting them back in the envelope and sliding it across the desk. "You should be careful how you deal with this guy, Ms. Santora. You never know what will push his buttons."

He was most definitely angry, and although his build was not large he appeared to be a guy you shouldn't piss off. His change of temper confused me, but when Lisa stood up quickly, she was the one that alarmed me most.

"Good advice," Lisa said, taking the envelope from him. I started to put the picture frame down, and did a double take when I realized the picture was of Katie and her son Buddy. Horrified, I kept my mouth shut as I numbly followed my sister out of the office.

It wasn't until I was walking through the station that my knees went weak as I realized Lisa had just bribed a police officer with fifty thousand dollars. She walked ahead of me with her envelope in hand, and her walk had the same *Don't fuck with me* strut she had after beating the crap out of a playground bully in fourth grade.

When both car doors were closed, I turned to Lisa, not raising my voice because I was much more scared than angry. "I can't believe what you just did. Do you have any idea how much trouble you could get in if he reported you?"

She nodded her head, and for the first time I saw she had been hiding her fear. A sheen of sweat was on her face and her hands shook a little as she reached into her bra and pulled out a small digital recorder. She shut the machine off and stuffed in her glove box. "Insurance on my fifty thousand," she said.

I remembered something I had not thought about in years. After she had beat up that playground bully, she made us cut through the woods on the way home. Then she'd insisted I hit her in the face until her lip split. It was insurance so she wouldn't get in trouble, since, of course, the bully hadn't landed a single punch against Lisa. Today, Lisa had gone a bit more high tech. Her split lip had matured into a digital recorder, and her best insurance had been in her bra.

Thirty-Three

Hoisting The Boobs For a Clearer View

It was the end of October, and Camptown Ladies and Camp Camp were finally officially closed to the public. Lisa had served her last dinner for the remaining small group of hardcore season campers the previous weekend, which now included a large pack of hardy lesbians. There was not a gay boy in sight once a bona fide nip had settled in the air, as they'd all tucked their tails off to warm weather the second they could no longer adequately show off their shaved chests. (I expressed to Lisa how glad I was there was no pressure for lesbians to shave their chests, being Italian and all.) Trailers were once again buttoned up for the winter and everyone had moved on, leaving rows of permanent vehicles as collateral promises that everyone would be back in the spring. I was there when they had checked out, and all they could talk about was the food, especially the lesbians: they would be back in droves, and next year, they would come prepared with larger, eco-friendly takeout containers.

I had permanently moved myself into the log cabin, and Vince had moved Katie and her son into the condo after Lisa decided to be a snowbird and spend the winter in Florida. Lisa's exact words had been: "I'm taking a lesson from the fairies and heading where the bitches are wearing less clothes." And off she went. (Lisa's snow-bird was more like a rooster . . . with the mind of a cock.)

Uncle Freddie had left long before for Italy and I settled into a solitary existence I assumed I would dislike. Remarkably, it ended up being a relief not to have to act cheerful around Vince, when I really just wanted to sit and brood over Erica. I did lots of that, since one of the many advantages of being wealthy was I didn't have to do anything but make sure I had food in the cabin, and wood for an occasional fire. When I was feeling particularly industrious, I would bundle up and clear portions of the grounds surrounding the cabin, which eventually gave me a cleared path all the way to the main road. It was an improvement on the path Erica created when she built the place, since she had to clear enough trees to get equipment through to build. When it could almost pass as a driveway, I moved my car from the Campground Ladies to make the trips out for food much simpler, and hikes only for pleasure.

One afternoon, I was walking back from the car toward the log cabin when I pictured Erica standing up on the roof, sunglasses perched on her head, looking down at me with that smile. I put my things down on the porch and surveyed the railing around it. Before I could talk myself out of it, I climbed onto the railing, and gripped the edge of the roof to attempt to pull myself up.

Images of the night of the storm kept going off in my head like flashes of lightning. I coached myself out loud, but it turned out I was the type of coach that would get shit canned from even the worst community college: *Come on, you fucking weakling, pull yourself up! What is wrong with you? You climb like a fucking girl! What kind of lesbian are you anyway? A disgrace to your kind! You were always a wimp!! It's those tits of yours. Listen, if you can't haul them around, you have no business having those fun-bags!*

When had my inner voice turned into Lisa?

Negative coaching was not very inspiring, and my arms were too weak to haul myself over the edge, and the closest I got was on the first try. Even the image of Erica up on the roof, hands sarcastically planted on her hips, couldn't give me the strength to hoist myself up. I couldn't do it even when I imagined getting over the edge would allow me to kiss her again.

When I had lowered myself to the porch railing, I realized my arms weren't the only failed extremities. My legs had also gone weak with the memory of almost falling off the roof of the Dove, saved only by Erica's grip, then later by her kiss.

I attempted this silliness every day, and every day I got closer. By the second week, I decided I'd better get a TV, that the alone time was taking its toll. Would I someday be the spooky weird lady in the woods, the Freddy Kruger of Camptown Ladies? Would the young campers tell stories about how I would wait on rooftops for an unsuspecting person to walk below, before swooping down for the kill? All good questions, I thought as I prepared to attempt my roof walk again. I positioned my hands closer together this time, having learned I had more leverage that way, and reminded my legs that on three, I would have to spring as hard as I could, as the first attempt would be my best chance of success.

"Mare, what the hell are you doing?"

"Mom won't let me say that word," said a tiny voice, and I knew without turning around that it was Vince and Buddy. I imagined Erica on the roof, my brother behind me, having changed his mind about giving her up, and my legs sprang with the adrenaline rush from being watched. I was determined to get up this time, and I did, easily. After I'd pulled myself up, with feet pumping an invisible bicycle, I spun myself around into a seated position, like I had been doing this effortlessly for days.

"Hey, Vince. Hey, Buddy," I tried to control my breathing from betraying the Herculean effort it took to propel a large set of Italian breasts over the best quality roofing shingles money could buy.

"Problem with your roof?" Vince asked, as he shielded his eyes from the lowering sun. Buddy looked over at him and put his tiny hand up to his forehead too. Since he didn't know why he was doing it, he looked like he was reenacting the John-John Kennedy salute.

"Problem with your roof?" Buddy echoed, and Vince beamed down at him.

"Nope," I said, "just checking the view. I come up here sometimes." I casually swayed my legs back and forth over the roof edge.

"Can I go up with Auntie Marie?" Buddy asked.

Warmth spread through me as it did every time he said that. Auntie Marie. Sure, it sounded more like a rotund Italian relative with the female beard-growing skills of Johnny Depp, but I'd never been called Auntie before. Mom and Dad had accepted the fact that our generation would end the Santora lineage with a grandchild that was a Miniature Pincher named after a Christmas special, so hearing Buddy call me Auntie made my heart grow ten sizes that day.

Vince said, "Sorry, Bud, your Mom would have my ass."

Buddy moved his saluting hand to cover his mouth. "You said a bad word again," he said, as he giggled through his fingers.

"That'll have to be another thing we don't tell your Mom," Vince said, making wide eyes showing this was something that happened quite often. "So, really, Mare, what are you doing up there?"

"Just wondered what the view would be like," I said. "You know, if I were the type of person that could climb a roof."

Buddy was used to being disappointed by his dad, so he rarely asked for anything, but on this he was relentless, "Can I please see the view! Please?"

Vince and I had an entire wordless conversation with our eyes: *Think we should?* He would love it. *His mother will kill me.* Oh, he'll be fine. *I could hand him up to you.* Just for a minute or two. *Don't you dare let him fall.* I would never let him fall.

Vince scooped him up, and Buddy let out a high-pitched yelp of joy, and while my new nephew looked just like a child, right then he seemed more like a wriggling puppy. This was a creature I understood, I thought, as Vince easily lifted him to me. Vince kept his hands open to catch him, until well after I had pulled him safely into my lap.

"Wow!" Buddy said, as he took in the view, "This is the best house ever!"

"Sure is," I said, keeping a hold on him with both my arms wrapped around him from behind, as if he might need a chicken bone released from his throat. I saw the view from Buddy's perspective, the long stretch of woods, the horizon oddly lower than us, and the feeling that if you could climb a roof, you could have anything in the world you wanted. I wondered if I had ruined that feeling for Erica. Even the scent of pine was heavier from this vantage, or maybe it was Buddy's hair. A closer look revealed a sticky patch of tree sap leftover from his salute.

Vince hopped up on the rail, and, after a bit of struggling, he was sitting next to us. "On the first try, just like me. Impressive," I said.

"Wow," Vince said, "Buddy is right, this is the best house." I could feel Buddy tense with the excitement of having Vince join us, or maybe because Vince had copied him. The three of us were quiet for a minute before Vince put his arm around me, and, with just enough detail to keep Buddy in the dark, he asked, "Did Lisa tell you we finally got those papers finalized?"

"That's so great," I said.

Vince said, "We don't know why. Or how. One day the papers were signed and left under the door."

"Creepy," I said.

"You don't seem surprised. Funny, Lisa wasn't either," he said, and then he raised an eyebrow at me.

I said, "Your girl is a capable woman. Good for her for getting that monkey off her back."

"There's monkeys up here?" Buddy said, searching the trees.

"She's capable of kicking my a—, butt, if she finds out I let her son on a roof."

"A really, really high-up roof," Buddy said.

"That's one more secret we don't need Mommy to know, OK, Bud?" Vince said and Buddy nodded seriously at him.

"I'm cooked. He'll serve me up," Vince mumbled to me as I nodded back. Then he smiled at Buddy again, knowing the view was made more exciting because his mother was not supposed to know.

Vince asked, "So, when you're up here, are you remembering that thunderstorm, the night before we opened the Dove?"

Right on target. That scene had gone through my head a hundred times.

"I guess so," I said.

"You guess so?" he said, as he tightened his arm around my neck, "I would think you'd remember kissing Erica, seemed like a good one from what I saw." When I turned to look at him, he was gloating just a little. I, on the other hand, felt sick.

My throat tightened up when I tried to speak. "I know you're happy now. But that doesn't change what I did. And since I can't take it back, I've been trying to think of a way to tell you, and to prove to you that hurting you was the last thing—"

"You proved that," Vince said. "You let her go."

I leaned my head on his shoulder, remembering how I had leaned on him when Lorn left me the first time.

Vince gave my neck another squeeze. "What were you thinking?" he asked, as I waited for the talk I had been dreading: the one where he asked me how I could let anything happen with the woman I thought he loved.

Vince continued, "How on earth could you do it? You get a woman like Erica, and then you let her go? She dumped me, so I have an excuse. But you are an idiot."

I tried to stop my lip from quivering as I felt a tear roll down my cheek. And I imagined my body as an air mattress with the plug pulled, and all the guilt finally rushing out. "I love you, Vince," I choked out.

"I can say the word 'idiot,' too," Buddy said.

"Go for it," I said, wiping my eyes behind him so Buddy wouldn't see. I still had my arm tightly curled around his waist.

"Idiot!" Buddy yelled, and we all laughed when it echoed back to call me an idiot again. Buddy thought it was magic, while I thought the trees were finally making some fucking sense.

I exhaled heavily, realizing how much the guilt had still been weighing on me. Now, all that was left was the misery of losing Erica. "Ain't love grand," I said.

Vince said, "It is for Uncle Freddie."

"What?"

"Well, it turns out that he wasn't just going back to Italy for the winter to help build a house for his niece," Vince said. His eyes were gleaming with the thrill of breaking news before Lisa, a rare accomplishment indeed. "There's a new woman in Uncle Freddie's life."

"Get out!" I said, and laughed in spite of my own pathetic love life. I thought about how our other Uncle Tony had found love with Lorn's mother, Katherine. What was it with these old Italian guys?

"Yup. Uncle Freddie's exact words to Mom was that he was going back to Italy and taking a young woman with him to boss him around."

I smiled serenely at this news before it struck me, just like lightning on a rooftop. I hugged Buddy more tightly and leaned over to kiss Vince on the cheek, "Oh my God, Vince! *Erica's in Italy!*"

Thirty-Four

When Your Ball Hits Your Thigh, Like a Big Pizza Pie . . .

Vince volunteered to go on the trip with me, and just a few days after I'd guessed Erica was in Italy, we were booked on a flight to Naples. I picked Vince up at his condo and watched him kiss his new little family goodbye. Vince whispered something into Katie's ear that made her smile, lean into him, and kiss him again. Then he crouched down to Buddy and mimicked our dad, telling Buddy he was to take care of his mommy, the house, and his new bulldog puppy. (To Lisa's delight, Buddy had insisted on naming the pup after her.) We were running a little late, so Katie held on to Buddy who wanted to get in the car to visit. She told him to wave to his Auntie Marie. Then Katie shouted, "I'm counting on you to make sure your brother behaves! And hey, Marie, I'd feel better if that woman were off the market, so, really, good luck!"

"Good luck!" Buddy repeated as he copied his mom's wave, and I was glad he'd said it. I would need all the help I could get. Then Vince bent down to Buddy, and Buddy yelled out to me, "Where's Uncle Lisa?" I shook my head at my brother, in a silent warning that he was going to get his ass kicked. It could have been worse. Vince had been debating whether to have Buddy call her Guncle (Gay-Uncle) Lisa.

The only one who was completely against us going to Italy was Mom, who said, "You don't go flying across the entire world hoping to find somebody."

I answered, "It's Europe, Mom, we're not crossing the globe, it's an eight-hour flight."

"Besides," Vince said, "it's not just somebody, it's Erica."

"Still," Mom said, "we were supposed to go outlet shopping together. I need good shoes and your father needs underwear. And your brother was going to come with Katie and Buddy and me to the movies on Sunday."

Later, Dad pulled me aside, looking concerned. He looked around suspiciously, like we were two spies meeting on a park bench, before he explained: "It seems your mother has come up with a reverse case of agoraphobia. Ever since Camptown Ladies closed for the season, she never wants to be in the house anymore. She always wants to be outside or heading somewhere. She acts like she is afraid to be alone in her own house."

This was the first I had heard of it.

Dad continued, "Your mother drags me around with her all over the place. I'm friggin' exhausted! If you kids take off to Italy, it will all be on me to keep her busy!"

I told Dad I would discuss it with Vince and Lisa, and that if it was still going on when I got back, we would address it.

"Oh, it will still be going on," he said. "Yesterday, she followed me into the bathroom, and I had my newspaper with me! That is a sacred time for a man."

Vince and I drove to the airport, armed with information Mom had reluctantly supplied, which was the married name of Uncle Freddie's niece, though she was recently divorced, and a vague reference to a village just south of Naples. Vince said it amounted to no information at all.

Vince waited until we were walking toward our gate before he said, gently, "You should be prepared we might be wrong, and that she might not be there."

"She's there," I said.

I tried not to think about how I might have stupidly convinced myself she was there, just to have one more shot at finding her. I also knew Vince was coming on the trip because he thought I might be wrong. I didn't care. As we walked, an announcement came over the loud speaker that caught our attention: "Will Asini Stupidi please meet your party at gate B12. Asini Stupidi, your party is waiting at gate B12."

Vince and I stopped dead in our tracks, then simultaneously asked, "Did you hear that?" We must have looked like we were in a comedy routine, as our eyes bugged out. "Holy Shit!" we both said, before we busted into a competitive run toward Gate B12.

Gate B12 is where we found Lisa hitting on the young woman behind the ticket counter. She spotted us barreling toward her, but she took the time to turn back to the girl to say something charming before turning to us.

"What are you doing here?" I demanded as Vince and I hugged her. She ignored my question to introduce us to her new friend.

Lisa said, "Stupid Asses, meet Natalie. She's great with a loud speaker. Natalie, these are my siblings. We're heading to Italy so my sister can bang my brother's ex-girlfriend."

Natalie said, "Oh. That's . . ." and looked back and forth between Vince and me.

Lisa said, "I know, kind of an extravagant trip, especially when there are so many good-looking women right here in the airport."

"I'm OK with it," Vince assured the girl.

Lisa had gotten our flight information from Mom and Katie and made them promise to keep quiet until she could fly from Florida to meet up with our flight. With Lisa joining us, her over-confidence was contagious, which made me think we could pull anything off. Lisa rarely failed. Like her building a four-star restaurant at a campground that catered to gays and rednecks alike; bringing Erica out to work on Camptown Ladies to play matchmaker again (OK, wrong sibling, but still); bribing a cop to sign his own divorce papers, etc. Now finding Erica seemed much more possible, and I could see by the way Vince was smiling, that he thought so, too.

The flight was packed, so we weren't able to sit together, but Lisa had finagled a seat up front in the exit aisle, and Vince and I sat on opposite sides at the rear of the plane. We didn't know it at the time, but Lisa knew slipping a nice tip to do thy bidding was just as effective as flirting, and quite a time saver, especially with the Italians. I was fighting hard not to drift off to sleep when the Italian pilot, with a melodic accent that reminded me of Uncle Freddie, made the usual announcements about safety and the weather.

Then, there was one not-so-usual announcement.

"We will be touching down in Naples on schedule. I want to give special thanks to the Santora family, who are traveling with us today." My eyes popped open and I craned my neck to lock eyes with Vince, who was sporting an identical *what-the-fuck* look.

"The Santora family has made a generous donation to cover any food or drink you may like on your way to Naples, so la prego, quindi mangiare e divertiti!" Upon hearing "so please eat and enjoy!" the passengers burst into applause, and a few passengers shouted Italian cheers of bravo, as the pilot continued. *"The Santora famiglia is traveling to the Naples area in search of their only living Italian relatives. If you have any connections in that area that might help them find their uncle, or his niece, kindly please alert your flight attendant."*

An hour later, when the flight attendants were inundated with free food and drink requests, Lisa joined in to help the two attractive women serve the crowd. She ran drinks and food to the passengers, despite making time to flirt with her new co-workers, who instinctively treated Lisa like the restaurant manager. I marveled at how my sister had assembled an efficient (though mediocre) cuisine version of the Dove Gaio Mangia at forty thousand feet.

When Lisa came to my row to take my order, she indicated with hubba-hubba eyebrow moves which flight attendant she had her eye on. The woman was watching Lisa with a mix of rapt interest and fear, a look I had seen at the beginning of all my sister's relationships. I laughed as I thought how, whenever Lisa was around, every day had its dog, and the dog was Lisa. When the woman winked at her, Lisa proved my point by crouching down low, to say toward her crotch: "See, vagina, there really is a Santa Claus."

After we landed, Vince and I waited by the VIP Lounge, well

beyond the limits of my patience, as Lisa exchanged numbers (and probably body fluids) with her flight attendant. She came out of the room forty minutes later and Vince said it looked like the VIP (Very Immediate Pussy) Lounge had served her well. When Lisa wasn't forthcoming with any details, Vince and I silently agreed with our eyebrows that there might be something a little different about this hook-up.

Lisa led us to the correct luggage carousel and traded in the driver I had found for one she said wouldn't gouge us. She rattled something off a piece of paper in Italian, and as she did, I realized it hadn't even occurred to me to ask where we were heading. Lisa had taken over this trip, and I, with a lifetime history of this type of thing, had completely turned it over to her.

"We're going to Uncle Freddie's niece's house, of course," she said, like I had asked the stupidest question she had ever heard.

"But how?" I asked.

"She probably bribed a cop," Vince said.

Lisa answered, "Someone on the plane knew somebody in Frederica's village. We're heading there."

There were times when I couldn't imagine doing anything without my sister. Times like this. Not that this was always the case. When Lisa made a debacle, it was usually a goliath one that Vince and I could laugh about for years to come. Vince and I liked to goof on those times so we didn't feel so inept during at times like this. Also, they were fun to relive.

There was the time she scored a date with a woman she had been stalking for weeks. Lisa was so mesmerized by her looks that she never bothered to ask for a name to go with the coveted phone number. Lisa had to call her "sweetheart" from the first phone call, which was fine with Lisa: "Dumb as a box of rock but hotter than an August pussy planted on a pavement." But after her second date, the woman disappeared on her. Lisa insisted she had only sent her a charming text message about how pretty she was, only to receive a message back that she would like Lisa never to contact her again. Ever. It wasn't until weeks later, when Lisa was scrolling her sent messages, that she saw the text she'd sent to the unnamed beauty:

"If only you weren't so damned petty." Petty—so similar to the word pretty, and yet, so very, very different. (Lisa guessed the woman had had this happen a few times before.)

Right out of college, on her first "real" job, Lisa tried to bond with the boss's daughter by taking up smoking on coffee breaks. Like ex-president Clinton, she had all the moves except for the inhale, and she was working toward the stain on the dress. On day two, Lisa felt she was gaining ground charming the girl with her smart aleck remarks. So when a guy from accounting walked by, Lisa shared her observations about him. "Damn, that guy creeps me out. He looks like a child molester."

The woman asked, "Why would you say that?" and Lisa mistook her stunned expression for admiration of her cutting-edge humor. (Lisa has had this happen a few times before.) Lisa took a fake pull on her borrowed cigarette and said, "Obviously, the creepy longish nails, but mainly it's the stink of his cologne, Ode de Candy and Lost Puppy." The woman stomped out her cigarette, and before she stormed off, she said, "I will let my father know you don't like his cologne."

As our taxi cruised along and Lisa attempted to make conversation in her broken Italian, I had to admit that Lisa's blunders did not nearly outweigh her victories. The longer we drove, the harder my heart pounded in my chest, like a blip on the radar getting closer. I believed we might actually find Erica, and realized I hadn't believed it before right now.

Vince squeezed my hand, and when I looked at him he was wearing his most confident face. But better than that, I could see he really wanted me to find her. I took a deep breath and he nodded at me, smiling. I wondered if Vince knew exactly what that smile meant to me. It meant that even if I couldn't find her, at the very least I could still love her without hurting my brother. Maybe that would have to be enough.

It was late afternoon by the time Dominic, our taxi driver, deposited us in the center of the beautiful little village. We had no specific address, so we'd asked him just to leave us on the first corner in the center of town. He refused, deciding it was best instead to deposit us at a busy café, where we hoped to find a local who could lead us to Frederica's home. Dominic was hesitant to do even this but finally relented after he'd had long talks with several of the café staff. He did not know them, but Dominic spoke with the familiar way of a bossy relative. (He spoke like Lisa, in fact.)

When we got out of the car, Lisa said to Vince, "Damn, it's humid. Good day to be a girl, cuz I'm betting you've got a severe case of batwing."

Vince had the afraid-to-ask look that we grew up seeing on each other's faces. He asked, "You're a girl?" but then his curiosity finally won out and he had to ask. "All right, what the hell is batwing?"

Lisa said, "It's when your balls stick to the inside of your thigh."

"Aaah. Of course."

"Want to hear the song? It's to the tune of 'That's Amore.'"

"Um. No. But thanks."

"Well, I'd love to hear a song," I said, and Lisa belted it out, complete with a softer high-pitched echo on the last line.

"Wheeeeeen yooooour ball hits your thigh, like a big pizza pie, that's a baaaaatwing! Thaaaat's a batwing."

Then she spanked him on the back, indicating he should sing it with her a second time, and I felt obligated to join in as a backup singer, for fear of risking the same slap that was probably still ringing in Vince's ears. I took a second to look around, fearing we looked like loud Americans in Europe (this had happened before), but the patrons were smiling and some raised their glasses to us in salute. I loved Italy. It was the only place on the planet our family could *not* stick out like a sore thumb.

Once we'd said our goodbyes to Dominic and we were settled in at the café, it became clear it would be a waste of time to continue questioning the staff without eating first, since Dominic had left them strict instructions, and nothing was going to happen until after the raven-haired waitress sailed over to our table with a large mustard-colored ceramic platter dotted with the most beautiful olive, cheese, and meat assortment in the free world. After bite one, we realized Dominic might not know what a batwing was, but he may have been the smartest man on the planet. In heaven from first bite, the three of us sang out at the exact moment, *"That's Amore!"*

Thirty-Five

Pasta, Pot, Pee & Me

After we had eaten our fill of the antipasti, with hunks of crusty bread that made Lisa downright weepy, the owner of the café came over to tell us our taxi was waiting outside.

"But we don't know where we're going," I said.

The café owner said something in Italian and Lisa rose to gather our things. I repeated myself as I grabbed her arm, and she said to me, "We don't have to know where we're going, the taxi driver knows."

"How did that happen?" I asked.

Lisa said, "For fuck's sake, Mare, I honestly don't know how you are able to even drive a car."

"Why the hell not?"

"Because you get distracted looking in your bag." Lisa demonstrated an impression of me looking in my bag, in case I wasn't clear. "Oooo. What's that? It's sooooo shiiiiiiiny."

All this because, one time, about six years ago, I forgotten I'd bought a fancy chrome pen that had settled to the bottom of my bag. I made the mistake of gasping when I rediscovered it in front of Lisa.

I had to be so careful around her. One false move and I would hear about it for years. Like the time I decided to smoke my first joint. A friend in high school had borrowed my jacket and left a joint in the pocket. (Really, it happened, though it's exactly what I would have told my mother had she found it.) I'd wrongly assumed Lisa was being very self-righteous when she refused to try smoking pot with Vince and me. Now I realized she wanted to remain alert for any material she could throw back in my face when I got stoned off my ass. And oh, there would be material.

Vince and I each took several puffs. When I said I didn't feel anything, Lisa convinced me I should take several more hits. I then made the mistake of saying: "Doesn't it feel like we've been doing this so much longer than this?" Then, a few seconds later, "Why don't people do this all the time?" Then, in a fit of paranoia, "Wait, are you judging me for this? Wait—what did I just ask?"

This was only the beginning. Lisa was in for some pure gold, literally.

We had come home from the beach, and my shoes were still wet. Apparently, I started talking a blue streak about how wearing wet shoes was making me have to pee very badly. After much debate about the cause and effect of wet shoes and urinating, Lisa finally convinced me to go to the bathroom. Lisa also convinced Vince they should follow me, since her stupid-sister sensors were flying off the charts. (Lisa is never wrong in cases like this.) We were still in high school, so I had to navigate the living room carefully so I would not wake my parents, and move past the coffee table and television as if they were booby traps. (I had convinced myself they were planted by Lisa.) I could vaguely hear Vince and Lisa giggling behind me, but was much more concerned about the suspicious-looking furniture.

Lisa says that when I reached the bathroom, assuming I was out of earshot, I started mumbling to myself that the first order of business, regardless of what anyone else in the room thought (I was in the bathroom alone), was to take my take my shoes off. I did this with much effort, since it didn't occur to me to untie the laces and the shoes had shrunk from being soaked. Once they were off, I thought it might be best to dry them on the baseboard heater, but then I went into another series of paranoid ramblings about how they could cause a fire, if not placed correctly. I kept turning the shoes to lean on the heat from the front, then from the back, and Lisa said it was like I was roasting meat on a grill, debating in a whisper which way was less flammable.

Finally, after trying several more configurations, laces out, laces tucked, rubber sole heel up, rubber sole heel down, I blurted "Oh!"

as I realized I didn't have to lay the shoes directly on the heater, but instead, placed them out of harm's way in the middle of the bathroom floor. Lisa says I stared at them, like a timid dog waiting for a bird to stop nesting in his supper dish. Then I said in a loud whisper: "Whew. That's safe, I can finally pee!" Which would have been a fine conclusion, *if* the thought had occurred to me to go over to the toilet, instead of peeing right then, though my shorts onto the bathroom floor. At that point, Lisa and Vince yelled, which freaked me out, and sent me into an athletic dive onto my shoes, totally bare ass, convinced they'd yelled because my shoes caught on fire. (Of course, they hadn't.)

This commotion woke up my parents, with my mother screaming a more shrill echo version of my *"Fire!"*, and the whole night resulted in all three of us getting grounded. This was totally worth it from Lisa's perspective, since the ammunition she had would be good for years, and my mother had Dad hold a two-day long inquisition to find out where Vince got the pot, but Vince never served me up. (Later, when Mom was not around, my father's cross-examination morphed into an investigation about how available the pot was at school, and could Vince score some for Dad without Mom finding out.)

Such was life with Vince and Lisa. One day I was feeding from their strength, the next day I'd say or do something that would give them ammunition for years to come. However difficult they could be, I was so grateful to have them with me—though I would never admit such a weakness to my sister. We were pretending this was a road trip they wanted to take, and all the while Vince was sweetly pretending to be our male escort to keep us safe, while we all knew this was Lisa's job.

Our new taxi driver wasn't talkative like Dominic. I could see that his constant warm smile made Lisa fear he was not very bright. As we drove through rural streets surrounded by beautiful fields, even Lisa seemed worried if we would get to Frederica's home. As history has shown, when Lisa is concerned, it's often too late for the rest of us to start worrying.

The taxi slowed in front of a tiny stone villa, with thick laces of ivy tracing it like a coloring book. The small wood-slatted door swung open and out stepped a woman who could only be our cousin, Frederica. At first she looked concerned and I guessed this quaint village didn't see taxis very often, and I wondered how often it signaled bad news. She shouted something to the driver in Italian and he shouted back a long explanation, which included him reading each of our names off a scrap of paper, while her face brightened to a wide smile as she clasped her hands together.

She left her door wide open and bounced toward the taxi. Her mound of wavy brown hair was tousled, and it whipped back and forth as she trotted up the driveway. She kept her elbows bent and tight to her ample sides, using the top of her forearms to cradle the underside of her breasts to lessen the bouncing, which looked like a pair of puppies fighting under a floral sheet. (I knew that move; I had done that move a thousand times, minus the floral housecoat.) When she got closer, we recognized her face was a gleaming, younger, feminine version of Uncle Freddie's. We laughed with relief, knowing that this woman was family, just as much as any family we had known our entire lives.

Since he was the first to emerge from the taxi, Frederica grabbed Vince in a giant bear hug that nearly knocked the wind out of him, since when he tried to say her name, no sound came out. Lisa and I laughed again. She was rattling off Italian in a blue streak singsong voice that made it hard to pick out even one recognizable word. I got my bear hug next, and I saw from Lisa's raised eyebrows and shaking head that, except for our parent's names, she couldn't understand a single word either.

Lisa pulled the suitcases from the taxi, set them down, and was nearly knocked over by Frederica's hug. Lisa tried to speak a few Italian words, but Frederica's expression of wide-eyed wonder didn't change. We understood that we could have said, "Hello, how are you" and got the same understanding as "Ravioli are running on trees."

Vince attempted to speak to her, asking about Uncle Freddie, but Frederica thought he was attempting her name and she said, "Si, si, si!" She grabbed Vince's cheek in a death-grip pinch that reminded me of Aunt Aggie. Then, she easily hoisted up the largest of our suitcases and carried it up the walkway. Clearly we would be staying with her.

Lisa reached for the rest of our bags and followed our exultant cousin down the long walkway. The walkway was ten times the length of the house, the warm orange stones turning to cool blue under the quickly fading light. It was early evening and the country road didn't have a single streetlight, so the darkness had come quickly. As we approached her home, Frederica had left her front door open as wide as possible, and it seemed a sign of how she welcomed us. If she could have taken the door off its hinges to make it more hospitable, I felt in my heart she would have done so.

The villa's inside reminded me of a Hobbit's residence, or Yoda's more tastefully decorated summer home. There was not a stick of furniture, piece of wall décor, or artifact that didn't look hand-crafted from a natural material, and, like my log cabin back in New England, the inside of the home exactly resembled the outside, missing only the ivy crawling on the fieldstones. If it hadn't looked centuries old, I would have wondered if my Uncle Freddie had built the place, but it was more likely his father before he had been tragically taken from his family at such a young age. Despite its obvious age, the walls were still flawlessly sealed, and the floors beautifully broken in, like distressed leather.

Frederica's singsong voice trailed off to her kitchen, and before we'd even set our things down, she had magically appeared with a tray of fresh-squeezed lemonade. The beverage was served in jelly jar glasses that may have been hand-me-down relics to her, but would have fetched a nice price at an antique show. She sang more Italian at us and we could tell from her hand movements that she wanted us to sit down.

Frederick knew, like Dominic the taxi driver, that making time for refreshment was always a wise choice. She watched our faces as we drank, her thick eyebrows raising to her hairline with expectancy, then lowering notch by notch as we each nodded our heads in agreement. That lemonade, which Lisa said was spiked with bits of sugared ginger, was the finest drink I had ever tasted.

When our drinks had been drained, she scampered off to pour us more and I signaled to Vince to try communicating with her again. She came back with the pitcher and he said, "Frederick, our uncle?" Then he winced when she put the thick ceramic pitcher down with a heavy thud so she could accost his cheek once again. Through gritted teeth and a painful smile, Vince said to me, "I'm not asking again."

Frederica filled our glasses to the brim before disappearing into the kitchen. Within moments we heard the crackle of a cooking fire and smelled simmering garlic. Lisa sprang up like she'd received an urgent call from the mother ship that complimentary authentic Italian cooking lessons were to begin around Yoda's antique stove. We heard Frederica's singing protest, but Lisa didn't return to the living area. We heard the sounds of two chefs chopping, stirring, and scraping, all attempts at language abandoned. The kitchen was one place Lisa needed no words, unless it was to call everyone to the table.

Vince and I stepped outside to watch the stars come out over the surrounding fields. "She may not even be here," I said to him.

He shook his head with more confidence than he had. "She's here. Who else could boss Uncle Freddie around besides Aunt Aggie?"

I wanted to believe, but there was an ache deep in the pit of my stomach warning me otherwise. Or, maybe I was starving from the intoxicating smells coming from Frederica's kitchen window. Vince had his hand on his stomach too, and in a few minutes we almost forgot our mission here. Wasn't our mission to eat?

I asked Vince, "Ever wish you could cook?"

He gestured over at Lisa and answered, "Thank God, no. It would be like wanting to be an actor and being Meryl Streep's brother."

Back inside, the unmistakable smell of Lisa's roasted red pepper boats with goat cheese filling mingled with the smell of spicy sausage searing on a cured pan. We gathered in the kitchen, making a chorus of "mmm" sounds, well understood in any language. For now, we wouldn't worry about communicating beyond the languages of our stomachs.

Later, much later, when we had eaten what Vince and I agreed was the best meal of our lives, Frederica kicked us out of the kitchen with playful shooing motions and demanded with various other hand signals that we settle in for the night into two small guest rooms, Vince in one, and Lisa and I in the other. With our bellies full, we were too tired to protest, and after using the washroom (located outside the house, adjoining a fairly well-kept chicken coop) we collapsed on our guest beds and fell asleep.

Thirty-Six

Bang-Bang-Tap

Despite being in the birthplace of my ancestors, and one of the most beautiful places on earth, my recurring dream took me back to a cabin nestled in a pine-tree-filled wood in Rhode Island. The cabin was near a playful little campground, and on most summer evenings it smelled very much like Frederica's kitchen. In the dream I'd been searching for Erica, night after night. I always convinced myself she was nearby, but most nights I couldn't find her. I would find a note she'd left on a bureau I'd purchased for the cabin, a bureau she had never seen.

Sometimes I would catch a glimpse of her in the woods, before she disappeared again. Other times, if I was lucky enough to catch her, she would shake her head no and her voice would grow faint as she explained to me as if I were a child, "You can't love me, you need to let me go now," and before I could tell her things were different, that Vince had found love, she would disappear again and I would awake with a hunger that ran so deep for her, I could feel nothing else.

Tonight, the dream was a little different. Instead of being at night, it was the full heat of a summer day, and throughout the dream I could hear the tapping of Erica's hammer on a distant roof. It started as a sweet sound, a sign that she was near—was she signaling to me? But as the dream went on and I searched from roof to Camptown Ladies roof with no sign of her, the tapping became maddening.

Then a beautiful woman was approaching me, the sun blazing behind her. Was it Erica? No, she was much too large to be Erica, much, much too large, a quite rounded silhouette, so dark I could not see from the bright light around her, and so familiar and beautiful to me. I loved her, though not in *that* way. Who was this?

When she spoke, there was no mistaking her.

"Marie, what the fuck are you doing in Italy?"

I bounded over to Aunt Aggie and she wrapped me in a smothering hug, then she pulled back to nail me with a painful pinch on the cheek. It was so painful, I felt myself stirring in my dream state, almost waking from my sleep. No, I thought, just a minute more with her—and, like magic, I was back with my Aunt, hugging her hard, not letting her go, smelling the dust and tomato scent of her house that clung to her clothes.

Aunt Aggie said, "Christ, Marie, let go of me. Might be your idea of heaven, but not everybody's a lezzie like you!" And then she laughed, her deep and raspy-cruel laugh that I'd had no idea how much I missed, until right then.

"Are you OK?" I asked. It was all I could think of to say.

And she answered, "Of course not, I'm dead!" and she laughed even louder into my ear and finally, I could let go of her, because anyone who laughed like that, had to be OK. She winked at me from behind her glasses, the only pair I had ever known her to wear. "You still need glasses here?" I asked.

"Nah, they're for you. The clothes too."

"Thanks for that," I said, and this time she laughed at me.

"I love it here except for the food," she said, "because there isn't any fucking food! I'm afraid I might be losing weight."

"No worries," I said, and she cackled and pinched my cheek even harder. I'd awake from this dream with a bruise, I thought, but as I was thinking this, I doubted something this real could ever be a dream.

"Who the fuck would be afraid of a skinny ghost? I don't know how I'm staying this way with no food, but thank Jesus. He's here too, by the way, he says hi." She winked at me. "Hey, I can't stay long, so tell your mother to be good or I'll keep haunting her boney ass. Can you imagine how much fun it is being a ghost chasing your mother around? And she knows I'm there, too."

I had to laugh with her. That explained why Mom was acting so strange lately, asking for Lisa and I to visit more, not wanting to be alone in the house!

Aunt Aggie said, "Once I figure out how to do some real tricks, I plan to move all her kitchen stuff, piece by piece, so she can't find anything and I just figured out how to make a tomato roll off a counter and splatter on her foot! I'll get your sister Lisa, too."

Just when I was thinking how I wished Lisa and Vince could see her right now, Aunt Aggie got weirdly quiet and surprised me more than a vision of a ghost ever could.

She softly said, "Tell your Uncle Freddie I love him. And tell him I'm glad someone else is bossing him around until I can have him back." I thought I heard her voice crack then, making my own tears come, but then she waved me off with her hand, as if I was annoying her, her doughy arm never looking so lovely in the bright white light.

"You don't get it, honey," she said. "You can't understand how happy I am, how happy you all will all be someday. Tell everyone, OK? I guess even your Mom."

"But, I have so many questions," I said. "You used to think Lisa and I would never get into heaven, you know, because of the whole gay thing."

Aunt Aggie said, "Oh, there are tons of homos here. Turns out just because some assholes down there post a sign that says 'Keep Out,' doesn't mean those are the rules. It was the first thing I checked on when I got here, since I wouldn't want to be in a club that didn't allow you and Lisa as members."

"And what about the argument that it's in the Bible?" I asked.

"Marie, don't be an idiot. Jesus was a carpenter, not a publisher. You may learn just as much standing on a roof. It's closer to God, with less men standing in-between."

"True," I said.

"Guess who else is here," she said.

I was thinking Elvis, but braced myself, since the expression on Aunt Aggie's face was the happiest I had ever seen, on any face. Ever.

Her lower lip was quivering with joy as she said, "My twin sister Etta is here."

"I'm sorry Aunt Aggie, I didn't know she finally passed—"

She laughed at me again, "No, no. She's not dead. She just gets to spend time with me while she's in her coma. Great deal, actually. She'll get to see both sides when they send her back."

"Send her *back?*"

"Word up here on the clouds is that she'll be waking up one day, so this is just a visit. Of course, everyone will think she is nuts when she says she saw me up here in bright lights, but that's earth for you. Of course, in the end, I'll see you all up here."

"So, one other question," I said. I was talking fast, instinctively knowing our time was ending soon. "What's the point of life, anyway?"

What the hell, she was making so much sense, I just thought I would throw it out there.

"Love," she answered, without hesitating, and because it was Aunt Aggie, who'd never spoken of love in my presence before, I was strangely embarrassed for her. In contrast, I could see she wasn't embarrassed at all; in fact, she flew into one of her rants I had so sorely missed.

"So, now that you know that you know the secret of life, I'm counting on you to tell that silly brother of yours to treat that new girl of his right. I know he'll be the best dad to that little boy, so tell him to marry that woman quick and tell him that I forbid him to fuck it up. Tell him I said being a man is the easiest job on earth, so there's no friggin' excuse. For Christ sakes, they make Valentine's cards that say 'Sorry I take you for granted' and, 'I know I'm a dipshit and never show you I care, but you know I love you!' For fuck's sake, they even have TV commercials reminding fathers to 'Take time to be a Dad today.' Can you imagine some organization paying to remind women to 'Take time to be a mother'? I didn't see this so clearly when I was down there with the morts, but women are programmed to be thrilled by the simplest God-damned gesture from a man."

Aunt Aggie realized she said God-damned, but it only slowed her down for a second before her rant returned, at double speed.

"A handful of cheap carnations will get a man out of the doghouse after weeks of acting like an ass. But tell him never to buy his girl carnations because it's the only flower God makes fun of, and, between you and me, it's the fault of the gay guys. They were the ones that realized you could dye them all different colors. Tell Vince that. Tell them he has it made. Also, when it comes to sex, to get pleasure all a man has to do is stick their pee-pee in a hole, so he better take his time to do that right. And men aren't that bright, so have that crass sister of yours remind him of which hole."

I let myself laugh at that one. Up till now, I was afraid I would miss a word.

"But seriously, Marie, tell Vince he'll have to deal with me if he fucks this one up. It's the easiest thing in the world to love a good woman."

I nodded, but I said, "It's not so easy, sometimes, but I'll make sure he doesn't fuck it up."

"Don't you fuck it up either," she said.

I nodded again. "If I can find her," I said.

"And tell that sister of yours she needs to just love one woman or she'll never be happy. One. That's the secret for her."

I said, "Go figure, all this time it was just a math problem. I'll tell her, but she seems pretty happy."

"Then just mess with her and tell her I said the big guy upstairs says she's actually straight, and that's her problem. She's repressed and she needs some dick."

Aunt Aggie roared at her own joke as the sunlight grew intensely bright behind her, turning her floral housecoat back into a round silhouette. I knew then without a doubt she was in a good place, the best place, and I felt Aunt Aggie's joy and peace in my heart. I also knew it was just a glimpse of her happiness. Still, it was more intense than any a person could handle in the waking world . . . and it was right then that my dream ended.

My dreams had let me down so many times, but this may have been the hardest fall. I wanted to go with Aunt Aggie, instead of waking with the same emptiness in my chest and a damp pillow flecked with tears. The dream was barely fading, and already the idea that I had been with my Aunt Aggie didn't seem as believable as it had been only seconds before. I wondered if, over time, I wouldn't believe it happened at all, and maybe seeing my Aunt had been just a sad dream, though it hadn't been sad, not at all.

As my eyes adjusted to the morning light, I remembered there was one great difference to waking up on this particular morning. I was in Italy, in a charming old bedroom, splintered with bright shards of sunlight from the shutters in need of repair. Had the bright morning sun shining in my eyes created the entire dream?

Even though there was a heavenly scent of bacon and polenta pancakes wafting up from the stairway, I was drawn instead toward the shutters, and pulled them open to reveal a small, sun-drenched balcony. The cracked plaster was so picturesque and uniform that it appeared like an expert faux finish. Except unlike the faux plaster finishes Erica had taught me to do back in LA, this was the real deal.

I felt the sun through my thin nightgown as I leaned on the railing, my arms tickled by the tendrils of ivy, which had climbed up the house and grasped onto the rail like two hands perfectly spaced. The very tips of the ivy fingers seemed no longer growing, they were dry and curled upward into delicate spirals, as if they were thanking the heavens for giving it the strength to get where they wanted to be. It wasn't getting onto the balcony that was the point; it was the journey.

I breathed the air, and I told my heavy heart that even if I never found her, maybe this was about my journey, to be here with Lisa and Vince and our new cousin Frederica. Maybe something in my DNA had sent me to be here to heal, maybe it was to have a moment with Aunt Aggie. If only the hammering in my heart would quiet. And if it did, I was left with a question: if I was here for my heart to heal, why had the faint sound of Erica's hammering followed me from my dreams?

I knew what I was here for—*fuck the journey!*

I spun around, holding the rail to steady myself, the familiar hammering now syncing up my heart. Bang-bang-tap—bang-bang-tap. The hammering becoming a pounding in my chest when I saw, far in the distance, a beautiful half-stone and half-wood home, and the unmistakable dotted silhouettes of my Uncle Freddie and Erica perched on the roof, while a small crew attempted to hammer along to Erica's signature beat. I only paused one second to make sure it wasn't the heat, or another cruel dream.

Then, I ran.

I ran across the room, not stopping to change my white flimsy nightgown, and flew down the stairs, skipping several, nearly plowing over my brother, who was heading up the stairwell. "Jesus!" he said, pressing himself to the wall, so I could fly past him. "Like you've never smelled bacon before."

I ran through the living room and into the kitchen, nearly knocking over Lisa, making her fumble her handful of tomatoes, sending one rolling off the counter to splatter dramatically on top of her bare foot. I howled with laughter as I ran through the rest of the kitchen, backward, pointing to her tomato-splattered foot.

"Aunt Aggie did that!" I screamed at her.

"No, you did it, you fucking idiot! Why are you running in your friggin' nightgown, blaming your klutziness on your dead aunt?"

I yelled back, "Erica!"

Frederica was at the stove and shouted back, "Si, si, Erica!" as she pointed out the window, toward the house in the distance. My sister spun around to the window as I blasted out the door.

I ran up the dirt road toward the house, barely aware of my braless and barefoot state, and I stopped running only when I could clearly hear Erica's voice, chastising the workers as she always had—only Erica was shouting one insult at a time and Uncle Freddie was translating in Italian—and the sound of her teasing the men was like music to my ears.

"Rocky and I could have had this done hours ago!" she yelled, "Come on girls, learn from the old guy and pick up the pace before the rain comes! This roof is getting done today, or I'll toss you off it one by one!"

I let myself walk the rest of the way to the house, breathless, knowing that I had her cornered; she would not get away from me. I could hear Uncle Freddie's "heh, heh, heh" laugh as he came down a ladder, and he didn't spot me until he reached the last few steps.

"Marieooche!" he called out, as he hopped the last two steps like

a young man. I looked for Erica over his head, but I was too far under the roof to see her now.

Uncle Freddie spread his arms as wide as he could before clasping them around me in a bear hug. "She said you were here!" he shouted into my ear.

I looked up for Erica again. "She knew I was here?"

"No, your Aunt Aggie! She was in my dream last night, asking me why you were here. I told her you weren't here, and she called me a 'stupid tool.'" He cackled and joy spread across his face at the fresh memory. "Did you or Vince teach her that word?" He laughed again, and I realized how much his laugh had become my aunt's, or maybe her laugh had become his over the years. I kissed him a proper hello on both cheeks.

"She came to me too, Uncle Freddie. She told me to tell you she loves you."

"Hmm. You sure it was her?" he laughed, but he was touched by the message.

"She also said she was glad someone else was bossing you around until she could have the job back."

He smiled and nodded, "That's your aunt."

"I came for Erica," I said.

He nodded again as if he had already known, and he said, "It's all or nothing, with that one, too," he cautioned me. "So much like your Aunt Aggie, only she's a hottie, heh, heh. Don't tell your Aunt I said that. Even now, she seems to know everything I do." Then he gently patted the house with pride, and seemed to look at me for approval.

I said, "My uncle is finally a carpenter. You're living your dream."

"Except Erica won't let me forget I'm a stone mason. She insisted we build the houses half and half like this. Our signature style. She might be right. People love them. She calls me Rocky to remind me that I'm still wet behind the ears as a carpenter." I felt him watch me as I stared up to the roof looking for her.

"Seconda opportunità," he whispered.

Second chance. He told us this so many times as kids when we made a mistake and we were given one more chance. Then he pulled me close to repeat the secret he had told Vince, Lisa, and me what seemed thousands of times. "My father used to say, *In life there are only two things: I o fuori?'* Because in life, either you're in, or you're out."

I nodded, hoping I would get the chance to hear him say that a thousand more times. "I'm in," I said. "I just hope she is."

He nodded back at me. "I'm in, until they take me out, heh, heh. Then Aggie can call me all the names she wants." I saw a tear glint in the corner of his eye, but I knew by the bounce in his step when he walked back to the ladder that he was happy.

Uncle Freddie called out to the crew in Italian and all but one hammer stopped, and the crew began to climb down the ladder one by one, the few youngest hopping off the side of the roof to the porch railing below.

"Rain is just starting," Uncle Freddie said, "we have to call it a day soon, anyway. Erica hates that, she always wants them to keep working."

Just then I heard a loud scraping sound, and I ducked my head instinctively, thinking the ladder was falling. But the ladder wasn't falling. My back was to the house, but I could tell from my Uncle's face that I wasn't in danger; he just looked surprised. He called up to the roof, "Erica, what are you doing?"

Erica was pulling the ladder up on to the roof and I turned in time to see the last few steps disappear over the edge. Then I heard the ladder make an angry thud onto the roof, a thudding Erica would have yelled at her workers for, for taking the chance on damaging shingles, especially, a beautiful terracotta roof like this one.

Uncle Freddie gave my cheek a good luck tweak filled with love and maybe a pinch of pity. He of all people knew what it was like to be outmatched by a strong woman. He walked away to rejoin his crew as I heard hammering begin again on the roof.

I carefully avoided stray nails as I walked around to the porch. In one smooth movement, I easily hoisted myself onto the porch railing and when I straightened up, I hopped hard once with my bare feet to pull myself up onto the roof with the strength of my arms. Erica was crouched at the far end of the roof, her back to me, hammering roofing nails at double her usual speed, a speed fed by anger. I also knew she would have several nails in her fist and a few between her lips.

"Erica."

I had surprised her by getting on the roof without the ladder and she stopped nailing for a moment, but she didn't turn around. Instead, she shook her head no, her back still toward me, continuing to hammer away.

"Erica," I said, louder.

She finally turned, as she spat the nails onto the clay. She spat her words, too. "Why the fuck did you come here?"

It had been so long since I had seen her face, I was equally startled by her anger as I was by her perfection, so much I had forgotten about her. Her face was reddened and I wondered if a few of her tears had hit the roof along with the raindrops that were now pelting us both.

Erica yelled, "Answer me! Why did you come to the one place where I finally stopped thinking I'd see you everywhere went? Now you ruined that. Why?"

"Because I love you," I said.

"You think I didn't know that, Marie? That's why I left!"

"What you don't know—"

"No! What you don't know is that I can't hear any of this!" Then she said to herself, "I did the stupidest thing imaginable."

I said, "Running away to Italy—"

"No! I kissed you on a rooftop in the middle of a storm. I came to that campground for you and kissed you, knowing I couldn't ever have you. Running away was the smartest thing I ever did! Until you followed me here, and now I have to start over again."

I moved toward her and she stood up so quickly near the edge of the roof that she startled me. Gently, I said, "Erica, listen to me—"

"No! Go! Will you just go? Take the ladder, and go. Please. Go before Vince finds out you came for me. I won't ruin what you have with him, with your family, just because you think you can't let this go. Because you can, just like I have, or like I did."

Now Erica was crying hard and I wanted to move toward her again, but she was too close to the edge and my stomach lurched at the fear of her falling backward to get away from me, not to mention my own memory of falling for this woman on a roof, in more ways than one.

Instead of moving toward her, I lowered myself down to the roof until I was kneeling on the shingles, still warm from the disappearing sun. I imagined I looked like one of those tacky religious paintings, a woman kneeling in a nightgown with the backdrop of an Italian garden and countryside in the distance, the thick and dramatic clouds in the sky leaving open areas where the sun still blasted through in rays, like God was shining a spotlight down on his flock. (Except that I was on top of a roof, begging for a lesbo lover.)

I also imagined my Aunt Aggie peeking through one of the holes in the clouds, her giant eye behind her horn-rimmed glasses that, by some miracle, seemed comically back in style, and I imagined her shouting down that I was making a fool of myself in the rain. She would have been right. I knelt there and waited, knowing that while I'd had days to think about the possibility of finding her in Italy, Erica had only minutes to absorb the idea of me being here.

When she finally seemed convinced I would not come any closer, she calmed down a little as she wiped her face with the shoulder of her t-shirt. Then she shook her head again, this time slowly, sadly as she said, "You can let this go, just like I did." she said. "I just hate that I have to do it all over again. Now I have to imagine that you could be here, too, instead of just in my dreams."

Then she moved closer to me and grabbed me by the shoulders and pleaded, softly, but still so angry, "Why did you have to come here?" Then she knelt down in front of me as if she had given up, and hung her head down, crying invisible tears as the sky opened up and dumped buckets of heavy rain on us.

I was about to answer, to tell her everything, when the increasing roar of what I assumed was insanely close thunder turned out to be the engine of a speeding flatbed truck below us. We looked over the roof edge to the gravel road, where the careening truck sent workers scattering as it made a wild half-circle close to the house, kicking up mud, and finally skidding to a hard stop. I heard Uncle Freddie's laugh as Frederica leaned out and waved wildly to us from the passenger seat, shouting God knows what to us in Italian. When Lisa jumped out from the driver's seat, I knew Erica was thinking what I was: She should have recognized her driving.

Lisa yelled casually, "Hey there, Erica, hope you're not getting too comfy here! We'll be needing you back at Camptown Ladies. I have *huge* expansion plans!"

Erica looked back at me, confused. Her cheeks, which before were streaked with tears in the dust, were now washed clean by the rain. Erica looked back to the truck to see Lisa prying Vince by the seat of his pants as he backed out of the tiny back seat. Lisa took joy in flinging him into the rain. He lost his footing and landed on his ass on the ground. He looked up at us with a giant smile and awkwardly waved his hand covered in mud.

"Hey, Erica," Vince said, "I thought I'd bring both my sisters over, you know, so you could take your pick." Then he laughed at his own joke as Lisa helped him up.

I said softly to Erica, "Vince is happy. He fell in love with Buddy's mom, Katie. And he wants us to be happy, if you still want to be with me."

She blinked at me, bewildered, and I leaned closer to her, taking her face in both of my hands. "Will you let me love you? It's OK now, if you still want this. I love you, Erica. If you still want this."

Erica breathed out a gasp of air and said, "Is this really happening?"

"If you want it to," I said.

She slowly nodded yes as I felt my own tears warm my cheeks in the rain.

Vince yelled up, "Mare, friggin' kiss her already before you both get struck by lightning!"

We both knew I had already been struck by lightning. Still, I kissed Erica anyway and Erica fell against me at last, her arms no longer holding me stiffly away, and we kissed as the sheets of rain washed over us both. It was sweet how she tightened her grip on me as if I might pull away. Not a chance. Not ever. This was the woman I would spend the rest of my life with. Even as I was ecstatically holding her, I knew also that my happiness came from knowing my brother and sister were sharing this with me.

With her impeccable timing, Lisa bellowed from below, "Marie, you fucking imbecile, you really need to get some clothes on!" She was pointing up to me. "Your wet nightgown is giving the crew a perfect view of tits and ass crack! Then, in case they missed it, Lisa turned to the crew and yelled, and pointed, "Look, a vagina!"

Vince and Lisa's laughter mixed with Erica's, which was warm against my neck, as she still gripped me tightly. I could hear Uncle Freddie laughing as he translated to his niece, Frederica, so she could laugh at me, too. At Lisa's call, the crewmen circled the house to see what a woman in a completely transparent nightgown looks like holding a gorgeous woman on a rooftop. A few seconds later, although she had been the one who called them over, Lisa now swatted and chased them away from the view, and Frederica joined her as they made the workers scurry back under the roof of the house. The whole scene was bursting in equal parts laughter, fear, love, and chaos: Lisa's favorite recipe.

I held onto Erica as I looked over her shoulder, up to the sky, silently thanking the heavens of Italy raining above the expertly shingled clay roof. It was more than just knowing I had found the love of my life. It was knowing that my sister, brother, and even my Aunt Aggie would always be there to watch my back—ass crack and all.

A Note From The Author

After *Greetings From Jamaica, Wish You Were Queer* was published, I asked readers to drop me an e-mail (specifically, only those who'd liked the book), then reaped the rewards, since my e-mail address is hard to forget if you read the entire address out loud: MariLaughs@cox.net Go ahead, I'll wait as you try it. Getting feedback from readers turned out to be a bit addictive too. I loved finding out what particular thing a reader liked or what made them laugh, and some readers went so far as to supply quotes from the book, which I read, of course. Some extra-conscientious readers took the time to list any spelling or grammar mistakes, and those were fun to read, too. (Not really.)

However, it takes a brave (or idiotic) woman to admit my favorite thing to read was the downright ego-stroking letters that made writing the book worth all the weekends spent staring at my computer. I have to say, I'm tempted to print out these gushing letters, get naked, and roll all over them like a pig in—well, you know. Would that be wrong?

OK, I'm back. And it didn't feel wrong. Not at all.

Back to my story. On the arrival of the ninetieth fan e-mail from my first book (yes, I was counting back then), I found out I was getting a bit cocky. This was the day an e-mail arrived with the subject line: *"Greetings From California!"* This was also the day I leaned back in my chair and sang out to myself: "Another faaaaan letterrrrrr!" (Now, in my defense, this was a legitimate assumption since many of the letters had come with headings that made had made this play on words from the title of my first book, tied in with the state where the reader lived. (For example: *Greetings from New York! Greetings From*

Colorado!) Just as I settled myself in, sighing as if the hardship of preparing for another ego-stroking had become a bit of an imposition on such a lovely day, I was promptly deflated, much like the appendage the e-mail was marketing to:

> *Greetings From California!*
> *Mister Mario Sangloviany, YOU WAN BIG-LONG HARD COCK THAT NEVER GET THE SMAL ALL THE NITE LONG??!*

Well, maybe. Never get the small all the night long would certainly be nice. But, that isn't really the point. I saved that e-mail with the other "fan letters" and if there is a moral to the story, it might be: Just when you expect to get your ass kissed, you might be getting your big, long, hard cock (or vagina) swindled. Or maybe the message is: My apologies to anyone who took the time to write me one of the *awesome* letters I received, since this one has become my favorite. What does that say about me? Not sure. What does it say about you? Well, you were crazy enough to buy the sequel, so, you are loved (by me). Now, please go tell all your friends, and also tell them F-ing no way, they can't borrow your copy. Thanks.

Once again, I dyke-gress, since the whole point of this author's note was to thank readers of my first book for taking the time to write me, or visit me at a book signing, or for harassing me, ever so gently, to write another book. This book exists only because readers told my publisher they liked the first book, or because they took the time to post a kind review. And thank you, sincerely, for being kind enough to buy your own copy of this book, instead of borrowing a friend's copy, even in this crappy economy. You are a friend to writers everywhere when you "Recommend; Don't Lend" a book you like (especially mine). As the specialty publishing industry struggles, getting the word out about books and independent films you like, will help more to get made. Trust me, it isn't about the money (because there is none). It's all about getting more copies of the book out there so the demand will be there for the next book, or possibly, a film.

This book is dedicated to my number one partner in crime, Kim

(Amylon) SanGiovanni, who does not legally have my last name, but who gives a flying F what the government thinks. Kim is the love of my life, the best person I know, my biggest (and totally undeserved) cheerleader, my first reader-editor and "fan," and I owe everything to her, especially my happiness. At the time I am writing this, she faces the health battle of her life, and faces it every day with a reassuring smile for the people around her to see. Brave is a ridiculous word for me to use—she is the happiest person I know, even now, even with this hand she was dealt.

Now for some other buttocks-smooching. I'd like to thank some amazing people who have gone out of their way to encourage me, promote my stuff, or, more importantly, to help me get through a most difficult year: A huge thank you to my sister, Nisa SanGiovanni, for her constant support of Kim and me, and her *relentless* promotion of my first book, and to my publishers Kelly Smith and Marianne K. Martin for their continuing commitment and support of my ludicrous stories and sophomoric boob jokes and their love and support throughout this year. They believed there were enough people who shared my (sick) sense of humor, so thanks to you for proving them right. Thanks also to the amazing promotional efforts of Michele Karlsberg and comedian Kate Clinton.

Thanks also to the fabulous women at Womencrafts store in Provincetown, MA for making us feel so welcome to share their beautiful store during our author events—*they* support women's fiction, and now more than ever, independent bookstores need *us* to support them. Thanks to the ladies at Gabriel's at the Ashbrooke Inn (also in Provincetown, MA) for their hospitality and for one of my favorite places to write, especially in the winter, and for their permission to include their Inn (and themselves) in this book.

Thanks also to my agent Lou Viola, who took on representation of my screenplays, even with the challenge of marketing a subject matter to Hollywood that does not target comic-book-reading, 18–21 age males. Might there be producers, directors, or investors that feel the same way we do? (**Insert cricket noises here**) It never hurts if readers ask for movies to be made in the reviews of books that they like. Hint, hint.

Beyond my entire family, both the Italian side and the non-gifted side (but especially my sister Nisa and my brother Tony, who have pushed my book like Italian thugs to a bunch of their friends), I want to say thanks to the following people who went out of their way to read my book and go overboard with their encouragement in so many ways: Debbie Riley, Carolyn Williams, Joan Opyr, Bett Norris, Andi Marquette, Val McDermid, Stacy Homan, Rachel Henry, Cynn Chadwick, Loretta Stromberg (and her mom), Valerie Graff (who gets the long-distance award), Keith Cameron, Kellie Schumm, Debbie Druce, Frann Stahlbush, Vivian Nolan, Gerri Marcoccio, Yvonne Perry from Writers In Sky, Liz & Danni from Pancakes and a Valium, Melinda Finnegan (who wants to cast the movie), Dolly DiSantis DiPrete (my aunt, who wants to be in the movie), Julie Twombly, Qrkiegrl, Mimi Torchin, Liron Cohen, Kimmy Turrisi and Crystal Chappell. Thanks also to Options News Magazine, Out & About Travel, and AfterEllen.com for their great review of my first book, and thanks to *all* my Facebook and Twitter friends for their continued support and friendship, some who continually promote my writing for me every week—I wish I could name every single one of you here!

A special mention to the people from whom I have "borrowed" an anecdote, fictionalizing and totally mangling all the details to suit my idea of what is funny. Beyond my immediate family, who I steal stories from all the time, thanks to: Debbie Riley, Sara Riley, Clara Mederois, and also to Adriana, my "sister" from way, way, way down south. (Disclaimer: they did not contribute any of the tales of bad taste; I take sole and full credit for these.) Thanks also to the brilliant Donna Deitch, the director of *Desert Hearts,* the film based on the book by Jane Rule. No infringement intended, as this is a total homage to one of my favorite movies and the first lesbian movie I ever saw in the theater, way back in the mid-eighties—and it blew my mind. I was five. (OK, I was a teenager, but who's counting?) Also, a random, but very special thanks to Howard Stern from the *Howard Stern Show* for promoting my book on his show. Check it out on YouTube or on my website and make sure to hang on till the end to hear how Howard says he will never read the book followed by his juicy burp.

My brothers and Dad were so proud, as was I. The real shocker: He pronounced my name right. I can die a happy woman.

I hope I get the chance to meet more readers who have contacted me or taken the time to post a kind review of my book, and if we do meet, be sure to bring a copy of your review so we can put them on the floor, get naked, and roll all over them right in front of you, or at least give you a hug for your effort. Please hunt me down on Facebook or GreetingsFromJamaica.com, or marisangiovanni.com—especially if you have a way to help the Santora family become a film. I know it's a long shot, but I would love to see a movie theater, or, at least my living room, filled with a bunch of loud (Italian) lesbians, who I hope will leave their tomatoes at home.

xoxo
Mari